A BONAFIDE DETECTIVE

TIM TWOMBLY

ILLUSTRATIONS BY BRAD ARNOLD

Acclaim for *A Bonafide Detective*

Tim Twombly's debut novel sizzles with wit and charm. It dazzles with provocative images and entertains the way comedy should. But don't be seduced by what you might think is a coming-of-age romp. Darker elements run through this story, undercurrents of murder and abuse that keep readers on edge.

The central character, Doc, suffers the misfortunes that, all too often, come with falling in love. He has the longings of a would-be rock and roller, does his best to avoid being pulverized by the town's badass bully. All these, he knows, come with the territory. But territorial boundaries break away, the landscape of reality changes, and now Doc must decide if he has both the imagination and the courage to solve a mystery, and in doing so, save the life of one girl who is living, and one who is dead.

Readers of *The Catcher in the Rye*, *Harry Potter*, and *Huckleberry Finn* will love this book. *A Bonafide Detective* is one of the best coming-of-age novels I've ever read. An instant classic.

- Louella Nelson, best-selling author, creator of *The BestSeller Secrets Series for Writers*

Tim Twombly's *A Bonafide Detective* is a bonafide classic, a literary experience that brings readers pure pleasure. Set in 1960, Orange County, California, the novel is simultaneously a love letter to the past and an intriguing mystery deftly drawn with a brush dipped in magical realism. Through the adventures of Doc, Margaret Ann, Jimmy and their other teenage friends, we live through an era America will likely never see again. We run into iconic figures from the past, laugh out loud as the characters try to survive those awkward, coming-of-age moments, hold our breath when it seems our hero has no way out. This book is an instant treasure. It leaves the reader with only one hope: that there will be more.

- Herb Williams-Dalgart, author, *The French Girl's War*

Timothy Twombly is my favorite kind of writer: the kind who makes me laugh and cry on the same page…every single page! In *A Bonafide Detective*, he reconstructs one week in 1960 and populates it with characters we deeply care about and root for. His lyrical prose lifts us to poetic heights, and then *wham!* He drops us into a funhouse of giggles. His mastery of plot, turn-of-phrase, and humor make this book an effortless delight. Yet, like all good novels, the tale leaves us much to ponder; indelible memories linger on. *A Bonafide Detective* is a coming-of-age story that is shockingly fresh and downright delicious.

 - Deborah Gaal, author of *Synchronicities on the Avenue of the Saints, The Dream Stitcher*

To my angel in Heaven, Robin Collier –You gave up all your Sundays to make sure I'd finish this book. Your hands-on-hips encouragement, the pure magic of your laughter, kept my pencil moving across the paper. I will hold you in my heart forever.

To my daughters, Haylee and Kiva – Thank you for believing I had a story worth telling. This novel would not exist without your guidance and inspiration.

ACKNOWLEDGEMENTS

I remember thinking, "You've got to be kidding," when Twila Tate, my freshman English teacher, told me I would need to write a four-page essay on the use of symbolism in *The Mill on the Floss*. Who could write that much about anything?

I feel just the opposite way when it comes to listing those who've inspired and encouraged me to write. Life has been so generous to me when it comes to having wonderful friends, friends who dragged me, kicking and screaming, into dangerous territory.

To my mentor, the fabulous Louella Nelson, and to the members of my writer's group, I thank each of you for your insights and fresh perspective. My heartfelt appreciation to Debby Gaal, Herb Williams-Dalgart, Rosie Lewis, Blake Bullock, Beverly Plass, Brad Oatman, Fiona Farrell Ivey, and Mary Myers.

To my editors, the irascible and utterly charming Jack Barnard, Erin from CreateSpace, Paul Saevig and the amazing Christopher Steele, I thank you for making sure what was in my mind made it to the page.

To George Campanis, Glenn Gelman, and Ed Sweeney. The greatest friends a guy could ever hope to have.

To my fellow Doctors, Kevin Parker and Ken Erickson, for their support and willingness to look the other way when I took office time to work on this project. Thanks to Victor, too.

To my mother, Marie Twombly, for teaching me about storytelling.

To my illustrator, Brad Arnold, for the brilliant artwork.

To my childhood friends, Allen Crutcher, Larry Brehm, Jim Bucheister, Tom Jewett, Larry Loeck, Dennis Miller, Greg Lorton, Don Martin, Rich Lippi, Mickey Patton, Greg Getz, and Marc Levitan: without you, I would have no story to tell. But of course, as we all well know, this novel is pure fiction.

CONTENTS AT A GLANCE

A Dewey "Doc" Ruggles Poem (circa 1960)

Don't leave the theater.
Stay one more moment.
You'll witness,
be able to pet,
the sable-soft pelt,
the notorious ears
of the impossibly pink rabbit that pops out,
(all smiles for you)
from the magician's empty hat.

SHE GUINEVERES A SMILE

September, 1960. Orange County, California.

Dewey "Doc" Ruggles didn't need a gypsy to tell his fortune, didn't need a genie to grant his wish. He placed his trust in the winds of Fate and in the kite he and Jimmy had built. The plan would fall into place like the tumblers of a lock. The kite would find the girl, the girl would lead them to the car, and the car would lead them to the man who'd killed Jimmy's sister.

Jimmy, who always acted like life was a joke, a game he didn't care about, would get what he really wanted: dark, delicious revenge. Somewhere along the way, Doc would find true love. That's how the story goes. That's how it turns out for the heroes in the magazines. He was the detective, and a detective who chases down pure evil always attracts its opposite along the way.

From the pinnacle of Lemon Hill Terrace, from atop the roof of Jimmy's grandparents' house, Doc let the string slide through his fingers, watched Lancelot climb, rifle its way into a sky as brilliant as the blue Pacific.

The kite's tail flicked back and forth, wicked as a stingray's barb.

Fair winds prevailed.

Even the sun overhead seemed to know some things could not be stopped.

The kite was on a mission.

The kite was bait.

Nearby, Jimmy, shirtless, tanned, a purple beach towel draped across his shoulders, paced the shingles. He had scissors in his hand. He'd named the game they played "skyfishing," said it would be a game with rituals, a secret purpose. The game would be their cover, a preoccupation everyone would understand. Boys will be boys, right?

They'd use the kite to hunt for girls, all kinds of beautiful girls: sugar-and-spice-and-everything-nice girls, experienced girls, curvy girls, daddies' girls, wayward girls.

"Even girls that make passes at boys that wear glasses. Bet you'd like that, wouldn't you, Doc?" Jimmy had once said, and Doc, adjusting his glasses had said, "Yes."

He always said yes to Jimmy.

Somewhere beyond the house, below the hillside, laundry snapped on a clothesline, a chain clanged against a metal pole, a gate rattled on its hinges. Out in front of him, so small now it could have been a mile away, the kite skittered on, skittered skyward, its paper skin buzzing on the wooden frame.

Jimmy looked up at the sky, then glanced down at the scissors in his hand. He was listening too, but not to the sounds Doc heard, not to the rush of the wind, but to sounds ancient, haunting and further away.

Circling around Doc in the same way he often circled around the truth, Jimmy began chanting Pig Latin parodies of the Mass, passages from Revelation, prayers to Augustine, the patron saint of playboys. The words were spoken to bring Doc luck. Doc needed luck. Jimmy, the Prince of Sunny Hills, heartthrob of this year's sophomore class, didn't.

Jimmy turned. "We need one last invocation, Doc, a fable to inspire us. How 'bout you tell me your latest dream?"

Doc's connection to the kite reduced itself to a single thread of sensation: a sweet burn across his palm. He looked out on hillsides garlanded with orange trees, bridle paths lined with eucalyptus, post-war pastel homes, a horizon steepled by the spires of Sleeping Beauty's Castle, then nodded, played his part, spoke the dream as though he saw it as a movie in his mind:

> *I cut the string. The kite races beyond the orange groves, soars over the town. Suddenly, Lancelot flutters, falls, skims over a pond, cartwheels over lush green grass. It lands next to a girl with the face of a perfect angel. She's lying on a blanket reading a poem written in future perfect tense. I skid to a stop, hop off the Schwinn, remove my glasses, walk over to her slowly, and say "I see you've found it."*
>
> *The girl smiles at me, admires the kite's hand-hewn balsa struts, the heraldry adorning it. "Beautiful," she says.*
>
> *I kneel. Tell her I built the kite from native wood. Egyptian parchment. Named it after the hero I most admire.*
>
> *She Guineveres a smile.*
>
> *We talk awhile. I lie on the blanket next to her and together we look up at the sky.*
>
> *A caravan of lavender clouds passes overhead.*
>
> *"That one," I say, pointing my finger. "That over there looks just like a hippopotamus."*
>
> *She looks at me curiously. "I love the word 'hippopotamus.' How could you know that was my favorite word? Are you magic or just funny and cute?"*
>
> *Then she looks at me again, her lower lip trembles, her eyes fill with tears. "I'm in danger. I need someone to help me..."*

Doc took a breath, a sigh of sorts, and turned to Jimmy. "That's the dream I hope comes true."

Jimmy pointed the scissors at him. "Don't get your hopes up."

It was supposed to be a joke.

GRAVITY PULLED THE SWITCH

Earlier in the day they'd been at a pool party. Jimmy still had swim trunks on. Three of the mothers who'd chaperoned the party had taken turns rubbing Coppertone on Jimmy's back and shoulders. Arms folded, their daughters had looked on from behind dark glasses. Doc had offered to put lotion on one of the girls, and he recalled saying, "I'm sure your mom doesn't want you to burn."

Staring daggers at her mother, the girl had said, "I'm already burning," then shoved Doc into the pool.

He'd spent the rest of the party practicing holding his breath underwater.

Jimmy snap-snapped the scissors. "Pay attention, Doc. I'm cutting the string."

"Hold on. Gotta get it through this crosswind."

Jimmy's eyes stayed steady on him. "You're going it alone today, Doc. I got things to do." He snipped the line. "It'll be good practice for tonight."

The string fell limp in Doc's hand. The spool at his feet spun, rattled to a stop.

He stared at Jimmy. "But we always go skyfishing *together*."

Jimmy's body stilled. The wind changed direction. Harsh, cold. The kite drew back, hovered high above them, threw its shadow across

4

Jimmy's face. "Meet you at the tracks. Seven-thirty," he said. "We'll leave the bikes there." Jimmy walked across the roof, leapt without hesitating from the eaves to the lawn.

Doc looked up. The kite was gone. Perspiration fogged his glasses. He wiped his hand across the lenses, frantically searched the sky.

From out of nowhere the kite appeared again. It ducked behind a distant palm tree, taunted him with an aerial game of hide-and-seek, then sailed away. He recalled the girl on the blanket, the girl with the face of a perfect angel. Maybe this time his dream wasn't just a dream.

Doc took off running across the shingles. Jumped. Landed hard. Came up limping.

A moment later, he was on his bike, pounding the pedals. His mind, like the gears, hummed in synchromesh.

He whipped around the corner onto Highland Avenue, gritted his teeth against the wind. He dodged a red ball that bounced into the street, outpaced a black dog that tore out from between two houses, changed lanes without using proper hand signals. Today he would have no regard for the law. Today he was all grit. Today he was his own man.

In the past, whenever the kite landed in a tree next to a girl's bedroom window, he'd always let Jimmy climb up and smooth-talk her. When it landed in a park, girls would scurry to pick it up, run right past him, and hand the kite to Jimmy. Jimmy would flirt. The girls would blush and giggle, scrunch little painted toes into their sandals. Candy hearts would float from their mouths when they talked to him.

He pedaled faster. The wheels of his bike smashed those stupid candy hearts into the pavement.

He was tired of being the invisible best friend, tired of tagging along, fed up with living life holding his breath underwater.

From out of nowhere, a delivery truck swerved into his path, "Red's Sanitary Supply" painted on the side panel. Inside the cab, three burly Latin men jostled into one another. The driver jerked the wheel. The tires screeched, and the chassis tilted, leveling out with a *bang*. The men shook fists at him, stared daggers through the driver's side window. The driver pointed something at him. A gun?

He didn't care. He stared right back at the guy, claimed his right of way, then steadied his eyes on the kite as it dipped and danced above the power lines that rose above the buildings along Commonwealth Avenue.

Under his breath, he growled one of the annoying limericks Jimmy sometimes used to embarrass him: "There once was a girl from the city, her lips were as nice as—"

He hit the brakes. The words fizzled in his lungs. The kite had reached its destination. It was tangled on the cross atop Saint Mary's Catholic Church.

Doc's heart sank. What girl was he supposed to meet up there? Saint Mary?

He could imagine Jimmy teasing him, saying, "I hear older women are really nice, Doc. But isn't Mary about two thousand years old—and already taken?"

Doc shook away the thought. Even if he fell trying, he had to get to the kite. Technically, it hadn't touched the ground yet. Its flight wasn't over.

He marched his bike across the street and into the alley next to the church, slammed down the kickstand, and furiously stacked metal trash cans, one on top of the other. Climbed.

Standing on tiptoe, Doc stretched out his arms. His fingers grasped for the rain gutter that ran below the second floor balcony. Beneath him a vibration built, the earth shook, trash can lids slid like tectonic plates.

Gravity pulled the switch.

Doc fell, everything collapsing around him like a clattering, clanking, ignominious house of cards. Deflated, he lay flat on his back, pancaked on the asphalt.

The world went dark.

"Are you all right?" a voice asked.

He opened his eyes.

An angel in black stood over him…well, not quite an angel.

The young nun knelt. Up close, she was prettier than most penguins. Round, pink sugar-cookie cheeks. Oval eyes, shiny black like a stuffed animal's.

"Engineering problem?" she asked, glancing around. "I mean the way you stacked the barrels."

Doc got to his feet. "More like faulty depth perception," he said, pointing to his glasses.

She rose, reached out, took Doc's glasses off his face, and examined the frames. "Like Buddy Holly's, like Clark Kent's, aren't they?" She looked through them. "Powerful. Bet you could start a fire with these."

He noticed flecks of pink polish in the beds of her fingernails. An odd adornment for a nun.

She caught him looking at her hands, frowned, replaced his glasses, and snugged them over his ears. Her fingers were like ice.

"So, who are you?" she asked.

"Doc. I'm Doc," he said.

Her eyebrows, like little curvy caterpillars, crawled together.

"Not like a doctor, a medical doctor," he said. "It's a nickname. It means…more like, professor." He pushed his glasses up his nose. "See, when I was a kid, I had polio. Spent a lot of time in bed. Nothing much to do but read and—and make stuff up in my imagination."

"I guess you *need* an imagination if you don't see very well. Anyway," she said, "we have nicknames, too. Mine's Sister Theresa."

"My real name's Dewey Ruggles. So what's yours?"

She didn't answer. Instead she looked up at the roof.

A sheet of newspaper blew past, John F. Kennedy's name in the headline. "Diamonds are a Girl's Best Friend" played on a car's radio as it passed by the alley. Overhead, the kite rattled in the wind.

"I have to get to the cross," Doc said.

"We have a perfectly nice cross inside."

"What I need's up there. I'm on a mission."

"Got an idea," she said. "Be right back."

I ONCE WAS A GIRL
FROM THE CITY

True to her word, Sister Theresa came huffing up the alley toward him, a ladder propped lengthwise over both shoulders, her neck pressed back against its weight, her outstretched arms threaded through the rungs.

When he saw her, he regretted letting her go alone to get the ladder. She looked pilloried, like a victim of the Salem Witch Trials, or a refugee from Heaven.

Panting, she stopped in front of him and set down the ladder. Strands of her damp, dark hair trailed in ringlets from beneath the crown of her habit. Her chest heaved. An earthy smell of incense hung in the air around her. "They can't know I'm helping you," she said. "They can't know I'm here."

"I don't want to get you into trouble."

"No trouble, Doc. This is fun. Makes me hot." She wiped her brow. "In fact, I have half a mind to find a pond of Holy Water, strip down naked, and just throw myself in."

Doc said nothing, tried to keep his mind absolutely totally blank. It was hard.

"That's a baptism you'd like to see, right? Naughty boy. You do have an imagination."

"I better get going."

He lifted the ladder, clunked it against the second-floor balcony, ticked up a few steps, then paused. He stared down at her.

"You're not like most nuns, are you?"

She shrugged. "I once was a girl from the city."

Doc's hands went numb. He almost lost his balance. "What did you say?"

"I said, you better get going."

"No, you started to quote a limerick."

"Concentrate, Doc. What you want's up there. Don't let your imagination keep you here. Get going."

Doc took a step up. Stopped. He suddenly felt compelled to tell her something. "I was on this roof once before," he said, "after funeral services for my friend's sister. She was killed in a car accident. They never found the guy who hit her." Doc looked up at the roof. "Jimmy went up there to be alone."

"Jimmy's Catholic?" she asked.

"Told me he was about ten days old when they baptized him. Guess he didn't have much say in it."

"And you climbed to the roof to give him comfort?"

Doc nodded. "He's my best friend."

"And today?"

"It won't sound very nice, but today, I'd like to show him up."

"Then do it. Just don't get yourself killed. Remember, you owe me one."

A SHAPE SHIFTED

When Doc reached the second-floor balcony, he tightroped the top railing to the point where it bolted into the wall, and then, like a circus monkey, shinnied up the drainpipe attached to the side of the steeple. Hooking his hands into a gutter anchored to the roofline, Doc pulled himself to the summit, to the roof of the church.

He stood there, amazed, on top of the world, holding in his triumphant heart the memory of a girl he'd met without Jimmy's help. A girl that was darn cute to boot. It didn't matter she was a nun. He'd leave that last detail out when he told Jimmy about her.

Turning, Doc took a dizzying look over his shoulder, over the edge of the roof. Below him, tiny as ants, children played hopscotch and Double Dutch on the asphalt playground behind the church. A tetherball spiraled around a metal pole, the chain clanking in the wind. He could hear the girl's choir practicing. Across the roof from him, the kite's frame tapped the cross in rhythm to their high-pitched "Hallelujahs."

Though Lancelot's tail had tangled high on the cross, the kite it-self dangled upside down like a trophy fish. It swayed above skylights made of stained glass. He'd only seen skylights like these once before, in the dome of a Greek Orthodox church. He didn't know Catholic churches had windows like these, but Saint Mary's did, and they were beautiful.

He approached the kite cautiously, crept forward. Below his hands were scenes depicting Bible stories. In one multicolored panel, Jesus consorted with Mary Magdalene. In the next, the Prodigal Son approached his father's open door, and in the third, Lazarus was rising from the dead.

Something moved beneath the panes. A shape shifted. He found a diamond-shaped frame of clear glass and peered down. Below him was the prelate's study. A girl about his age, maybe sixteen, maybe a little older, sat behind a desk in a leather chair. She had short dark hair, wore large hoop earrings, her shoulders draped in a choir robe. She held a vanity mirror in one hand and was applying lipstick with the other. When she finished, she lay the mirror down, spun in the chair, stood, and walked over to a wardrobe closet. She removed the robe, placed it properly on a hanger, and stood there completely naked.

LASSOED BY THE HAND OF GOD

Doc jerked back, came forward slowly again on hands and knees, his jaw slack, his heart thumping.

He searched for the small slice of clear glass he'd been peeking through.

It was gone. It wasn't there. It had been right beneath his hands but now he couldn't find it. She was still there, though no longer made of flesh and blood. Obscured by colored glass thick as a gumdrop, she'd dissolved into fractured bits of fawn-colored light. It was like looking into a kaleidoscope. It was like trying to decipher modern art.

Frustrated, Doc stood. "What kind of God lets you see a naked girl, then just takes her away?"

He stared down at the panels, implored the figures in stained glass, one of them at least, to speak up, to point the way to a pane he could see through. He wasn't asking them to sin. A naked girl in a church could be part of a crime in progress. This was no time to be holier than thou.

Lazarus was no help. Recently resurrected from the dead, the guy apparently wasn't taking any chances. The Prodigal Son, conveniently repentant, kept his head bent at his father's knee.

Doc felt a shudder in the sky, heard a whirling sound.

The tail of the kite whipped down, slapped the back of his head. His chin hit his chest. Images swam, his eyes refocused.

Directly below him, a single leaded frame of ruby red glass slowly bled clear as crystal. Doc dropped to his knees. There she was again.

She was lying on a blue velvet couch facing away from him.

Gazing down at her, Doc's consciousness expanded, traveled to that sacred place where a boy's imagination justifiably goes to memorialize something worth remembering. After all, there was something wrong here. Something was going on. Detective work was absolutely required. He did what he had to do: he sleuthed her body, mapped every curve, savored every pink inch. A machine in his belly started up, hummed, churned whipped cream.

The girl on the couch began to roll onto her back. He looked away the instant before their eyes met, prayed that if he stayed stone-still she wouldn't see him.

When he looked again, the game had changed.

A priest's back blocked his view of her. For a moment he caught a glimpse of the man's face in profile. He was young, strong too. He grabbed her arm, pulled her up from the couch, dragged her across the room into an abstract world of slivered light.

It was difficult to see them. The panes were too thick, too drenched in color. There was no way to hear them either.

Where prisms crossed, the priest broke into swirling black sticks, his movements staccato. His head, sometimes disembodied, bobbed up and down as though he was biting off consonants, yelling at her. She was like liquid. If she made sounds, they were all smooth vowels.

Who was she? Had the priest made her a sex slave of the Vatican? Doc had read of such things in the magazines he'd come across in Stone's Barbershop, magazines like *True Detective* magazine and *Real Crime*. Now he knew what had brought him to the roof. She was the girl he was meant to meet, the girl in trouble, the girl worth fighting for. He'd solve the mystery. Save the girl. Write the story. It would make the cover of a magazine. It would be an excerpt from his first novel.

A gust of wind popped the air. Over his shoulder, Doc saw the kite rise again, swirl above him like a giant serpent. It came down hard, cracked him on the side of the head.

He fell backward, slid headfirst toward the edge of the roof. Frantic, he extended his arms, dug his heels into the clay tiles. He fanned his legs apart, spun like a starfish in shallow water. His mind became a white scream. He whispered goodbye to his parents. Recalled every summer of his all-too-short life. Remembered the Christmas he walked without his leg brace. He wished, for God's sake, if he was going to actually die he could have at least seen the face of the girl he was dying for. One last scrap of justice. Was that too much to ask for?

The wind blew the clouds apart.

A scribble of white cloth flurried over him.

He torqued, twisted, slammed to a stop.

Lifting himself onto his elbows, Doc looked down at his ankle. The kite's tail had twisted around his left leg, his polio leg. He'd been lassoed by the Hand of God.

HELLO, MARGARET ANN

Doc dropped the last eight feet to the asphalt, landed hard on his heels. Spikes of pain shot up both legs into his groin. He grabbed a breath, bent at the waist, and walked gingerly in small circles.

He looked up at the roof, turned, and glanced over his shoulder. No one in the alley, but somewhere a door flew open, banged against a wall. He heard the sound of heavy feet moving quickly in his direction. Maybe in all the commotion the priest had seen him. He ran to his bike, popped up the kickstand, got a running start, and pedaled, pedaled, pedaled.

He skirted the edge of town, took the back way through older neighborhoods.

Too many questions if he went home now looking the way he did. His pants were torn and the back of his shirt was smeared red from the clay roof tiles.

Crossing Harbor Boulevard, he turned onto Pomona Avenue and coasted the Schwinn into a wrought iron bike rack at the west end of the mission-style building. He dismounted, tucked in his shirt, and limped toward the massive wooden doors of the library.

Light streamed in behind Doc as he entered.

Clearly annoyed by the blast of sunshine, the girl with cat glasses, the girl who was always there, squinted back at him. She was sitting in

17

her usual seat at the large oak table. Today, she was reading the *News Tribune*. She shielded her eyes, pinched her face, shook her head. He could read her mind: Here he was again, she was thinking, the kid who thinks he owns the place.

She lowered her gaze and pretended to return to her newspaper.

For now, he let her have her way. But he wouldn't look at her. He'd leisurely take in the interior architecture, the vast room with vaulted ceilings, a space as impressive as a ballroom in a Spanish governor's palace. He panned the WPA murals depicting early California history: Cortez gazing out over the blue Pacific, the conversion of the Indians, the Gold Rush, rolling hills dotted with orange trees. All around him, cathedral columns of books rose to meet chandeliers shaped like wagon wheels. There was a skyline of books in Doc's room, too, and he'd read them all, but there were more here. He loved this place. It had always been his church, his sanctuary.

From across the room, the girl he loved to hate was staring at him: a well-practiced look of disdain. Just looking at her face drove him crazy. She had a mouth made for talking, movie star lips, lips a little too red and ripe for his tastes. Across her nose there was a dusting of freckles that, she insisted, replicated the Milky Way. One feature was indisputable: she had ears that stuck out a little too much. She made a pathetic attempt to conceal them beneath shoulder-length brown hair, hair some might have called a lustrous sun-kissed auburn. He thought the color was, and would forever be, mousey brown.

Doc walked up and took the seat across from her. "Hello, Margaret Ann."

She turned the page of the newspaper. Not looking up, she said, "Kennedy's traveling on a train through Central California. He's heading this way. Says, if he's elected president, the pope won't be running the country. Words to that effect." She pulled a linen handkerchief from her pocket and blew her little freckled nose: a tiny, annoying squeak. "You smell like dust," she said, tucking the handkerchief away. She smiled, a self-satisfied, smarty-pants smile. He'd always thought one upper incisor was a little snaggled, not quite aligned. He'd told her that several times. She'd denied the tooth was anything but perfect.

"I assume you've been out hunting for girls, playing with your imaginary friends, and now, as usual, you're going to tell me there's more to the story, not that I have time to listen. As you can see, I'm immersed in reading." She patted two thick books. "I've got Kinsey's book on sexuality and a pictorial volume on injuries to the male anatomy, which I plan to reinterpret in watercolor for my college admissions portfolio. I expect to be accepted into the prestigious nursing program at Indiana University. I'll be living outside of Bloomington, staying with my aunt and uncle. They have a farm, a huge house. An artist's studio where I can paint."

Tiring of her self-serving monologue, Doc had focused on the far end of the library. The three Latin men who'd nearly run him down less than an hour ago sat at a large circular table, their fingers tapping maps spread out in front of them. Their whispers, like spits from a machine gun, ricocheted across the room. One of them glanced at Doc, then silenced his compadres with an icy stare.

"Reds," Doc growled.

Margaret Ann looked from Doc to the men, then back to Doc. "You're so typical. You think Communists are everywhere."

"No, 'Red's Sanitary Supply.' They nearly ran me down. The guy with the gold tooth pointed a gun at me...Wonder what they're doing here."

"Maybe reading up on how to improve their aim?"

Doc frowned, reached out, took Margaret Ann's hand and placed it on the lump on the side of his head. "I nearly fell off the roof of Saint Mary's."

She wasn't impressed.

He stood and begrudgingly turned around. He had no choice. It was the way they did things.

She clucked her tongue. "Your shirt's filthy and you're exposed on the back side, but I guess you know that." She clicked open her purse and looked inside. "Well, I've got a fresh handkerchief and a needle and thread." She glanced up. "In case you didn't know, I come from a long line of Irish tailors."

"Yeah. Apparently you come from a long line of everything."

"So it seems."

She'd tried to slip it by him. Tired as he was, he'd still caught the play on words. "*Sew it seams?* What's that? A tailor's joke?"

"I'm going to the restroom," she said. "Meet you on the back patio. While I stitch, you can confabulate."

This was an example of her annoying vocabulary. But at least she hadn't said, "So you can blow smoke up my ass." She'd said that to him once. Apparently, she'd enjoyed the look of shock on his face. "It's an old Irish expression," she'd said casually, then added, "You know, for a supposed playboy, you're kind of a priss."

'TWAS BEAUTY KILLED THE BEAST

Waiting for her on the patio, Doc recalled a thousand conversations they'd had like the one that had just happened. Duels that went back and forth, verbal thrusts and parries. Margaret Ann usually got the better of him.

When they'd first met, she'd made it abundantly clear she was fourteen months older than he was and had already skipped two grades. They'd met at the library when he was eight. That day, she'd glared at him as he tried to sneak from the children's room into the adult section. The head librarian, a flinty old hen, had seen him too and grabbed him by the ear. Margaret Ann had come to his rescue.

"How dare you," she'd said. "What? You think he comes here to leer at girls in *National Geographic*? My friend reads Dostoevsky, *Crime and Punishment*. Release him now or I'll tell my father you assaulted him, tried to abridge his rights." With one last full-throated breath, she'd declared, "Grant this young American, this son of a war hero, a full privilege card!"

The librarian had relented. They'd been friends, of sorts, ever since.

Arriving on the patio, she told Doc to lie face down on the bench. While she stitched, he told her everything, the whole story: Jimmy sending him out to chase down the kite. The kite on the cross. Sister Theresa. The naked girl he'd seen through the stained glass. The priest who'd joined her. Priest and girl together in some wicked water-color dance. His brush with death.

Finishing, he sat up. He couldn't wait to hear her response.

"Wanna share a tuna sandwich?" she said, digging around in her purse.

"That's the only thing you can think to ask me?" He shook his head. "No. I don't want a tuna sandwich. I want to know what you think."

She unwrapped the sandwich, meticulously folded the wax paper. "I think you hit your head. Your furtive juvenile imagination took over from there."

Doc stared at her.

"You're sure it wasn't a flesh-colored leotard?" she asked, one big bite into her sandwich.

"It wasn't a leotard."

She patted her lips with a fresh handkerchief. "Well, assuming this wasn't all a hallucination, I'll start with the priest." Margaret Ann stood and paced back and forth, tapped her chin with a mayonnaised index finger. "Have you ever considered upon whom a priest models his behavior?"

"No, Socrates, I haven't."

"On the pope. Now I don't know much about Pius the Twelfth, but I heard a story about the last one." She stopped, raised one eyebrow. "Remember Fay Wray, the actress?"

Doc nodded. "*King Kong*. 'Twas beauty killed the beast."

"Yes, the film's love interest." She cleared her throat. "In the late nineteen thirties, Fay went to Rome, gained an audience with the Pope. He gave her absolution, forgave her for all that monkey business. Afterward, he took her aside and whispered in her ear, 'Shirley Temple's a midget, isn't she?'"

"So? What's your point?"

"My point is, priests don't get out much. Most are probably as innocent as you. If what you're saying is true, I blame the girl."

Doc looked at Margaret Ann with disgust. "You would," he said.

She smiled. "I love it when you're miserable."

THE MAHARAJAH
SPOKE TO HIM

Back at home, Doc stood with his face to the shower head and let the hot water pound away. He was sore all over. No great surprise. Still, he ached more than he expected. The washcloth came across strange bruises in mysterious places, tender spots for which he had no explanation. He had to wonder if Margaret Ann had somehow left her mark.

He squished a glob of Prell shampoo into his hand, lathered it into his scalp, shaped it till his blond hair formed a white turban. He became a maharajah in one of Kipling's tales of India. He loved pretending he was a character from one of his great-grandfather's stories.

In the condensation that filmed the glass door, Doc wrote, "confabulation," Margaret Ann's word. He stared at it, wiped the word away. Beneath the smear, he added a few "con" words of his own. "Confection," "concupiscence," and "concubine": Words that evoked his memory of the girl he'd seen at the church.

He picked up the shaving mirror, stared into the soap-crowned face. The Maharajah spoke to him.

"For now tell no one. Destiny will cause your paths to cross again."

He hoped, for God's sake, the Maharajah was referring to the naked girl, not Margaret Ann.

There was tapping at the bathroom door.

"Dinner's ready."

His mother's voice always reminded him of Elizabeth Taylor's. She looked a little like her, too.

"There in a minute," Doc said, toweling off. He slipped on beige Corbin pants and a blue oxford button-down shirt. On the way through the living room, he plinked out "Heart and Soul" on the family treasure: Kipling's grand piano.

THANKS FOR THE HOMILY

His father sat erect at the kitchen table, reading the *Los Angeles Times.* He glanced up, frowned. "Where are your shoes?"

"I left them in India."

The frown didn't budge.

"In the closet on shoe trees. I'm waiting for the polish to dry." It was a lie, but so what?

"If you managed time better, they'd be on your feet."

"Didn't want dinner to get cold, Dad."

"Barefoot's no way to come to the dinner table. You're not a farmer."

"No, I'm not. But farmers are the backbone of the nation."

His father stiffened, turned a page of the newspaper, tapped an article. "What do they teach you in school about Castro?"

"Don't know, Dad. School only started three weeks ago." He sat down.

His father's blond butch cut bristled. Behind rimless glasses, one eye twitched. "Intellectual curiosity isn't dependent on how many weeks you've been in school. Want to get somewhere in life, keep up with world events—What do you know about Cuba?"

"An island of farmers?"

"Communists," his father said. "They probably come to dinner barefoot."

Doc gave in, got up from the table, and went back to his room. He was tying the laces of his oxfords when he heard a cry from down the hall, from the room that, until eighteen months ago, had been *his* bedroom. It began as a faint, fussy whimper, then escalated into a tirade of tears. Snowball was awake. He could just see her standing in her big-girl crib, rattling the bars, the overhead light illuminating the shock of white hair that haloed her head.

Doc stepped into the hall. The odor of ammonia wafted from his old bedroom, converged with the smell of butter burning in a skillet. His mother, a few steps ahead of him, carried the little usurper toward the kitchen. Snowball peeked back over his mother's shoulder, gummed him a sly smile, goo-gooed the word, "Bad."

"That's not Dad. That's your brother," his mother cooed.

Snowball knew what she was saying. She was a midget Margaret Ann.

In the kitchen, he watched his mother place Amanda in a highchair, then ferry dinner to the table: fish, rice, hominy. The white meal matched everything in the kitchen except the daffodil-print fabric his mother had used to make the tablecloth and curtains she'd hung above the sink.

She brought him a glass of milk: more white food.

"So, Dewey, I mean Doc, guess tonight's the big dance at the Teen Center. Don't forget to carry a fresh handkerchief in case a young lady needs one. You're fifteen now. You need to be prepared to act gentlemanly."

"Okay, Mom."

His father set down the paper.

"What's this 'Doc' your mother's talking about?"

"It's his nickname, honey," she said. "It's always been his nickname. Like the boys call Amanda 'Snowball.'"

"Let the boy speak for himself."

"It's just a nickname," Doc mumbled, looking down at his plate.

"Did you tell your friends you plan to be a physician? Don't you think it's a little presumptuous of you to tell your friends to call you Doctor?"

"Dad, it isn't a nickname if you give it to yourself. Your friends come up with it. And it's not 'Doctor,' it's 'Doc.'" He dreaded these conversations.

"So now you're one of the seven dwarfs? Great accomplishment."

"It would be if I was trying to become a dwarf, Dad, but I'm not. See, a nickname just fits. You know how it is." Apparently his father didn't.

"So 'Doctor' fits? Fits into what?"

"It's not engineering, Dad, it's a nickname. I think the guys mean 'Doc,' like professor." He'd left himself wide open.

"Well those that can't do, teach."

Beneath Doc's elbows the daffodils wilted across the fading tablecloth.

"Maybe it's the glasses, honey," his mother said. "They make him look so scholarly." She lifted Snowball from the highchair and bounced her on her lap.

"You mean his *new* glasses."

"Honey, he's had them for almost two years now. They're not that new. And he needed them. Just look how much his face has grown since fourth grade."

"The fact that his face has grown isn't the point. He was irresponsible."

The sacrosanct nature of prescription eyewear was a subject his father never seemed to tire of. There were recurring themes, elements of family history. Doc had broken his first pair of glasses not long after he'd gotten them, but never told his parents. He'd never worn the glasses at school, anyway. Guys who wore glasses were called "four-eyes," were picked last at recess, played chess against imaginary friends. Girls, axiomatically, didn't make passes at boys who wore glasses. Rather than wear glasses, Doc had decided he'd rather not see.

On the last day of junior high school, he'd pulled his glasses from their case and found the lenses shattered.

He'd asked his father for new glasses.

What had ushered forth was a diatribe on responsibility.

His father was reprising the familiar, impassioned monologue now at the dinner table. Doc didn't need to listen; he knew the story by heart: His father had been issued corrective lenses by no less than the US Army and he'd worn the said lenses all through World War II. The rest of the lecture was filled with varying versions of his father's recollections of hand-to-hand combat with Nazis, vivid descriptions of being blown backward repeatedly by exploding grenades, and yet despite all the horrors of war, his father had never broken his glasses.

Swallowing the last of his fish, his father said, "*You*, young man, couldn't preserve the gift of vision through elementary school."

Doc lay down his fork. "Thanks for dinner. I especially enjoyed the homily."

"You mean hominy?" his father said.

"Yeah right, Dad."

Doc set his plate on the counter, stroked Snowball's dandelion hair, then left the kitchen.

In a low voice, he heard his father ask, "You giving him a ride?"

"No," his mother whispered. "He's going with Jimmy."

Doc heard his father push back his chair, heard the click as he flipped the lid of his Zippo lighter. "When's he gonna realize that kid's got a piece missing?"

"More like a piece torn out, Dad," Doc said, closing the front door behind him.

YOU MIGHT CHECK
AESOP'S FABLES

Doc stashed his bike in the stand of scrub oaks just behind the row of houses that snaked the crest of the valley. Jimmy had apparently arrived ahead of him. His bike was already tucked in among the branches.

Except for the tracks of the Southern Pacific Railroad, the valley below Doc was virginal, untouched since the days of Cortes. Lavender clouds drifted over acacia, sycamore, and jacaranda. The sky above was the color of peach jam. In the air, he smelled sage, wild mustard, a hint of smoke from steaks searing on a backyard barbecue. He liked this world. Here, no one told you who to be, what to do.

He spotted Jimmy sitting on a large saucer-shaped rock halfway down the hill. He was wearing a white dress shirt, the sleeves rolled to the elbows.

Doc ambled down and sat beside his best friend.

He nudged Jimmy's shoulder. "Wanna hear about the kite?"

Jimmy didn't move, didn't speak. He continued to look out over the tracks.

Doc followed Jimmy's line of sight.

From where they sat, the tracks shot straight eastward. No bends. No curves. At the point where the rails seemed to converge, Doc could see something coming up the tracks toward them. It moved quickly, its head low. Even at a distance, he could hear its paws clicking on the wooden cross ties.

"He's been following me all day," Jimmy said.

The coyote stopped thirty yards from them, stared motionless yellow eyes up at Jimmy.

"You sure it's him?" Doc asked.

"Look at the scar on his flank."

Doc could see it. "You're right," he said.

Jimmy stood, slapped the dust off his pants. "I'm going down."

"Want me to come along?"

"No. He wants me alone."

The valley changed as Jimmy made his way down to the tracks. It was as though some primal law required the two of them to meet in an altered world. Tulle fog funneled toward them through the sawgrass, shadows on the hillside became raging rivers of black paint. A thousand crows gave up flight and filled the trees. Even the tracks, now barely visible through the swirling fog, seemed to lose their way. Sections of rail gaped apart like a poorly stitched wound.

Doc had read things like this happened when boy and beast met to talk about the dead.

"What's the holdup? What's with the weather?"

Doc glanced around. A crow had dropped down onto the rock next to him and was surveying the valley. With his beak tilted up, the little creature projected a certain military bearing. He stood legs apart, the tips of his black wings touching behind his feathered back. A sort of bird version of parade rest.

"My friend's down there talking to a coyote," Doc said.

"This gonna take long? Some of us have migration schedules to keep," the crow said, his scratchy voice pouncing on every first syllable.

"No, probably not. He just needs some information about a murder."

The crow stared up at Doc, his eyes bright black BBs. "So, the coyote's what? An accomplice, the perpetrator?"

"No, a witness. In fact, he was probably hit by the same car that ran down Jimmy's sister."

"And you know that how?"

"We were there. Just got there a little too late. The night it happened, Jimmy and I were on our way down to the stables to bring Cindy back for Christmas dinner."

"Shorty's stables? Three years ago?"

"Yeah."

"I remember the fire," the crow said. "The nativity scene burnt to the ground. Heard about the girl, too. It was all over the newspapers."

"You read newspapers?"

"Magpies read newspapers. The bottoms of birdcages are lined with newspapers. Word gets around."

"Remember the 'bloodied coyote on the hill'?"

The crow nodded, then puffed his chest like a bandstand orator. "Captured for a fleeting moment in the squad car's spotlight, only the wounded wolf knows what really happened."

"That's almost an exact quote from the *News Tribune*, except it was a coyote."

"I was quoting the magpies."

"Yeah. Well, that's him, the one the papers were talking about. Jimmy thinks the coyote's been following him ever since the night it happened."

"Stalking her memory, as it were."

"Exactly. He believes if our kite doesn't lead him to the killer, the coyote will."

"Listen, kid, Coyote's never gonna be the boy's hound dog. Not to say he couldn't conjure up another way to help. You might check *Aesop's Fables*. I don't pretend to understand the four-legged types." The crow looked up. "Fortunately you have another clue, right?"

"How'd you know that?" Doc asked.

"I can read your mind. Not hard to do, considering part of me is a projection of your imagination." The crow rolled his beady eyes. "Tell me what you think I don't already know. Go ahead, reiterate."

Doc sighed. It troubled him that he'd created an imaginary being that could do no better than feed him a series of straight lines. The dialogue between them was just slightly better than a bad vaudeville act. While Jimmy's imagination had come up with a heroic beast, a beast with *scars*, Doc found himself struggling to make his mission sound interesting, not to an eagle, but to a preening dilettante, a wise-cracking crow. He took a breath and answered what the bird had already decided was a rhetorical question: "Jimmy saw the taillights of the car that hit his sister. We look for those taillights every time we fly the kite. See, we cut the string, ask Fate to help us find this certain girl. The idea is she'll lead us to the car. We'll recognize the taillights and…"

The crow wasn't listening. He'd taken flight, his black wings lost among the shadows of sycamores.

HE GOT PHYSICAL

Over the valley, the fog was lifting.

Jimmy was coming up the hill. Doc yelled out, "What happened?"

"He got physical," Jimmy said.

"He bit you?"

"Yeah, I'm a werewolf."

"What?"

Jimmy smiled. "Nothing happened. He just wants us to go to the dance."

"You're sure nothing else happened?"

"Sure I'm sure," Jimmy said, buttoning his cuffs. "We just looked at each other. It was up close and personal. Then he ran off."

In Doc's mind, Jimmy's words floated in the air between them, the letters separating, moving independently, working hard to rearrange themselves into something closer to the truth. Jimmy was lying to him. At least part of what he said was a lie.

Doc knew it was possible he'd imagined the mystical transformation of the valley, maybe even the crow, but there *were* things he knew for certain. Jimmy's sleeves were now rolled down and, in his irises, flecks of yellow-gold had appeared. Jimmy was different, a little scary. More like the Jimmy that Doc's dad had spoken of: the kid with a screw loose. "How 'bout we just go to the show?" Doc said. "See *The Time Machine*. It's playing at the Fox."

Jimmy threw his arm over Doc's shoulder, his animal energy pulling Doc down to the tracks. "No way," he said, in a gravely voice. "Got this feeling we're the show tonight."

HEY, PRETTY BOY

Surrounded by palms and eucalyptus, the Teen Center was snugged into a rock outcropping above a flagstone parking lot. Looking down from the trail they'd taken through Hillcrest Park, Doc thought how different the building looked at night. In daylight, the Center seemed so ordinary. Now, lit by moonlight, the setting seemed romantic, the architecture reminiscent of a Spanish hacienda, a place Zorro, living as the mild-mannered Don Diego, might have used to entertain the government officials he hoped to someday overthrow.

From the looks of it, the evening had already started. Beneath lantern-lit balconies, souped-up cars swirled in all directions, growled, flashed high beams, brandished colors like midnight blue, pearlescent lavender, and candy apple red. The air pulsed with the rumble of glass-packed mufflers, the revving of high octane engines, the dissonance of competing car radios blasting rock 'n' roll.

Clearly the older guys held reign. Their cars battled like chariots in the Coliseum. Hot rods with four-on-the-floor lurched toward automatics. Cars with flames menaced sedans painted in Easter pastels. And all around him, beautiful girls spilled from backseats of sedans, hiked up skirts three, some four inches; undid top buttons of blouses; and swung their hips toward the tiled staircase that led to the entrance. Doc, glad he hadn't arrived on a bike, followed.

Just beyond the gaggle of girls, something caught his eye. A '50 chop-top black Mercury angled out a baby blue Chevy Bel Air for prime position at the base of the stairs. The Chevy shuddered on its axles, its paint paled, its carburetor choked. It backed up.

Doc knew why.

The guy behind the wheel of the Mercury was Junior Mentz. Doc had never seen the notorious badass before, but the Wanted-Dead-or-Alive description was a perfect fit: inky-black pompadour, hatchet-shaped sideburns, a face chiseled from a tombstone.

Junior was every kid's worst nightmare. At Boy Scout campouts, when ghost stories weren't enough to constrict your testicles, older guys told stories of Junior.

He'd once heard Junior made a kid rip a mole off his own cheek, made another take back puberty. Stabbed some guy in Tijuana with a switchblade he'd named *Persuasion* just to see if the blade was sharp.

Through the open driver's window, Doc saw a vestige of Junior's latest act of cruelty: a short plaster cast on his right forearm. Rumor had it Junior busted the bone savagely beating in the face of a kid who'd failed to correctly answer the question, "What are *you* lookin' at?"

Right now, Junior and the three other guys who filled the car were staring down a string of girls moving toward the stairs. Doc, now two steps behind Jimmy, tried to blend in, disappear among the little lambs Junior was eyeing.

It didn't work.

When he crossed into Junior's line of sight, Junior's features retracted, flattened against the bones of his skull. His lips slicked with saliva. "Hey, pretty boy."

Doc felt Junior's eyes on him, knew he'd been cut from the herd, singled out as the weakling "pretty boy." Fear played his ribcage like a xylophone, turned his bone marrow to oatmeal.

He looked at Jimmy.

Jimmy's eyes flicked from him to Junior then back again. A glint of coyote-gold flashed in his irises. His shoulders rose, his neck muscles thickened.

Doc watched Jimmy turn and walk straight toward the Mercury. If Jimmy were a snake, you'd only hear one rattle before he'd strike.

"I think you got it wrong, pal," Jimmy said. "If anybody's 'pretty boy,' it's me."

"Okay then, pretty boy," Junior repeated. "Wanna do somethin' about it, pretty boy?"

Not breaking stride, Jimmy shot back, "Yeah."

Junior started to open his car door.

Jimmy closed the distance, kicked the door shut, broke off the side view mirror.

Doc winced and felt the contents of his stomach curdle as he watched Jimmy pick up the mirror, hold it out, and gaze at his own reflection. "You're right," he heard Jimmy say. "I am a pretty boy." Then Jimmy stepped back and rifled the mirror at Junior's head. There was a bone-chilling scream. Junior grabbed at his ear. The Mercury vaulted forward, accelerated, and slammed into the base of a palm tree.

Glass tinkled to the ground.

Every car radio in the parking lot went silent.

A dozen girls stopped on the staircase and stared open-mouthed at the Mercury, then at Jimmy.

Jimmy yelled out, "Did just like you told me, Doc. Busted his ugly ass up, just for you."

Doc froze, felt the universe throw a spotlight on him. In his mind, he saw himself transformed into the carnival freak, who, tonight, for reasons beyond his understanding, had been dragged to center stage and proclaimed the main event. Blinking, he looked around.

The open-mouthed girls turned and stared at him.

The guys climbing out of the Mercury iced him with their eyes.

For some ungodly reason, he looked back at them. Beyond his control, his eyes drifted, locked on Junior's. In slow motion, Junior, holding his bloody ear, silently mouthed, "What are *you* lookin' at?"

Doc lowered his head and slowly walked toward the staircase. His right hand fumbled in his pants pocket for a dime to call his parents.

Jimmy bounded up the stairs, slowed, walked next to him. "Nothing to worry about, Doc."

"Who's worried?" Doc said with a thin chuckle. "There's adult supervision inside, right?"

IN CASE YOU'RE INTERESTED

An implausible blonde in a pink angora sweater sat behind a card table at the top of the stairs. She was fondling a stack of quarters, her cinnamon-colored eyes fixed on Jimmy as he climbed the steps toward her. Doc followed a step or two behind. His bad leg spasmed, his spine wobbled like yellow Jell-O. Waving an arm at the blonde, he squeaked out, "Pay phone?"

Any moment now, he expected to see Junior and his henchmen come bounding up the stairs toward them, tire irons swirling above their heads like scimitars. If Doc were lucky, he'd only end up disfigured, partially paralyzed. Even now, he could imagine the aftermath, his father standing above his hospital bed asking him if he knew what had happened to his glasses, if he knew where they were. Toothless, left with only a bloody stump for a tongue, he would slur something unintelligible. His father would shake his head and walk away.

"Jimmy, you *do* know that was Junior Mentz, don't you?"

"The guy rubbed my fur the wrong way," Jimmy said, then stopped in front of the blonde.

She looked up at him from beneath mascaraed lashes. "There's a prophecy, ya know. Word is, witches told Junior no man born of woman will ever take him down."

"Sounds like mumbo jumbo," Jimmy answered back.

"Or maybe Shakespeare." She looked past them down the flight of stairs. "Anyway, turns out tonight's your lucky night. They're going, going, gone…I've seen you play baseball, sugar. You're really good."

Doc turned. She was right.

Junior and his gang of thugs had gotten back into the Mercury. He heard the starter grind, the engine growl. Watched the Mercury peel out, the rear tires squealing, a twisted piece of its grill sparking as it clattered over the pavement.

The chop-top's taillights faded into the darkness below the park.

"I think we played it just right," Doc said, adjusting his glasses.

The girl raised an eyebrow at Doc. Melted as she looked at Jimmy.

Jimmy handed her a crisp twenty dollar bill and pointed to the open cash box on the table in front of her. "Two tickets and I'll take that roll of quarters, please," he said.

She handed him the cylinder of quarters, two tickets, and change. "Have a nice time at the dance, tough guy."

Because it was Jimmy, she mouthed "tough guy" as though it was a soft-centered chocolate.

Suddenly, as if a dike had broken, jubilant teens pushed up the stairs toward them. Standing to the side, Doc watched tickets sell like hot cakes. Girls he didn't know smiled, eyed him with coquettish curiosity. "I'm here with Jimmy," he said to one of them.

BABY POWDER AND BLACKJACK GUM

To the right of the ground floor entrance was a brightly lit community room. During the day, this was the room where Cub Scouts and Boy Scouts met. There was a makeshift kitchen, tables for Ping-Pong, checkers, and crafts. At night, this was the last outpost. Here was where the rejects, the spazzes, and losers congregated. It was Boys' Town for the socially inept. You stayed here if you were afraid to go upstairs and ask a girl to dance.

Doc couldn't help but look in. The longer he looked, the weaker his leg felt.

A dozen guys, maybe more, sat frozen in chairs that lined the walls. Others huddled in corners. A few laughed, made armpit sounds, pretended they were having fun. Most looked hollow-eyed, drained of blood, their gonads sucked dry of testosterone. It was a sorry sight.

"Coming upstairs?" Jimmy asked.

"Think I'll hang here for a while."

Jimmy gave him a look of concern.

"You go on," Doc said. "When the music's right, I'll make an entrance. Might be a good idea I act as lookout in case Junior shows up." The truth was, down deep, he knew he was a lot like these guys. The only difference was, he hadn't given up. Unlike them, he *would* go upstairs tonight. Jimmy's shirttails would carry him there.

From across the room a skinny guy with braces waved at him, yelled out his name. It was Herb Melch. Jimmy had nicknamed him "Grill." A Polaroid camera hung from a shoulder strap. In his hand, he toted a long cardboard tube filled with blueprints; Grill always carried blueprints. His smile and those blueprints were signature pieces of a life characterized by bizarre schematics and failed orthodonture. It took him only seconds to corner Doc.

"So what's the bright idea this time, Grill?" Doc asked, nodding at the tube.

"Chinchilla ranching. I've designed a whole new concept in breeding pens. Fur's the future. Gonna make a million, and when I do, I'm going upstairs."

Doc watched his mouth as he spoke. It was a snarl of metal and red, raw gums. He'd worn braces since the fourth grade. As if he could read Doc's mind, Grill added, "You know, I'm in the final phase. A few more months and they're coming off. I got it all timed out. I see a future where there will be more photographs of me than dental x-rays."

"Good for you," Doc said.

"You wanna join us over in the corner? I'm about ready to unroll the plans and I've got pictures of Jimmy playing the guitar. We're startin' a band, ya know."

"A band? You and Jimmy?"

"You too, Doc. Today, while you were out chasing the kite, Jimmy bought you a guitar: a Fender Bass. Jimmy picked up a Stratocaster. He's been takin' lessons in secret from some guy he calls the Coyote. Hope I didn't blow the surprise. Anyhow, it's all decided. We're resurrecting 'The Four Teens.' Remember how we wowed 'em in elementary school?"

"Yeah, I remember," Doc said, wondering why Jimmy had kept the idea for a band secret.

"My voice is changing, mellowing out," Grill said. "How 'bout, right now, you and I try a little duet?"

A vile goo congested around Doc's vocal chords. He tasted strychnine. The idea of a duet with Grill was so repellant, so horrifying, even his bad leg had the sense to say, *Get out of here now.*

"No thanks. Maybe later," Doc said, as a force that commanded him to claim a better life pulled him toward the stairs.

As he climbed, he could hear Bobby Freeman on the record player singing "Do You Want to Dance?"

The answer tonight would be yes.

Reaching the second-floor landing, Doc paused beneath a Casablanca fan then peered through the arched entrance. The dance floor was packed. He assumed Jimmy was walking the perimeter, scoping things out.

When Doc tried to enter, his path was blocked by a girl who'd suddenly appeared in front of him. She wore pink lipstick, had Cleopatra eyes. Large hoop earrings dangled beneath short black hair. Standing beneath the fan, her hair whipped around her face as though it were a cap made of raven's feathers. She was exotic, a little terrifying, somehow familiar.

"Excuse me," Doc said.

Rather than step aside, she moved closer. She smelled like baby powder and Black Jack Gum. She looked him up and down, chewed, reached into a small velvet clutch bag and produced a fresh stick.

"So *do you?*" she asked, popping the gum into her mouth.

"Do I what?"

"Wanna dance."

"I'm not much of a fast dancer."

The Bobby Freeman song ended. Johnny Mathis began singing "Chances Are." A slow song.

"Any other excuses?"

She didn't wait for his answer. She pulled Doc onto the dance floor, placed his hands at her waist, draped her arms over his shoulders. She led. A few dizzying moments later, she'd spirited him onto the balcony. They danced beneath a canopy of stars.

He felt blood circulate in his sore left leg. His dance muscles fired in a syncopated fashion. Light on his feet, he recalled how guys who stuttered could sing without faltering, and now, though he limped when he walked, he could dance. She looked into his eyes. "Have you ever been this close to a girl?"

"Just my dental hygienist."

"There's something you need to know," she said. "I don't always chew gum. When I'm in the bathtub, I chew red licorice. Wha'da ya think about that?"

He couldn't think. He could only picture her in the bathtub. Did she want him to imagine what he couldn't help imagining? He didn't know. Wanting to appear unflappable, urbane, sophisticated, he said, "Uh…yeah…seems like a good idea. Licorice is sort of waterproof. If you got soap bubbles on it, you turn on the tap and rinse it right off."

"I've done that," she said, pressing her cheek against his. Her cheek was warm and, between chews, soft.

The song ended.

Still embracing him, she asked, "Have you ever been wet kissed by a girl?"

"I've been licked in the face by a French Poodle. Her name was Ruffles." He'd done his best to say this in a suave sort of way, though it came out sounding stupid.

"The first time I was kissed," she said, "the guy held me down."

Her words sent a chill up Doc's spine. His mind flashed to the girl he'd seen from the roof of the church. He wondered if her reference to the bathtub was code for being naked. Like this girl, the naked girl in the arms of the priest had worn hoop earrings and had short dark hair. It struck him this could be her. Sure, it was farfetched, but it was possible. Had fate delivered him to his damsel in distress? Was this the moment in which the hero says something momentous? Yes it was. He gave her his best wise-beyond-his-years look, and said, "I think the right kiss can awaken a girl from a bad dream. I think the perfect kiss can make all of history vanish."

She looked deep into his eyes, into his naked, unprotected soul. "You mean what you say, don't you?"

Doc nodded.

She pressed him up against the railing of the balcony, pushed her tongue between his teeth, added to the kiss something slippery, something strangely substantial.

She stepped back, looked at him as if doubly mystified, slapped his face, then disappeared into the darkness of the dance floor.

He just stood there chewing her gum, enjoying the confluence of flavors, savoring the sting that lingered on his cheek. No girl had ever liked him enough to be really angry with him. You'd have thought he'd tried to stick his hand up her blouse, the way she'd slapped him. Could the truth be, when they'd kissed, a voice inside her head had whispered, *He knows*? Just maybe.

Doc tried to go inside, follow her. He couldn't. Something sacred, something profane, some curare-like substance in the juiciness of her kiss had paralyzed him. He couldn't walk and chew her gum at the same time.

Looking through the open archway, Doc could see the powdery silhouettes of dancers bumping to the sounds of Ricky Nelson's "Be Bop Baby." He squirreled the gum into his cheek, steadied himself, and walked inside.

The girl who'd kissed him was gone, but he did see Jimmy. He sat in one of the folding chairs that lined the walls, his body facing a blonde in a sky blue dress. She looked like Alice in Wonderland. Jimmy was talking to her, reeling her in. The girl seemed nervous, a reluctant wallflower not used to attention. She fidgeted, looked around as though wary of something in the room. Her hands trembled in her lap. Even above the music, even standing ten feet away, Doc could hear her charm bracelet chattering on her wrist.

Doc stepped closer, leaned in, "We need to find this girl I danced with. Her life may be at stake."

Jimmy, his eyes still focused on the blonde, wasn't listening. "Let me introduce you two," he said. "Doc, this is Raylene. Says she's Junior's girl, not that she had any choice in it. Says if I know what's good for me, I'll go away."

"I couldn't agree more. Come on. Let's get out of here. I need your help."

Jimmy wasn't about to budge. He was nuzzling Raylene, whispering something in her ear.

Color rose in Raylene's neck and face, igniting her perfume. Doc recognized the fragrance. It came in a little bottle with the Siamese cat on the label: My Sin. Perhaps the coyote part of Jimmy had had a say in picking her, had sniffed out her scrumptious kitty cat scent.

"Okay, I get it. She smells nice. Let's go."

Jimmy leaned back in his chair and stared up at him. "So now you're stickin' your *nose* in my business?"

"Yeah, that's what you smell with," Doc said.

"Go live your own life, Doc," Jimmy said. "You met a girl? Fine. We don't need you."

"We? You and the coyote? What's with you? Twenty minutes ago you almost got both of us killed."

Jimmy looked at him through slitted yellow eyes. "Go play with your imaginary girlfriend. There is no *us* tonight, Doc."

Doc felt his skin prickle, the muscles in his hands tense. "You're possessed by the Big Bad Wolf, and *I'm* the one with the problematic imagination? My girlfriend isn't imaginary, but you know what is...? Our friendship." Doc turned his back to Jimmy and surveyed the room again. "I'll get my own ride home," he muttered, and walked away.

He hurried to the steps, his leg barking as he took them down two at a time. Before going outside, he glanced into the community room, though the chances she'd gone in there were slim to none. It was a fatal mistake: Grill saw him.

"Doc, get in here."

"Sure," he sighed. "Just for a minute."

Grill came forward. Trailing him were three scrawny freshmen, their faces scorched with acne. "The lepers and I have completed our poll," he said. "Check it out. We've got the new name for the band: Jimmy and the Gigolos."

"Swell," Doc said. "See ya later." He started for the open doorway. Stopped. Straight ahead, at the base of the stairs, stood Junior, the Bluto brothers, and Junior's twisted cousin, Frankie "Fang" Faletti. The bad guys were back.

Doc spun to the side, flattened his back against the wall just inside the arched entrance to the community room. Over his pounding heart, he heard Junior order Fang upstairs.

He felt someone's breath on his cheek, smelled the stench of vaporized metal, heard a sound like a gas leak.

"Pssst."

Doc looked to his right. Grill and his three friends had plastered themselves to the wall alongside him.

"Here," Grill breathed, handing Doc his long cardboard tube. "It's not just for blueprints. It doubles as a periscope. Take it. Hold it sideways."

Feeling like an idiot, Doc fed the end of the tube around the corner, then looked through the eyepiece. It worked. He could see Fang coming back down the stairs. Between steps, he poured M&Ms into his mouth from a five-cent bag. Through wet brown teeth, Fang reported, "He's with Raylene, Junior. Got his hands all over her." Junior pushed past Fang and headed up the steps. His goon squad followed.

Doc's shoulders slumped as he handed the tube back to Grill. He wondered what he should do. He was torn. He could yell up at Jimmy, warn him Junior was on his way. But what good would it do? Over the dance music, Jimmy wouldn't hear his "imaginary" voice. And why should he worry about Junior's "imaginary" fist smashing into Jimmy's face? Jimmy didn't care about him. But he wouldn't lower himself to Jimmy's level. He looked at Grill. "Aren't there any adults around here?"

"Haven't seen one," Grill said. "Some lady from the PTA is supposed to be operating the record player."

"Could you get her? Tell her what's happening?"

"No problem. If you want, I'll throw a slug in the payphone, call the police."

"Take your best shot, Grill. I gotta go. A matter of life and death."

Grill grinned. "Really?"

"I think the girl I danced with is a sex slave for the Catholic Church. On top of that, she hates me with a passion."

"Cool," Grill said. "Want to take the periscope?"

CHECK IT OUT

Doc walked all the way down to the road below the Teen Center, came back and looked in the windows of every car in the lot. He tramped the perimeter of the building. He shouted out inane things like, "Where are you?" then kicked himself for never having asked the girl her name. Now, coming up the hill toward the Teen Center, he saw a pulse of red and blue lights. He heard the wail of sirens. From the other direction, he heard the thudding of feet. Grill was running down from the Teen Center toward him, gasping for breath.

"What's going on?" Doc asked.

"You're missin' the whole thing. Jimmy's up there standin' his ground, ready to fight Junior. It's like watchin' Davy Crockett grin down that psycho Creek Indian, Red Stick. I got pictures," Grill said, shaking the Polaroid.

From inside the Teen Center there was a thunderous crash. Lights in the building flickered, glass shattered. There were hoots and screams.

As Doc ran toward the building, he saw Jimmy leap from the balcony and tumble down the hill. When Jimmy came to a stop, he was on all fours. It may have just been his imagination but Doc could swear he heard a howl, saw a lupine shadow wrestle free from Jimmy's body. Whatever the shadow was, it scampered off into the darkness between the trees. Jimmy tried to stand. He staggered. Doc got there just in time to grab Jimmy under the arms. With Grill right beside him, Doc hoisted Jimmy up and carried him to a cluster of palms. Exhausted, disoriented, Jimmy crumpled, and his eyes turned from yellow to brown again. They fluttered, closed.

Two police cars whipped into the parking lot. At the top of the tiled steps, Doc saw Raylene and an older woman, probably the PTA lady, waving their arms. They motioned the cops inside as dozens of guys and gals beat feet out a side door.

Grill thumped Doc's shoulder. "Check it out."

Coming around the other side of the building was Junior Mentz. He had his arm wrapped tight around the waist of a girl with short dark hair and large hoop earrings. Junior pushed her forward toward a blue Buick parked at the curb beneath a streetlamp. The driver got out. The man, stick-like, wore a Roman collar.

Doc's knees went weak. He stumbled back deeper into the shelter of trees.

There was nothing he could do. It was as though a thousand branches suddenly bent down and formed a cage around him. There was no way he could break through the branches, no way he could stomp down the hill, fight off Junior, take on the authority of the church.

All he could do was watch as Junior pushed the girl into the car. Slamming the door closed, Junior pointed a finger at the priest.

"You want it your way, you'll listen to me," he said.

Without replying, the priest stepped back, went around to the driver's side of the car and got in. Junior got in on the passenger's side. With the girl Doc had kissed between them, the car pulled away from the curb and drove off into the night.

As the Buick faded, the cage that held Doc fell away from his body. The trees that ran up the hillside above him straightened, vaulted toward the heavens, their blue-green branches now threaded with silver light cast down from the moon.

At Doc's feet, Jimmy dozed, a midsummer night's dream refilling the place in his brain the coyote had occupied. Grill, like some ancient mariner, stood scanning the horizon with his periscope. Doc heard the bells of Saint Mary's, thought of the kite tangled on the cross above the church, remembered the way its frame had tapped in rhythm to the choir singing. The song of the kite hadn't ended. Some things could not be stopped. Tonight, in his dreams, he'd build a campfire in a sacred wood, and forge a plan to set his mystery girl free.

SCARLETT

Doc kept Jimmy hidden among the palms until the police had left, didn't emerge from the shadows until Jimmy was his old self again. With Grill jabbering beside them, they worked their way back to the parking lot and blended in among the stragglers.

Sunny Hills High School's "Ken" doll quarterback, Rusty Richards, approached them and offered to drive them home.

Doc, last to get in the car, sat in the front seat next to the glamorous, leggy redhead Scarlett Brisco. Her shoulders were draped in Rusty's letterman's sweater, her bare knees, alien green in the nuclear glow of the dashboard lights, brushed against his. There was only one way to describe Scarlett: she was sexy as sin. The star of almost every local theater production, he'd seen her seduce audiences in a hundred different ways. A senior now, she'd lived across the street from Doc his whole life, though he doubted she knew he existed.

They sped out of the parking lot. Grill and Jimmy rode in the back, Grill snapping Polaroids of God-knows-what, then tossing the snapshots over the seat onto Scarlett's lap. Rusty talked nonstop, going on and on about Jimmy and Junior: the fight, the police busting in. Doc was aware only of one thing the whole time: Scarlett's bare leg as it pressed against his.

Rusty turned down the radio, slapped the steering wheel with the palms of both hands. "That was truly bitchin'. What a night." He glanced at Jimmy in the rear-view mirror. "You were Spartacus, man."

"I love that 'pretty boy' thing you guys did," Scarlett said, twisting in her seat to face Doc. "You plan that out?"

Doc hesitated. "We improvised," he said.

"Oh, really? So when did a bookworm like you get so interesting, so bold, so ready to do whatever it takes to get a 'rep?'" She didn't wait for an answer. Instead, she clicked open her purse, took out a tube of Maybelline and slowly, theatrically applied lipstick. When she finished, she let Rusty's sweater fall from her shoulders. Smiling at him as though they were about to share an inside joke, she said, "Risky business being a social climber. Hope you're up for it." She gave his leg a squeeze.

A chill ran through Doc. Had he just experienced an eerie déjà vu? Had Scarlett just replicated what he'd seen the girl at the church do: paint on lipstick, then drop a garment from her shoulders? He moved his leg away from hers as he pushed away the thought.

Rusty downshifted, rounded a corner. "Wha'dya hit Fang with, Jimmy? Brass knuckles?"

"Wrapped my fist around a roll of quarters. Meant to hit Junior."

Rusty slapped the wheel again. "Airborne. The guy went airborne. Flew clear across that cardboard table, crashed all the way down the stairs. Raylene hanging all over Junior, yelling for him to help Fang. And the Blutos running in circles trying to catch you. It was like a Chinese fire drill."

"It's all kind of a blur," Jimmy said.

The Ford Fairlane turned onto Crestview Drive, drove halfway down the cul-de-sac, pulled to the curb.

Doc and Jimmy climbed out. Doc held the door for Scarlett.

She slid out, extracted a house key from her purse. "Daddy's out for the night," she said. "Guess I'll just have to open my bedroom window and snuggle down in bed." She took a few steps. "Hope my body heat's enough to keep me warm." She turned and gave Rusty a wink.

Grill picked up on the invitation. He leaned his face out the back passenger window, yelled out, "Scarlett, nothin' chases away the shivers like the insulating properties of a chinchilla muffler. I have several fresh pelts tucked away in the science lab."

Reaching the front door, she looked back at Grill. "Any of them still need their heads chopped off?"

"Sorry. No."

"Too bad, Grill," she said. "It might have made for an interesting date."

Rusty shot a cold glance at Grill, but spoke to Doc and Jimmy. "Sure you two don't need a ride home?"

"I'll walk from here," Jimmy said. "I live at my grandparents' place over on Lemon Hill Terrace. Doc's just across the street."

"Really?" He looked at Doc. "You live across the street? Scarlett's never mentioned you."

A flash of white light froze Rusty's profile for posterity. The tiny motor of the Polaroid whirred. From the backseat Grill said, "Looks like it's just you and me, Rusty. How should we play it? Chauffeur or shotgun?"

Blinking away the spots in front of his eyes, Rusty started the car. "Listen up, metal mouth, I want you flat on the floor, out of sight. Mention my girlfriend's name again, I smash your face in. Got it?" He eyed Jimmy, dropped the car into first gear. "Heard Junior say when he gets his cast off, he's coming after you. Good luck, Spartacus."

The Fairlane sped away.

Doc shoved his hands into his pockets, glanced at Jimmy. "I'll get our bikes tomorrow after school." He crossed the street and looked over his shoulder one last time as he stepped onto the lawn that rimmed the semicircular driveway in front of his house. He'd caught a glimpse of Jimmy kneeling, picking up what looked like a length of clothesline that lay coiled next to the Brisco's mailbox. He knew Jimmy would turn it into a makeshift lariat, knew what he would do with it. Sure enough, for the second time today, Doc heard a whoosh of wind. From ten yards away, Jimmy lassoed him.

"Yes, we all know you won the raffle last year," Doc said. "Spent the day with some hotshot stuntman at Knott's Berry Farm."

Coming up from behind him, Jimmy gave the hose a pull. The slipknot cinched Doc's elbows to his sides, a jerk set him down on the grass. "Not so fast," Jimmy said. "I want you to tell me a story."

Doc looked up. "You were the story tonight. I think Rusty said it all: 'You were Spartacus, man.'"

Jimmy loosened the knot and slipped the rope over Doc's head.

"No, Doc. I want to hear about *your* girlfriend."

"It was nothing."

"You wouldn't have left your best friend upstairs for nothing. Even if I was being kind of a jerk."

"A colossal jerk."

"I made up for it in advance. Bought you a guitar today." Jimmy smiled. "The coyote picked it out."

"Really? While I chased the kite, you two went shopping?"

"Just 'cause Coyote's got a mind for mayhem doesn't mean he's got no taste. He's been teaching me a few things, showing me a few 'licks.'" Jimmy sat down next to him, lay back on the grass. "Come on, Doc, tell me about the girl. You met her at the Teen Center, then what happened?"

"She left with Junior Mentz."

Jimmy pushed up onto his elbows. "You're kidding?"

"No, Spartacus, I'm not kidding. And I didn't meet her at the Teen Center. I think I may have run across her when I was chasing our kite."

"Oh yeah?"

"Yeah. I'm chewing her gum right now. You wanna hear the whole story?"

"Shoot."

Doc told him everything. The kite, the nun, the girl, the priest. The girl saying how she chewed licorice in the bathtub. Her running away when he told her, "I think a kiss from the right guy can awaken a girl from a bad dream, change the course of history."

"You laid some pure poetry on her and she still ran off."

"And there's something else," Doc said. "Scarlett had her hand on my leg the whole way home. Said something that struck me as kinda weird. Said something about climbing being a risky business…I was climbing today. Think I'm overthinking things?"

"Stop thinking. Surrender to the moonlight." Jimmy leaned his head back and howled.

"Maybe you're right." He leaned back and let out a series of yips.

They laughed and their laughter sent sparks into the night. Chained dogs joined in, baying and barking from behind backyard fences, and up and down the block, porch lights snapped on with disdainful "flicks" and bedroom windows slammed shut in a disgruntled succession of bang, bang, bangs.

Doc gave Jimmy a push. "Shhh!" he whispered. "We'll get in trouble."

Falling back, Jimmy said, "You're a peeping Tom, you're already in trouble, and you thought trouble was *my* middle name." He howled again. *Aaowww* straight up into the darkness, and every dog answered back, each with their own call of the wild.

AT THE EDGE OF SLEEP

Doc clicked off the porch light, eased the front door closed. The entry was dark, but beyond it he could see lamplight. His mother was alone in the living room. She was sitting on Kipling's piano bench wrapped in a white chenille robe, her back to the beloved Steinway they'd inherited from Doc's great-grandfather. She looked like she'd been crying.

"Your father needs to see you," she said. "He's in his study."

Doc's heart, warm from the night's adventure, cooled, constricted, its vessels twisting into the most dreaded of mandatory Boy Scout knots, the one knot he'd failed to master: the Sheepshank.

"Everything's okay," she said. "It'll all work out. He just wants to talk to you."

It was the worst thing she could have said. Her words, like an eraser across a blackboard, swept away the magic of the day: the birth of "Jimmy and the Gigolos," the girl with hoop earrings, the night that had seen him rise from just some nobody to someone notorious... all now reduced to chalk dust. Left with only one memory, he found himself saying, "Mom, I almost fell off the roof of Saint Mary's today. God saved my life."

From the back bedroom came the sounds of his sister Snowball crying. His mother got up. "That's nice, honey," her voice trailing off as she hurried down the hall toward the baby's bedroom.

"Gotta be worth something, right?" Doc yelled, then watched his words slide down the dark walls of the empty living room.

He tucked in his shirt, straightened up, headed for his father's office. Reaching the door, he tapped twice, stepped in. His father, still in dress shirt and tie, sat at his desk. He didn't look up. His left hand held a coffee cup, a sharpened pencil in his right tapped the frame of the glasses the Nazis had been unable to break. There was paperwork spread in front of him: ledgers, graphs, bills, reports, lists of inventory. He pointed the pencil at Doc. "Sit down," he said, and returned to his paperwork.

Doc swallowed the last vestige of the evening: the girl's Black Jack Gum. So long, sweet memory. He sat, looked around the room, stared at the top of his father's head. The crew cut was intimidating. Trim around the ears and collar, his father's hair possessed a certain fearful symmetry. Each shaft stood stiff, purposeful, like a soldier in a regiment. His father cleared his throat, looked up, took a sip of coffee, looked down again. Doc's eyes broke rank, moved up to the wall behind his father's desk. Three plaques hung in a straight line: The Eagle Scout certificate, the Bronze Star for heroism, the *cum laude* diploma from Stanford.

His father lifted his head, studied Doc. "I'm revising the plan for the company's operations," he said. "There've been some setbacks... exigencies." He took off his glasses, cleaned the lenses with the tip of his tie. An odd, almost ironic smile crept across his face. "Exigencies," he said again slowly, his voice barely above a whisper. "Not exactly a word you run across in your fairy tales, is it?"

"I don't read fairy tales, I read novels."

His father's eyes darkened.

"No, sir," Doc said. "No, it isn't."

"So you understand it's time to get down to business." He looked into Doc's eyes. "It shapes up like this: Until further notice, I'll be spending more time at the plant. Long days, nights, weekends. Your mother has taken a nursing position at Cottage Hospital."

What was he talking about? Doc thought. Whatever it was didn't sound like a problem. "I'll be fine on my own," he said.

"You're not on your own. Think. Use your head." His father stared at him.

Apparently the word *Duh* was written across his face.

"You're babysitting your little sister," his father said. "Every day after school. Every night till your mom gets off work. Eleven p.m."

"I can't babysit. I'm a guy."

"You're a boy with a stupid nickname. You live in books. You daydream like a girl. You think everything rhymes with moon, spoon, and June. Well, it doesn't."

Seeing red, Doc stood and headed for the door.

"Understood?" his father said.

His mother was just outside the door. She drew her robe tightly around herself as he passed by.

He marched down the hall to his bedroom.

Just like that, his life was over. Forget cruising in Rusty Richard's car. Forget prowling around with Jimmy, looking for clues to solve a murder. Forget skyfishing, the band. There'd be no sporting life. Just Pablum. His life had been reduced to Pablum.

He stood in the middle of his room, turned in a circle. An I-get-it smile played across his face. Now he knew what his "new" room really was: servant's quarters. No, more like the maid's quarters.

He wouldn't sleep here, not tonight. He grabbed the framed photograph of Kipling from his nightstand, went into the living room and lay down on the white couch that faced the piano.

From his parent's bedroom, he heard whispers, then the sound of his mother's slippers padding up the hall. Oblivious to him, she walked through the room, his father's coffee cup in her hand. She pushed open the swinging door that led into the kitchen. It swung on its hinges like a perpetual motion machine.

The light in the kitchen went on.

He lay back and stared at the swinging door, watched it rock back and forth like a metronome. Spears of light angled into the living room, swept across his face. The light vanished, reappeared again. He was tired. He closed his eyes. The kettle rattled on the stove, its breathy whistle like the sound of a train traveling through the night.

The door click-clicked, click-clicked.

At the edge of sleep, his mind drifted back in time. He was eight years old again. Wearing his Cub Scout uniform, he saw himself push through the same swinging kitchen door into the living room. Above his head, he carried a tray with glasses filled with Hawaiian Punch. He held the tray high like a waiter in a classy hotel.

His den of Cub Scouts sat on the living room floor in a semicircle. Jimmy, Slatz, Grill, eight other boys, all his best friends. Behind the Cubs, their fathers sat in folding chairs. Everyone was watching a slide show. A guest speaker was showing them photographs of men who had careers in science.

"These are America's hcrocs," thc man said. "They're helping us beat the Russians, ensuring we win the 'Space Race.' The man on the screen is the man you want to strive to be." Doc, tray in hand, was standing in the projector's beam, his shadow blotting out the face of a man named Oppenheimer. The boys laughed. Doc felt like he was on stage.

His father yelled, "Sit down," but Doc didn't want to. It was all so funny, the way his face had replaced Oppenheimer's. The other cubs began answering the speaker's quintessential question: "Young men, what will you be when you grow up?"

He heard Bobby "Slatz" LaDesma say, "An astromoner!" A deeper voice behind him echoed the correction, "Astronomer."

Jimmy said, "Jet pilot!"

Grill's metal mouth tried to wrap itself around "Aeronautical engineer!"

They answered like sheep. They told their dads what they wanted to hear.

"What about you, Doc?" Jimmy asked.

Doc stood in the spotlight of the projector, the tray of glasses clinking above his head. "A butler," he announced, grinning. "I want to be a butler."

His friends laughed. He laughed. He'd been funny. His answer was original.

The room fell silent. The fathers were silent. All of America went silent.

His father grabbed the tray from his arm. Doc's polio leg gave out. He fell. The glasses toppled. Red punch spilled onto the carpet.

His father glared down at him. "Look at the mess you've made. You'll never be anything but a little girl."

Doc lay there stunned, staring at the red punch, like spilled blood soaking into the carpet. His skin felt like it was on fire; it hurt like the sting of a thousand bees. He looked around. Everyone had heard what his father had said. Some of them stared at the floor, others fiddled with the buttons on their uniforms. A minute ago, he'd been the coolest of cool cats, smart as a whip, leader of the pack. But now his friends would never look at him again in the same way.

"Go to the kitchen and get some towels." His father was on his knees sopping up punch with a fistful of paper napkins. "You heard me. Get towels and get back in here."

Doc limped into the kitchen. He looked over his shoulder at his father. I'll get towels, he thought. And I'll come back, but not to you, not tonight, maybe never.

HE LIKED WHAT HE
SAW IN THE MIRROR

"Must I remind you, boy? Call me Kip. The Maharajah does and, I dare say, he does this with much affection."

Somctime during the night, Doc had woken, stumbled from the couch back to his bedroom. He was dreaming. This time, the dream was the stuff real dreams were made of. No more reliving a bad memory, a pronouncement by your father that'd you'd never be anything but a little girl.

In the dream, he was with his great-grandfather, Rudyard Kipling. They were sitting in an outdoor café in colonial India, sipping black tea and watching natives, bustling and busy, in an open-air marketplace. The novelist, dressed in a white linen suit, was going on and on about lost rubies and his adventures in the Punjab District, telling tales of dangers barely averted.

"I doubt I will ever write of these things, my son," he said. "But you may fashion what you hear into stories of your own. Maybe one about those Cuban devils, the ones you saw in the library, the ones who tried to run you down. After all, we share one intellect and storytelling is in our blood."

Doc had stopped listening. His eyes were on a girl, a princess. He'd noticed her moments earlier strolling past vendors' carts and ragged shop stands, her feet floating several inches above the ground. She wore a turban of coiled red licorice, her ears adorned with large hoop earrings that flickered silver in the sun.

The crowds fanned back as she approached and Doc saw why. Three regal Bengal tigers preceded her. She walked two of them like dogs, their necks tethered to satin leashes. The third tiger, sporting a black tuxedo jacket and a Roman collar, roamed unrestrained.

Kipling slid back his chair, stood, clapped his hands. "Levitation! A jolly good illusion. Bravo!" His voice, loud, jarring, caught the attention of the crowd.

The third tiger spun his head, eyed Doc warily, slowly advanced toward their table.

"So there's to be a second illusion," Kipling said. "Well come on, kitty. Show us your best stuff!"

Doc stopped breathing. His heart pounded. "Quiet," he said. "You're provoking it."

"Me?" Kipling asked. "What? Have I said something?"

In the crowd, a baby began crying. The wail grew louder and harsher.

Doc opened his eyes, his heart still thumping, a vague sense of uneasiness lifting momentarily as his vision cleared.

It was morning.

He was in his room. The sobs and wails had come from the kitchen. The dream, the antidote to a bad memory from his early childhood, had turned into a daytime nightmare, a preview of what his future held. He could hear Snowball pounding on the plastic tray in front of her highchair, screaming to high heaven, demanding God-knows-what.

Through the Venetian blinds, blades of sunlight raced across the room in diagonal lines, painted shimmery butterscotch prison bars on the walls. Even the light conspired to remind him his room was not a haven. It was a jail cell. He sat, picked up the small framed photograph of Kipling from his nightstand, looked through his own glasses at the spectacled face that looked back at him. "How 'bout tonight a dream with a different story?" he said. "One that gets me out of babysitting."

Suddenly, the yelling stopped. Perhaps, he'd entered the eye of the hurricane, the freaky silence before the little banshee really went berserk. Doc listened, waited, decided, for now, the storm must be over. In the distance, he heard his mother's soft voice speaking pretty baby talk and Snowball's alter ego cooing. He could smell coffee, heard bacon pop and sizzle in the pan, and the *chuk, cha-chuk, cha-chuk* of the Rain Bird sprinkler arcing plumes of water across the backyard lawn.

Doc stepped into a pair of khaki pants, reached into his closet and pulled out a short-sleeve white dress shirt. He walked to the mirror, ran a comb through his hair with one hand, buttoned his shirt with the other. Something was different. He stopped, ran the comb through his hair again. It glided through smoothly. He stood in front of the mirror and looked at himself. His hair looked great. It was sort of silky blond and he could swear there were lustrous sun-streaked highlights. He looked older, stronger, tougher, too.

Maybe the girl's stick of Black Jack Gum had infused his hair with some secret salivary source of lanolin. Maybe, like the apple in the Garden of Eden, the gum contained knowledge of a world beyond any hope of innocence. He liked what he saw in the mirror.

Doc walked into the kitchen. His mother was at the stove stirring something that rose bubbling in a pot. Snowball was chewing bits of bacon and sipping from a Tommee Tippee cup. Her white hair stood not only straight up, but straight out in all directions: dandelion hair. Snowball looked up at him. "Dumb-dumb," she said, then resumed nibbling.

His mother reached for a bowl in the cupboard. "Cream of Rice?"

Having tasted the apple, Doc wasn't in the mood for more white food. "No thanks," he said. "Got to get to school." He grabbed a fistful of bacon from Snowball's tray and gobbled it while she stared up at him. "Yum-yum," he said, smoothed down her hair, and headed for the door.

TRAVELIN' JAVELIN

Doc met Jimmy at the corner of Crestview Drive and Valencia Mesa. As they walked side by side toward the high school, Doc told Jimmy about the one-way conversation with his father, the fact that he'd been ordered to spend the rest of the meaningful part of his life babysitting.

A parade of cars rolled past them heading toward the school. Girls leaned out windows, hooted, pushed each other, blew kisses at Jimmy. Guys honked, gave Jimmy serious, knowing nods. Word of what had happened at the Teen Center had apparently gotten around. Last night had added to Jimmy's big-time reputation.

"Any ideas?" Doc asked.

Jimmy stopped smiling at the girls, turned to Doc. "You mean, how we get you out of babysitting?"

"Yeah. It's a raw deal, right? We can't stop skyfishing. A naked girl. A priest. I'm onto something. Something big. I can feel it in my bones."

"Your bona fides?"

"Yeah," Doc said.

Jimmy looked up the street. "Sorry. Got nothing for you. But I think I see someone who might."

At the next corner, Doc saw a rail-thin guy leaning against a fence. The travelin' javelin, Bobby "Slatz" LaDesma, was apparently back from his summer in New York, a summer that had lasted almost a month into the new school year. Never subtle, Slatz wore a canary-yellow shirt, green corduroys, a white belt, and blue suede shoes. His black hair was styled in a pompadour, the sides, the "fenders," as he called them, slicked back into a perfect "ducktail." He rebounded off the fence and walked toward them.

"So how was Juilliard?" Doc asked.

Slatz didn't answer. He never talked about the piano. He looked Doc up and down. "New clothes. Momma take you shoppin'?"

"They're *not* new clothes," Doc said.

"Doc's got big problems," Jimmy said. "He's got to babysit pretty much from here to eternity. He's gonna be a prisoner. No way he'll be able to be my shamus, work the skyfishing project, play bass in the band."

"You're lucky I'm back," Slatz said. "Doc, know what you need? Better representation."

"So wha'da I do, Slatz?" Doc asked. "I can't let this happen. I can't babysit."

He ran a comb through his hair, smoothed his ducktail, thought for a moment. He weaseled a smile. "Simple. We find some trailer skag who's already babysitting. We slip her a few bucks, dump your sister with her. She keeps her mouth shut. The beat goes on."

"Lie to my parents? Lead a double life? I can't do it," Doc said.

Jimmy eyed him. "Not even if it means you'll never solve the case, never see another naked girl?"

Slatz raised an eyebrow. "Not even for 'Jimmy and the Gigolos'?"

In the distance, the first bell rang. Doc had six minutes to get to class.

JESUS EQUALS NOT A NEGRO

"You got your Fertile Crescent and your tight end. One's where Cro-Magnon first sunk his plow. The other marks the beginning of the modern game…You think there's a difference? You're wrong. Who am I? I'm the wet towel that's here to snap your bare butts. I'm here to teach you one lesson, to cram one thing down your throats: Understand football, you understand history."

Doc sat third from the left, front row in first period Western Civilization. "Big Bob" Ugler, the Lancers' varsity coach, stood in front of the class, the blackboard behind him confettied with x's and o's, arrows that curled then shot out in all directions. Caught up in listening to Slatz detail his plan, Doc had gotten to class late and hadn't made it to his seat until a minute after the tardy bell rang.

His late arrival hadn't gone unnoticed, and now Ugler, rolling up his sleeves, was eyeing him again. He hoisted his massive Adam's apple above his open shirt collar, cracked his neck from side to side, tugged down on the chain that held his "championship" whistle. Giving Doc one last steely squint, he looked out at the class.

"In front of each of you's your new playbook." Ugler paced, smiled, rolled his tongue in his cheek. "In here, that's what we call your textbook. These just arrived today, special delivery from the commie sympathizers that control the school board. Turn a few pages, you'll find some color illustrations: Sumerians, Hittites, and Meso-potatee-ums. They look like a bunch of 'darkies.' This is a lie, perpetrated by East Coast commie publishers who want to undermine America. Well, it's not gonna happen here." He stared at Doc. "From the get-go, let me make one thing clear: I'm not gonna tolerate some pansy pinko strollin' into this classroom with his Arthur Miller glasses...Arthur Miller, the Trotsky playwright who stole Marilyn Monroe from Joe DiMaggio...tryin' to start some rumor that Jesus was really a Negro."

Doc rolled his eyes. Ugler was a jackass, a moron with a crew cut just like his dad's. Doc looked around the room. The girl next to him wrote, "Jesus equals not a Negro." Doc sighed, gazed up at the patch of blue sky he could see through the window above the door. A caravan of clouds drifted by. He thought about the girl, the mystery surrounding her life, Jimmy's sister's death, songs he could write about love and freedom if he played in the band. Some part of his soul would die if all he had to live for were school and babysitting. He'd find Slatz between classes, tell him he was right, give the okay to track down a babysitter. Doc realized now that the only way to lead any life would be to live a double life. He'd lie to his parents and that lie would be his liberation.

After class, Doc searched the hallways for Slatz, then remembered they were both scheduled to be in Miss Mooseman's second period, English.

Coming into Miss Mooseman's classroom, he glanced around. Slatz wasn't there yet, but Grill was. He was chatting up girls who, if they said anything to him at all, asked only his last name, hoping, Doc guessed, alphabetical seating would put them rows away from him. Doc took the opportunity to look around, too. Maybe a girl here was the babysitter he needed.

He searched each female face for eyes that said, "I'd love to help you." No sparks, just polite smiles.

The second period tardy bell rang and Miss Mooseman took roll. She reminded Doc of the subject in a nineteenth century portrait, a young woman who, throughout the sitting, would have been suspicious of the artist. Pretty in a reserved sort of way, she wore her dark hair up in a bun, a green silk blouse buttoned to her throat. Still, there were aspects that hinted at a daring Bohemian side. She cinched her black skirt with a leopard belt, wore cat glasses like Margaret Ann. Her earrings were tiny mobiles. Each danced differently when she turned her head. Mildred Mooseman was avant-garde.

When she called Bobby LaDesma's name, three girls—a blonde, a brunette, and a redhead—raised their hands. The blonde said Slatz was helping Mr. Clegg in Auto Shop. He was reversing the shackles on a '40 Ford, a tricky operation that only a guy from Brooklyn would know how to perform. The brunette disagreed. "He's preparing several of his signature Hispano-Italian dishes for Miss Anderson in Home Economics. Cilantro Manicotti Suizas and Toltec Cannelloni." The redhead shook her head and announced with confidence Slatz was creating some new arrangements for the a cappella choir. "You know, Miss Mooseman," she said, "Slatz was a finalist in the Van Cliburn Competition."

"I look forward to meeting this apparently talented young man," Miss Mooseman said, glancing around the class. "If...Slatz is unable to attend, is there someone who could pass on his homework assignment?"

Doc slowly raised his hand.

She looked at Doc, checked the roll sheet. "Thank you, Mr. Ruggles." Her gaze lingered on him a moment. "I like your glasses," she said. "A little like Buddy Holly's, though on you, perhaps more like Arthur Miller's. Perhaps both music and writing are in your future." She took off her glasses, removed the clasp from her hair, then clipped a "Kennedy for President" campaign button to the front of her blouse. "Before we get started, I want to remind you that, in this class, we will be looking at literature in the context of contemporary thought. Historically, most Americans have viewed life through a Christian perspective. In recent decades, this view has been challenged. The educated community has come to believe this rather antiquated, certainly naïve view of the world has lead us into wars, been a justification for slavery and has thwarted sexual expression. The religious person, conditioned by the power structure, sees life as an arc beginning with birth, followed by a period of time during which the individual attempts to follow commandments while bearing witness to God's wonders. After death, the baptized person enjoys eternal life. This may be fine for the simpleton and the superstitious. Sophisticated people and social scientists of today have offered up a different point of view. It is one that puts the emphasis on existence, not essence. The arc in this model begins with birth, then a near eternity of torment characterized by abject terror, despair, and meaninglessness. Life ends with death and nothingness. Works of poetry and literature that celebrate this model are frequently described as brilliant, evocative, and soul-wrenching."

Doc listened, did his best to nod along with her presentation, but found himself wondering, how can poetry and literature wrench the human soul if that soul doesn't exist in the first place?

Miss Mooseman stopped and looked out at the class. "Do you have a question, Mr. Ruggles?"

"No," he said.

A girl from the back of the class cleared her throat and asked, "Now that we've finished the short stories from the anthology, will we be reading *The Mill on the Floss*?"

"Despite growing objections by the Board of Education, the answer is an unqualified yes. As some of you know, having talked to older sisters, Mary Ann Evans wrote this novel at a time when women were, shall we say, discouraged from publishing. She wrote it almost exactly one hundred years ago using the pen name George Eliot. She wrote in the 'realist' tradition. Perhaps too real for the times. The young woman at the center of the novel is caught between the world of convention and the world of her desires. Now, a century later, many young women feel the same 'realistic' tug. Let's get it out in the open, right?" She glanced around the room, raised an eyebrow. "Some of you have perhaps stolen a peek at your mother's copy of Kinsey's *Sexual Behavior in the Human Female.* Others have been reading about the birth control pill about to be released. I see no reason to avoid any aspect of this book, including references to deviant sexual relationships."

"*All right Miss Mooseman!*"

The shout, slurred through wired teeth, came from Grill.

Miss Mooseman called him to the front of the room. "Herb, I need you to apologize to the class for your outburst."

Coming forward, Grill pleaded, "Gosh, Miss Mooseman, I'm sorry. I was overcome by your willingness to champion our First Amendment right to free speech." He gave the class a wink. "Frankly, your words touched me, touched me deeply, touched me where it counts."

Miss Mooseman, a good reader, read between the lines.

Grill spent the rest of the period with a smile on his face and a bar of soap between his teeth. Unlike the "modern" novel we were about to read, the punishment she selected was old-fashioned, puritanical, demeaning.

Grill didn't seem to mind. He asked if he could keep the soap as a souvenir.

After the bell rang, Doc and Grill stepped outside. Slatz was there. Leaning against a pole, he had a look of satisfaction on his face. "I found a babysitter," he said. "It's all set. You're gonna meet her after school at Ascension Park."

"I'm meeting this girl at a cemetery?"

"Doc...think about it. This way, you've got it made. What kinda girl says 'no' in a graveyard?"

THE ELEMENT OF SURPRISE

"Rusty Richards is drivin' us," Slatz said, looking back over his shoulder. "You know him, don't ya?"

Taking two steps to Slatz's one, Doc nodded.

They turned a corner in the hallway, worked their way down the crowded corridor past open classroom doors. Slatz waved away the acrid smell that came from the chemistry lab, flamboyantly breathed in the apple-pie aroma wafting from Home Ec. He blew a kiss at a ten-foot-long banner tacked to a wall: "Homecoming Dance Friday, Autumn Reign," then gave a thumbs-up to a second banner that arched over the hallway: "Campaign Comes to Town. Kennedy in Person at Amerige Park." They burst through the last gate. Slatz was done with school for the day.

Earlier, at lunch, with Grill and Jimmy gathered around, they'd sat on benches in the sweltering heat, the Santa Anas blowing, Doc listening as Slatz talked about the girl. "Her name's Bonnie," he'd said. "She lives across the tracks. Dad split years ago. Went out for a loaf of bread, never came back. Mom's a barmaid, works someplace in Anaheim called 'The Farmer's Daughter.'" Slatz Grouchoed his eyebrows, leaned back. "And she's already babysittin' a little brother. Way I figure it, we slip her a few coins, it's in the bag."

At that point, everyone having put in their two cents worth, they'd made a pact to keep the Gigolos together come hell or high water, to end Doc's nursemaid days before they began. To celebrate, they'd mowed down sandwiches and potato chips from grease-stained paper bags.

Classroom buildings behind them now, Doc and Slatz crossed the strip of lawn that ringed the campus, hurried down to the parking lot. Doc, excited and nervous at the same time, knew if he dumped Snowball with a babysitter, traded his family's trust for a chance at love and a spot in the band, there'd be no turning back. But how much less could his father respect him? Why go home to a *parent* so utterly *transparent*? Why go home to a man who wanted his own son to live like a girl? He wouldn't babysit, not now, not ever.

Parked amid the cars beating it out of the lot, Doc saw Rusty's Ford Fairlane. Rusty, wearing a black turtleneck sweater, paced back and forth on the driver's side. Jimmy, his shirt off, sunned himself on the hood. Spotting them, Jimmy called out, "Get a move on, guys. Rusty's got to get back for practice."

They piled into the Fairlane. Doc took the backseat behind Jimmy. They sped back up Valencia Mesa, Jimmy and Rusty talking back and forth about sports, Jimmy, for some reason, working hard to pump up Rusty's spirits for the big game Friday night.

"Does anyone know why this girl's going to a cemetery?" Doc asked.

Sitting across from Doc, Slatz shrugged. "Scarlett didn't say. Visiting some dead relative would be my guess."

Rusty's eyes narrowed. He glared at Slatz in the rear-view mirror. "Scarlett?"

"Yeah. She's the one who tipped me off to Bonnie."

Rusty gripped the wheel, sped through a red light, wheeled sharply onto Brea Boulevard.

"Tell your girlfriend thanks," Doc said.

"She's not my girlfriend," Rusty muttered. "Not anymore. The chick's just plain weird."

Slatz slapped the back of Rusty's seat. "Won't put out, huh?"

Doc cringed.

Tight-jawed, Rusty whipped off the highway. The Fairlane bounced down a dirt road lined with signs that said over and over again, "No Trespassing." Heat, dust, and the smell of dry grass swirled in through the open windows.

"So this is what…a short cut?" Doc asked.

Rusty said nothing. He punched buttons on the radio, looking, Doc guessed, for a song to drown out whatever was playing in his head. The car kept going. It bounded across a dry creek bed, stones pelleting the undercarriage.

Through the windshield, Doc saw a sweeping rock wall, a giant oak where the rutted road came to a dead end. They fishtailed over combed gravel the last fifty yards. The Fairlane stopped.

Pointing to a wrought iron gate, Jimmy said, "Used to be the back way into the cemetery. Nobody comes this way anymore."

"Gives you the element of surprise, Doc," Slatz said.

Jimmy opened the door, let Doc climb out.

"Surprise? Why do I need the element of surprise? She knows we're coming, right?"

Jimmy looked at Slatz, back at Doc. "You're on your own. Rusty's taking us to Fullerton Music. We've got band practice."

"My mom will pick you up at the front entrance in an hour," Slatz said. "She'll run you down to the store. We'll be in the percussion practice room."

Jimmy slid back into the Fairlane, closed the door.

Spitting gravel from the rear tires, the Ford spun in a circle. As it roared past, Rusty gave Doc a long slow-motion stare, tugged down the collar of his turtleneck. His eyes, red-rimmed, conveyed a sense of warning. He pointed to his throat, mouthed the name Scarlett. A welt like the mark left by a hangman's noose raised the skin around the base of his throat. His last look said, "Stay away from her."

Doc stood alone next to the stone wall. The wind blew hot as a blast furnace. Branches of the oak creaked above his head. He wondered what Rusty's final look was supposed to mean. Was he supposed to stay away from Scarlett or Bonnie? He couldn't figure out how to stay away from a girl he was supposed to meet.

He watched the Fairlane fade into the distance, its form wobbled in heat waves rising from the ground.

"She *does* know I'm coming, right?" he yelled.

His words floated, blew back over his head, the letters disassembling as they scattered across the dead, dry brush.

A gust of wind shoved him sideways, tossed him like a scrap of paper against the wrought iron gate. He took the path of least resistance, wiggled his way between the bars. With no way back, he might as well go forward. Kill an hour in the cemetery. Maybe the dead, those who'd gone to the grave having never brought their own dreams to life, would understand why he was here. Maybe the dead would bring him luck.

Doc crunched along a gravel road onto a flagstone path that led up to a visitor's center and patio courtyard overlooking an expanse of lawn that swept out like an emerald sea. He breathed in the heady tide of freshly mown grass, listened to the hum of a million busy bees. Ahead of and below him, white crosses, like masts of sailing ships, dotted the landscape. To his left, on the opposite hill, there was a mausoleum and a rose garden with a statuary.

He saw movement, narrowed his focus. Someone was down there, someone was moving among the statues: a distant figure dressed in black.

Descending from the crest, Doc worked his way between the crosses to a cluster of palms that surrounded a small lily pond at the edge of the rose garden. He knelt, hid. The fronds, like a fan made of peacock feathers, waved back and forth in front of his eyes. It was like he was behind a screen.

Among the flowers, marble saints, and seraphim, a nun turned in circles, waltzed around a gravestone, her arms held outward as though draped over the shoulders of an invisible dance partner. The wind chased the hem of her habit, billowing it several dangerous inches above her knees. She was barefoot. Pink polish adorned her toenails.

Doc stepped out from his hiding place.

The nun stopped, looked at him. "Care for the next dance?" she said.

"Sister Theresa?"

"Hi, Doc."

Doc's eyes panned the rose garden, then met Sister Theresa's. "You're not...Bonnie, are you?"

"No...Who's Bonnie?"

"A girl I'm supposed to meet here. Never know if the guys are playing a little joke on me, sending me on a wild goose chase."

"Haven't seen any geese." She leveled the crown of her habit. "Did see some ducks down by the pond."

"What brings *you* here?" Doc asked.

She trailed her hand above a row of roses, plucked a pink one, leaned against a sepulcher. Her eyes got a little dreamy. "Reliving a few memories," she sighed. "You won't tell anyone you saw me?"

"Who would I tell?"

She seemed to study him. "By the way," she said, "you ever make it up to the cross?"

"Yeah. Thanks for the ladder...That's right, I owe you one."

"So I can ask a favor?"

"Sure."

"I want you to introduce me to Jimmy."

Now Doc sighed. "Why does every girl want to meet Jimmy?"

She started to speak, but Doc stopped her.

"Nevermind. I get it. I understand."

"No," she said. "No, you don't. What I mean is I need to tell him about his sister. I know things. The angels speak to me."

Doc shook his head. "I don't know. Jimmy's not too crazy about religious stuff. He might have been baptized Catholic, but he never had much faith."

"I'd still like to talk to him if you can arrange it. You think about it, okay?" she said.

A rush of wind raced past Doc and tugged the rose from Sister Theresa's hand. It spiraled off like a little cocktail umbrella, disappeared among the reeds and palms that surrounded the pond.

"My corsage. Oh no," she said, her voice tinged with sadness. "It was so beautiful."

Doc looked at her. "Would you like me to find it for you?"

Her lips got pouty. "Please."

He'd forgotten how pretty she was.

"Sure," he said.

Doc trudged down to the pond, looked around, stepped in among the reeds. He bent, raked his arms through wet marsh grass and cattails. His shoes sucked mud. A frenzy of gnats cycloned around his face, covered his forearms. Dragonflies buzzed his ears.

No rose in sight.

Doc stood, looked back. "Sister Theresa?"

The garden was silent. She'd disappeared just like she had after she'd given him the ladder.

He took a few steps up the hill, stopped at the outer border of the garden, and sat down on a stone step. He kicked off his shoes, peeled off his mud-soaked socks, banged the soles of his shoes together.

"Barefoot's no way to come to a cemetery."

Doc looked over his shoulder. Perched on the same headstone Sister Theresa had danced around, sat the crow he'd met at the railroad tracks.

"You sound like my dad," Doc mumbled. He stood and stared at the creature. "So where are *your* shoes?"

"Ever tried to scratch for worms with shoes on? Balance on a branch wearing boots?"

"Excuses. In life you either produce results or excuses."

"Now," the crow said, "you sound like *my* dad."

"Don't pay any attention to me. I'm havin' kind of a rough day." He looked at the crow. "So your dad was hard on you, too?"

"Put it this way: He didn't think I was much to 'crow' about."

"My dad doesn't think I live in the real world," Doc said. "Maybe he's right. Look at me now. I'm talking to a crow…Who does that?"

"Who does that?" He locked his beady eyes on Doc. "The word 'nevermore' come to mind?"

"Edgar Allan Poe? 'The Raven'?"

"It wasn't a raven. It was a crow: my great-great-great-grandfather to be precise. He was the poet behind the poet." Wistfully, the crow lifted his eyes to the heavens. "And the silken sad uncertain rustling of each purple curtain." He looked over at Doc, shook his head.

"The opening of the third stanza. What a great line."

"My grandpappy's idea. Every word…Try gettin' that lyric through to a drunk poet when your palate's the width of a pencil."

"You're saying a crow wrote 'The Raven?'"

The bird nodded. "Before he settled on 'The Raven,' Poe had the nerve to suggest to my grandpappy that they call the poem 'The Parrot.' Talk about adding insult to injury."

"Why didn't Poe just call it 'The Crow'?"

"'Quoth the crow' supposedly sounded too scratchy. Wasn't sonorous enough. In the end the guy with the pen had the power."

"Tough break," Doc said.

"Yeah, like they say, art hurts."

"Some days it all hurts," Doc said, looking out over the cemetery. "You haven't seen a girl about my age wandering around, have you?"

"She have something to do with your murder mystery?"

"No. I just need her to help me buy some time so Jimmy and I can keep looking for answers."

The crow sat, dangled his bird feet over the top of the tombstone. "Ever thought you might have missed a clue to your murder mystery along the way? Maybe something right under your *nose*?"

"Don't think so," Doc said.

The crow rolled his black BB eyes. "How about something right under *my feet?*"

Doc looked at the gravestone, studied the inscription. "'Tommy McLean, born January fifth, nineteen thirty-seven, went to join Our Lord September twenty-first, nineteen fifty-four.' So?" Doc said.

The crow torsioned his shoulder joints, tilted his head from side to side as though trying to unravel a spasm that was creeping up his neck. "Didn't that nun say she *knew* something about Jimmy's *dead* sister?"

"I think she meant something spiritual."

The crow looked exasperated. "And I thought my grandpappy had it tough working with a rummy." He stared at Doc. "You want my feathers to fall out? You want my immune system to weaken to the point I'm infested with mites? Ever heard the phrase *chain of evidence?* Ever thought a mystery from one death might hold the clue to solving a death that occurred at later point in time?"

"Sounds complicated," Doc said. "Kinda hard to follow."

"Think about it. The dead move on but maybe something stays in the physical world and this thing is connected to a second death. But this second death is no accident, see? It's a murder." The crow sighed. "I'm trying to be your mentor, your muse. You want to solve the mystery, write the story, get published?"

"I'd love to get published," Doc said. "It's something I've always dreamed of."

"Well stop dreaming and check out the story behind this dead kid here. The one the wacky nun was dancing with. Think she was trying to tell you something? Maybe? Duh?"

"Sister Theresa *is* a little odd," he said. "And now that you mention it, the bare feet, the disappearing act, and the pink polish have always kinda bothered me."

"And don't you think she's a little young? A little too sexy?"

"She once told me she wanted to strip off her clothes and throw herself into a pond of Holy Water."

"There you go."

Doc leaned forward, looked the crow right in his squinty eyes. "So you're my muse?"

"Patton's the name. Great-granddad's blood flows in my veins." He lifted from the tombstone, flapped up to the bare branch of a sycamore. He scanned the horizon, hesitated a moment. "I think your girl just arrived." He pointed a wing westward. "Better get going."

Doc looked. Patton was right. There was a girl. "You've given me something to think about. Thanks for the tip."

"I'll give you one more. Don't forget those 'quaint and curious volumes of forgotten lore.' It's from the opening of 'The Raven.' It is important you remember those lines."

Patton spread his wings and rocketed into the sky.

GIMP CARD

The girl Doc saw in the distance held three bright balloons in her hand, their strings stretched out in front of her, taut as tightropes, by the force of the wind. She walked in Doc's direction, her head down, her hair whipping around her face. The gusts nearly levitated her feet from the grass.

A shiver of excitement, a vague sense of remembering coursed through Doc's body. Something about the look of the girl, her face veiled by her windblown hair, her feet defying gravity, her body tugged forward by the balloons...It all seemed eerily familiar. Doc recalled the dream he'd had the night before: he and Kipling in the café, the three tigers testing the satin leashes, the princess whose feet had floated just above the ground, the tiger who'd broken away from the others and menaced him. The dream had ended abruptly, left him with the feeling he was about to be eaten. Maybe last night had been a premonition, somehow symbolic of what would happen in the cemetery today.

The girl, closer now, walked through the grassy depression just below the rose garden. She stopped at a gravesite, tied the balloons to the simple white cross affixed there, and knelt down.

She began to pray.

Her words seemed to affect the world. The wind stopped its incessant blustering, its breath taken away by the beauty of her sorrow.

Mockingbirds rose from trees, spiraled skyward, their white wings banded in black feathers. Great sighs of purple clouds shouldered their way to the rim of the valley and stopped to witness her mourning. Somewhere in the distance, a church bell rang.

He couldn't imagine approaching her now. How could he ask her to be complicit in a lie, do a favor for a sneaky little ingrate? How could he take advantage of a girl from whom so much had apparently been taken? He doubted she'd been told he was coming. He'd go. He'd leave her alone.

Her prayer concluded, she stood, looked around. Turning, she walked back down the hill toward the main gate.

The wind began to howl again. A dust devil touched down, cycloned between the elongated shadows of the tombstones. Its force tore one of the balloons away from the cross. The red balloon skipped over the grass, bounded up the hillside, and sailed over Doc's head. It struck the top of the sycamore, lodged among the branches.

Doc looked back at the girl. Unaware of what had happened, she was still walking away.

He felt sorry for her; he couldn't bear the thought of the balloon, this symbol of her reverence, being popped by a branch or remaining there only to have the helium fizzle out. He'd make up for spying on her. He'd rescue the balloon, return it to its rightful place.

Still barefoot, Doc walked to the tree, grabbed the lowest limb, pulled himself up, reached above his head again. Branches clawed at his face, scratched his skin, knocked his glasses cockeyed. Above him, the balloon thrummed among the limbs. He extended his arm, stretched his fingers, caught hold of the string, pulled the balloon down. Holding the string between his teeth, he descended.

Dangling from the lowest branch, Doc looked down. The girl stood there beneath him. His eyes met hers. It was the girl he'd danced with at the Teen Center: the Black Jack Gum girl.

He dropped to the ground.

"So you can dance *and* climb trees," she said.

Doc took the string from his mouth. "Your balloon blew away. I wanted to put it back with the others…Here," he said, holding out the string.

She didn't take it. She seemed more interested in watching the balloon climb. He watched it, too. The balloon continued to float upward, the string attached to it seeming to grow longer and longer, as though they were witnessing a magic trick. It disappeared among the branches. He tugged down on the string, smiled at her, tugged a little harder.

Pop.

Her eyes lowered to meet his.

A red worm of rubber dropped from the sky and fell to the ground between them.

Doc looked down at the remains, at what was left of a good idea.

Without thinking, he offered her the limp string.

She started to cry.

"I'm sorry," he said. "Please don't…weep."

She turned away from him. "I'm not 'weeping.' It's just the wind in my eyes."

Doc reached into his hip pocket, pulled out a pink handkerchief. He studied it a second, recalled it was the one Margaret Ann had given him at the library. "Here," he said.

She shook her head.

"It's not the string, it's a handkerchief."

She looked over her shoulder at him, frowned. "I really don't want something you blow your nose on."

Doc reached back into his pocket, produced a second handkerchief, a white one. "This isn't a blowing-your-nose handkerchief. It's a handkerchief for girls in case they start to…get wind in their eyes. In fact, it's great for girls with wind problems."

She took the pink handkerchief and dabbed her eyes. "You always carry two handkerchiefs?"

"It's a family tradition. It was passed down by my great-grandfather, Rudyard Kipling. I think he came up with the idea when he was in India."

She nodded her head. "Ya know, I think I read somewhere it's very windy in India."

"Really?"

"No, not really," she said sarcastically, a grin tugging at the corner of her mouth. She lifted Doc's glasses from his face. "Here, give me those. They're all sweaty and sappy."

Doc watched the wind blow through her hair and studied her hands as she cleaned the lenses of his glasses, the handkerchief she was using still damp from her tears.

"I'd love to go to India," she said, without looking up. "Someplace you could go and they'd never find you and you'd never want to come back." She lifted her head. "Where'd you like to go?"

"I just want to go to band practice."

She smiled, set the glasses gently on the bridge of his nose. The last of her tears evaporated from the lenses, and Doc saw his world crystal clear with her in the middle of it.

"Scarlett says your band's pretty good."

"Right now the band's more like an idea than a reality. We've never actually played together. We just need time to write some songs. Practice a little."

"That's where I come in, right? You need a babysitter."

In the distance Doc heard a horn honk, saw the priest's car pull up to the entrance at the bottom of the hill.

"Got to go," she said.

Doc blocked her way. "Wait."

"Don't worry. I'll babysit. You need me. I need the money. Simple as that."

"No. No it's not as simple as that."

She tried to walk past him. Doc grabbed her arm. "You don't understand."

She shook his hand away. "There's nothing *to* understand."

"Bonnie. That's your name, isn't it?"

"So what?"

"You kissed me last night. You left, ran away without telling me your name."

"It was late. I had to go."

"So you slapped me goodbye?"

"Someone's waiting for me. And don't ever grab me again."

"But *he* can grab you?" Doc said, gesturing in the direction of the car. "I saw him do that to you at the Teen Center. And he's done it before, hasn't he?"

She stiffened. "I'm leaving. Goodbye, Doc."

"Are you in some kind of trouble? I can help."

"I'm not in trouble, but I did make one mistake: kissing you."

Doc looked around at the cemetery, down at the car idling by the gate. "I don't think so."

"Don't flatter yourself," she said.

"What I mean is, it was destiny."

She stomped down the hill. "Oh! You're my destiny. Wouldn't want to confuse that with flattering yourself."

Doc shook his head. "Our *meeting* was destiny."

She waved "I'm coming" at the car.

Doc followed. "Want to know a secret?"

She walked faster.

Doc stepped in front of her, walked backward. "You're the girl who says she wants to run off to India. At the dance, you said the last guy to kiss you held you down. And don't you think it's kinda like destiny that you offer to babysit not knowing that what it does is give me time to help you?"

"You make so much out of a kiss. It's all about love, gettin' lucky. For me, a kiss has always been the beginning of pain and sadness."

"Then why did you kiss me?"

"Pay me for babysitting: that'll solve my problems," she said, breaking into a run.

Doc took off after her, his polio leg stiffening with each step.

She was fast.

"I want to meet this priest. I'm serious." His words nipped at her heels, but she got away.

The priest's car pulled closer to the entrance as she neared the gate.

Doc was still on the grass when her hand touched the car's door. She got in.

The Buick rolled away.

Doc stood on gravel road. "What about the gum?" he yelled. "What about the handkerchief? In my world those things mean something."

The priest's Buick rounded the corner, picked up speed.

"What about destiny? What about fate?" he shouted.

There was silence. A long silence. In the distance, Doc heard the rumble of a car coming up the hill, coming closer. Was she coming back? Had she made the priest turn around?

The answer was no.

The chop-top Mercury zeroed in on him, skidded to a stop. There were five in the car: Junior, his three goons, and Raylene.

They all got out, Fang last to emerge, Raylene pleading, tugging at his arm urging him to stay in the car. Junior opened the trunk, handed each thug a baseball bat.

The two Bluto brothers came toward Doc in some sort of pincer maneuver, their arms spread wide, their weight shifting from foot to foot. Fang waved the bat above his head, juked from side to side.

Junior's gunslinger eyes locked on Doc. He pointed the barrel of the bat at Doc's head. "So where's your friend, pretty boy? Got a message for him."

Doc didn't answer. He looked past Junior at the Mercury parked in the lot, at its busted headlight, its dented front fender. He prayed

Slatz's mom would choose this moment to arrive. But there was no sign of Bunny LaDesma's pink Coupe de Ville. Only one option left. He wasn't proud of what he was about to do.

"Hey, four-eyes, we're talkin' to you," Fang yipped.

Doc squinted through his glasses at Junior, gazed around vaguely as though, seen through his coke-bottle lenses, the world was hardly more than a blur. Facing certain death, he had no choice: He played the blind card, the gimp card, the infectious disease card.

"Sorry, I'm having trouble hearing," Doc said. "Sometimes the fever just comes over me. The virus." He phlegmed a consumptive cough. "It's never really gone."

Junior's eyes flicked from side to side. "What are you talkin' about?"

"The polio. It's back," Doc said, a tragic tone of acceptance tingeing his voice. "Didn't the priest tell you?" He extended his arms to Junior, limped a few syphilitic steps forward. "It doesn't matter now. What matters is you're the only ones who've come to join the prayer group." Doc raised his voice in praise. "Yea, though germs slime my body, yea, though contagion seeps through every pore of my skin, I thank you, friends, whoever you are, for coming to me in my hour of need…Let us pray."

The Blutos knelt, made the sign of the cross.

Fang poured M&Ms into his mouth, chewed slowly.

Junior smirked. "So you're sayin' you don't know us?"

Doc shook his head.

"Well, you're gonna *remember* us," Junior said, "'cause when we're though with you, you'll be back in one of those iron lungs. And when I catch up to your pal, pretty boy, he'll be lying right next to you."

Fang laughed, his open mouth all wet brown M&M teeth. "Iron lung? Heard those machines turn you queer…Bet you're daddy's little girl, aren't you?"

Doc exhaled slowly. He'd given it his best shot at being a wimp. Now he was reminded of something else: He'd recently become "interesting," become a guy who wouldn't stand for someone holding a girl down. He wouldn't go back to being invisible. He smiled at Fang, smiled because he saw in Fang's eyes the same weakness he saw everyday in the mirror. "No, Fang," he said calmly, "M&Ms turn *you* queer."

Fang exploded. "Just the green ones. Everyone knows it's just the green ones. I toss those out. You can check the bag."

"Show the bag to the police," Doc blared triumphantly, "'cause here they come!"

Junior, Fang, and the Blutos whipped around.

Doc spun, sprinted back through the open gate into Ascension Park. They'd fallen for the oldest trick in the book: He'd "made them look." Now he could only hope the hours he'd spent pedaling after the kite would pay off. He'd try to outrun them. Just because you limp when you walk doesn't mean you can't run.

His toes caught traction in the grass. He found an angle up the hill where the wind was at his back. With a little luck, he could make it to the rose garden, lose them among the statues, climb the sycamore, hide among the branches.

He looked over his shoulder. The world behind him melted into a nightmare, a waking slow-motion dream where he moved through molasses while his pursuers walked faster than he could run. He saw Fang jump from the tops of tombstones like a demented demon. The Blutos, like monoliths unearthed from Easter Island, lumbered forward chanting, "Fce-fi-fo-fum." Junior was nowhere in sight.

Doc scrambled past the grave marker with the balloons attached, skirted the palms at the edge of the pond, charged the hill that led back to the rose garden, the mausoleum, the sycamore. Head down, he climbed the stone steps, almost tripped over the muddy shoes he'd left there. He lookcd up.

Three feet in front of him, Junior leaned against the sycamore, bat raised.

Doc braked, slipped, fell back against a marble statue.

He heard the whoosh just above his head. Wood smashed against marble.

Stone fingers, splinters of Louisville Slugger exploded in all directions, rained down on his chest.

Doc scrambled to his feet, backed up, spun around. His eyes met Fang's. Head down, he freight-trained Fang, drove his head into the weasel's sugar-saturated gut. His momentum took him to the mausoleum's door. He grabbed the knob, turned. The tomb was open.

Doc scrambled into the darkness, his footfalls echoing off walls that formed a high-rise for the dead. He turned a corner, spotted a shaft of light that sliced its way in through an open door at the far end of the corridor. He dug deep, willed himself to keep running.

With every step, pain literally stabbed at his heart. His fingers fumbled in his left shirt pocket. He pulled out a thin dagger of pine, a remnant of the shattered bat. He burst through the partially open door. Stopped. Something had caught his eye.

The knob on the door had been installed backward. The keyed side of the lock faced inside the tomb. He looked at the sliver of hardwood in his hand, turned, reached back, jabbed the jagged pine shard into the lock, twisted. Something clicked. He tested the knob. It wouldn't turn. Somewhere in the darkness he could hear them coming. He snapped the stick off at its hilt, slammed the door. If Junior and his minions tried to follow him now, they'd have to negotiate the pitch-black tomb, shoulder their way through a locked door or turn around and go back the way they'd come. "Yes!"

Having a few seconds to spare, Doc stopped at the crest of the hill, grabbed a breath, looked toward the visitor's center on the opposite ridge. Why was there never adult supervision? How could this place be deserted? It was the middle of the day. Didn't people die in the middle of the day?

He spun around, looked in all directions. Beyond a grove of oaks, a patch of white the size of a small circus tent captured his attention. He heard the snap of canvas.

He sprinted toward it, dodged the trees, reached the clearing. In front of him, a wind-blown canopy shaded an open grave. Off to the side, a shovel speared a mound of dirt, a curled green hose lay next to it. Looking back up the hill, he saw Junior and the others stumble out of the entrance to the mausoleum. Shielding his eyes, Junior pointed in Doc's direction.

Doc looked over his shoulder. Surrounding him on three sides was a stone wall not even the dead could climb.

So this would be it, Doc thought. A gravesite would be his Little Big Horn.

As they closed in, Doc considered his options. Like Robin Hood, he could use the shovel as a staff. No, he'd use the hose. Like Jimmy, he'd use it to perform a few cowboy tricks, a little Wild West roping. The whole idea was a ridiculous long shot, but had had to try something. Lifting it, he whirled the eight-foot length of green rubber above his head. Its nozzle whistled in the wind.

"Whatcha gonna do?" Fang chattered, strutting toward him. "Water us to death?" The Blutos, transfixed, watched the wheeling motion of the hose. Junior, his eyes like cylinders of twin revolvers, took dead aim at Doc. He picked up the shovel, stuck it out.

Doc lashed out with the hose. Its initial trajectory was right on course, true as a rifle shot. Junior defended, snagged the hose. In twists and turns it wound up the hilt of the shovel like stripes up a barber pole. The nozzle smacked the shovel's blade. *Whack.*

"If that had been someone's head," Doc said, "that smack would have really hurt. All of us might want to think about that."

Junior shoved Doc down on the grass. He tried to pull the end of the hose from Doc's hand.

Doc turned on his stomach, wouldn't let go.

Junior kicked him in the back. The heel of the same boot pushed Doc's face into the wet grass.

Fang tugged at the cuffs of Doc's pants. Without shoes, his beige Corbins slid over his hips, down his legs. The Blutos tore at his shirt.

In his grass-stained underwear, Doc crawled toward the open grave.

The Blutos grabbed his legs, Fang cinched them with the long end of the hose, kept wrapping till Doc was mummified. With the toe of his black boot, Junior rolled Doc toward the edge of the grave.

He dropped six feet, thudded onto his back.

In the rectangle of light above him, he saw the elongated forms of Junior, Fang, the Blutos.

Doc spit out grass, wet dirt. "I think you guys have made your point. So what's the message for Jimmy? You need me to pass it on. Fine, I'll do it."

The figures above him had disappeared.

"Okay," Doc said. "I take it this was an object lesson…Hello?" He tried to Houdini free of the hose. Nothing budged. "You just gonna leave me like this?"

The first shovelful of dirt came down on him.

Surely, Doc thought, the act was meant to be symbolic, a ghoulish punctuation mark, Junior's finishing touch. He writhed futilely against the constraint of the hose, lifted his head. "Okay, I get the metaphor, you bury your enemies. That's the message you want me to deliver to Jimmy? No problem. I'll do it…Now get me out of here!"

Backlit, the four cutout figures hovered above him.

The Blutos began chanting, "Fee-fi-fo-fum." Fang, cackling like a madman, ran in circles kicking dirt down on him. More dirt, avalanches of it, spilled in. An ominous rhythm rose from the mountain of earth next to the grave. Doc could hear the *chunk* as the heel of Junior's boot stomped the spade. Doc's pulse raced, panic squeezed his throat. "Someone could get hurt here…You hear me? Enough of the fun and games."

Brandishing the shovel, Junior looked down on him. "We don't play games." A thud of dirt knocked his glasses sideways; mud smeared the lenses. He glanced down at his chest as another shovelful landed on him. His body was disappearing. They weren't through. They *were* going to bury him alive.

A voice in his head screamed, "No!"

He couldn't, no, wouldn't just give up. He had band practice! His life had just begun. He was on the brink of leading a secret life! He almost had a girlfriend!

Doc's hands found another gear. He throttled the nozzle, squirmed, twisted his body. One arm burst free of the rubber wrapping. He shoved his fist through the layer of dirt that covered him. A cool breeze blew across his forearm. Only a few inches of earth still covered him.

He pulled his arm back, stuck the nozzle of the hose into his mouth, prayed the other end of the hose wasn't screwed into a faucet, that it still snaked up over the lip of the grave. He sucked, spit out water, grit, sucked again. Oxygen! Just enough to keep him going. Still, he was at the bottom of an hourglass filled with earth. Time was running out.

He sucked on the hose, inhaled, Dizzy Gillespied his cheeks to the limit. With all his might he trumpeted through the mouthpiece of the hose one long word: "Helllp!" The sound gurgled the length of the hose.

In the distance he heard his wet, rubbery voice emerge from the other end, the sound forlorn as a foghorn: "Helllp!"

Out of breath, Doc's mind spun. Dizzy, he felt himself sinking. In his imagination, even as he heard Junior yell out, "This is just a warning," he felt his lungs fill with the dust of decayed bone, his mouth fill with the taste of metal leached from the blood of corpses. He saw his body sink through the earth, pass through generations of the dead. He saw artifacts, relics, prehistoric fossils trapped in tar. In his thoughts, he traveled downward through the Earth's bubbly, molten core.

The planet rolled through half a full rotation. Gravity pulled him on. He knew he must be imagining all of this. What he couldn't imagine was that he could actually die beneath a few inches of dirt. But he knew things like this happened. People drown in six inches of bath water. No way could he picture himself dead. This, he told himself, was just an experience, something you later tell other guys about and they say, "Come on, man, you're exaggerating."

Faint in the world above ground, he heard someone speaking. Was it Chinese? Had he actually fallen all the way through planet Earth?

The voice grew louder, barked something he couldn't understand. He could hear thumping above him, the sound of a stampede.

A tug on the hose.

His grip reflexively tightened.

He came out of the ground like a turnip pulled from a farmer's garden.

Doc blinked away dirt, wiped mud from his ears and face. An Asian man the size of a sumo wrestler stood over him. He wore gray overalls; the name "Ricky" was stitched above the pocket.

"You're in luck," he said.

Doc spit dirt. "Where am I? China?"

"You survive fraternity prank. Initiation…yes? You lucky." A smile like a haiku spread across the giant's face. "Underwear boy make me laugh."

THE GIRL IN THE
PINK FORMAL

Ricky walked Doc up to the visitor's center.

"You have shaky legs. Sure you all right?"

"I'm fine. Thanks for running those guys off," Doc said.

"I tell them, you go now or I get hedge clippers…" Ricky looked down on Doc. "They almost bury you in dirt. This was just prank, right?"

"Sorta."

Inside the visitor's center, soft music piped from unseen speakers. Desks were positioned around the room, stiff-backed chairs placed opposite them. Double doors opened into three separate chambers: a small chapel, a room that displayed coffins, another room with headstones and easels that supported plastic flower wreaths.

In the back of a custodian's closet, Ricky found a black suit coat for Doc. He held out the "mortuary jacket," displayed the front, then the reverse side.

"Go on easy. See slit up back…Sorry, no pants."

The coat was extralong and fit Doc like a hospital gown. He rolled the sleeves, glanced down at his bare legs. Looking at him, Ricky gestured for the coat again.

Laying the jacket on a bereavement bench, Ricky made a few deft tucks and folds, concealed the "vent" by overlaying the fabric. He *cha-chunked* the whole thing together with a stapler.

"I'm gonna see if I can find my shoes," Doc said, trying on the coat. "My friend's mom's picking me up."

Ricky frowned. "Not good go to lady with no pants. I look again."

While Ricky fumbled through the closet, Doc wandered to the center of the room. Covering the top of a large table was an architectural replica of Ascension Park. It was like a salt-and-flour map made by hands as skilled as Michelangelo's. Pins marked gravesites. The tiny buildings were reminiscent of a model railroad village. "You are Here" was written on a small plastic arrow.

Looking down on the topographic display, Doc rewound the day. He envisioned all that had happened: He watched a miniature version of himself slip through the back gate of the cemetery, replayed the surreal encounter he'd had with Sister Theresa and Patton, the crow. He saw himself climb the tree to retrieve the balloon, relived the moment he'd met Bonnie, the ordeal at the gravesite.

For some unknown reason his mind kept going back to the rose garden and Sister Theresa. The image of the nun dancing around the grave persisted. Something a little bird had told him percolated in his memory.

"Ricky, I need to ask you something."

Ricky emerged from the closet empty-handed. "Sorry, no pants."

"That's okay." Doc pointed to a small red pin. "Know anything about the guy buried here in the rose garden? I think his name's Tommy McLean...Is there stuff you can look up? Records or something?"

Ricky looked from the pin to Doc. "No need look up. Dead boy famous."

"I don't think I've ever heard of him."

"You hear of him, but you hear about *her* more. Every boy know 'Girl in Pink Formal.'"

Doc did know the name. Though the scariest tales told around campfires revolved around Junior Mentz, the ultimate ghost story was "The Girl in the Pink Formal." Years ago, according to the legend, a Homecoming Queen and her date died in a fiery crash in Carbon Canyon. The boy's mangled body was found at the scene. The girl's wasn't. The only things left untouched by the blaze were her pink high heel shoes, size six and a half.

"Legend say ghost of 'Pinkie' wander canyon looking for shoes…"

"And the guy who brings them to her is…"

"Ah, yes. The most tantalizing part." Ricky finished the prophecy. "This boy given total knowledge of women and timeless moment of unbounded joy."

"You think that means ghost sex," Doc said.

"Ghost sex. Most gratifying."

Doc paced the room. "And that's her date's grave?"

Ricky nodded.

"You see a nun here today?"

"No nun come here today. Ricky see everything. I see you, fraternity brothers, right? No nun ever come here. Ascension not Catholic cemetery."

"Interesting," Doc said, nodding. "Gotta go. Thanks for everything, Ricky."

"You welcome." Coming forward, Ricky buttoned the black jacket, smoothed the labels. "I wish you long life."

WHAT "X" EQUALS

Bunny LaDesma's flamingo-pink Coupe De Ville idled just beyond the entrance to Ascension Park.

Doc got in, squished his mud-caked feet into his wet shoes, folded his hands on his lap. Even though he was drained, could have broken down in tears, he wasn't going to act like a sissy in front of Bunny.

She glanced at his bare legs, took a drag on her cigarette, put the car in gear. Perry Como sang as they wound down the hill.

"Sorry I'm not wearing pants, Mrs. LaDesma. Some guys tried to bury me alive."

She took another drag, honked, sped around a car in front of her. "They tried to do that to Big Lou once in Jersey, another time in Sicily."

Slatz's folks, Bunny and Big Lou LaDesma were from New York. They'd come out West with the Dodgers. Big Lou was in the vending machine business. When they were kids, Slatz's dad provided Doc and Jimmy with candy cigarettes, wax lips, musky lubricants, and nylon stockings. Doc used the lubricants for his bike chain. His father had never bought his explanation for why he had nylons in the bottom drawer of his dresser.

Today as always, Bunny was luscious. There was no other word for it. She reminded Doc of Veronica Lake in those black-and-white mob movies. She looked like a gun moll, a woman who, no matter how much the Feds slapped her around, would never rat out her man. It was hard to think of her as Slatz's mom.

"Stopped at the dry cleaners on the way," she said. "In the back, there's yellow Capris on a hanger. Try 'em on."

Doc climbed over the seat. The Capris were a little tight in the waist, big in the rear, but they fit okay.

Doc hopped back into the front seat.

She looked at him. "I like the glasses. Make you look like a blond Arthur Miller. You know, the playwright married to Marilyn Monroe?"

"Heard of him," Doc said.

"I heard she didn't just marry him for his mind. Know what I mean?" She blew out a smoke ring, poked her finger through the center of the smoky donut, glanced over at him. "So what's new?"

"Well, like I said, I was buried alive today. Junior's gang's trying to kill Jimmy and me. Oh, and I saw a naked girl with a priest. I think she might be my new girlfriend."

Bunny nodded. "So how's school? Reading anything interesting?"

Doc loved Slatz's mom. Nothing fazed her. "We're reading *The Mill on the Floss*," he said.

A hint of amusement crossed her face. She gazed out the window, was silent for a moment, looked back at him. "Sort of ties it all together, don't you think? Naked girls with priests. Boys trying to bury another boy alive."

Doc didn't understand. He guessed she could see the confusion in his face.

"I went to college, Doc. I've read that book. The novel's about deviance," she said. "Forbidden relationships, incest, perverse inclinations. And burying you alive, choking off your air...The act is loaded with overtones. Do you think it's possible this gang has a thing for boys?" She turned onto Harbor Boulevard.

"They got a thing for guys, all right. They kick your ass if you look at 'em cross-eyed."

"No, I mean something more repressed. Could they be driven by homosexual confusion?"

Doc thought a moment. "They didn't seem confused. This guy, Fang, did sorta go berserk when I said green M&Ms turn you queer. But he started it."

Bunny gave him a long look.

"Gosh, all I know about *The Mill on the Floss*, Mrs. LaDesma, is lots of parents don't want us to read it."

Bunny stubbed out her cigarette. "*They* all read what they want. Everyone's reading Kinsey, Masters, and Johnson. *They* all want to know about sex. They eat it up, can't wait to know what's going on behind closed doors, even church doors. But they don't want you to know anything, do they?"

"My dad thinks I should concentrate on stuff like learning what x equals. Science. Things like that. He's worried about the communists."

"You can worry about communists later," she said, pulling up in front of Fullerton Music. "You don't learn how sex makes the world go 'round now, you *will* end up buried alive. Big Lou's got the scars to prove it."

Doc got out of the Cadillac, looked back at Bunny through the open window. "You give a guy a lot to think about," he said.

She leaned across the front seat. "You're a thinking man, aren't you, Doc?"

He shrugged his shoulders.

"I love Slatz," she said. "I'd like him to be a thinking man, too. He's sweet in a conniving, slippery sort of way, and he plays the piano beautifully, but he's not a thinking man. His father convinced him he's dumb as a post. You'll be with him for hours practicing with the band. Help him out, won't you?"

"Mrs. LaDesma—"

"Call me Bunny."

"Bunny, Slatz already thinks he knows everything."

She put on dark glasses, slid them down her nose, looked over them. "How stupid is that?"

She blew Doc a kiss, turned up Sinatra, and drove away.

A RIP CURRENT OF WORDS

Fullerton Music took up the entire ground floor of the three-story office building at the corner of Harbor and Wilshire. Refrigerated air blew on Doc as he entered. Fans whirled above his head. The music store was cool; it kept the instruments in tune.

Doc walked through the display of grand pianos, between lacquered Baldwins and Steinways, rosewood and mahogany uprights, past a restored player piano that looked like it once resided in a frontier saloon. But the pianos didn't call to him. He was here for the birth of the Gigolos. He was ready to strap on his new guitar. A few weeks of practice and they'd bring down the house. He'd build on his experience from earlier in the day. He'd write their opening song: "Buried Alive."

Near the back of the store, the girl with cat glasses stood behind the counter. Arms folded, Miss Know-it-All, Margaret Ann, the girl he could never wedge from his life, guarded the cash register, the hall to the practice rooms, and the staircase that led to offices on the upper floors. Music drifted from behind her. Woodwinds squealed out scales, fingers plinked out melodies: "Heart and Soul," "Chopsticks."

As Doc approached, she reached into one of the glass cases below the counter, pretended to organize clarinet reeds and brass mouthpieces.

"I didn't know you worked here," he said.

Margaret Ann looked him up and down. "So what are you supposed to be? A beatnik bumblebee?"

"Unconventional. I'm on the verge of being a rock 'n' roll star."

"I see you more as a novelty act. Someone with a kazoo and a red rubber nose—besides, you don't even play an instrument."

"I played clarinet in the fourth grade."

"Well, whoopee for you…I think Elvis was just in here looking for someone who could really groove on the ol' licorice stick. Funny, I never thought to mention you."

"Where's the percussion practice room?"

"Sorry, you're too late."

"Wha'da ya mean, 'too late'?"

"Your friends were kicked out."

"Thanks to you, I bet."

"They were too loud. Especially that Herb Melch: 'Jazzman Grill.' Did you know that's what he calls himself? And that stupid beret. Anyway, I asked him politely to keep it down. He pointed a drumstick right at me. With the other stick he tapped out a backbeat on the high-hat, drowned me out. While I tried to explain the rules, he intentionally mocked me. Then your friends, Jimmy and Slatz, came in. I calmed myself, explained to Jimmy that I was the assistant manager, and that, since the owner was at lunch, I was in charge. I told Slatz I knew how nicely he played piano, and could they please play nice while they were practicing. Slatz asked if *I* played nice. Was I a nice girl or a good girl? Well, I know that old joke and I told him so in no uncertain terms, and he said he liked the way my lips moved when I was mad and did I play the upright organ? Your two other sick 'friends' just smiled at each other."

Doc had to give her credit for lung capacity, the rip current of words, the little smirks twitched in between syllables, how much came out of her mouth in a single breath. And she was still talking.

"When I turned to go back to the register, I saw the whole thing. *That's* when I tossed them out."

Doc threw his arms out to the side. "What whole thing?"

"The three of them were standing just outside the practice room door when Scarlett, with two *t*'s, came walking down the stairs. Jimmy started crooning." Margaret Ann put her hands on her hips and glared at Doc.

"And…?"

"And that's when Scarlett lifted up her skirt. She showed them her underwear. The front of her underwear. And then they all said, 'Monday.'"

"Monday?"

"Monday was stitched on her underwear. They make underwear for every day of the week."

"That doesn't make sense, Margaret Ann."

"It's a fashion trend. Keeps girls organized."

"What I meant was, girls just don't do that stuff. Maybe she was rehearsing for a theatrical production. She plays the lead in practically every play the school puts on. She's played Lady Macbeth, Annie Oakley, that girl in *The Crucible*. She's a thespian."

Margaret Ann's face was expressionless.

"I don't know, maybe steam blew up from a vent or something. Maybe she was a victim of circumstance. It happened to Marilyn Monroe."

Mumbling "victim of circumstance" and "thespian," Margaret Ann grabbed Doc's arm and, pointing up, marched him to the staircase. "She came down these stairs. And like I said, Jimmy started singing 'There She Is, Miss America,' then Slatz said something about Playboy Centerfolds, Miss September. Then Jazzman said, 'September? Man, I don't even know what day it is…' And that's when she did it. She showed them what day it was all right." Margaret Ann turned and stomped back to the cash register. "Girls like that are just plain weird."

The bell over the front door clanged.

The showroom had been empty since Doc had arrived, but now a mother and daughter had come in, and behind them another customer, a man almost as huge as Ricky.

Margaret Ann gave them an across-the-room smile, picked up a cloth and began cleaning the glass display case. She lowered her voice to a whisper. "I think Kinsey's to blame. Masters and Johnson, too. Girls like Scarlett and, I'm not saying it's true, but that girl you think you saw with the priest, the way they act—it's all just like something straight out of sexology. The down and dirty stuff." Margaret Ann shook her head. "Bet her father, Dr. Brisco, has all the books. He's a psychologist, you know. His office is upstairs, and..."

Doc waited for a break in her monologue. All this talk about sex and sexy things. The closest he'd ever gotten to sex was "Spin the Bottle." He'd played the game once at a party, but the bottle had never pointed his way. Now, suddenly he was tangled in a web of intrigue, folded into a dark tapestry of events that he couldn't help but believe were tied to the prophecy of the kite: The kite was supposed to lead him to a girl. The girl would lead him to the car. The car would lead him to the person who killed Jimmy's sister. Sex and death: he'd never thought of those things being twined together. Who *was* the girl he'd seen through the stained glass windows? She was the girl the kite had led him to. His *eyes* had convinced him it was Bonnie. She looked like the girl. She had short dark hair, wore hoop earrings. He'd seen her with the priest twice since last night. But Scarlett's *words*, what she'd said to him as they'd driven home from the Teen Center still haunted him. She seemed dangerous, eager to flirt with both sex and death. Hadn't she said to Grill, an evening spent chopping the heads off chinchillas might make for an interesting date? On the way to the cemetery, hadn't Rusty said Scarlett was just plain weird? Now Margaret Ann had said the same thing.

"Doc? Are you listening to me? You think I talk just to hear myself think?"

Margaret Ann was glaring at him. Her hands were on her hips.

"Yes. I mean, yes, I'm listening." A few music students exiting the back practice rooms bumped past him. His mind kept going back to what Rusty had said, how Scarlett was "just plain weird."

"Can I ask you something? What could a girl do to a guy that would leave a rope burn around his neck?"

The woman's daughter walked to the counter, bought a metronome. The man ordered a Concert Master microphone stand and told Margaret Ann to bill it to the Elks Club.

The bell above the door clanged again.

Margaret Ann looked out across the showroom. "The manager's back," she said. "I just need to catch him up on things. In answer to your question: erotic asphyxiation. Look it up in Masters and Johnson, look it up in one of Kinsey's books, prissy pants. They say people engage in weird stuff like that more often than you'd think. And they say it's normal."

Doc watched her walk away, her Irish legs pale as pipe cleaners, her shoes a little big for her feet. He wanted to yell out, "It's not normal. It's not good for girls to believe sick stuff is normal." But he didn't.

The manager nodded as she approached, kept nodding as she pointed around the room, then at Doc. A minute later she was back.

"The owner says you can help me in the stockroom. When we're done, I can clock out. I'll give you a ride. You can't walk home in that stupid costume; you'll get your ass kicked."

KIPLING'S PIANO

They walked down the hall, past the practice rooms, through the double doors and into the stockroom.

"All in all, I've had a pretty good day," she said. "I got to see you looking like an idiot and I threw your friends out. I make commission, ya know, along with the hourly rate, ninety-five cents an hour. Pretty good, huh? Got a big commission today. Sold the piano your dad brought in. First customer that saw it bought it. I told him all the cool stuff you told me. How it once belonged to Rudyard Kipling, how the piano had traveled from England to India and how a maharajah had once played it...I think all that provenance sealed the deal. Proud of me?"

Doc's body turned cold. "That's impossible. My dad wouldn't sell our piano. It's like a legacy."

"The man who brought it in had your last name. Said his son went to Sunny Hills High School." She pointed. "It's over there. I'll show you."

In a dark corner, between a stack of amplifiers and an old church organ, was Kipling's piano.

Doc slumped onto the piano bench, sat facing away from the keyboard. He couldn't bear to look at the beautiful ivory keys, the gleaming polished wood. Stupid. All of his dreams seemed stupid. He wasn't caught up in a web of intrigue, he wasn't on a noble mission. His life was a few grandiose words smeared across a crumbled scrap of paper, bitter kindling for a fire that would never warm a single person in this world.

Margaret Ann knelt in front of him. "I'm sorry. I thought you knew."

"No," Doc said, shaking his head. "No one told me."

"Your guitar came in today," she said softly. "That's good, isn't it? With everything going on I forgot to…You don't even play the piano, do you?"

"That's not the point."

"Maybe I can stop the sale. We'll get it back for you."

"Don't think my dad wants it back."

"I don't understand, Doc. If nobody plays the piano, why is it important you keep it?"

"Because…I guess because to me Kipling's piano made music just standing there, just being in the house. I know it's silly, but sometimes at night, I find myself imagining it sings stories to me, brings Kipling to me in my dreams. And don't say he's an imaginary friend. He's not a friend; he's my great-grandfather."

She placed her hands on the knees of Bunny's yellow Capris, rubbed the sides of his legs. "I'm going to clock out. I'm going to take you home."

TELL ME THAT'S NOT YOUR HOUSE

Margaret Ann drove Doc home in a '55 Chevy, the exterior painted a shade of mint green that reminded Doc of a stomachache.

Around cars, Margaret Ann was a disaster. She closed the hem of her skirt in the door when she got in, spent five minutes adjusting the seat and the mirrors, turned the headlights on after looking up something in the owner's manual, then said, "You just sit back and relax." If he hadn't been numb, if his life hadn't been robbed of meaning, if he didn't feel so all alone, it would have been funny.

Out on the road, she changed lanes without looking, made hand gestures he'd never seen before, wrinkled her nose every time the gears ground, as though the transmission should have known she was going to shift. She was the worst driver he'd ever seen.

"Know where Crestview is?" Doc said.

"Off Valencia Mesa, by the high school?"

"Yeah."

Tommy Dorsey's "So Rare" came on the radio. She turned up the volume, swayed in her seat. The Chevy drifted from lane to lane.

"Benny Goodman's playing clarinet," she said. "It's kind of an old folk's song, but I love the way he breathes the melody."

"My dad says I don't have the lip for the clarinet."

"I think your lips are very nice. Maybe no one's given them enough encouragement." She quickly turned up the radio, clamped her lips together and stared at the road ahead.

Doc, looking out the passenger window, his mind a million miles away, said, "We're having money problems. My mom starts work on Wednesday. I have to babysit my sister." Doc glanced over at her. "Bet *your* mom doesn't have to work."

"I don't have a mom." She gave her head a little nod. "It's okay."

They were silent until the Chevy turned on Crestview.

Halfway down the block, she clicked off the radio, coasted the Chevy to a slow stop. "Tell me that's not your house," she said.

Through the windshield, Doc could see a police car parked in front of his mailbox and a second car, a dark sedan, in the driveway. His stomach tightened; worry made his ribs hurt even more than they already did. He hoped Snowball wasn't sick, that something hadn't happened to her.

"The flashers aren't on, so it's not an emergency, but they're investigating something." She looked at him. "Or someone. You're not in trouble, are you?"

"I haven't got the nerve to do anything wrong."

"Better let you out here. When you get inside, my father's going to introduce himself. I'd appreciate you not telling him I brought you home."

"Your father? Your father's a cop?"

"Detective Quinn. And don't lie to him; he'll sniff it right out."

A RIVER OF NITROGLYCERINE

When Doc came through the front door, two men, a porky-pig faced cop and an older man in a tweed jacket, sat on the couch next to his father. Each face, in its own way, said, "We've been waiting for you." Porky jerked forward, touched his hand to his holster. The older man, his eyes like Sherlock Holmes's, crossed one leg over the other, leaned back.

His father barked, "Sit down," then muttered, "My God, he's wearing women's pants."

Doc walked to where the piano bench wasn't, to the place it used to be. He turned in a circle, stared at his father. "Where would you like me to sit?"

They all stared at him.

"There used to be a piano bench here," Doc said, "and a piano. But they're missing. So if you'll excuse me a moment, I'll get a chair." Doc didn't wait for an answer. He turned and went into the kitchen.

He heard Porky say, "Should I write down there's a missing piano?" In a louder voice, he barked out, "You're facing some serious accusations, kid, it won't do you no good to lie. You know what happens to liars, don't ya?"

Returning from the kitchen with a chair from the dinette set, Doc said, "Their pants catch on fire?" He was being a smartass, but he didn't care. He'd been stripped, buried, beaten. The only thing he cared about in this house had been sold out from under him. Besides, he hadn't done anything.

"Thank you for your cooperation, Dewey," the detective said. "We're from the police department. This is Officer Lyman Sleeve and I'm Detective Quinn. Do you know why we're here?"

He looked down at his pants. "Dress code violation? I have no idea."

"Do you need to use the restroom before we begin? Would you like to change clothes?"

"No."

"Would you care for a glass of water?"

"No, sir."

"Do you plan to set your pants on fire?" Quinn said, a twinkle in his eye.

"No." Doc smiled a little. "Not these pants, they're Capris. They're Bunny's."

Quinn glanced at Doc's father. Porky fingered his holster.

Out of the corner of his eye, Doc saw Snowball toddle into the room, climb onto his father's lap. He was glad she was okay.

"We took a report yesterday over at Saint Mary's," Quinn said, flipping through a few pages of a small notepad. "A priest reported a teenage boy 'skulking' around, 'peeping' through the windows where the girls change for choir practice."

"Peepa! Peepa!" Snowball squeaked excitedly, pointing her finger at Doc, her little bottom bouncing on their father's knee.

Quinn looked at Snowball. "Maybe, Mr. Ruggles, it would be better if you took the child to her mother."

Doc's father stomped off with the wiggly witness for the prosecution.

When they'd left the room, Quinn turned to Officer Sleeve. "Stay with the boy's father. Dewey, let's you and me go outside."

"You want me to search his room?" Sleeve said.

The detective exhaled. "No, Sleeve, that won't be necessary."

The two of them stepped out onto the front porch. Quinn looked up at the twilight sky. Venus, the evening star, sparkled above the horizon.

"The same priest called a little over an hour ago, reported this afternoon that a boy matching the same description was 'shadowing' a choir girl who was at Ascension Park visiting the grave of a deceased friend. I guess the girl was alone and the boy's actions made her nervous."

"What actions?"

"So that boy was you?"

Doc bit his tongue. Margaret Ann was right. He'd been sniffed out. "Look, I wasn't 'shadowing' anybody," Doc said. "And I wasn't skulking around the church. My friend Jimmy Vaughan and I were flying a kite. It got caught on the cross above Saint Mary's, so I climbed up to get it down. Simple as that. A nun, Sister Theresa, I think that's what she said her name was, gave me a ladder. You can ask her."

"I will," Quinn said, writing in his notepad.

"She *knew* my name because I *introduced* myself," Doc said. "'Hi, I'm Dewey Ruggles. I'm a skulker, a practicing pervert. Where do the girls change clothes? I'd like to take a peek.' Does that make sense?"

Quinn seemed to study him. "Your friend Jimmy Vaughan? His sister was Cindy Vaughan, the girl killed a few years ago? Died on Christmas Eve?"

"Yes."

"Do either of you know this priest, Father Stephen?"

"No."

"Well, he doesn't seem to want you around. Can you think of any reason why?"

"A reason why?"

"I want to know if you can think of any reason Father Stephen would want you to stay away from this girl. Any reason he'd want to see you get in trouble."

"I'd have to think about it."

"Go ahead." Quinn lit a cigarette, inhaled slowly.

Doc pretended to think, gave it his best acting job. He looked upward, paced, opened his mouth occasionally as if to speak. He pointed his index finger skyward, then, as though he'd drawn a blank, vigorously shook his head.

Silence stretched out between them. In the shadows crickets bet on who would speak first. Time ticked by. Eternity looked down on the chess match, yawned, twiddled its thumbs. Two eavesdropping moths, bored with beating their wings against the porch light above the detective's head, fluttered off.

Quinn looked at the luminous dial on his watch.

"I'm still thinking," Doc said.

"I can see that. I appreciate you giving your 'best' effort. Perhaps I'll come back tomorrow. Maybe I'll pay a visit to the girl in question before I stop by." Quinn walked toward the front door.

Doc's mind churned like a river of nitroglycerine. He couldn't just blurt out that the priest who was fingering him was the priest he'd seen with a naked girl. It would just mean more grief, more time under hot lights in some interrogation room. And if Quinn buttonholed Bonnie, his father might find out about the plan to have her babysit. "No."

Quinn stopped, turned around. "No?"

"I mean, I think I *know* what happened. It was a coincidence: a co-incidence of misunderstandings."

"That's your theory?"

"Makes sense," Doc said. "The priest wouldn't lie and I didn't do anything wrong."

Quinn took a long look at him. "Okay. Let's leave it at that. I'll get Sleeve, you and your family get on with your evening. I'm sure you have homework to do." He crushed out his cigarette, tucked his notepad into his inside jacket pocket. "And I'll let your father know, as far as the police are concerned, you're in the clear."

Doc tried to keep a smile off his face. So much, he thought, for the nose that could sniff out a lie.

Quinn started for the door again, stopped. "Funny you mention- ing coincidence," he said. "Did you know Father Stephen's younger brother, Buddy, committed suicide the same night Jimmy's sister was killed?"

"No." Doc could feel his heart pounding in his chest, remembered Patton saying a mystery surrounding one death might hold a clue to solving the mystery surrounding another death. "No," he said again, "I didn't know that."

"You boys were first on the scene that night, weren't you? You saw the car that hit Jimmy's sister?"

Doc nodded nervously as Quinn's eyes took on that Sherlock Holmes look. "We just saw taillights, sir; we couldn't tell who was in the car."

"Today, that same priest becomes concerned about you being with a girl who I suspect was visiting his brother's grave."

Doc stared past Quinn into the darkness. He heard the sound of black wings beating overhead and wondered if Patton was nearby.

"I've often asked myself," Quinn said, "what it must be like for a young priest to live and die knowing his church believes he'll never meet his brother again in Heaven. Dewey, you understand Catholics believe suicide is a mortal sin, don't you? A sin for which there is no forgiveness. You don't get to Heaven if you kill yourself."

"Are you saying you think Father Stephen's brother didn't kill him- self, or are you saying there's a connection between Buddy's death and Jimmy's sister?"

"I'm not saying one thing or the other, Dewey. I like your theory. Unless you haven't told me the truth, I'm sure it's just a coincidence both died on the same day." Quinn lit another cigarette. "On the other hand, it might be interesting to see what happens if you keep making the priest nervous. I'm not suggesting you break the law."

"Of course not."

"But you like this girl, right, Dewey? It's an honest affection?"

"Yeah, I like her."

"Well, let's just see what happens. We'll put the charges against you off to the side for now."

To Doc it seemed like Quinn had picked him up by the ears, dropped him down some rabbit hole of logic, and now he was supposed to feel what? Relieved? What was going on here? Did Margaret Ann's father think he knew something, or the priest knew something? Was he supposed to go undercover, or did Quinn just need a patsy, some dumb kid who'd keep making the priest nervous? Doc took off his glasses; they'd steamed over a little.

"So that's it?" Doc said.

"That's it," Quinn replied, his words light as air, a cat-and-mouse smile tugging at the corners of his mouth. He stretched to his full height. "I'll let your father know there's been a meeting of the minds. Why don't you stay out here while us boring adults talk?" He glanced around. "It's a beautiful night, isn't it?"

"Couldn't be better."

The detective reached out his hand. They shook, Doc all fake smiles, wanting Quinn to know he'd taken the deal whatever it was. What choice did he have?

Quinn turned away, walked up the front steps. "Beautiful night," he said again as he walked back inside the house.

Doc walked halfway down the driveway then looked back.

Quinn was inside the house telling another lie, telling his father what a fine, upstanding young man his son seemed to be. No need to put a kid like Doc on restriction. Let him be free. Let him be bait.

Overhead, the moon rose. Kipling stepped from the shadows.

"Beautiful night, my eye. Rather more like the stroke of midnight in some dark fairy tale would be my guess. Or say, some scene from one of those raunchy crime thrillers you love to read. You're in the thick of it, that's for sure."

"It *is* getting a little creepy," Doc said.

"All that talk about mortal sins and murder. Yes, lad, I'd say so."

"So what am I supposed to do?"

"You might begin by answering the man's question. The one he can't push without playing his hand."

Doc thought a moment. "You mean, why the priest doesn't want me around Bonnie?" He shook his head. "I already know the answer to that."

"Ah, yes. The Vatican. The conspiracy. All that tawdry sex slave business."

"I know what I saw. At least I think I do."

"Yes. But do you know *who* you saw with the priest? A little uncertain there, aren't you?"

"Yeah. You're right. Bonnie just doesn't seem the type. She's…not that…weird."

"But we know someone who is, don't we?" Kipling glanced at the house across the street.

THE WEIGHT OF HIS TOUCH

The sound of a car charging around the corner chased away Kipling's voice.

Doc looked up, saw light from the distant streetlamp reflect off the hood of Rusty's Fairlane. The car accelerated, side-swiped a few trash cans, rocketed past him. It fishtailed around the cul-de-sac, came roaring back up the street. A beer bottle sailed out the driver's window as it sped by, its target the house across from Doc's: Scarlett's house. Scarlett, the actress who could play anyone. Doc watched the bottle cartwheel across her lawn, clink off a sprinkler, gurgle to a sudsy stop.

Rusty was losing it.

Something had happened between yesterday and today, something that had left him with noose marks blistering his neck. What had Margaret Ann said? Erotic asphyxiation? He had no idea what the words meant. He did know one word: "Monday."

In his mind, he watched the word "Monday" slowly embroider itself on a field of sheer white cotton. All he could see was Scarlett's underwear.

For a moment the image floated there, undulating as though worn on the hips of an invisible belly dancer. Then a thread uncoiled from the waistband, traveled like some mythic snake through time and space, connected two things that hadn't occurred to Doc until just now.

He recalled it was Slatz who said Scarlett was the one who'd suggested Bonnie as the perfect babysitter. Scarlett was the one who'd placed the call to Bonnie, set up the meeting in Ascension Park. Could Scarlett have been the one who'd told Junior that Doc and Jimmy would be at the cemetery? Jimmy'd come along for the ride. He just hadn't stayed. Maybe she'd assumed Jimmy would hang around while he talked with Bonnie. They'd be sitting ducks for Junior.

Doc considered the neighborhood, reflected on everything that had happened since he'd climbed to the top of the church, gone after the runaway kite. He studied Scarlett's house, remembered the wink she'd given Rusty, how she'd told him her father was away for the night. Scarlett had done something to him. It may have started off as down and dirty fun. In the end, it had hollowed Rusty out.

Doc had another thought: In stories and in movies, the girl-next-door is always the wholesome one, America's Sweetheart, the one you can trust. But what about the girl-across-the-street? Maybe she's a different sort of female force. Maybe she's not like the girl-next-door. Doc needed to find out.

Doc glanced back at his house.

Quinn was still inside talking with his dad. There was still a little time.

He walked across the street and knocked on Scarlett's door.

Her father answered. He wore a red velvet smoking jacket with black satin lapels, held a book in his hand: *Anomalies of the Pelvis*. Through eyeball-magnifying glasses, he considered Doc's outfit: the mortician's jacket, the yellow Capris.

"I'm in a play, sir. It's absurdist. Like *Waiting for Godot*."

"Hmm."

This was something he probably said a lot, Doc thought. Scarlett's dad, Dr. Brisco, was, after all, a psychologist.

"I was wondering if I might speak with your daughter. I have a question about homework."

The man didn't blink, didn't appear to have eyelids. He just kept staring down at Doc as though he were a specimen, a smear on a rectangular piece of glass he'd slid beneath the lens of a microscope.

"I need to know about symbolism in *The Mill on the Floss*. I live across the street."

"Across the street?"

"Yes."

"Where the police are?"

"Yes."

"Hmm." Dr. Brisco opened the door a little wider. "Come in," he said, his voice like the gentleman frog's in Disney's *Mr. Toad's Wild Ride*.

He led Doc, the kid from across the street, now Doc the detective, through the living room. There were blackout curtains on the windows, lots of smooth glass objects on glass tables, several of which Brisco caressed as he passed by. The white sectional sofas and overstuffed chairs had clear plastic slipcovers. The place was simultaneously sterile and, at the same time, wicked as a dirty secret.

In the den, there was more hermetically sealed furniture. A sixteen-millimeter movie projector mounted on a gray metal cart had been rolled to the corner of the room. Doc could see the cart's track marks on the rug. Like almost everything else, the projector had a clear plastic hood over it. Doc touched the hood as he walked by. The plastic was sticky and warm. He wondered what type of home movies were watched in this house. Not the type that went well with buttered popcorn and chocolate chip cookies, he guessed.

"Scarlett's bedroom is down the hall, last door on the left. Just go right in."

"Just go right in?"

"It's our home," her father said, walking away. "There's no reason to knock."

Arriving at Scarlett's bedroom door, he knocked. The weight of his touch, soft as his taps were, was enough to cause the door to open on its own.

Scarlett was sitting cross-legged on the bed. She wore skimpy, scoop-necked, babydoll pajamas. A loose-fitting chenille robe was draped over her shoulders.

The room was like a little girl's room, everything frilly. Porcelain dolls with French faces looked down from shelves, plastic horses of every breed, size, and color filled display cases. The music on the record player was grown up, classical. On a dressing table, various styles and colors of wigs crowned Styrofoam heads. One wig had short black hair.

She noticed him looking at it. A self-satisfied smile played at the corners of her mouth.

"The wigs are for playing make-believe," she said. "Bet you're drawn to the black one...You like Beethoven?"

"Who doesn't?" Doc said.

"Want a cigarette?"

"I don't smoke."

"That's a good boy." She smiled, patted the bed.

"Thanks anyway. Think I'll stand."

She got on all fours, slowly lowered her blossoming chest to the comforter that covered her bed. Resting her chin in the palms of her hands, she looked up at him with eyes that matched the style of her pajamas: babydolls.

Doc cleared his throat. "How do you know Bonnie?"

"We're in choir together. She doesn't come much anymore."

Above the bed was a framed print: a depiction of the Holy Mother. Beams of light burst from a blood-red heart in the center of her chest. Given the mission he was on, the image was as scary as Scarlett was. "You still sing at Saint Mary's?"

"Like an innocent little songbird."

"Were you at Saint Mary's yesterday afternoon? Before the dance at the Teen Center?"

"Yes. Were you?"

"I think you already know the answer to that."

She batted her eyelashes. "Whatever do you mean?"

"I think you know what I mean." Doc glanced over to Styrofoam heads. "You were the one, weren't you? You wore a wig. That black one."

"Hmm." She made the sound just like her father. "A wig like that with those hoop earrings *would* make me look a lot like Bonnie. If the stories are true, looking like her might resurrect a few fond memories for that nice young priest."

"What's that supposed to mean?"

She lifted a wisp of hair from her face. "Oh my, don't you just get so cute when you're serious?" She made a pouty face. "Wanna kiss me?"

"No. I wanna know what makes you tick. Why you were in the priest's office with no clothes on, why is Rusty acting crazy, why he has a welt around his neck. I wanna know if you told Junior that Jimmy and I would be at the cemetery."

Scarlett sighed. "Your first two questions would require an adult conversation. You're not ready for that. As for Junior, maybe I told him, maybe I didn't. Now that I think about it, Bonnie knows Junior, too. You saw her leave the Teen Center with him last night."

"She was taken by force."

"Maybe she likes a little force. Most people do…except for boo-hoo Rusty. Did you know he came back last night, after he dropped you off? I invited him in for a little neck-tie party. He got all choked up and left. It was a shame. The fun had just started. How 'bout you, Doc? Wanna play a game called 'kiss me or I'll scream'?" She sat up. "I mean it. Kiss me right now or I'll scream bloody murder."

Doc took a step toward her. The detective inside him panicked, took off running for the front door. The part of him that stayed pleaded, "Please, please don't."

She scooted back, sat up, took in a quick I'm-going-to-scream-right-now breath.

Doc lunged, his hand reached out to cover her mouth.

Scarlett twisted away from him, threw off her robe. As she turned, the back of her elbow whacked Doc across the nose. He felt a sting, a warm, wet feeling above his upper lip. He swiped his hand across his face. His nose was gushing blood.

Leaning back on her elbows, looking up at him, she drew in another here-comes-the-scream breath. Desperate, Doc fell on her, pressed his hand over her mouth. He couldn't believe what he was doing. It was impossible to fathom how quickly what was supposed to be an interrogation had gotten out of control.

Through his red, sticky fingers she mumbled, "I love to get boys in trouble." Her eyes fluttered, closed. Her skin turned pale as the porcelain dolls on the shelf above her dresser. She sagged, slumped back on the bed.

He looked down on her. His blood polka-dotted her face. She went from looking bad to looking really bad. "Scarlett?"

No response.

"Scarlett, are you all right?" He shook her, pressed his fingertips first to the inside of her wrists, then to the soft flesh at the edge of her jawline. He palmed the front of her pajamas, felt around for a heartbeat, then brought an ear near her lips. Was she still breathing? Yes. He felt little puffs of air touch his skin, whispers of breath, and words.

"Cut me free, Doc. Watch me fly."

The bedroom door opened. Doc glanced over his shoulder. Her father stared down on him from the threshold.

He froze. His mouth went dry. His lips, his tongue slicked over with a substance gummy as glue.

His mind intended to say "help," but the word came out sounding more like "hell." He tried again, shouted twice: "Hell, hell!" Even to his own ears his voice sounded like a crazed, demonic rant, but it wasn't his fault, it wasn't what he intended. It was just that his lips were stuck to his gums. He couldn't pucker out the *p*.

Dr. Brisco came over to the bed and stared at his daughter. "Hmm." He looked at Doc. "My daughter is subject to familial vasovagal syncopy."

Doc worked the muscles his mouth, summoned a trickle of saliva, freed his lips. "Believe me sir, I have total 'sympathy.' You can't imagine how much 'sympathy' I have at this very moment for everyone concerned here. But you've gotta believe me, I wasn't yelling out the word 'hell.' I was trying to call to you for 'help' and honestly I didn't do anything. She just spazzed and went limp. She caught me in the face with her elbow. It was an accident."

"Not sympathy, you idiot," Brisco said. "Syncopy. She's fainted." He felt Scarlett's forehead, lifted her eyelids. "She'll be fine." Dr. Brisco's eyes slowly rotated Doc's way. Suspicion brought his eyebrows together. "Something must have overwhelmed her. Do you know what overwhelmed her?"

"I can assure you, sir, nothing about me is overwhelming. I'm not even popular." He pinched his nose, tilted his head back.

"I'm talking about causation, young man. I'm asking if you can ascribe causation."

"Huh?"

"Did she, for example, change positions?"

"We weren't doing anything that involved changing positions."

Brisco frowned, looked exasperated. "I mean, did she perhaps stand up suddenly?"

"No."

His eyes magnified beneath the lenses of his glasses. "What was the question you asked her?"

"The question?"

"You had a homework question. You said that was why you came over. Something about *The Mill on the Floss*."

"Oh, *that* question." While the scared part of Doc's mind tried to form an answer to Brisco's question, another part, the detective part of his brain, retraced the path he'd taken from the front door to Scarlett's bedroom. Everything he'd passed by seemed too sanitized, too silent; the couch, in its prophylactic wrap, the stag-film projector, the phallic objects on the tables, the fleshy drapes all forced to become unwilling players in something sadistic.

Brisco was still waiting for his answer.

"Well," Doc said, "I can tell you for sure it wasn't remotely related to the relationship the book is supposed to be about. You know, a girl who has a thing for her brother. That would be really wrong, right? Pretty much impossible? I think I asked her about water imagery."

Brisco wasn't listening anymore. He was giving his daughter that "specimen" look.

"We'll just let her sleep," he said. "I think it's time you go."

"Okay, sure. Sorry about the blood."

"I have a compound that will remove every trace from her night-wear. The mattress will be fine. It's wrapped in plastic."

SEE YOU IN CHURCH

Doc clicked closed Scarlett's front door, slowly negotiated the down slope of the lawn. It wasn't easy. His limbs zombified. His brain felt fried. His imagination, somehow still functioning, traveled to the inside of his skull and wandered through rubble. The landscape of his brain was reminiscent of burnt-out Dresden right after the Allies' last bombing run: not a pretty sight. He wiped his bloody nose, kept moving.

A few steps down the lawn, he stopped and, without thinking, picked up the beer bottle Rusty had thrown from his car.

He kept his feet moving, his legs steadier with every step he took. The ten minutes he'd spent at the Brisco's had been like a visit to a house of mirrors, a spiraling fall to the center of a hypnotist's wheel. It had been insane.

As he crossed the street, Kipling's voice spoke, "You're lucky her dad didn't call the cops."

"Luck had nothing to do with it," Doc growled. "The guy's a freak, the patriarch of weird." He trudged up his driveway, passed beneath the porch light, opened the front door. He was home.

The detective, the cop, and his dad were sitting on the couch just as they'd been when he'd first come home.

Sleeve tensed. Quinn looked amused.

His father shook his head. "You've been drinking?"

Doc glanced down at the beer bottle in his bloody hand.

"No, 'course not, Dad."

Officer Sleeve came across the room, snatched the bottle from Doc. "Your prints are going to be all over it."

"It was on the lawn. I slipped on it, hit my nose on the concrete. It's dark outside; I didn't see it. Someone must have thrown it there, or the bottle didn't make it into some neighbor's trash." He looked at his father. "I didn't want you to run over it, Dad. Didn't want you to end up with a flat tire."

Sleeve sneered, gripped the bottle, held it to the light. "So it's gonna be the ol' flat tire alibi, is it? We'll just put this baby in an evidence bag, let the lab guys lift the prints. Anyone wanna guess whose prints we'll find?"

Quinn sighed, then spoke to Doc. "You might want to get a towel for your nose."

Doc shook his head. "I've got homework to do, Dad. Mind if I go to my room? If you want to talk, we can talk about this later."

"Go ahead. I'll walk these gentlemen to their cars."

Quinn stood. "See you in church, Doc."

"Church?" his father asked.

"I was a little surprised, too," he overheard Quinn say as the men walked out the front door. "Talking with your son, I learned we both share an interest in religion."

The front door closed. Adult voices faded up the driveway, all of them commiserating over the state of today's youth.

The more Doc thought about it, the less he liked the detective's comment about "religion," the inside joke about their mutual interest in the priest. The whole thing was designed to seal the deal he and Quinn had made and make his dad look like a fool at same time.

Quinn was tactical. Part of his plan was to drive a wedge between Doc and his father, one Doc knew Quinn would someday want to exploit. But to what end? He thought about the piano lost to him forever. Quinn could work whatever racket he wanted. And his Dad could believe what he wanted to believe. In the end, Doc believed Destiny would be on his side.

CINCH

Sitting at his desk, Doc heard the front door close, heard his father clear his throat as he walked down the hall toward the back bedroom. Doc ground a pencil into the pencil sharpener. His father cleared his throat again. This exchange, tantamount to a conversation, meant they would talk tomorrow. That was fine with him.

Doc finished off his math assignment, reviewed the achievements of the "meso-potatoe-ums," then read the first chapters of *The Mill on the Floss*. The writing was stiff, kind of old fashioned, but the heroine Maggie Tulliver sizzled. Her mother calls her a "wild thing" and her father worries her dark skin makes her look like a "muleteer." When people "vex" her, she stomps to the attic and shoves nails into her voodoo doll. Her best friend at "Floss" High is a girl named Scarlett. Not really.

The idea of a friendship between Maggie and Scarlett was a joke, something sick his mind came up with as he set the novel down. There was no Scarlett in the novel, but there sure was a girl named Scarlett in Doc's life.

He clicked off the desk lamp, leaned back in his chair and wondered what sort of character a writer could create if he combined the two girls into one. She'd be pretty scary, he thought, a girl drawn to forbidden relationships with boys, but at the same time a girl who gets turned on at the thought of getting those boys in trouble. She'd thrill at the idea of someone seeing her naked with a priest, just like she'd love it if her father caught her in bloody babydolls with the boy across the street. What had Margaret Ann said yesterday when he'd described the scene he'd witnessed from the roof of the church? "If what you're saying is true, I blame the girl."

Margaret Ann had been right. It was Scarlett he'd seen at the church, not Bonnie.

Doc changed out of the blood-stained mortuary jacket and Capris, grabbed a fresh notebook and lay on the bed. It was time to start the next installment of the true-crime story he'd sell to a magazine. But this time he'd incorporate the adventure he was actually living. When he finished, he'd change the names to protect the innocent.

The hero of the story, the guy who in reality would be him, he'd call "Cinch." Cinch's real identity would be forever a mystery to the grateful citizens of the mythical town, Centerville. He'd be a crime fighter, streetwise, extremely cool. His alter ego, a guy not unlike himself, would appear to all the world as a bumbling nobody, though girls would find him strikingly handsome. His disguise would be simple: He'd simply put his glasses *on*. Why wouldn't that work? Clark Kent became Superman by taking his glasses *off*. He'd do the opposite.

Doc wrote for hours, jazzed up the details, but in essence stuck to the truth:

> *Cinch jumps from the disabled, home-built, futuristic glider to the roof of Saint Mary's. Leaping to his feet, he pulls a "remote control" detonator from his skin-tight jeans and blows up the cartwheeling glider seconds before it crashes into a bus filled with young nuns, orphans, and animals rescued from the pound. He watches the tangerine ball of flames vaporize in the sky, then glimpses, quite by accident, a disturbing scene play out before his eyes: Through a stained glass window, he sees a near-naked teenage girl in the clutches of the young*

priest, Father Stephen. He doesn't get a good look at the girl's face, but he does glimpse the word "Monday" stitched on her underwear.

Wanting to intervene, hoping to rescue her, Cinch uses dazzling technique and unbelievable strength to descend the interior shaft of the bell tower. He's too late. The girl and priest are gone. They've disappeared into a maze of catacombs beneath the church.

Needing to avoid detection, he disguises himself as a mild-mannered organ tuner and continues his search for the girl.

Before he can leave the church, he's stopped by a mysterious nun, the dreamy-eyed novitiate, Sister Theresa. She says she knows why he's here—but more than that, she has information about the only crime Cinch has failed to solve: the hit-and-run that killed the sister of his best friend, Jimmy. The young nun strikes Cinch as otherworldly, but at the same time, credible. She asks him to pray for guidance, to kneel before the altar and accept the Eucharist, the body of Christ. "Sorry, Sister," Cinch says, "I don't play 'swallow the leader.' I only kneel when I'm tuning organs."

She blushes.

They agree to meet the next day at the cemetery. She says it will be among the gravestones that she'll tell him what she knows about the murder.

That night as "Doc," Cinch goes to the Teen Center. On the way, he and his not-so-handsome best friend Jimmy are followed by devious Cuban communists, the same foreigners Cinch suspects sabotaged his glider.

They bamboozle the commies, arrive at the dance safely. But things turn bad when Junior Mentz, the town's psychotic bully picks on the shy, forever-grieving, socially awkward weakling, Jimmy. Cinch wants to step in, protect his friend, but must avoid giving away his true identity. He uses jujitsu *and Chinese magic to incapacitate Junior, then acts surprised to have defeated the bully. Shrugging his shoulders, he explains his deft moves were just dumb luck. The amazed but naïve crowd buys his story.*

Shaken up, Jimmy stays downstairs, content to hang out with the other losers who inhabit the game room.

Doc goes upstairs to dance.

Moments after the music starts, he finds himself in the arms of a girl named Bonnie, and wonders if fate has brought him to the damsel in distress he saw at the church. He cleverly finds a way to nonchalantly ask, "Does your underwear say anything?"

She looks into his eyes, "I'd like to think I leave my underwear speechless." She pauses, adds, "I won't say they don't occasionally 'panty-mine.'"

They both laugh because they share a taste for sophisticated humor.

The magic moment is broken when Doc hears Jimmy cry for help. Junior has returned with a gang of thugs. A melee ensues. Cinch, unable this time to act without betraying his true identity, holds back. Junior takes Bonnie away in a car driven by Father Stephen.

At three in the morning, Doc put his pen down and closed his eyes.

Tomorrow night he'd write the next chapter, explain how Cinch meets Scarlett, gets her to confess she was the one he saw with the priest. He was proud of the narrative, though there was one moment during the night when he'd been unclear as to how to order the sequence of events. Patton the crow had tapped at his bedroom window, squawked through the glass how much simpler and more lyrical the story would be if there were more "rhyming words." While Patton pleaded his case, Kipling appeared in the mirror over Doc's dresser to throw in *his* two cents.

Kipling vehemently disagreed with the crow. "My preference," he'd said, "would be to combine all the female characters into one. Perhaps you should move the story to India, lad. Change Slatz and Grill into talking jungle animals."

Doc gave them a "thanks but no thanks." He was going to write the story on his own. He was convinced all the characters were necessary, every element germane, certain everything that had happened so far somehow fit together, even the Cuban communists who both critics thought were a distraction.

Closing his eyes, Doc tried to visualize the "big picture" of the mystery he was trying to solve. The image that appeared was a clockwork of turning gears, a mechanism of spinning wheels with teeth that somehow interlocked, each wheel a separate plot within the story.

The story had started out with one dead person, Jimmy's sister. Now there were three: Jimmy's sister, Cindy; the priest's brother, Buddy; and the Homecoming Queen, immortalized in the legend of "The Girl in the Pink Formal."

Doc's eyes popped open. He had a revelation. Maybe, he thought, the dead aren't just dead. Maybe in the mystery he was trying to solve, the living weren't the only ones who turned the wheels within the clockwork. Maybe, for different reasons, each of the dead people still wanted something. Doc knew what he needed to do next: He'd stop trying to understand the living and concentrate on figuring out what the dead had left undone.

THE CAT WHO ROCKS
THE STICKS

The next day, school was a blur. It wasn't just that Doc was exhausted, all bleary-eyed from having been up half the night writing. He also had a mind-numbing headache. The pain started in the bridge of his bruised nose, needled its way into his frontal lobe. And it didn't help that the gas tank of his brain was on empty; he hadn't eaten since lunch yesterday. But what really put a fuzz on the day was that Doc had left home without his glasses.

First period, History had been a disaster. He'd fumbled into the room late for the second day in a row. Coach Ugler, in the middle of showing a filmstrip, spotted him as he took his seat. "Big Bob," going in for the kill, called on him to answer the first question. "Okay, Tardy Boy, what are we lookin' at here?" Doc, blind without his glasses, identified what he could only guess were the pyramids at Giza. It turned out to be the triangle defense of the Oklahoma Sooners.

Forty minutes later, in Dr. Sprowl's math class, the distant blackboard a chalky haze, he'd answered a ten-question pop quiz by writing down either x equals zero or x equals one. He'd gotten four right: a D-plus.

Betsy Biggers, the class suck-up, inadvertently, at least hopefully inadvertently, had added to his embarrassment by blurting out, "Gosh Mr. Sprowl, if this is how Doc handles one of your 'quizzies,' I'd love to see him try to handle one of your testes!"

There were snickers from some of the boys. The girl next to Doc looked at him, squinched her face, wrinkled her nose. The day was going from bad to worse.

After the bell rang, he slunked, slank, or whatever-ed from the classroom, Brailled his way through the halls, finally honing in on a flash of metal, a beacon of light that could only emanate from elaborate orthodonture; he grabbed Grill's shoulders, dropped his books.

"Take me to the office," Doc said, kneeling and gathering up notebooks and texts. "I need to call my mom. She needs to bring my glasses."

"Sure, no trouble," Grill said. "Just don't let her think you're sick. We've got band practice after school. You've gotta be there. The Gigolos are the only future for guys like you and me."

"I know."

"You don't know. See, we've got a problem. Slatz wants to kick me out of the band. I told Slatz you'd be on my side, you'd back me up." Grill took a breath, exhaled, escorted Doc down the hallway. "Here's the situation: You know Scarlett? The girl who lives across the street from you?"

Doc nodded, shuddered at the memory of her limp body, the indelible image of her bloody babydoll pajamas. "What about her?"

"She's into me, gotta thing for me. Showed me her underwear yesterday at the music store. Slatz said she 'Marilyned' *him*. It's not true. She wants me. She wants the cat who rocks the sticks. She's a drummer's girl. Anyone can see that."

"Right now, I can't really see anything."

Grill grabbed Doc's elbow, tugged him around the corner of the brick building at the front of the school. "Remember how she was after the Teen Center? When we were in Rusty's car? She was hot on the idea of stroking one of my chinchilla pelts. Tell Slatz she wants me. Tell him to back off."

"I don't know, Grill. I'd stay away from Scarlett if I were you."

"I'm not afraid of Rusty, if that's what you mean."

"I don't think she's going out with Rusty anymore."

"So, you're saying the way's clear for me?"

"No, I'm not saying that."

"But you *are* saying if the Scarlett thing comes up at practice, you'll back me?"

"Grill, the Gigolos need you and Slatz. Jimmy and I don't really even play instruments."

"Yeah, remind Slatz of *that*," Grill said, opening the door to Administration.

SIGN HERE

Mrs. Clegg, Principal Leseker's secretary, called Doc's mom, sent Grill off with a hall pass, then led Doc to a frosted glass door in the far back corner of the room.

"You need to be seen by a student nurse," she said. "Knock and go in."

Doc knocked, walked in, sat his books on a sink.

"Can I help you?"

The voice was annoyingly familiar, its pretentious pitch as irritating as an Indian arm burn. Coming closer, Margaret Ann's freckles came into focus. She wore a crisp white lab jacket, had one hand on her hip. With the other she shook a thermometer.

"So what's wrong with you? I notice you're limping. You look flushed."

"What are you doing here?"

"The nurse is at lunch. I'm certified to help you."

"I don't need help, and I always limp a little."

"You needn't be shy about discussing any personal health problems you might have. I could probe you for possible inguinal hernia, torsioned testicles. These are several of the diagnoses the nursing manual says should be ruled out. I'm also licensed to take your temperature."

"Anyone can take a temperature."

"Rectally?"

Doc's head pounded. His blood sugar plunged.

"I left my glasses at home. My mother's on the way here to drop them off."

Margaret Ann took a step closer. "What's wrong with your nose? It's all lumpy in the middle."

Irritated, he snapped, "Nothing's wrong with my nose."

She took a pen light from the pocket of her lab jacket, clicked it on, shined it into Doc's eyes. "You look a little concussed. Experiencing any visual problems...? Perhaps hallucinations involving naked girls with priests?"

"I'm just tired."

She clicked off the light. "You know what they say, 'fatigue makes cowards of us all.'"

"What's that supposed to mean?"

"Oh, nothing." Margaret Ann turned, walked into a wash of medicinal white, came back with a blank chart. "I'll just get a history of your nose injury. Test your cranial nerves. If necessary, I'll call an ambulance."

"I'm not hurt. I'm not sick. I'm not a coward."

She set the chart down. "Then why were you too chicken to tell my father what you saw at the church?"

"Sure. Why not? Tell the police the same story *you* didn't believe? Tell Detective Quinn I was a Peeping Tom, but for a good reason?"

"You can trust him," she said. "And you didn't have to tell him that stupid story about talking to some imaginary nun."

"I did talk to a nun. I told her my name. She told me hers: Sister Theresa. She got me a ladder. I wanted your dad to know the only reason I was at the church was to get the kite."

"Unfortunately, like your head, your alibi has a few holes in it. Last night, after my father left your house, he went by Saint Mary's. No one there's ever heard of Sister Theresa. She doesn't exist."

"Really? I talked to her yesterday at Ascension Park. The nun you say doesn't exist was there in living black-and-white dancing around a grave."

The door opened.

Doc and Margaret Ann shut up.

Doc's mom walked in. Snowball was in her arms. She handed Doc's glasses to Snowball. Snowball, her dandelion head of hair fluffier than usual, begrudgingly held them out to Doc.

"Are you all right?" His mother said, in her Elizabeth Taylor voice. "Your face is red…and your nose looks…funny."

"I've been squinting. Squinting takes a toll on your nose. Sighted people don't understand." He put on his glasses. "Mom, I'm fine. I'm not sick. They make you wait in the nurse's office if you can't see. That's all."

His mother seemed to study both of them. Snowball eyed Margaret Ann, chattered something that sounded like "kissy girl."

"See you at dinner?" his mother asked. "We're having egg white omelettes with mashed potatoes."

"Don't think so. I'll be at the Melch's kinda late. Grill and I have a science project. Won't have much time to work on it once I start babysitting."

Margaret Ann laid a chart in front of Doc's mom. "Sign here, Mrs. Ruggles. It's a release so your son can get back into class." She smiled, held out a pen.

"Give your sister a kiss," his mother said, signing, handing the pen back to Margaret Ann.

Doc tried to give a peck to Snowball's cheek but she turned away.

When his mother left, Doc sat down on a cot in the corner of the room. "I guess I should head to class."

"You're not going back to class." Margaret Ann said, holding up the slip of paper Doc's mother had signed. "You've been formally dismissed for the day. You have to leave campus. You're 'sick.'"

"What are you talking about?"

"You're coming with me. You're going to do what you promised my dad you'd do. You're going to find a way to make Father Stephen really nervous. And I'm going to help you. I think we should start by focusing on the church itself. Find out, once and for all, if this mysterious nun really exists." She reached for her purse, pulled out her keys. "Ready? I'm driving."

LA PALOMA

It took Margaret Ann forever to back-and-forth her way out of the space in front of the school where she'd parallel parked. At some point, probably about halfway through the maneuver, she'd stopped abruptly, turned, and pressed her index finger to Doc's lips. He'd been trying to get an answer to the same question he'd asked over and over since they'd left the nurse's office: How in the heck did she know what he and Quinn had talked about last night? Frustrated, silenced by her wagging finger, he'd sat back, folded his arms and muttered, "So who says I promised your dad anything?"

"I'm not listening," she chirped, "I'm concentrating. Some of us realize driving's a full-time job."

"You're not driving," Doc said. "You're unparking."

She pulled out, made a Y-turn in the narrow street, bumped the flagpole with her rear bumper, drove down the hill.

"Perfectly executed, if I do say so," she said.

He looked over at her, shook his head. Even her profile made the bones of his skull throb.

"How's my patient's headache?" she asked.

"Pounding along quite nicely, thank you."

"Let's fix you up." She took her hands off the wheel, clicked open the purse next to her on the seat, shook out a few pills from a small bottle. "Try these."

Doc took the tablets, crunched them in his mouth, gulped them down as the Chevy drifted into oncoming traffic.

"Aspirin?"

"Midol," she said, taking the wheel again. "They're for menstrual cramps. They'll get the 'flow' going, clear your mind. Your nose might spot a little, and, come to think of it, your voice might squeak for a few days, but the relief should be worth it."

He stared straight ahead, worried for a moment she might be serious. Smiling, she said, "Did you know there's erectile tissue in your nose?"

"No, can't say I did."

"Didn't you ever wonder why it feels so good when you sneeze?" She glanced at Doc, turned south on Harbor Boulevard. "I find little anatomy tidbits interesting. Some people find that quality in me rather enchanting."

"About as enchanting as a curse."

"Another tidbit. Among girls, 'the curse' is colloquial for menstruation…Lunch?"

"I've lost my appetite."

"Well I'm hungry."

"I thought you wanted to find Sister Theresa."

"While we eat, we'll formulate a plan." She held up her index finger again. "An army runs on its stomach."

"This man's army's not going anywhere until you tell me how you know what your father and I talked about. Isn't that stuff supposed to be confidential?"

"It's supposed to be, but I sneaked a look at his notebook. He writes everything down. I pretty much peek at it every night after he falls asleep. A girl's gotta watch out for her dad. His work puts him into contact with some rather unsavory characters"—she glanced at Doc—"not to mention idiots that get in over their heads."

Ten minutes later she turned left into the parking lot of La Paloma, stopped beneath the brim of a giant plaster sombrero. "How does Mexican sound?"

"Fine."

"Has the Midol kicked in? Is the little prince feeling better?"

Doc stared at her. "I thought you wanted to get serious about solving a mystery, but you just want to keep stickin' it to me. You can't be nice for five minutes."

Margaret Ann's freckles faded a little. "I've been nice for ten minutes," she said. "And I do want to help you; it's hard to explain why." She looked into his eyes. "Doc, the stuff in my Dad's notebook is pretty scary. Thinking about it makes me nervous, mostly for you. But teasing you relaxes me. It just does. When we sit down to eat, I'll be all business. I promise."

La Paloma had a peppery, yeasty, tomato-and-onion smell. Paper-mache piñatas in the shape of donkeys and little mustachioed Pancho Villas hung from the ceiling. Behind a red Formica counter, a heavy-set Mexican woman in a poofy fiesta blouse patty-caked tortillas and tossed them on a grill. She stared at Doc suspiciously, then nodded. Doc guessed the gesture meant, "I instinctively don't like you but you may as well take a seat." Of the twenty or so tables in the restaurant, only four or five were occupied.

They sat in a booth in the back. A boy about twelve years old took their order. Doc wanted the combination plate, "No white food, please," he said, handing back the menu, adding, "I mean the color white." Margaret Ann, in Spanish, requested, *por favor*, chile rellenos and pumpkin pie. Though she didn't know how to say pumpkin or pie in Spanish, she spoke the words with her tongue flicking the roof of her mouth so it would sound Spanish. She was so annoying.

While Margaret Ann sipped a coke, Doc told her about seeing Sister Theresa dancing in the cemetery, what Ricky, the Japanese

giant, had told him about the boy buried in the grave, the disappearing act the nun pulled when he'd searched the pond for her "corsage."
"You can't make this stuff up," Doc said.

"And she wants you to introduce her to Jimmy?"

"She says she has information about his sister."

"What do you think that means?"

"I have no idea."

"You know what I think?" Margeret Ann said. "I think she talks to
the dead."

"Who talks to the dead?"

She took a bite of pumpkin pie. "Other dead people."

"So now Sister Theresa's a ghost? Gosh, it wasn't that long ago she
was a lie, an imaginary friend I'd made up."

Margaret Ann chewed placidly.

"What? No comeback?"

She held up her index finger, chewed some more, swallowed. She
sucked a little Coke through her straw. "You know how I ensure good
digestion? I 'Fletcherize' each bite, masticate each morsel thirty-two
times before I swallow." She pushed her plate aside. "It just seems
logical."

"If you're a cow."

Margaret Ann sat back. "You're so, so young. You know what your
problem is? You're too easily distracted. And this is a perfect example.
I'm not talking about my digestion. I'm talking about your so-called
nun. I'm talking facts, facts like no one's ever heard of her, no one's
ever seen her but you. She appears and disappears." Margaret Ann
patted her lips with a napkin. "Can't you see I'm trying to give you the
benefit of the doubt? I'm skeptical, but I'm willing to go along with
you. I'm willing to accept the possibility that there are entities not
quite of this world. *The Bible* says that an angel spoke to Mary. History
books tell us an angel appeared to Joan of Arc." She put her napkin
down. "Complete this prompt: The first time I saw Sister Theresa, I…"

Doc groaned.

"If you want me to believe you, you'll have to help. Think back to Sunday, you're at the church. You're climbing, climbing. Now complete this simple sentence: The first time I saw Sister Theresa, I thought…" She raised her eyebrows, kept them elevated.

"This is stupid."

"Indulge me. Close your eyes. Go back to the moment you met her."

Doc grudgingly closed his eyes, took a few slow breaths, drifted back in time. "I'd crashed through a bunch of trash cans. I was lying on my back. I opened my eyes. The first time I saw her, I thought she was…an angel."

"An angel in *black*. That's what you told me on the patio behind the library. Remember what else you said?"

"That she was weird?"

"She told you she wanted to strip down, throw herself into a pond of Holy Water. She had polish on her nails."

Doc nodded. "Little pink flecks in the nail beds. I remember."

"She's not a nun, Doc. Nuns don't wear polish. They don't tell impressionable boys they want to frolic around naked. See, ghosts have bigger goals. That's what makes them different from your ill-conceived, one-dimensional imaginary friends. Unfortunately, your conscious mind isn't conscious enough to perceive the difference. But maybe, with a little time and patience, I can delve your subconscious, probe and probe until…"

In his mind, Doc watched a babbling ribbon of ticker tape spill out from between Margaret Ann's teeth. Her words garbled together until all he could hear was a thresh of noise, a smear of sounds indistinguishable from the commotion in the room. Nouns became bits of meat sizzling in a fry pan, verbs the clatter of plates in the kitchen. The overhead fan thrummed, moaned adverbs that declared they absolutely knew how, when, and where. He watched her mouth parade out words wearing big boots. She diatribed, pontificated, conjugated, strung together "ipso factos" and multi-syllabics with pompous Latin derivatives.

"Stop. Stop right now," he said. I'm in charge here, not you."

Margaret Ann's mouth fell open.

"And I'm not that young." He picked up his fork, carved off a piece of her pie. He swallowed it without Fletcherizing. "You're only a year older than me."

"Fourteen months to be precise," she said meekly, using the side of her hand to scrape crumbs off the table.

"Don't forget to tell me you've skipped two grades," he said. He reached for her plate again.

"I'd prefer you not touch my pie."

"I'll touch your pie if I want to." He grabbed the last piece and popped it into his mouth. "This isn't school, Margaret Ann. And your father didn't pick you to help him. He picked me. So for now, we'll solve this mystery my way."

She mouthed something.

"What did you say? I didn't hear you." He felt like he was on a roll.

"I still think it'd be a better mystery if it had a ghost in it."

"It doesn't need a ghost. It's already got everything. There's a disturbed priest with something to hide; a detective tormented by an unsolved murder; a young hero, namely me, whose mere presence has cracked a wall of silence; and a beautiful girl, who finds yours truly irresistible."

Margaret Ann's nose crinkled, her freckles pulsed.

"First," she said, gathering steam, "you haven't cracked any wall of silence. So far you've been nothing more than a fly in the ointment. An irritant. That's what my father thinks of you. It says so in his notebook. And who says I find you irresistible?"

"Not you," Doc snorted. "I'm talking about Bonnie."

Margaret Ann blinked, brushed away a flop of hair that had fallen over her eyes. There were bits of piecrust stuck to her forehead.

"Who's…Bonnie?"

"She's my destiny." Doc grabbed her hands. "Haven't you ever had the crazy feeling you were connected to someone? That you were meant to be with that person?"

Margaret Ann looked away. "No."

"Bonnie's the girl I met up with at the cemetery. She's gonna babysit so I can practice with the band. She's the girl who kissed me at the Teen Center."

"A girl voluntarily kissed you?"

"Yeah, she kissed me, all right. French kissed me. I slept with her gum in my mouth."

Margaret Ann's freckles faded like drops of invisible ink. Her voice became a syrup of sarcasm. "And it all began after you saw her naked, got a real good peek at her from the roof of the church. How romantic."

"That wasn't Bonnie. In the beginning I thought it was. Turned out it was Scarlett I saw naked."

"Did that little adventure come with a piece of gum, too? Another trophy, another souvenir you could sleep with?"

"What are you talking about?"

Margaret Ann stood, grabbed her purse, leaned across the table, got right in his face. "I'm leaving," she said. "You can walk home. Better yet, why don't you hitchhike. Maybe some tramp will pick you up." She poked a finger into his chest. "You, you and your tight jeans. You'd like that, wouldn't you? Another notch on your gun belt."

"I don't even own a gun belt."

She slid out of the booth and stomped toward the door.

Doc followed her.

The fat woman making tortillas stared at him.

Everyone in the restaurant stared at him. He'd plead his case to anyone who would listen. Diners. Kitchen help.

No one seemed to care. Maybe it was because they didn't speak English.

Margaret Ann stopped, turned. "Did you say it was Scarlett you saw with Father Stephen? That's who you saw at the church?"

"Found out last night," he said, relieved the subject had shifted away from Bonnie. "I went over to her house. She pretty much confessed. I took action because I couldn't get her underwear out of my mind."

Margaret Ann stiffened.

"What I mean is, I couldn't get what you *said* about her underwear out of my mind. Remember? The 'Monday' thing at the music store? You were right. You were the key. I think Scarlett takes off her clothes, does crazy stuff like that 'cause she knows it'll get guys in trouble, knows that if anyone finds out, it'll be the guy everyone blames. You blamed the guys in the band, right? I blamed Father Stephen."

"I was the key?"

"You were brilliant."

Margaret Ann nodded. "So she's an exhibitionist. I'm not surprised." A smirky, little self-servicing smile rippled across her mouth. "So much for your 'Sex Slaves of the Vatican' theory."

"Come back to the table," Doc said. "I'll tell you what else I know. We'll make an outline. We'll add in ghosts, all the dead people you want."

"Maybe I'll find another key."

"Wouldn't be surprised."

Doc guided Margaret Ann back to the table, pulled out a chair for her, then walked over to the jukebox. He shoved in a quarter, punched in three Mexican songs he'd never heard of. If she started up again, he hoped the blare of trumpets, the insufferable squawk of accordions would drown her out.

When he got back to their table, a Holy Mother candle flickered brightly between two orders of flan.

Margaret Ann unfolded a fresh napkin, glanced over at the young waiter. "Apparently," she said, "the dessert's compliments of the house."

Doc sat down. "I didn't say you weren't beautiful."

Margaret Ann looked across the table at him, slurped a spoonful of flan. "You think that's why I'm mad at you?"

"It was a guess."

"Well you guessed wrong."

"Then I have no idea why you're mad."

A song played on the Wurlitzer: The Flamingos' "I Only Have Eyes for You."

Margaret Ann took a moment and swayed to the music, then reached across the table and grabbed Doc's hands. "You're in the middle of something big, maybe a breakthrough in a murder case," she said. "But here's your problem: You get distracted. Look at what you just did. You subconsciously picked my favorite love song to play on the jukebox because you know you have a crush on me."

Doc glanced back at the jukebox, shook his head. "I didn't pick this song."

Looking down at her plate, she said, "I know it's hard for you to speak honestly about how you feel about me." She lifted her head, took a breath. "But I want to speak honestly to you. The truth is I wasn't in the least disturbed by your feeble attempt to make me jealous. I was mad because my father asked you to help him find out who killed Jimmy's sister. He's never asked me to help with anything."

Somewhere, deep in his heart, Doc felt a warm feeling, and a certain sadness, too.

"That's got to be tough to handle sometimes. I'm sorry."

"That's my point: You should be sorry. While I get a raw deal, you just stumble along fantasizing you're as cool as Jimmy, thinking Kipling's piano sings songs to you, believing a magic kite will lead you to some hot chick. You think life's a fairy tale."

"A fairy tale? Yesterday, I dug myself out of a grave. How's that a fairy tale?"

"Let me put it another way: girls, girls, girls. You can't see past a pretty skirt."

The warm place in his heart turned to heartburn.

"Not true!" he said. "I've seen through more than one pretty skirt since this whole thing started."

Margaret Ann scowled. "I guess that's true in the literal sense."

"What I mean is, I've uncovered a lot of stuff, gathered a fistful of puzzle pieces. Paid a price for gettin' 'em, too. I know things I can't tell your father about, at least not yet. But I've told those things to you. You wanna help me or not?"

"Why would you want me to be your partner?"

Doc wanted to say, because you're infuriating, because you make my mind crazy. He exhaled.

"Because...you're the smartest girl I know who's also pretty."

"Really?"

"Really."

"And you won't get distracted by kite flying or that stupid band, wha'da ya call yourselves, 'Jimmy and the Jockstraps'?"

Doc frowned. "'Jimmy and the Gigolos.'"

"Do I have your promise or not?"

"I promise."

Margaret Ann grabbed a fresh tablet of notebook paper from her bottomless purse. "I'll make an outline."

Doc called the waiter over, thanked him for the flan, ordered two more cokes. He slid his chair over next to her.

In the upper left corner of the first page, Margaret Ann drew a large Roman numeral one. Below it, she quickly sketched out something that looked like a scene with him running through the cemetery. When she stopped drawing, he watched her pull a ruler out, drop down two lines, indent exactly one inch and make a capital A. She started to measure again.

Doc stopped her.

"I want you to draw circles," he said. "Big ones. I want you to cut them out and write a name in the center of each one. Make one for Father Stephen, one for Junior, one for Bonnie, and Scarlett. Make a bunch of them. We'll fill in the names as we go."

"I'd rather indent."

"You'll cut circles and like it," Doc said, leaning in, adding, "I'll tell you what I've seen, what I've heard. You'll slide the circles over each other. It'll give us a picture of where the suspects intersect, who overlaps with who, or whom, however you say it. Don't you see, it's all wheels within wheels."

"You've gone completely mad," she said. "And who carries scissors with them?"

"You do."

They stared at each other. Doc scooped a spoonful of her flan. She nabbed a spoonful of his: a Mexican standoff. *Segundos* ticked away.

"Okay," he said. "How 'bout this? You make a circle for the ghost Sister Theresa. Make it as big as you want. Does that make you happy?"

Margaret Ann smiled, reached into her pulse. "Will pinking shears do?"

"Fine."

"And I'll use a compass. I just happen to have one with me."

"Why am I not surprised?"

Margaret Ann drew perfect circles, cut them out. The "pinked" edges gave the rim of each disc little triangular teeth.

Doc picked up one of the paper gears, rambled, free-associated as he studied it.

"I figure," he said, "Father Stephen knows I was there the night Jimmy's sister died. Maybe he thinks I saw something, that over the years I've put some sort of two-and-two thing together."

"That fits with my dad's idea that something about you makes the priest nervous." She wrote Doc's name on one circle, the priest's on another.

"Overlap us," Doc said.

"Done. What's next?"

"Junior's involved with Father Stephen, too. Sunday night at the Teen Center, before Junior got into Father Stephen's car, I heard him yell at the priest. He said something like, 'You want it your way, you'll do what I say.'"

"And wasn't your 'Miss Destiny' there with them?"

"Junior kidnapped her."

"And the priest drove the merry trio away? The way it went down tells me Junior didn't care what Bonnie heard because it wasn't news to her." Margaret Ann slid Bonnie's circle into Junior's. "There she is. Little Miss Wheel Within Wheels."

"Bonnie was probably in shock. A victim of circumstance."

"And pure as the driven snow." She shook her head. "Why is it all the girls in your stories are three-dimensional, have backstories and childhood wounds, while the villains have only two dimensions? Here's a prime example." Margaret Ann touched the disc with Junior's name.

"Junior doesn't need a third dimension," Doc said. "He's just psycho."

"Maybe this time 'the psycho' has motivation. Maybe *why* he wants to kill you is connected to the reason you make the priest nervous. Personally, I think this Bonnie girl put him up to it." She laid the circle with Jimmy's sister's name on it very near to Bonnie's and Buddy's.

"No way."

"No way? Look at your stupid discs."

Doc looked down. It was all there in front of him. Bonnie's circle overlapped everyone's, the living and the dead.

"Gosh, your Bonnie looks more like a cog than a wheel. And there she is again in the cemetery."

"She was visiting a grave: Father Stephen's brother."

Margaret Ann touched the circle with "Priest's Brother, Buddy" written in the center of it. "That's two circles with the names of dead people." She picked up Sister Theresa's circle, dangled it between two fingers, let it flutter in the breeze from the overhead fan. "Sister Theresa sorta floats around the edges of everything, doesn't she? Which group should I put her in? With the heres or the hereafters?"

Behind them, Doc heard the door to the restaurant fly open.

He turned.

Three men brandishing *pistolas* burst in. They shouted over each other in Spanish.

Margaret Ann reached out, grabbed Doc's arm. "They're robbing the place! They want us down on the floor!"

"It's the Cubans," Doc exclaimed, sliding under the table, pulling her down with him.

"Who?"

They lay side by side on the floor facing each other.

"The Cuban communists," Doc whispered, their mouths barely a breath apart. "Remember I pointed them out to you in the library? The fat one with the gold tooth tried to run me down when I was chasing the kite."

"Reds!"

"Exactly," Doc said. "Red's Sanitary Supply."

The cash register *cha-chinged*.

More words in Spanish. The thunk of boots on the wooden floor.

Margaret Ann's lips were less than an inch from Doc's. "They want everyone's money."

"I've got maybe six bucks," Doc said.

"Give it to them. Just stick your hand out with the money in it."

Doc fumbled in his pocket, stretched out his arm.

A boot came down on his wrist.

He winced, twisted, writhed. Electrons shot through his brain. An image formed in his gray matter: Margaret Ann holding up the disc with Sister Theresa's name on it. He saw Sister Theresa morph into Pinkie, "The Girl in the Pink Formal." That was it. He knew the truth in that instant. The epiphany of pain had brought with it a realization. Margaret Ann was right: Sister Theresa *was* a ghost. She went to the cemetery to dance with her Homecoming King, the boy she'd died with in Carbon Canyon. He managed a look back at Margaret Ann. In the midst of the robbery, with a wrist on fire with pain, he had the perfect idea. He whispered to Margaret Ann, "Wanna go to the Homecoming Dance with me?"

"What?"

"It's this Friday. Do you wanna go with me?"

"I haven't got a dress."

The Cuban reached down and dragged Doc out from beneath the table. He shoved Doc across the room and pinned him to the wall.

The fat man yelled something in Spanish.

Margaret Ann peeked out from beneath the tablecloth. "He wants to know why you're following them."

Doc shrugged his shoulders. "Make something up!"

"First, I want to know why you asked me to Homecoming."

The man held a gun to Doc's head.

START COUGHING

Cinch, cool as a cucumber, winked at Margaret Ann. He wanted his little compadre, the cute freckle-faced brunette who stared wide-eyed at him from beneath the table, to relax, not to worry. He had the situation well in hand. Even if the Cuban had the huevos to pull the trigger, even if this no good commie wanted to blow his brains out, Cinch knew the gun would fail to fire. Cinch was certain of that.

The last round his gold-toothed attacker had fired, the one that had burst the candy-filled piñata that dangled from the rafters, had made a distinctive, high-pitched pinging *sound. The report had been music to Cinch's ears. Well versed in weaponry, he knew that* ping, *C-sharp two octaves above middle C, signaled the death knell of the Luger P08 pistol's breechblock mechanism. The next shell would never advance into the chamber.*

The smirk on the commie's face told Cinch his adversary was unaware the gun had jammed, unaware of the fatal mistake he'd made when he'd loaded the Luger with inferior, foreign-made, low-pressure cartridges. The weapon he held was as worthless as a wet match.

Cinch took one last glance over at Margaret Ann. She was kneeling, praying, blinking away tears. He wished there was some way to signal her, to let her know it would be only a matter of minutes before they'd sit across the table from each other again, smiling, sharing the last morsels of flan, while the authorities led the bewildered robbers away in shackles. But he also knew her happiness would be short-lived.

Disabling the Cuban, Cinch knew, would be far easier than explaining the real reason he'd invited the shy, soft-spoken girl to Homecoming. Momentarily, he would dispatch the Cuban with a Manchu wristlock, followed by a sword punch to the man's carotid. Dealing with Margaret Ann, however, would require a special touch. The truth might break her heart.

How could he tell her they weren't actually going to the dance? That fate had cast her, not as his date for Homecoming night, but as his driver. He'd just have to hold her close to him as he spoke the truth, assuage her broken heart with the finesse he'd developed through the years of attending Cotillion. Instead of going to the dance, they'd go out to Carbon Canyon. Sister Theresa would be there. This time, she would appear as who she really was: Pinkie. In an aside, Cinch made a mental note to bring the pink shoes. Maybe he'd find time to fulfill the legend, have conferred upon him total knowledge of women. That would be nice. A little bonus. Margaret Ann would hate that.

Pleased with the "fiction" he'd written, Doc smiled, set his pencil down on the oak table, and gazed out over the library.

He caught sight of the nonfiction Margaret Ann, just the top half of her at first. She was huffing up the stairs from the basement, her arms loaded with the newspapers he'd asked her to ferret from the stacks.

One look and he knew she was still mad at him.

He avoided her eyes, pulled out a chair for her.

"If my dad comes in," she said, "I walk from this table. I don't know you."

"Fine."

"So where were you?" she said, her whisper a vapor of snake venom. "I thought you were coming downstairs to help me. You have any idea what prolonged exposure to mold and dust can do to a girl's sinuses, let alone her skin?"

"Sorry," he said, taking the newspapers from her. "My leg's kinda hurtin'. Got twisted up when I wrestled that fat commie over to the wall."

"*You* wrestled *him*? That's a laugh." She settled into the chair. "You're lucky those guys took off when they heard the sirens." She looked down at the table. "What's my notebook doing out?"

"I was going to make a wheel for the Cubans."

"The Cubans don't have anything to do with the priest or the ghost or whoever killed Jimmy's sister. They're extraneous. Stick with the chain of evidence."

"You're probably right."

Margaret Ann looked down at the notebook, then at Doc. "You don't have scissors out. I don't believe you were making a wheel."

She waited for an answer.

"I was thinking about turning what we're doing into a story," Doc said. "Maybe a novella. A slick murder mystery. When this is all over, I plan to sell what I've written to *True Detective* magazine."

"As literature?" Margaret Ann drew in a breath, held it until her cheeks nearly exploded, then burst out laughing.

Doc felt his shoulders sink. The chuck of each of her chuckles sticked-and-stoned him.

He forced a thin smile. "I guess being my partner doesn't include propping up my ego. Just forget I brought it up. It's a stupid story." He

164

opened the notebook, ripped out the pages he'd written, tore them in half.

Margaret Ann fell silent. She looked at him in the oddest way. "I'm sorry the idea of you being a writer strikes me as funny, but that doesn't make it stupid. And you certainly weren't stupid today. Actually you were quite brave. Even though you just stood there while that guy pointed a gun at your head, I thought you did it in a very noble way. And if you wrote in your story that today you saved my life, I'd say, to anyone who asked, what you'd written was true because, no matter what did or didn't happen, you never let anyone point a gun at me."

Margaret Ann reached into her purse, withdrew a roll of Scotch tape, and began mending Doc's torn pages.

"You don't have to do that," he said.

"Yes, I do. If I don't, we'll both have to keep feeling sorry for you." She glanced at the stack of papers. "Anyway, I thought we were here to solve a mystery, though I can't fathom how dragging out a bunch of old *News Tribune*s is going to help."

"We're going to research the Homecoming Queen, the first dead person...The Girl in the Pink Formal."

"That whole legend thing's silly and you know it."

"It's mythic."

"About as mythic as *Playboy* magazine. That rag's a bedtime fantasy for adolescent boys."

"Boys didn't write these newspapers, Margaret Ann. Reporters wrote down the facts. I'm just asking you to read the facts."

"But we're *here* because you had some epiphany, right? Some sort of vision."

"I believe it was a near-death experience. Very cool. When that Cuban stepped on my wrist, my whole life flashed before my eyes. The last thing I saw was you."

"You saw me? Hmmm." She seemed to think a moment. "I guess that would make sense."

"Well not exactly you," Doc admitted. "What I saw was you holding up that circle with Sister Theresa's name on it. And, remember, you asked me where you should put it? With the heres or the hereafters? That's when it came to me. The answer to your question was *yes*. She's here *and* hereafter. She's both. Sister Theresa's the nun *and* the dead Homecoming Queen. She's Pinkie. She was practically telling me that when she was dancing around the grave."

"Then why didn't she just say it: 'Hi, I'm Pinkie the ghost?'"

"I don't know. Maybe to her it's like she's in a fog. Maybe being dead is like having a concussion. Maybe the best ghosts can do is be mysterious. Maybe she needs us to figure out why she's here. I don't know the rules for dead people."

"And you know for sure Pinkie's date, what's his name...?" She studied one of the newspapers a moment. "Tommy McLean is the one buried in the grave she was dancing around?"

"Ricky, the guy at the cemetery told me so. It's gotta be a clue."

"A clue to what?"

"I don't know," Doc said. "That's why we're here. That's why we're going to read what was written about the accident. There's got to be a connection between the past and the present. We'll know it when we see it."

"Your idea might have some marginal scientific merit. Let's give it a try." She looked around the library. "I'm serious. If my dad comes in, I walk from this table. I don't know you."

"Fine. I get it."

They started with the first article, the one written for the afternoon edition of the *News Tribune*, the day following the accident. The headline read, "Homecoming Tragedy, Fiery Crash in Carbon Canyon Ends Lives of Fullerton Teens."

The reporter began, "They would never make it home from Homecoming."

The column went on to describe what firefighters and police investigators found at mile marker forty-three: the skid marks; the twisted wreckage of the sports car, a Studebaker Starliner Coupe; the bat-tered, burnt body of the high school quarterback who, only hours ear-lier, had been crowned Homecoming King.

Running his fingers across the bottom of the page, Doc read the last line out loud: "The name of the young woman presumed dead in the accident has been withheld."

The following day's edition had a single photograph above the fold: a picture of the car, wrapped around the oak tree, nearly split in half by the impact. On the next page there were two more images: a smudge-faced fireman kneeling, his head in his hands, and a close-up photo of the pink high heels, the winding road behind them twisting off to eternity.

"Thus the legend begins," Doc said.

"Yellow journalism," Margaret Ann sneered. "Blatant sensationalism."

"They never found her body. That's pretty sensational."

"It happens."

"No, it doesn't."

They stared at each other, then read on.

The following edition named the girl, Sandy Taylor. There was a photo of her.

"She looks like Sister Theresa." Doc said. "I would almost swear it is the same girl. Hard to tell. Does your face get older when you're dead?"

"It does if you're dead dead."

"What about the initials, S.T. and S.T.? Sister Theresa, Sandy Taylor?"

Margaret Ann shook her head. "Pretty thin."

There were eight more stories about Sandy Taylor in the days fol-lowing the accident. In one article, a reporter speculated on the ru-mor that Sandy's body had been dragged off and devoured by wolves. Another reporter, a woman who'd gone to college on the East Coast, had supposedly followed up on an anonymous phone call. In her col-umn, she wrote of the rumor that, secretly surviving the accident,

Sandy, weary of the life of a shallow debutante, had hitchhiked with a beatnik to Mississippi to become an agitator in the Civil Rights Movement. An editorial, written by a local minister, expressed concerns about the fate of her soul; Sandy had apparently never been baptized. The last article, a single column on page twelve, entitled "Dead End," carried with it a small grainy photo of the Studebaker. The car lay tilted on its side in a wrecking yard in Santa Ana.

Doc sighed. "Dead end is right. If I *do* write a novel about us solving a mystery, I'm leaving this chapter out." He started to close the page.

"Wait," Margaret Ann said, extracting a magnifying glass from her purse. "Wait just a minute. Let me see that photo again."

Using the magnifying glass, she focused in and out, stopped, smiled. "Take a look at this."

Doc looked through the lens. "What am I supposed to see?"

"The sign."

"A sign? Like from God?"

"No. The *sign* on the building behind the car: Mentz's Tow and Salvage."

Doc wasn't looking at the sign. He was staring at the taillights of the Studebaker. In the black and white photograph they blinked to life, burned red. "Holy crap, Margaret Ann. You're not going to believe this, but I could swear these are the same taillights Jimmy and I saw the night Jimmy's sister was killed." Doc jabbed his index finger at the photograph. "I'm certain of it. This is what Pinkie wants me to know: The car Pinkie died in was the same car that ran down Jimmy's sister." He grinned at Margaret Ann. "Start coughing."

"What?"

"Just start coughing."

GET OUT OF THE CAR

Margaret Ann stared over the steering wheel. "We could have gotten in big trouble."

"But we didn't."

"Doc, you destroyed, defaced, and illegally removed library property. Forced me to cough in complicity so you could tear that page out."

"I can't wait to tell Jimmy."

She ran a red light, pulled to the curb, and started to cry.

"What's the matter?" Doc asked.

"I'm late for work."

"So? I'm late for band practice."

"Yeah, well you'll just have to make a grand entrance. Tell your friends everything. Show Jimmy the picture and then you, Mr. Hero, and the stupid Gigolos will take it from there. You'll all go to the salvage yard. Probably solve the whole thing with the evidence you'll find and I'll be left on the sidelines, left out 'cause I'm a girl."

"Since when arc you a girl?"

She glared at him. "You think I'm a sexless cardboard cutout, don't you? Well, I've got boobs and an ass in case you haven't noticed. And feelings, too."

"Look, I only meant you're not a typical girl. You're not fragile... persuadable. And that's good. You're feminine without being girlie. You have a unique solidity."

"Solidity?"

"If you were a rock, you'd be a diamond. Okay? No one's leaving you on the sidelines. I'm not gonna say anything to Jimmy. Not now. Not even close to now. You and I, just the two of us, we'll go to the salvage yard together. I promise."

"I don't believe you."

"Look at it this way, Margaret Ann. I can't tell Jimmy a ghost led me to the photograph. He's not going to believe the whole 'Girl in the Pink Formal' thing. We need more proof. We'll go to the salvage yard, then on Friday night..."

"We'll go to Homecoming?"

"Sort of. We'll *leave* for the dance. We just won't get there. I see you driving us out to Carbon Canyon. Pinkie will be there. It's the anniversary of the night she died. Every version of the legend puts her there that night."

"Get out of the car."

"What's wrong?"

She pulled to the curb. "I'll tell you what's wrong, and you can call me a sniveler if you want. I wish my mom would come back from the dead. And if I could pick one night for her to visit or see me, it would be Homecoming. But I won't be there, and it's all your fault. She'll never see me in a formal. I hate you."

"Would you feel better if you took a Midol?"

QUINN CRANED OVER HIM

Doc walked the last few blocks to the music store. Icy air hit him in the face as he entered. The chill didn't just come from the air conditioning system.

Margaret Ann had already arrived and clocked in.

Head down, she was standing behind the register fiddling with something in the display case. He tiptoed past her and joined the Gigolos in the percussion practice room. Rather than explaining why he was late, Doc recounted the song-worthy, buried alive incident at Ascension Park. He stayed away from ghost stories and any mention of Margaret Ann.

As Doc spoke, Slatz played a dirge, a lament with a blues beat. Grill stirred brushes over the snare. The instrumental theme was a tasteful soundtrack to Doc's "cemetery" story. It sort of set the mood.

Jimmy plugged in his guitar. "I like the idea of setting your 'buried alive' story to music."

"It's not just my story, Jimmy," Doc said. "Junior thought *you* were going to be there, too. I think mostly he wanted to kill you."

"We can throw a mistaken identity theme into the song," Jimmy said. "Either way it should make for a great tune." Jimmy turned to Slatz and Grill. "A little rock 'n' roll rhythm, maestros? In E."

"Already in E," Slatz said, nodding. He improvised an upbeat melody with his right hand.

Beneath his beret, behind his dark glasses, "Jazzman" Grill set down the brushes, picked up his drumsticks, got in sync.

The volume rose. The air became electric.

Jimmy struck a chord. The sound was lush, brutal, sweet, wildly dissonant. Outside the room, every instrument in the store vibrated. He strummed the chord again. This time in key with the piano, in perfect rhythm with the drums.

Grill broke free, crashed the cymbals, thumped the tom-toms. Slatz Rachmaninoffed the keyboard.

The music was brilliant. It was hard to believe Jimmy had virtually never had a lesson, had never picked up a guitar until days ago.

"Sorry about that first chord, Doc," Jimmy said, shouting over a Grill drum solo. "I'm just getting acquainted with the strings."

"You're doing fine."

Jimmy winked, and a glint of coyote yellow flashed in his eyes. He slid his fingers up the neck of the guitar and bent off a series of notes, each one mournful and pure, unapologetic, answering only to itself.

The sound worked. Everything harmonized.

It was their first practice together and already the Gigolos sounded like a real band.

"Pick up your bass, Doc," Jimmy said. "Without a bass there's no heartbeat to the music."

Doc glanced around the room, saw his Fender tilted on a guitar stand next to the Baldwin.

Slatz stood from the piano stool, lifted Doc's bass, and handed it to him. It was as hefty as an axe. The sunburst finish greeted his eyes like the dawn of a new day.

Jimmy and Grill kept playing, gave Doc looks of encouragement.

"Just pluck the bottom string," Slatz said. "When the chord changes, play the string above it. On the third change, slide up two frets. That's all there is to rock 'n' roll: E, A, and B."

Slatz sat at the piano again.

Doc slung the guitar strap over his head.

"From the top," Slatz said. "'Buried Alive,' take two."

Doc, his fingers fumbling a little, played along—not too badly.

When the song ended, they all smiled at each other.

The door to the practice room opened. Doc expected it to be Margaret Ann coming in to say she was sorry, that she understood there was no way he could have known she was awash in memories of her own mother's death, that she was sorry she'd overreacted in the car, that deep down she believed in him both as a writer and now as a musician.

Instead, it was Scarlett who leaned in the doorway, all curves and bad intentions. She wore a plunging sleeveless blouse, tight black slacks.

"I was just going upstairs to my father's office when I heard you guys. Nice. Very nice." She tossed back a flame of red hair. "Love the drums and piano. Not sure which one I like best. A girl needs time to think."

Scarlett gave Slatz and Grill long, appraising looks, fingered the heart necklace that plumbed the space between her breasts then drifted back into the hallway outside the room. Like the others, Doc listened to the time-bomb tick of her high heels as she climbed the steps to her father's office.

Her exit had a predictable effect on the drummer and the keyboard player.

Slatz, ever the mix of gullibility and unbridled self-confidence, had lapped up Scarlett's seductive monologue without hesitation. He'd devoured her flirtations in the way a hound dog would snarf up a rump roast left to cool on a kitchen table.

Grill, on the other hand, was stunned, perplexed. He sat dazed, motionless, as if impaled by Cupid's first arrow.

"You okay, Grill?" Doc said.

A garble of words both sacred and profane slurred over Grill's lips, a wet sizzle of sparks arced across his braces, both aftermaths, Doc suspected, of some deep neuronal disturbance.

Scarlett had set the two against each other. She'd planned it that way. This was the encore performance to the monogrammed underwear incident she'd pulled off the day before.

Slatz slowly rose, put away his sheet music, his rail-thin body stiff, ascendant, triumphant as an exclamation point. "I think it's pretty clear someone, namely me, has just been invited upstairs."

Jimmy glanced over at Doc, shook his head.

Doc could only imagine what fate awaited Slatz if he followed Scarlett to her father's office. If this were New York's eastside, she'd probably ask Slatz if she could fit him for cement shoes. Trance-like, he'd likely nod "yes."

Carried forward by the momentum of the mind, Doc found himself wondering if, like the Gigolos, Father Stephen had been set up, lured to the prelate's study only to find Scarlett naked, salaciously unapologetic. The resulting situation would be hard if not impossible for the priest to explain to authorities, let alone to Scarlett's father. But then again, maybe there were things the priest knew about the man.

Thinking back, Doc recalled how Dr. Brisco had been oddly calm when he'd come into her bedroom, almost creepy calm when he'd found Scarlett and him virtually in bed together. Maybe at an earlier time, the priest had witnessed something similarly disquieting play out between father and daughter.

Bringing his mind back to the present, Doc realized tensions in the percussion practice room had escalated. What had apparently started as a "chop session," a battle of insults, had turned physical. He looked up to see Grill using a drumstick, lunging, thrusting D'Artagnan-style in a swordsman's effort to skewer his rival bandmate.

Slatz deftly swatted Grill back with a hard-cover book entitled *Beethoven's Bests*. Between swipes, Slatz occasionally stopped to retrieve his comb from his back pocket and lovingly style his ducktail, at the same time saying things like, "She loves real music, Grill. Drums don't make music. They make noise."

Grill answered back with "Drums were man's first instrument. Their pounding lured jungle women to their mates. Drums say, let's get it on, let's horizontal mambo."

"Think I'll go upstairs," Slatz said. "Ask Scarlett about that. Let her decide." He broke for the door.

Grill was right behind him.

Listening to feet battle for lead position on the stairs, Doc looked over at Jimmy. Kneeling, his friend was setting his Stratocaster into its case.

"Guess that's a wrap," Jimmy said, clicking the lid closed.

"Not bad for the first time we've ever practiced," Doc said. "Thanks again for the bass."

"Sure." He stood, faced Doc. "You wanna head back to my grand-parents' house?"

"We could take the tracks," Doc answered back. "No way Junior would find us there."

"And you could tell me the rest of the story."

"What story?"

"Why you left school today? What the police were doing at your house the other night? You've got secrets, Doc, and one of them's out there working behind the counter."

"Margaret Ann? There's nothing going on between us."

Jimmy handed Doc a quarter. "Really? Go out there, buy a few picks, then come back and tell me nothing's going on. I'll wait."

Doc hesitated. Why not? He wasn't afraid of Margaret Ann.

Approaching the counter, Doc saw she'd put on her cat glasses. She wore them when she wanted to be formal, when she was deter-mined to act like an adult.

"Can I help you?"

"I need a guitar pick," he said.

"Primary colors or tortoise shell?"

"Tortoise shell."

"Thick or thin?"

"I don't care."

"No, it seems you don't. Some people stick with you through thick and thin. Some could care less."

"I'm sorry. For what I don't know exactly, but I'm sorry."

"It doesn't matter." She scattered a handful of picks on the counter. "Two for a quarter." She looked up. "I think your friend is leaving."

Looking over his shoulder, Doc watched Jimmy walk to the front of the store and stare out at Harbor Boulevard through the plate-glass windows.

"He's watching cars brake at the signal," Doc said. "He's looking at taillights. Never misses a chance. I wish I could find a way to tell him I'm pretty sure I've got what he's looking for right here in my pocket."

"The picture of the Studebaker?"

Doc nodded. "I want to show him the clipping, but I want to keep the promise I made you."

"Go ahead," she said. "Tell him the ghost story. Tell him about 'Pinkie.'"

"But what about us?"

"'Us' will just have to be whatever it is."

"He's not going to believe a ghost wants to lead him to his sister's killer."

"Start with what my father said. Tell him about the connection with the priest. Go step by step from there. He'll want to believe you." She took off her glasses, folded them, and placed them in her purse. "By the way, I took a few Midol. They helped."

"Glad you're better. But, I'm telling you, if Jimmy believes me, he'll want to go to the salvage yard. I can't guarantee he'll want *you* to come along."

"Get away from the counter."

"I thought you said—"

"My dad just came into the store. Go."

Doc turned, took a few steps. Quinn blocked his path.

"You two know each other?"

Doc withered.

Margaret Ann's freckles scattered.

It was too late to lie. Quinn had Sherlocked them, had spotted the two of them talking when he'd first come in.

"He's a customer, Daddy," she said from behind the counter. "His band practices here and—" She clammed up, shot a quick glance at Doc.

"And that's about it," Doc said.

Quinn shifted his weight, tilted his head, studied their eyes.

For every second they remained silent, their eyes spoke a thousand guilty words.

"The truth is," Doc said, "I've invited the counter girl here to Homecoming."

Margaret Ann cringed.

Quinn cleared his throat. "This counter girl's my daughter."

Doc countered with bravado.

"So? The chick is solid. I like her grooves. She likes the way I rock 'n' roll."

Quinn craned over him. "So how long has this been going on?"

Jimmy's voice came from behind him. "For about forty-five minutes," he said. He gave Quinn a cool, calculating stare. "It went down like this: I dared Doc to ask her to the dance."

Margaret Ann blurted, "I said no, Daddy. But he wouldn't listen."

Jimmy grabbed Doc's elbow, "Come on, Doc, let's get out of here." He took a step, stopped, stared at Quinn with coyote eyes. "I know you, don't I? You're the cop that made that 'nice try' to find the guy that killed my sister. Wha'd you spend, maybe ten minutes on that case?"

Now Quinn was silent.

Dread, like a jagged rock, stuck in Doc's throat. Jimmy tugged his arm again.

Defiant, dismissive, Jimmy walked toward the front door. He flipped the start switch on a player piano as he passed by it.

Doc followed behind him, his pace at odds with the jolly rhythm of "Happy Days Are Here Again" playing on the piano. He wondered which Jimmy he was following? Jekyll or Hyde? Coyote or his best friend?

HIS FEATURES
HARDENED TO STONE

Doc and Jimmy took Harbor Boulevard north six blocks toward the viaduct that led up to the tracks. The streetlights were on though it wasn't quite dusk. Overhead, pink clouds feathered along in layers of grays and blues. Girls in a passing car, whistled, blew kisses at Jimmy.

Jimmy tipped an imaginary hat at them, then said. "You know which girl I like best, Doc?" He pointed up. "Venus."

The evening star winked above a moon the shape of a clipped fingernail.

"The Goddess of Love," Doc said. "Nice choice."

"A heavenly body. And she keeps her distance. Maybe someday I'll build a ladder tall enough to lean up against her, climb up and give her a kiss."

Only a few minutes earlier Jimmy had been cold, almost cruel. Now he was almost whimsical. Doc wondered which aspect of Jimmy would be listening when he told the story of Sister Theresa, explained the series of revelations that had led him to the newspaper clipping now folded in his pocket, the idea the nun he'd run into the day he flew the kite was actually a ghost.

"Let's cross the street here," Doc said. "The Turntable's still open."

"I'd rather find a place I could eat some meat. Rabbit would be nice."

"I need to show you something over there in the light."

Dodging cars, Doc crossed the street. Jimmy followed but not without elements of style. He spanked the hood of one car, played matador with another.

Doc waved him over to the halo of neon light that bathed the pavement outside the record store.

"What ya got to show me?" Jimmy said. He reached for Doc's shirt collar. "A hicky on your neck?"

Doc brushed his hand away.

Jimmy wagged a finger, a lupine grin spread across his face. "You spent the day with Margaret Ann. Risky. Bold."

"Jimmy, I need you to ask you something. I want you to tell me if you know what I want more than anything in the world."

"You want to find a girl with the face of a perfect angel. A girl worth fighting for. You've told me that a thousand times."

"There's something else. I want to be the best friend you've ever had. I wanna be the guy who never gave up, the one who stuck by you till we found out who killed Cindy."

"We go skyfishing. Most of the time together. Sorry about last time. Is that what you want me to say?"

There was too much coyote in Jimmy right now. It was hard for him to listen. Doc spoke slowly. "I need you to pay attention. What I'm talking about is the last time I chased the kite. It was different. It's brought me into contact with people and places I never could have dreamt of." Doc reached into his pocket. "I found this today." He handed Jimmy the clipping. "I want to know if you see what I see."

Jimmy stared the grainy photograph, held it up to the light. His eyes flashed with flecks of yellow. His features hardened to stone. "It's the car, isn't it? Those taillights are a dead ringer for the ones we saw."

Doc nodded. "Look at the sign." He tapped the clipping. "Know the legend of 'The Girl in the Pink Formal'? This was the car the girl was in when it crashed in Carbon Canyon back in nineteen fifty-four. My guess is it wasn't junked. I think someone restored it. I've got a pretty good guess who was behind the wheel of this car the night Cindy died."

Jimmy stared long and hard at the sign in the background of the photograph, read the words as though they tasted of acid. "Mentz's Tow and Salvage. Where did this come from?"

"Let's keep moving," Doc said. "We've got a lot to talk about."

THE DARK COLORS OF
LOST INNOCENCE

Supporting themselves against the rounded columns that formed the base of the Pacific Electric viaduct, they climbed the steep embankment that led to the tracks. As cars whipped beneath the overpass, Doc chronicled his encounters with Pinkie the nun, the ghost girl from Carbon Canyon. Detailed what he'd learned at the library.

Jimmy, clutching the folded clipping in one fist, listened.

Reaching the top, Doc paused in his story, gazed out over the city now ringed in evening light the color of cinnamon. He could see the shadowy terrain of Hillcrest Park, the lights of the Teen Center twinkling in the hollow just below its summit. He recognized the crisp-cut silhouettes of Fullerton Music, the bell tower of Saint Mary's church, each location now harder etched, redrawn in the dark colors of lost innocence.

Jimmy walked ahead of him. Placing one foot in front of the other, he balanced on the right rail.

Doc took the left rail, tightroped forward until the two were parallel to one another. "It's like Pinkie's drifting in a dream," he continued. "I'm not sure if even she knows what she's doing. My best guess is she wanted me to find the car. God knows she practically whacked me over the head with clues. Now she wants me to bring you to her. She has something to show you or tell you. That's what she says."

Jimmy looked over at him. "How do we make that happen?"

Doc stepped down from the rail. "You actually believe me?"

"I'm a guy who talks to coyotes. Not a big stretch to believe in one more crazy thing. Besides, he believes in you. Why shouldn't I?"

Doc stopped. "Who believes in me?"

Jimmy nodded over his shoulder, grinned. "Take a slow look back."

Doc pivoted ever so slowly.

Loping along the tracks, keeping pace, maybe fifty yards behind them, was the coyote.

"Oh, him," Doc said, a little nervously. "I guess it's a good thing he believes in me. Makes me feel a little safer when he's around."

"He doesn't *want* you to feel safer, Doc. He wants you to know he believes there's a part of you that's capable of being dangerous."

The click of the coyote's paws faded slowly into the distance as they drew closer to the homes that ran along the crest of the valley.

At the top of the last hill, when both feet were back on asphalt again, Doc, in a slightly gruffer voice, proposed his plan to have Margaret Ann take them into Carbon Canyon the night of Homecoming. "Pinkie will be there, Jimmy. She'll be waiting for you."

"Got a few more days till Homecoming, Doc. I say we start now. Come at this from the other direction. Do a little snoop around Mentz's garage. See what we can come up with."

"Or who we run into."

IN THE FADED PHOTOGRAPH

Jimmy's grandmother greeted them at the front door. She was about a thousand years old, the same age she was when Doc, just out of kindergarten, had met her. She held a disconnected phone in her hand, wore a full-length London Fog coat buttoned up to the top, her pale blue flannel nightgown visible below the hem. Pinned in her thinning hair was a tilted rhinestone tiara. She pointed at Doc.

"I told him if he was going to be late he might as well not come at all."

"You're absolutely right, Grandma. Doc has no right to waste your time. Let's get you back to your bedroom."

"I'll get ready as I please, and he'll just have to wait," she snarled.

"He'll wait, Grandma," Jimmy said, motioning Doc to come along.

They walked through the living room. Jimmy's grandfather, "Harry the Chair," was asleep in a brown leather La-Z-Boy, a novel by James A. Michener on his lap. He didn't move. Never did as far as Doc knew. As usual, Jimmy's mother was nowhere around.

Jimmy guided Grandma down the hallway. Displayed on both walls, Cindy's equestrian ribbons fluttered as they passed by. Doc stopped to look at a portrait of a young man in uniform. "Is…was that your father?"

"Casper, the friendly dad? No. Used to think so. Found out later the photograph came with the frame." Jimmy smiled. "Guess someone hung it up when I was a kid. Maybe they thought it'd make me feel better."

Doc stopped in the doorway of the master bedroom as Jimmy and Grandma went in.

Jimmy helped her remove her coat, pulled out a gold-gilt chair from in front of a vanity, and steadied her as she sat down.

"You were the hit of the party, Grandma. Everybody had a great time." Jimmy turned to Doc. "Grandma thinks every night's her birthday party."

"Happy Birthday, Grandma," Doc said.

She looked at Doc's reflection in the mirror. Eyed him warily.

"See how beautiful you are, Grandma," Jimmy said.

Slowly, she removed her earrings, placed them in a silver box. Jimmy unpinned the tiara, set it on the vanity next to a small framed photograph.

Hesitating a moment, she lifted the silver frame. Tilting her head, she gazed at the image.

"You'd like Doc to see this, wouldn't you?" Jimmy said. "I'll have him come over and you tell him about you and Grandpa on your honeymoon."

Doc came closer.

In the faded photograph, a Packard touring car was parked in a field of wildflowers. A young couple sat on the hood. A man wearing a stiff collar was eating a sandwich, and a woman in a flapper dress kicked one blurry leg out as she smiled at the camera.

"I don't know him," she said, "but I remember her. I think she was my best friend." She looked up at Doc. "Doesn't she have kind eyes?"

"Yes," Doc said. "She has very kind eyes."

"I wish someone could tell me what ever happened to her."

Doc didn't know how to answer, what to say. Just like he didn't know how to talk to Jimmy about the dad he never had, why his mom was always gone, or about the sister whose ribbons hung on the wall. This house, like Scarlett's, and Bonnie's, was a much tougher house to grow up in than his was. Unlike these places, his house, most of the time, actually felt like a home.

Jimmy tucked Grandma in and pulled up the covers. He ran a brush through her hair, all the while saying something soft to her. He laid the brush on the nightstand, walked to the door with Doc, and turned off the light.

Doc kept walking till he reached the front door. "I think I'll head over to Grill's," he said.

"Not hungry? There's TV dinners in the fridge."

"I'm fine."

"Be sure to ask Grill how he and Slatz made out with Scarlett. You never know," Jimmy said. "One way or the other, there's probably a song in it."

BUSBY BERKELEY STYLE

"Herb's still flossing. But do come in."

"Yes, ma'am," Doc said, thinking how, in the porch light, Grill's mother looked a lot like Janet Leigh in *Psycho*, but in color. She held a martini glass in her hand. Her breath smelled like butane. This was another tough house to grow up in.

He took a step forward. She stiffened in the doorway, blocked his way.

"You understand Dr. Melch isn't here?" She pressed down her skirt. "Perhaps my son mentioned that? He's out tonight with the Elks. As you probably know, they're a benevolent protective order. You're not tracking anything in, are you?"

"No," Doc said. "But let's be sure. He raked his soles on the door-mat and imagined her in the morning, downing a glass of tomato juice, then wobbling outside to inspect the flower beds beneath her bedroom window for the telltale imprints left by species of other protective orders: Moose. Lions. It was rumored Mrs. Melch was an animal lover.

He closed the front door softly behind him and they stood facing each other in the foyer. He couldn't tell if she was looking at him or off in dreamland listening to the music coming from the living room.

Guy Lombardo's orchestra played "Auld Lang Syne" on the stereo and in the air, the butane smell mixed with something else. Cinnamon? Sugar?

"Here. Hold this. I'm hot," she said, handing him her glass. She raised both arms, pulled the sweater she was wearing over her head, used her fingers to reset the tortoise shell clips that held back her hair. Doc hoped what he was looking at was the top of a red two-piece bathing suit. Then again, maybe other mothers were different than his. Maybe every home was as different as the people who lived there. Maybe his mind was making a big deal out of nothing at all.

"You can smell my sticky buns, can't you?" she said, smiling at him.

"Yes, ma'am."

"I know Herb smells them, too. But he can't have any. Neither can you, unless you stay over."

"I don't think I can, ma'am. It's a school night."

"Dr. Melch will be having them for breakfast, but if you stay, you're welcome to dig in. But nothing for Herb." She wagged her finger at Doc. "Nothing hard, nothing crunchy, nothing sticky until he gets his braces off. He's in the final phase."

"Yes, he's told me about the final phase."

"You're a good listener, aren't you, Dewey? And very polite." She took back the glass. "Did I tell you Herb was flossing?"

"Yes, you did."

She took Doc's hand and led him into the living room, motioned with her drink hand for him to sit down.

Doc sat on a blue crushed velvet couch facing the fireplace. Above the hearth there was a portrait painting, an overhead shot of six girls in formals clustered together, Busby Berkeley style.

Mrs. Melch collapsed into a red Queen Anne chair, the lacy fabric identical in color and texture to her "bathing suit" top. She crossed one leg over the other. The firelight flickered over the surface of the glass she held in her hand. "Notice anything interesting?" she said.

Doc looked at her bra, her top, whatever it was, then at the fabric in the chair. "When I look at you," he said, "it's like your bosom disappears."

"No," she corrected. "What you don't see is pink. Not a single touch of pink in sight. Now look behind you."

Doc turned around. On the opposite wall was a reproduction of the famous Gainsborough painting. The original portrait had been pointed out to him a hundred times at the Huntington Library.

"It's *Blue Boy*," he said.

"They told Gainsborough he couldn't paint a portrait without using pink. So he painted *Blue Boy*. Later, he painted *Pinkie* just to rub their noses in it. Has anyone ever tried to rub your nose in it?"

"I don't believe so," Doc said, adding, "I think *Pinkie* was painted by Joshua Reynolds."

She wasn't listening.

"Rudolpho, my decorator, told me the neighbors said I couldn't design a room without using shades of red. And do you know why?"

"No."

"Because they're jealous. They're jealous because I was Queen of the Rose Parade my senior year at Pasadena High School. Well, we showed *them*." She tipped her head back, emptied the glass.

Doc looked up at the painting over the fireplace. "But all the girls in the portrait are wearing red."

A voice coming from the hallway said, "My mom put the portrait back up after she fired Rudolpho. He turned out to be a cad."

Doc watched Grill cross the room. His hair was wet and he wore a smoking jacket that was eerily similar to the one Scarlett's father had worn the night before. He took the glass from his mother. From a silver shaker that seemed to appear from nowhere, he poured her a fresh martini.

Glancing at Doc, Grill said, "Come to my room while I dress." He turned to his mother. "Mom. Mom!" He spoke to her in a voice a deaf person could hear. "Doc and I are going to choir practice."

METAPHOR FOR A
BAD MEMORY

Grill's room was at the end of the hall.

"I need you to see my lair," he said, opening the door, flipping on the light. "It'll help you understand why the band's so important to me. By the way, Scarlett told Slatz and me to drop dead."

"Sorry," Doc said. "It's probably for the best."

"I'm not giving up. I'm gonna keep trying. There's chemistry there. I can feel it."

Doc nodded, looked around. What he saw in Grill's room was heartbreaking. Everywhere he looked were reminders of Grill's failed attempts with girls, mementos that spoke to the pitiful extremes to which Grill had gone to be desirable to the opposite sex: black figure skates, with the laces tied, hung over the bedroom's inside doorknob; bright plumed costumes draped a standing coat rack; a megaphone perched on a haystack of pompoms.

"Why do you keep this stuff?"

"For my biographers. But it's even worse than it looks." He pointed to a framed photo above an empty trophy case. It was a picture of Grill, his face made up to look Asian. He was wearing purple pantaloons and a sleeveless gold vest.

"Here I am in *The King and I* as Lun Tha," Grill explained. "Tuptim is supposed to fall in love with me. But the girl playing the part begged the director to have the king sentence her to death at the end of the first act so she could avoid doing a love scene with me." Grill sighed. "Instead, they executed me Act One, Scene Three. I sang 'We Meet in a Shadow' and 'I Have Dreamed' offstage. The director explained the audience would experience me as metaphor for a bad memory."

"But this is pretty cool," Doc said. He picked up a framed, autographed glamour shot of Marilyn Monroe.

"I forged the signature. Not likely my path will ever cross hers."

"What about this one?" Doc picked up the other framed photo on Grill's desk. In it, Grill sported a white shirt, pink tie, and white pants. "You sold ice cream?"

"No," Grill said. "I talked Saint Jude's Hospital into letting me be the first male candy striper. I'd hoped to be bedside when some girl came out of a coma. You see, there's this psychological phenomenon where a girl, when she returns to consciousness, associates her recovery with whomever's with her when she wakes up. Sometimes that psychological distortion of feelings blossoms into love."

"It didn't work?"

Grill squinted into the glare of the ceiling light. "I'd rather not talk about it."

Draped over the back of his desk were three small pelts stitched together. Grill held up the gamey patchwork. "As you know, I've recently tried chinchilla ranching. The idea was, give a girl a fur coat and maybe she'd feel like she owed you something." He tossed the pelt aside. "I can't even buy love." He looked up at Doc. "That's why the band's got to work. You've got to be there 'cause you understand what it's like to be me, 'cause we're in this together. I'm out of options, Doc. I think the band gives me a real chance with, if not Scarlett, some girl." He stared at Doc, shifted gears. "We're going to Bonnie's tonight to seal the deal on this babysitting. Come hell or high water, you're playing with the Gigolos." He held up a set of car keys. "Let's go."

"I think your mother's too drunk to drive."

Grill slipped on his pants. "My mother's not driving."

AN ORIGINAL GALAXY GLIDER

Doc stared out at the darkness through the windshield of Mrs. Melch's pink Lincoln Continental.

Neighborhoods streaked by, streetlights, stop signs, telephone poles blurred. Doc tried to picture someone else behind the wheel, someone more like James Dean or a young Marlon Brando. Someone savage, wild, competent.

He couldn't.

He tried to see himself as resolute, bold, a guy with nothing to lose. But that wasn't true either. As excited as he was to see Bonnie, he couldn't shake the feeling he was doing something that was stupid, wrong. He was about to put in place a plan that would leave his little sister in mortal jeopardy. He was going to leave Snowball with a girl whose life was tangled up with Junior Mentz.

Grill, a gloved left hand on the steering wheel, grinned metal at him. "Relax, Doc, we're closing in."

"You're sure you know where you're going?"

Like I told you, Bonnie lives in this shotgun shack down on Locust Avenue. I know the house. I was in the backseat one night when one of the choir moms dropped her off."

"You're in Saint Mary's choir?"

"Was." Grill raised his voice. "There was this little incident with the holy sacrament. Those little wafers?" He glanced over at Doc. "So a Jew got a little hungry. It wasn't like I ate that many of them."

"You're Jewish?"

"Adds an air of Old Testament mystery to me, don't you think?" He flicked his high beams at an oncoming car.

Doc shook his head. "I don't think you're supposed to do that unless the car has its high beams on."

"I'm having fun, Doc. That's why they call it joyriding."

The approaching car narrowed the distance.

Now its high beams *were* on. So was the cop-car spotlight on the driver's side.

The cabin of the Lincoln became a shock of white light. The squad car froze for a moment in time and space as it drew parallel to them, accelerated, hit the brakes, whipped a U-turn, and came after them.

If Doc wasn't mistaken, he'd seen Deputy Lyman Sleeve behind the wheel.

An explosion of flashing red light came in through the back window of the Continental.

In that moment, Doc saw his imminent future, saw himself being ripped from the front seat, slammed down on the hood of the cop car, his wrists handcuffed behind his back, Sleeve standing over him, baton in hand barking out the question, *"What's black and white and red all over?"*

"WHAT'S BLACK AND WHITE AND RED ALL OVER, PUNK?"

"The hood of your squad car with my blood on it?"

"You got that right."

The squad car sped up, rode the Continental's bumper then, siren howling, blew past them, its wail fading in the distance.

Grill seemed completely oblivious to what had just happened. He fiddled with the dial on the radio, finally settling on, ironically, Connie Francis singing "Stupid Cupid." Grill sang the title line, stopped. "I just can't make the 'esh' sounds, Doc. Don't know if you've ever noticed but my braces tangle my tongue."

"It's not that noticeable," Doc said.

"Yeah, but a lisp's just one more strike against me. Funny thing is it's only when my dad cranks up the tie on this incisor wire that I lisp." Grill pointed to a hunk of metal behind his upper teeth.

"Your dad's your orthodontist?"

"He wants me to be perfect, Doc. It's just, in the meantime, life hasn't been much fun."

"The meantime? Grill, 'in the meantime' has been more than half your life."

"Yeah. Sometimes I wonder if he's got it out for me. Think it could be a 'mirror, mirror on the wall' thing? Like he doesn't want me more handsome than he is?"

Doc looked into Grill's sad face. If any dog needed someone to toss them a bone, it was this guy. "I think that's exactly what he wants. He's afraid one of these days you'll rise up and be the stud of the family."

"Yeah. One of these days. Maybe next year."

The Lincoln thumped across railroad tracks, wound through a maze of dead end streets, then stopped beneath a streetlight in front of a house on Locust Avenue.

Grill switched off the ignition. "We're here."

Doc looked at the house through the open passenger window; the place was pretty shabby. Paint peeled from the trim around the windows, the lawn was patchy, overgrown where it wasn't dead.

Grill honked, honked again.

The front door opened. Bonnie stepped out. Shielding her eyes from the glare of the porch light, she peered in Doc's direction.

"Stay here, Grill," Doc said. "Let me talk to her."

Climbing out of the car, he yelled, "It's me, Bonnie. Doc."

Hands on her hips now, she yelled back, "Yeah. So what do you want?"

"A moment of your time?"

He didn't wait for her answer. He crossed the lawn, stumbled twice, once in a gopher hole, then on a toy truck half-buried in the grass.

From the porch, she said, "Let's go around to the back. I just got my little brother to sleep."

They walked around the side of the house, Bonnie leading the way down the narrow passage between her garage and a block wall that ran along the property line.

In the pitch-black night, Doc couldn't see a thing though he could hear Bonnie's footsteps ahead of him, could feel the lingering heat of her in the air: the savory slick, mouth-warmed aroma of her Black Jack Gum and the powdery pulse of the perfume she wore: Tabu.

They came around the corner. The light from a television in the living room beamed through a picture window and a sliding glass door. Its luminescence cast a blue-green haze over the patio.

Leading the way, Bonnie stepped over a child's wading pool that lay dilapidated, tangled in a heap on the cracked concrete, the air all fizzled out of it. She sat in a porch swing and motioned Doc to join her.

The canopy top over the swing was tattered, mostly torn away, and when Doc sat down beside her, he found himself looking up through flaps of torn canvas and taking in big pieces of the starry sky. He stroked the rusted metal frame. "I can't believe this," he said. "This has got to be an original Galaxy Glider. My grandmother had one of these."

Doc gave the glider a push with his feet. "You get one of these going just right and it's practically perpetual motion." He pushed again. "See? It feels like we're sitting on a Ferris wheel."

"Yeah. The thrill's almost more than I can bear."

"Guess that sounded kinda dopey. Sorry. I just came by to tell you I really appreciate you helping me."

"You mean by babysitting? It's no big deal. I love kids. I'm here. I need the money. Simple as that."

"Then we're all set? I'll drop off Snowball—I mean Amanda— tomorrow about three and pick her up at ten, if that's okay."

"Three o'clock's fine."

Bonnie leaned back, lay her head on Doc's shoulder. "Maybe to- morrow night before you pick up your sister, we could go for a swim. She nodded in the direction of the crumpled wading pool.

He smiled. "You're funny."

"Not really." She kissed him on the cheek.

Doc touched where her lips had been. He felt clammy, nervous, in over his head. "I don't know what to say."

"About a peck on the cheek?"

"About anything. Every time I talk to a girl, it turns into a disaster. The last girl I talked to thought I didn't care about her dead mother. I made her cry. The one before that passed out. I got blood all over her pajamas. Her dad said he had some chemical compound that would get it out."

"You're making that up."

"Wish I was. Funny thing is, that's the one thing I'm kinda good at. I can make stuff up."

"So you're a good liar?"

"I make up stories," he said, his voice sounding like an apology. "I do it all the time. Can't help myself."

"Well, the TV's on the fritz and I'm bored half out of my mind. If talking to me's a problem, why not tell me a story?" She settled back in the glider. "I need you to make up something about me in another life, maybe another world, a world where a nice guy like you falls in love with me. Just do your best to make me believe the story could be true."

"I'll *start* the story with something true, then improvise. How 'bout that?"

"Just put a little sugar on top. That's all I ask."

Doc thought for a moment, recalled the night they'd met, how she'd stunned him with "a kiss out of nowhere," had told him about the first guy who'd kissed her, the one who'd held her down. No way he could begin a love story where the hero had to overcome that dark truth.

He gave the swing a push with his feet. "You're older than me, right?"

"Definitely."

"Would you like this nice guy in the story to be at least as old as you? Someone ruggedly handsome?"

"But not so rugged he wouldn't wear glasses." She looked at him, touched the frame of his glasses. "I can't decide if these remind me of Buddy Holly, Superman or...what's his name...the writer who was married to Marilyn Monroe."

"Arthur Miller."

She nodded, closed her eyes. "Have you thought of a true beginning?"

"Remember when you came up the hill and you saw me in the tree?"

"In the cemetery? Yesterday?"

"Not 'yesterday,' Bonnie," he said in his best storyteller's voice. "It was years ago and thousands of miles away. You were in France, during the war. Think back."

"Oh, that's right, you're telling me a story."

The glider creaked. Above their heads, the heavens "boomed, crackled." Needles of light cut through the air. One edge of the night sky pulsed red, while along the western horizon, sprays of silver illuminated the undersurface of clouds.

Bonnie looked up. "They're shooting off fireworks at Disneyland. It's Mickey's birthday."

Doc shook his head. "It's artillery fire, Bonnie. Remember the war's still going on."

"Artillery fire," she repeated the words slowly, her eyelids closing again. "I remember now. And there was lightning, too. It's raining..."

"You're climbing over a low stone wall," he said. "You were on your way home. You were crossing a field."

"And I saw you…in a tree, right?"

"Yes, I was injured. Barely conscious. My plane had been shot down. I'd parachuted into occupied France."

"Your parachute was all tangled in the tree."

"My leg was broken. You cut me down."

"I hid you…in the barn."

"The barn behind your blind grandfather's farm house."

"How could I forget Papa? He was so kind."

"That was good," Doc said. "Nice detail."

"I just imagined him as Heidi's grandfather."

"You brought me water in a tin cup. Roasted chicken. A buttered chunk of brown bread. You wrapped my wounds. I asked, 'Who are you?'"

"So." She opened her eyes, smiled. "So, who am I?"

"You're this little ooh-la-la French girl named Babette. You milk goats."

Bonnie frowned. "Goats?"

Doc quickly added, "But at night you dance in the Follies."

"A can-can girl?"

"That's exactly who you are. In fact, you're the star of the show. You sing like a nightingale. They call you Beauty."

"That's good. Keep going."

"Now the tension builds. Turns out this Nazi commandant, this big bad wolf, has his monocled eye on you. He's at the follies every night. He's suspicious, thinks you may be a gypsy or a Jew, perhaps tied in with the Resistance. He keeps sniffing around. You tease him, flirt, buy time to nurse me back to health. Before I'm well enough to travel, he brings jackboots, storm troopers to the farm. They kick in the door. The commandant sees something in your eyes. You couldn't help it. You just took that one glance out the window at the barn. This guy doesn't miss a thing. His eye glistens behind his monocle. He knows. And you know he knows. He goosesteps out. Busts through the barn door."

She sighed. "Sorry about that pitchfork he kept stabbing into the hay."

"It was only a massive puncture wound in my broken leg."

"But you never let out a peep did you? You were afraid they'd kill me if you did."

"If I'd have 'peeped,' the story would be a tragedy, not a romance. No sugar on top."

Bonnie laughed. "A tragedy for you, soldier boy."

"For both of us. That Nazi would have killed you, too, remember?"

"I'm a Follies girl. We can always buy ourselves one more day." She set the glider into motion with her feet.

Doc's mind remained still, frozen on something he'd seen, something she'd said. He saw the image of Junior dragging her to the priest's car. He stood, turned and faced her. "You mean, you'd let some Nazi kiss you while he held you down?"

"I was kidding."

"How do you know Junior Mentz?" Doc asked.

The fireworks stopped.

Her features hardened. "This was fun for a while but now it's not."

"Maybe you could tell me why you were at the cemetery."

She climbed out of the glider, walked past him into the darkness. "Why do you want to know?"

"Just making conversation."

"So the story's over and now we're back here in my crappy backyard having one of those *conversations* you're not very good at?" She turned and glared at him. "The balloons were for Buddy, okay? Buddy was Father Stephen's kid brother. He's dead. Committed suicide. Don't get the idea it was some Romeo and Juliet thing. There was never any Juliet. And Junior…well, Junior's got problems."

"Yeah, I know. He tried to bury me alive."

"Don't take it personally."

She walked back to the glider. He sat down next to her. She squeezed his hand, said softly, "Sometimes in life things just happen:

You get buried. I go along for a ride. Things blow over. Eventually, Junior will get bored. He'll find someone else to scare. When he does, we'll both be okay." She gave him a weary smile. "Wha'da ya say we go back to France again. Take me away for just a little longer before you go home."

Doc pushed the swing. Bonnie closed her eyes.

He started slowly, described the barn where he waited for her, the way the moon looked through the broken wooden slats of the window, how it climbed above the rock wall that ran along the path she took home each night.

He talked about the food she brought him, the covered basket, the checkered cloth she spread across the bale of hay, how she'd giggled at the way he ate. "So hungry, my dear. Eeeze good your appetite comes back."

Bonnie leaned over and lightly kissed the corners of Doc's mouth. "I love the way you do my French accent," she said. "I love a mouth that speaks so many beautiful words."

"Wanna hear more?" he said, eagerly. "Got a million of them. I'm practically a walking dictionary."

"I've got a word for you: shhh." She pulled him close and kissed him again, a steamy, breathy kiss that fogged his glasses.

All sappy smiles, he swooned back against the cushioned seat of the glider.

"You better go. Duty calls," she said, pointing at the sliding glass door that led back into the house.

Bathed in the cathode blue rays emanating from the television screen, a toddler in the cowboy pajamas wandered through the living room. Rubbing his eyes, the kid wobbled over to the door, reached up on tiptoes, tried to open it by tugging the handle. He'd almost forgotten she was a babysitter, too.

He touched her thigh. "Just one more kiss?"

"She said *it's time for you to go*."

The man's voice pierced the blackness, struck like a fist.

Doc's hand jumped from Bonnie's leg.

The glider rocked like an earthquake had shaken its base.

From the edge of the patio, a dark figure separated itself from the shadows, came toward them.

Bonnie sprang to her feet, stood at attention.

"Father Stephen. Hi."

"Good evening, Bonnie," the priest said. He looked at Doc. "I was driving by. Saw a car in front of the house. Remembered your mother wasn't home."

Doc stood, tucked in his shirt. "I came over to help Bonnie babysit. I have my own baby sister."

The priest looked from Doc to the kid inside the house.

The little boy slapped his hand on the glass, sank to the floor, started to wail.

The priest brought his eyes back to Doc. "Help or distract? It seems the child feels more neglected than cared for."

"I'll have my friend drive me home," Doc said.

"I'm afraid your friend is gone. Did you know he was joyriding? The boy doesn't have a license."

"News to me," Doc said.

"News to you? Really? We'll talk that over while I take you home."

"I don't have to go with you," Doc said. "I'm not Catholic."

"Let him give you a ride," Bonnie said. She gave Doc a nod that conveyed it might be better for him, or safer for her, if he left with the priest.

"I'll come back later, Bonnie," Father Stephen said. "Just to make sure you're all right."

Doc came back with, "And when this priest leaves, *you* call me."

Bonnie looked at both of them. "I'm locking the door and going to bed."

While Doc stood there confused, feeling powerless, a brawl broke out in his mind: a blistering cacophony of brain-battering noise that nearly shook Doc's gray matter from its foundation. He recognized the competing voices of the crow, Kipling, and his alter ego, Cinch. They were shouting out to him, sniping, arguing among themselves as to what Doc should say next, which strategy would turn the tide in his favor, why now was or wasn't the time to draw a line in the sand. One thing they all agreed on: Whether she knew it or not, Bonnie needed him. Doc's blood swirled, his nerve endings sparked, his mind cleared.

He'd devise his own plan to keep the priest, who didn't look old enough to be a priest, away from Bonnie. He'd do what he did best. He'd duel the priest with words. Words had won him kisses from a girl worth fighting for, now words would be his saber. He'd insinuate, try that first. Even the word itself had thrust, a certain fleshy feel.

Doc drew back his shoulders. "Now that I think about it," he said, "I'd love a ride."

"Good choice," the priest said. "Wait here." He followed Bonnie into the house, drew the sliding glass door closed behind them. Doc watched Father Stephen pick up the baby, snuggle him, carry him down a dark hallway. Bonnie followed. She didn't look back.

Doc collapsed into the glider, gave it a push with his feet. Above his head, the torn canvas flapped and fluttered like the sails of a derelict.

Patton, the crow, landed on a strut of rusted frame just above his right shoulder, squawked "Nevermore." Kipling appeared in his wrinkled white linen suit, sat to his left, uttered several passages from his advice-laden, best-known poem: "If."

Doc groaned, got up, and walked around the side of the garage to the front of the house.

A ROCK AND A HARD PLACE

Standing in the middle of the driveway, thinking through his plan, Doc watched Father Stephen come out the front door. His blue Buick was parked a few feet from Doc. Grill's mom's Lincoln was gone.

"I hope young Mr. Melch made it home without getting arrested," the priest said, coming down the front steps. "Kid's got a bright future. Hate to see him have a criminal record."

"I have criminal charges pending against me," Doc said, moving to the passenger door of the Buick. He took a deep breath. "Thanks a lot for telling the police I was a 'Peeping Tom,' that I was spying on choir girls in some changing room."

Father Stephen went around to the driver's side, stopped, and lit a cigarette. "That was you? I must have given the police a pretty good description."

"And a name."

"How could I have known your name? We've just met."

"Just met? Bonnie never introduced us. See, I think you remember my name from a few years ago. Christmas Eve? I witnessed a murder the same night your brother committed suicide. If that doesn't ring a bell, maybe Scarlett mentioned my name."

The priest seemed to look past Doc, study something amorphous in the distance. He took a long, slow drag on the cigarette. Waited.

Doc dug deep. His knees trembled. He took another shot at the man in the collar.

"I wouldn't come back here 'later' if I were you. Wouldn't look right: a young teenage girl all alone with a guy your age. You never know who might be watching."

The priest flicked his cigarette away. "Anything else?"

"Yeah. I've changed my mind. Think I'll hitchhike. Maybe I'll run into someone driving a fifty-three Studebaker."

Father Stephen opened the driver's side door. "I'll pray for you," he said.

"What...? What's that supposed to mean?"

The priest slid into the front seat of the Buick, started the engine, and backed out of the driveway.

ENTROPY

Leaving Bonnie's, Doc wondered where he'd gotten the courage to talk back to a priest. Not even adults did stuff like that. Was it him, or was it the world that was changing?

He worked his way across the adjacent front yard, navigated among shadowy hedges, kept his eyes on the Buick's taillights as they disappeared into a tumble of fog that rolled toward him from the far end of Locust Street.

A wave of exhaustion swept over him. Acting fierce, standing toe to toe with the priest had taken its toll on him. His left leg dragged, his body shivered as he walked. Still, there had been exhilaration in the experience, a sense he'd achieved his goal. He'd shaken the priest, peppered him with innuendos. But there was a problem. Something didn't make sense.

The priest hadn't asked any questions, hadn't asked why, if Doc had seen the encounter with the naked Scarlett, he hadn't blabbed about it to the police. He hadn't asked how Doc had come to know about the priest's brother's suicide or the Studebaker.

Doc kept walking, kept thinking. His mind had no answers.

An eerie silence swirled around him. Porch lights ahead of him clicked off as he approached. No family dogs barked opposition to his trespass. The fog pressed closer. The dry-ice steam of it swirled around his legs.

There was a park entrance to his right. He'd get off this street, cross the park to Harbor Boulevard. He wanted out of this neighborhood. He wanted the company of traffic, noise, flashing lights, signs that screamed advertising.

He wanted to go home.

Slipping through spidery wisps of fog, he rattled the locked gate, gave up and climbed the chain-link fence. He needed to be in new territory.

The park he entered was rimmed in an ache of moonlight. Wind stirred the eucalyptus, swayed the swings, jostled the tetherball that hung from a pole in the center of a playground. Ahead of him, a winding stone path twisted off into the darkness. Above the trees, lights of tall buildings twinkled in the distance.

He picked up his pace. Two hundred yards to civilization. He stuck his hand in his pocket, felt for a dime he could use to call Grill. No change, only a guitar pick.

Behind him he heard panting, the slap of sandaled feet, the slow creak of revolving wooden wheels. A glow of lantern light bathed his shoulder. He glanced back.

Kipling, traveling by rickshaw, pulled alongside him. Doc slowed to a walk.

"Rather well done," Kipling said, leaning forward, bending down to Doc.

"I don't know." Doc said. "When I think about it, he was probably right to chase me away from Bonnie's. Guys and girls our age shouldn't be left alone to climb all over each other. Looks like he loves her little brother. And another thing: I think both Scarlett and Junior have some sort of hold over him. I think the guy's more troubled than guilty. Something tells me he's between a rock and a hard place."

"So turn over that rock," Kipling said. "Put yourself in his hard place and ask yourself what you'd do, what dark secret could keep you silent." Kipling sat back, snapped his fingers, cheered a "tootle-oo." The dark-skinned, turbaned man secured the bamboo poles to his leather harness and rambled off.

Doc walked toward the city lights, a gear work of wheels turning in his head. Fog misted the back of his neck, trickled ice water down his spine. He wondered what the priest's "rock" might be. The answer came back. What could be more like a rock than the unmoving dead? He thought of the priest's brother, Buddy.

Maybe Buddy was tied to the murder. He was Junior's friend. He was the connection between Junior, Bonnie, and the priest. Maybe Buddy was the killer or at least somehow involved in Cindy's death. Whether he'd driven the car into her on purpose or the act had been unintended, either way the guilt would have been horrible, maybe more than he was able to live with.

But if Buddy was the killer and Father Stephen knew the truth, why did he keep this secret from the world? Why would Junior be blackmailing him? Buddy's punishment had already been exacted: The sin of suicide would keep Buddy out of Heaven. No court would try a dead man. There had to be more. Another rock? Maybe Junior, maybe others were in the car that Christmas Eve. But if there were others, why would the priest protect them? Was there a second reason Buddy couldn't go on living?

He wished Margaret Ann was by his side with her bag of cogs and wheels. Though he hated to admit it, she could help him figure this puzzle out.

Reaching the end of the path, Doc tugged on another locked gate. He climbed the fence, walked out on to Harbor Boulevard and stuck out his thumb.

The first car that approached captured him in its headlights.

The car pulled over. Doc lowered his head. The car's passenger window buzzed down.

"Hi, Dad."

"Get in," his father said.

Doc climbed in, closed the door. Sat back between a rock and a hard place. What were the odds, he thought, his father, on his way home from work, would be the one to stop and pick him up? The whole thing felt contrived. Then again, maybe fate sometimes enjoys a wicked sense of humor.

Jaw clenched, his father stared nails through the fog-misted windshield, twisted his neck around as though his tie had been drawn too tightly against his throat. With a sigh, he heavy-footed the family car from the roadside back into traffic.

Doc awaited the inevitable interrogation. Prayed green lights would take him home.

His father stewed, let the silence between them gnaw the oxygen from the air. Faint on the radio, Vin Scully's voice called a double play: Gilliam to Neal to Hodges. The crowd cheered.

"Go Dodgers, right, Dad?"

His father clicked off the radio, ran a hand through his bristled butch-cut. "It's almost nine o'clock. What, for God's sake, are you doing out here?"

"I'm on a field trip. I get extra credit."

"You're on a field trip, at night, by yourself?"

"Modern education, Dad. It's different since you were in school."

"Does your mother know you're out? Did she say you could do this?"

"I told her I was studying with Grill...Herb Melch."

"So where is *he*?"

"On *his* field trip."

His father twisted his neck around again.

"I can't do this stuff after tonight, Dad. I'll be babysitting."

The sympathy card seemed to play well. His father's shoulders sank. He sighed, didn't even flash his headlights as a car with its high beams approached.

"I'm trying to get As for you, Dad. The extra credit helps. You were the one who said, learning's a full-time job. I'm just working the swing shift." He smiled.

The car stopped at a red light.

"Hmm. A field trip," his father said. "A project of some sort?"

"For English. An experiment in…experiential experience."

The light turned green.

The car crawled in the slow lane.

"I'm not quite understanding this project."

Doc could feel himself losing traction. Out of the corner of his eye, he saw a vein rise in his father's neck and start thumping. Not a good sign.

"Miss Mooseman gave us all an assignment," Doc said. "A variation of a French approach to cinematography: Cinema Verite. We wander around at night, in a place far from home, using our dominant eye as a roaming camera. We focus in on the raw, real moments of life. It helps develop an artist's eye."

"You haven't been peeping through windows again, have you?"

"I never looked through any windows. Detective Quinn told you that whole thing was a giant misunderstanding."

His father wasn't listening. He was undoubtedly incensed with what passed for modern education. Doc heard him grumble "artist's eye" and "French."

All Doc wanted was to get home. Maybe his father's frustration with the state of education, his son's lack of access to the magnificent world of science would occupy the man's mind till they got there.

"How are you doing in algebra?"

"I already know what x equals."

His father slammed the brakes as they approached the intersection at Harbor and Commonwealth Avenue.

"You could have made it through the light," Doc said. "It was still yellow."

210

"The color is amber. Streetlights are red, green, and *amber*. Artist's eye. What a joke. You don't even know colors." He glared at Doc. "And, for your edification young man, *x* isn't something you know. It's something you solve for. It's the unknown. An engineer gets *x* wrong when he's working on a real world problem and bridges collapse, planes fall from the sky, people die."

"I was joking. It was a joke," Doc said.

"Life isn't a joke."

"I know, that's why I'm spending the rest of my life babysitting."

This time, the sympathy card didn't work.

Tilting his head, his father raised a cupped hand to his ear, slowly stoked his middle finger over his thumb. "Know what I'm listening to?"

Doc saw red. No doubt about that color, and, though his dad hadn't a clue, he's been racking his brain for the last three days, solving for a real-world *x*. Get it wrong and people die? People were already dead.

"The sound of the world's tiniest violin," Doc said, begrudgingly. "Funny. Bet your dad picked a few cherry moments to finger a tune or two for you on that little violin. Then again maybe he didn't have your sense of humor."

"My father...my father thought it was important to keep things in perspective. Sometimes there are things you sacrifice for the big picture. Later when you look back, you realize what you did was a good thing."

"So, I should look forward to looking back?"

His father let the sarcasm slide.

They drove beneath the Pacific Electric Viaduct. The car climbed out of the fog as the road rose in front of them.

When they reached the corner of Harbor and Valencia Mesa, his father drove into the parking lot of the Ranch Town Market and stopped the car. He sighed, but this time the sigh was different. It came out tinged with resignation, a breathy mix of sadness and regret.

"How 'bout you drive us home?" he said.

"Really?"

"We'll be breaking the law together. *That'll* give you something to look back on. Something better than babysitting, even though I don't know why babysitting has to be the end of the world."

They traded seats. Excited, Doc curled his fingers around the wheel. It felt good.

"You know what you're doing?" his father asked.

"I think so." Doc slid the seat forward, adjusted the mirrors. I've been watching you drive for years."

"Just pull in a little on the gear shift. Bring it down to D."

"For drive."

"Be glad there's not an *x* on that steering column. We'd be here all night."

Neither could resist smiling.

"Dad, really. I'm doing fine in math."

His father nodded, leaned back. Exhausted, Doc guessed. He'd worked all day then had to deal with a roadside reminder of his greatest disappointment. As much as Doc was embarrassed at the thought of babysitting, he wondered if his dad wasn't embarrassed, too. Embarrassed his wife had to go to work, that he had to ask his son to babysit.

Doc drove, slowly at first, picked up speed, just a little.

"If we make it home, I'll fix us a late dinner. Pancakes."

"I love pancakes," Doc said.

"My dad called them flapjacks," his father said, wistfully.

"He fixed you flapjacks for dinner?"

"No, not that I can remember."

When Doc pulled into the driveway, his father sat up, said, "Do you know the word *entropy*?"

"I think it has to do with energy or momentum, something like that. Right, Dad?"

"It's the tendency of all things in the universe to move apart. It's why things rust, why perfume evaporates from a bottle. See, it's not just poets and philosophers that know 'now' is only 'now' once."

"Is that why you're fixing me pancakes?"

"In a way, yes. Could be I just think the condemned man deserves a hearty meal." He slapped Doc's leg, climbed out of the car. "I'll get the griddle going."

Doc sat behind the wheel. All he'd wanted to do was get home without his parents knowing. Now he was going to eat flapjacks with his father in the wake of some weird father-son, man-to-man moment they'd shared, in which, if Doc guessed right, his dad was sort of saying, seize the day, or I'm sorry. Something like that.

He stared out through the windshield at the stars. He thought about Pinkie, the ghost, saw her as molecules of perfume that had evaporated from a bottle. He saw Scarlett's lost virtue, not as rust, but as a stained white radiance.

"Entropy." It was a sad song of a word.

THE DARK SIDE OF THE MOON

The phone was ringing.

There was a clatter in the kitchen, the whir of mixer blades ticking along the inside rim of a glass bowl, the sizzle of butter skidding across a cast iron griddle.

The phone rang again.

Doc closed the front door behind him, slipped off his shoes and socks, breathed in maple syrup heating in a pan.

"I've only got two hands," his father announced. "Would someone get that, please?"

That someone meant Doc.

He hurried across the living room, pushed through the swinging door, reached for the wall-mounted phone just inside the kitchen. The bell stopped midring.

His father's smile faded as he looked down at Doc's feet. "Where are your shoes?"

"Living room."

His father wore carpet slippers.

Behind Doc, the door swung open. His mother, wearing a freshly pressed white nurse's uniform, the sales tag visible beneath the short sleeve, came in. In her arms, a bleary-eyed, disgruntled Snowball.

"Real nice, Mom," Doc said. "You look like Elizabeth Taylor in *Suddenly, Last Summer.*"

Snowball squinted at the uniform, glared at Doc, started to cry bad-actress tears. Snowball blamed him for everything.

Doc patted her head. "Don't worry. While Mom's at work, I'll take good care of you."

"Your friend Grill's on the phone," she said. "He's called several times."

Doc looked over at his dad. "The field trip. Grill and I need to compare notes."

"Five minutes," his father said, stirring the pan. "Get your slippers on, and tell your friend he woke your sister."

"I'll get it in my room."

Doc's phone was on the nightstand next to Kipling's photograph. He sprawled across the bed, lifted the receiver.

"Grill. What the heck happened? Where'd you go?"

"Had to get out of there," his voice a tinny slur through his braces. "How'd you get home?"

"Hitchhiked."

"Cool."

"Not cool. My dad picked me up. Thanks for sticking around."

"We came back. I picked up Slatz and came back to look for you. Bunny and Big Lou were out. Tango lessons or something. We drove by Bonnie's, then your place. That's why I'm calling."

"Yeah. Told my father you and I were on a field trip. Anyone asks, you back me up."

There was silence on the other end of the line. Congested breathing.

"Grill, are you still there?"

"We tried to find you."

"So?"

"A little favor in return?"

"Gotta go, Grill. Dinner's on the table."

"Could you get my underwear out of Scarlett's mailbox? Slatz's, too?"

"What?"

"Scarlett dared us. See, we sorta ran into her. We got to talking. She dared us."

"Dared you to do what?"

"Put our underwear in her mailbox. Apparently it's one of the Twelve Trials of Hercules. Guess it's the modern version of the myth or the story. Guess it's a classic. Slatz said he'd heard of it. What could we do, Doc? She dared us to do it, as proof of our love."

"You took off your underwear?"

"She said it would be symbolic. You shed all pretense. Slatz and I shed ours in the car. Not, you know, in front of her. Her dad's coming home at nine-thirty. She said she'd get our 'skants' out of the box before he got there, but could you make sure?"

Doc looked at the clock above his desk. 9:25. "You're both idiots."

"But you'll do it?"

Doc slammed the phone into its cradle, ran down the hall, through the living room, past the kitchen. He caught a glimpse of his father in midbite.

"Be right back," he said. "Left something in the car."

The front door made too much noise behind him.

His bare feet slapped on the concrete walkway, the asphalt street.

A dozen yards ahead of him, Scarlett's mailbox shone silver in the headlights of an oncoming car.

Doc flipped down the lid of the metal box, fumbled his hand inside. He touched envelopes, a magazine. In its deepest recesses he felt tangles of wadded cotton, something disturbingly silky.

He pawed everything out, two pair of boy's underwear, one pair of panties. He crammed everything fabric down the front of his pants, shook his head knowing Scarlett had come out of the house after Slatz and Grill had left to stir a little bit of herself into the mix. She was sending him a message, and the message was, she was in control.

The car stopped beside him. He felt its heat, tasted its exhaust. Doc turned around.

Scarlett's dad, Dr. Brisco activated the electric passenger-side window. It hummed down. The psychologist stared Mister Toad eyes at him.

"Your mail, sir," Doc said. "Service project. Cinema Verite."

"Cinema Verite to you, young man. Pass the mail through. Drop it on the front seat."

Leaning in through the window, Doc complied.

Brisco looked from the mail to Doc's eyes then at Doc's pants.

Doc looked down.

A curl of red elastic bloomed above his beltline.

"It's okay, sir, I live across the street."

Home, Doc closed the front door softly, slipped past the lit kitchen, ducked into his bedroom, quickly buried Grill's and Slatz's underwear in the drawer where he kept his ratty gym socks. He took his time extracting Scarlett's lacey red panties from beneath his belt, feathering them slowly from the darkness to the light, taking care not to whisper a word in the presence of her emerging "unmentionables."

Cradled in his hand, her "undies" felt like a spider web of fire and ice, as unstable as a vial of nitroglycerine, as unknowable as the dark side of the moon. He slid back his closet door, jammed the panties deep into the inside pocket of the suit coat he wore to church, turned, and walked to the kitchen.

The father-son moment had come and gone. The room was empty, no one there, just a plate on the table stacked with cold pancakes, a note next to it. In his mother's hand was written, "We love you. Please do the dishes." Below, in his father's definitive scrawl, "*Do* means wash, dry, and put away. *Dishes* does not mean just dishes." Every word was underlined...in crayon...by Snowball.

WHERE BON-BONS PLAY

The next morning, Doc, bleary-eyed, swung his legs off the bed, slowly dressed for school. It wasn't easy. His mind was a cotton ball, gummy with the remnants of half-remembered nightmares. Adding to this was the big mistake he'd made. Before going to bed, he'd called Margaret Ann. He was confused; he needed her. He wanted her to help him understand the implications of his conversation with the priest, what had happened at the mailbox. He'd started by talking about the "Twelve Trials of Hercules." The conversation was a disaster. She'd listened at first, uh-huh, uh-huhed him a dozen or so times, then unleashed a blistering tirade. The girl who, the day before, had been his partner had ended up calling him a sex fiend, a louse, truly disturbed. "If you like Scarlett so much," she'd said, "why don't you just 'make it' with her?"

Girls, he decided, didn't listen very well after you mentioned another girl's underwear, which, apparently, you're not supposed to call "panties." Girls, he was told in no uncertain terms, hate that word.

Hair combed, teeth brushed, now in the kitchen, Doc promised his mother he'd be home right after school, and yes he knew where the diapers were, yes he knew not to make the bath water too hot, yes he knew Snowball would fall asleep if he sang "The Good Ship Lollipop."

Behind his mother's eyes was an ocean of heartbreak. She wanted to be home with her baby. His mom didn't want to go to work.

"It'll be okay," Doc said. He gave her arm a squeeze, grabbed his books, exited the kitchen humming, then singing, "Where bon-bons play on the sunny beach at Peppermint Bay."

He could feel her smile warm the back of him.

WE'RE NOT SUPPOSED TO KNOW

At the corner, he met Jimmy.

"I don't know if I can do this," Doc said.

"What?"

"Leave Snowball with a girl I barely know, a girl that Junior Mentz keeps his eye on."

"Up to you."

"I know."

"And speaking of Mentz," Jimmy said. "Talked to Slatz last night. Filled him in. Not on everything. Just told him we had a lead, maybe the location of the car that ran down Cindy. He's gonna have his mom take us by the salvage yard. Only thing is, we can't go straight to the yard. We got to go to the Pike first. Some sort of favor for Slatz's dad. Clear change out of some Swami machines, drop off a briefcase crammed with cash. You still in?"

He wanted to say, Margaret Ann's gonna be livid, but then again she was already livid. He nodded at Jimmy. "Yeah. I'm cool. Whatever it takes." Doc looked back at his house. "Snowball's gonna be fine, right? Bonnie's got this little brother. She's takin' care of him. One more kid. That's no big deal."

"Girls are great at that stuff. They've got the instinct."

"Yeah. What do guys like us know?"

"We're not supposed to know," Jimmy said.

"Yeah, we're not supposed to know. We don't need to know."

Doc's eyes met Jimmy's. "We've got important stuff to do, guy stuff. We're gonna hound-dog that Studebaker. Catch ourselves a killer."

They walked side by side down Valencia Mesa toward the high school. Horns honked, girls whistled, hooted Jimmy's name. Jimmy stared straight ahead, jaw set, his carriage that of a soldier with vengeance on his mind. For the rest of the day, Doc knew his friend wouldn't be thinking about grades or girls, wouldn't be conjuring up new tunes for the band. Jimmy would be thinking about the night his sister was killed, about putting hands on, if not the killer, at least the car that struck her.

Doc put on his own dead-serious face and marched beside Jimmy. Overhead, the sky turned red, a thousand crows cawed in the eucalyptus, a howl of wind spiraled leaves into the air. Today they'd bust into Mentz's garage, take names, refuse to take no for an answer. Today there'd be a break in the case.

At the edge of the campus, they met up with Grill and Slatz. Grill looked anxious. Slatz, leaning against the flagpole, savored the comings and goings of every girl that passed by.

"Well? Did you do it? Did you get our stuff?" Grill asked.

"It's handled," Doc said. "The contents of the mailbox are in my sock drawer."

Grill looked relieved and at the same time disappointed. "I hope it still counts as us passing one of the Twelve Trials."

A PAINT-BY-NUMBERS PORTRAIT OF THE POPE

In History, Math, and English, Doc watched the clock like a death row inmate. He didn't know if he wanted time to speed up or slow down. At lunch, to punish himself, he ate the cafeteria special: Tuna Surprise. When the last bell rang, he walked home alone, his mind a mess. What was he going to do at Mentz's? Buttonhole a bunch of grown men? Demand to know what happened to a car towed there years and years ago? He was on his way home, not to stay, not to live up to his responsibilities, but to set in motion a plan to ditch his sister, then lie to Bonnie. It wasn't a big lie, but it was another strand in the web of misrepresentations.

Sometimes a detective had no choice but to lead a double life.

When he came through the front door, his mother gave him a hug. She was in front of the hallway mirror, hurriedly applying a fresh coat of lipstick. She put a dab of red on Snowball's lips, handed her to Doc. "Dinner's in the fridge."

"I know, Mom. Snowball likes the smooshed chicken and the peas, but not the beets."

She cradled Doc's face in her hands. "You're wonderful," she said.

Doc didn't feel so wonderful. He felt like a dog. But he had a murder to solve. He could only hope whatever Slatz had to accomplish wouldn't chew up too much of the day. He wished they were going straight to the salvage yard. He wished he didn't need to leave Snowball with Bonnie. But that's how it had to be.

Five minutes after his mom left, Doc bundled Snowball, walked outside, locked the front door behind him.

Right on time, just as Slatz had promised, Bunny pulled up in the driveway. Doc handed Snowball through the back passenger window of the Cadillac. Jimmy took her and bounced her on his knee. She giggled.

"Where's Grill?" Doc asked, climbing in.

Slatz turned in the front passenger seat. "At his dad's office, getting his braces tightened."

"Cruel and unusual punishment," Doc said. "Gives his son an underbite, then an overbite. Spreads his palate. The next visit he starts all over again."

Bunny, playing the part of silent chauffeur, drove them to Locust Street. Unlike Grill's mom, Bunny was cool, not crazy. They stopped in front of Bonnie's house.

Doc carried Snowball across the dead and dying lawn, the flotsam and jetsam from a not so "Good Ship Lollipop."

Before he got to the porch, Bonnie opened the front door. She wore black Capris and a sleeveless black top with frayed silver thread spun through the fabric. She looked as tired as he felt. "Come in," she said.

He followed her inside. Snowball sniffed the air.

The house smelled like burnt SpaghettiOs; the aroma, a little bit of Italy, was somehow congruent with the paint-by-numbers portrait of the Pope that hung in the entry.

Other than a rump-sprung couch and two folding chairs, the living room was almost bare of furniture. The moss green carpet, as weary as the front lawn, *cur-unched cur-unched* beneath his hard-soled shoes.

"Nice place," he said, trying to tread lightly.

She looked at his feet then into his eyes. "Cheerios," she said. "The vacuum's been broken awhile."

Doc nodded. "Bet no one can sneak up on you in this place."

She looked at him curiously. "Who'd do that?"

"No one. I was just joking."

She took Snowball from his arms, stood a few steps back.

"Maybe I could take a look at your vacuum," Doc said. "Try to fix it."

A smile as sweet as jam on toast spread across Bonnie's face. She gave Snowball a playful jiggle. "You'll stay and help? I could make us dinner. We could listen to records after the kids fall asleep."

From within Doc's heart rose the same confusion: a desire to be where he was when he was supposed to be somewhere else. He liked this sorry, sad house, this girl worth fighting for, could imagine no moment better than this one now. "I wish I could," he sighed. "I really do, but I promised my friends…the band. We gotta practice." Doc looked at his baby sister, stroked her dandelion hair.

"Can't blame a girl for asking." She moved a step closer. Everything about her was female. "We'll just have to miss you till we see you."

Doc loved how, when she spoke to him, she did it with her whole body.

Snowball looked up at both of them, groaned, wiggled free of Bonnie's arms. She tottered over to a coloring book that peeked out from beneath the coffee table.

Outside, a horn honked.

"Go," she said. "Hope your band sounds great."

"Does your mom know you're babysitting?" Doc asked, backing toward the entry.

"She won't care. She's never around. Even if she was she probably won't even notice."

PAYOLA

Mrs. LaDesma, Bunny to the boys, drove windows-down south on Brookhurst, north on Pacific Coast Highway. Doc rode shotgun.

In the backseat, his voice measured and serious, Jimmy spoke in low tones to Slatz. He explained how Doc had "run across" a photograph of a car with taillights that matched the ones they saw the night his sister died. He kept it simple, didn't mention the photo had come from a ghost.

Slatz, on the other hand, talked at full throttle, about freak shows, wild rides, prostitutes, sex, a deal to rival the dreams of Avarice, a record contract for the band.

Bunny, placid as a pool of clear blue water, took in every word, never blushed, didn't bat an eye. Slatz leaned over the seat, said, "Ready for a good time, Doc?"

"I'm only here 'cause we're going to the salvage yard."

Slatz snorted. "Would it kill you to have a little fun along the way?"

"For the last three days all I've been is a liar and a sneak. Sorry if I'm having trouble living with myself."

"So move out."

"Funny."

Slatz threw his arms in the air. "Talk to him, Mom."

Bunny put her hand on Doc's leg. "Did it all start with a girl, this lying and sneaking?"

Doc sighed, recalled the kite, the roof of Saint Mary's, meeting Bonnie at the dance. "How'd you know?"

"You're only human," she said.

Slatz slapped the seat. "There's your answer, Doc. You're only human. Slatz sat back and closed his eyes. "How 'bout a little mood music, Mom? I need to recharge the savage beast inside me."

Bunny dialed in Mario Lanza on the radio, turned up the volume and let "Be My Love" and the sea breeze blow through her hair.

Twenty minutes later, looking out through the windshield, Doc could see distant carnival lights winking through a fog bank, the scaffolding of the Jack Rabbit Racer backlit by a sun the color of a silver dollar.

Jimmy leaned over the front seat, whispered, "Find out what the future holds." He handed Doc a penny, hoisted one of the pot metal Swamis over the seat and set it in Doc's lap. "It's a replacement for a busted one. We're dropping it off at some bar called the Palomino Club."

About the size and weight of a bowling ball, the Swami had almost knocked his breath out when it landed.

Doc had seen these little mystic men before. Slatz kept a few of them in a trunk at the foot of his bed. His "inheritance," as he often called them, shared space with other specialty items from Big Lou LaDesma's novelty business: nudie playing cards, wax lips, cartons of candy cigarettes, edible lubricants, fuzzy dice.

Doc dropped the penny in the Swami's navel, stroked the turbaned head, pulled down on the pot metal arm. Like a theatre ticket, a fortune spooled from the Swami's mouth.

"Read it out loud," Jimmy said.

Doc read. "That which you are seeking is seeking you."

"See," Jimmy said. "The salvage yard is seeking us. Trust the fates. We'll get to the salvage yard at just the right time, so relax."

226

"Let me get a look at that," Slatz said, coming forward and snatching the fortune from Doc's hand. "This is perfect," he said. "The band has an audition today."

"How can we have an audition?" Doc said. "We don't have instruments. We only know one song. Grill isn't even here."

"We don't need Grill. And instruments are for suckers and chumps." He produced a satchel from the back. "All the talent and tunes we need are right here. It's called 'moola.'"

Doc turned to Jimmy. "What's he talking about?"

Jimmy shrugged his shoulders. "It seems Big Lou has friends in the record business."

"Works like this," Slatz said. "They'll pick a song for us. Encourage a few DJs to play it on air after we record it. You play any song enough times everybody's humming it. The song's a hit. It's all about repetition."

"It sounds like payola," Doc said.

"So? You gonna make a federal case out of it?"

"They *can* make a federal case out of it, Slatz."

"Don't blame me. You were the one that got the fortune." Slatz looked around. "Pull over here, Mom."

AND GOD CREATED WOMAN

Bunny let them off at a set of wooden steps that wound down to the midway. Slatz, barely able to contain the grin on his face, lugged the money satchel with one hand, cradled the Swami replacement with the other.

The smell of tar and seaweed gave way to the aroma of cotton candy, hot dogs, the earthy scent of sawdust and diesel grease. They passed the Nu-Pike Arcade, a bar called Lucky's, Seven Sea Tattoos, and the Majestic Theatre. Carousel music rode the air. The wooden framework rattled beneath screams that came from passengers riding high above them on the careening carts of the Jack Rabbit Racer.

Slatz stopped in front of the Palomino Club. A sign read "Absolutely No One Under 21 Admitted."

"We make both drops here," he said.

Doc shoved his hands in his pockets. "You hand over the money and the Swami, then we go, right? We clean the coins out of the other Swamis, head for the salvage yard?"

"Unless something better comes up." Slatz pushed past Jimmy, swept aside the saloon doors, slipped between the shadowy figures just inside the entrance, and disappeared into the velvety darkness of the bar.

Doc turned to Jimmy. "Do you think this is smart?"

Jimmy looked at him. "Who needs smart when there's dangerous?"

Doc shook his head and followed Jimmy inside.

Over the crack of pool balls, Doc could hear "Mack the Knife" playing on a Rainbow Ribbon Wurlitzer next to a shabby bandstand at the back of the room. He blinked away the darkness, turned in a circle, caught a glimpse of Slatz strolling up to a spot-lit teakwood long bar and a thick-necked man who was wiping out soapy shot glasses with a yellowed dish rag.

Words were spoken.

The exchange was made.

The bartender set the satchel behind the bar, slipped Slatz an envelope. The man rang up "No Sale" on the cash register and poured Slatz a carbonated drink.

The deal was done. No federal officers sprang from the woodwork to nab them, no vice-grip hands pinned Doc's arms behind his back. To his surprise, he found the lunacy of the moment more amusing than terrifying. So what if he'd taken his delinquency to the federal level. His week had already been filled with murder and mayhem, deviance and the undead. Love and lies. If he could find out who killed Jimmy's sister, he could live with the consequences of being in the music business with the mob.

Instead of fretting, Doc focused on the next important thing he needed to do: grab Slatz, find Jimmy, and get out of the Palomino.

Excusing himself, saying "pardon me, pardon me," Doc worked his way over to the long bar. He bumped past sailors on shore leave, a toothless woman with a parrot on her shoulder, a man with no arms who tried to sell him a "solid gold" wrist watch.

He tapped Slatz on the back. "Let's go."

Slatz spun on the stool, sipped his drink. "Relax, Doc. Celebrate a little. You're on your way to stardom." He raised his arm, curled a finger in the air. "Singapore Sling for my friend."

The bartender walked over and plopped down a tall glass filled with what looked like party punch. The miniature umbrella swirling in the center took a lap around the ice cubes.

"Check this out," Slatz said, producing a laminated card from the envelope he'd received in the exchange for the satchel. He slid the card over to Doc. "Welcome to the Musician's Union. As of today, you're a full-fledged member. Got your name and birth date already printed on it."

Doc examined the card. "According to this, I'm twenty-four years old."

"Yeah. That's why they call it a fake ID. Difference is, this is genuine."

Doc closed his eyes, mentally counted to ten. "A genuine fake ID. Just what I've always wanted." He stuck the card in his pocket. "Can we get out of here?"

"Polish off that drink and we'll see if we can pry Jimmy away from his new girlfriends," Slatz said, pointing to the far corner of the bar. "He's back there by the Wurlitzer playing pool."

Doc chugged down the drink, pulled Slatz from the stool. Something in the aftermath of the drink dizzied him. Momentarily, he felt like the miniature umbrella that had swirled around the inside of the glass.

Beyond the crush of people, the smoke, the bubbling colors of the Wurlitzer, Doc could intermittently see Jimmy. He appeared and disappeared in the cone of light that illuminated the green felt surface of the pool table. There were two girls with him. One, a balloon-breasted blonde, wore her hair clipped up in a French twist. The other, a brunette, wore a slinky red dress, sported lips as red as a fire engine.

The big blonde was chalking Jimmy's pool cue. The brunette made hand gestures like she was explaining a three-ball combination. Neither looked like they needed a union card to pass for legal in the Palomino.

Jimmy, looking up as he and Slatz approached, gestured to each of the girls.

"Doc, Slatz, let me introduce you to Teri and May."

May wasted no time. She snaked a bare arm around Slatz's waist and began whispering in his ear.

Doc flinched as he looked at Teri. Her face was eerily familiar: round sugar cookie cheeks, eyes shiny black, like a stuffed animal's. She extended a hand, her touch featherlight, as though her flesh was made of ether, her fingernails immaculately painted, perfectly, poignantly pink.

She smiled. "Teri's a stage name. My real name's Theresa." She took a step back, posed. "Like my dress?"

The room tilted a little, the world suddenly became dreamlike, everything slightly askew. The taste of punch expanded in Doc's head. His face felt numb. "The red looks good, but I see you dressed in black," he said.

"Teri's a professional dancer," Jimmy said. "Dances right next door at the Majestic."

"Really?" Doc slurred, steadying himself against the pool table. "Bet you haven't been working there long."

"I'm new in town. Barely know a soul."

"How'd I know you'd say that?"

Jimmy looked at Doc. "You all right?"

Doc shook his finger at Teri. "She's not who she says she is. I can see right through her." He laughed at his ghost humor.

Slatz, his arm draped over May's shoulder, leaned in. "Sorry 'bout Doc's bad manners. Had Max, the bartender, pour our friend here a stiff one."

Doc, not listening, studied Teri. "What are you doing here?"

"Told you," Jimmy said. "She dances at the theater next door."

Teri came closer to Doc. "I'm sure what Doc means is, what's a nice girl like me doing in a place like this. The answer is I came here to meet Jimmy."

"And May came to meet me," Slatz said.

"That's a laugh," Doc said.

No one laughed.

Slatz frowned. "We need to talk." He pulled Doc aside, whispered, "Don't blow it for us. Get cool with the booze. Just go with the buzz."

May leaned in, gave Slatz a peck on the cheek. "We girls need to get going, honey. See you soon? Apartment Three Twenty-Two."

The girls disappeared into the crowd.

Watching Teri and May wiggle off, Slatz nodded, leered. He said to Doc, "We got a sure thing here."

"I thought we had a *plan*," Doc said. "Clear the coins from the Swamis, head for the salvage yard."

"Don't worry, Doc. We'll empty the Swamis right now," Jimmy said. "The girls say they need about thirty minutes to get ready for us. The timing's perfect. Plenty of time to get to the salvage yard."

"We made a deal. Handle the Swamis then go to the salvage yard."

"Listen, Doc," Slatz said. "We got a good deal here. The girls are going swimming at the 'Plunge.' Before they go, they want to model their new swimsuits for us. Ya know, see if they fit right."

Doc wasn't listening to Slatz, he was staring at Jimmy. He took a step back. "We're so close to finding out what happened," he said. "After three years of 'skyfishing,' we're about to reel something in. You do believe the car I showed you in the photograph is the same car that hit your sister, don't you?"

"I want to believe," Jimmy said.

"I don't think you do. I don't think you believe in me or the car or anything."

"Doc," Jimmy said, "you're drunk."

Doc's mind sloshed, his lips rubbered into a smile. "Wanna hear something funny? Here it is: The real reason I wanted to find out who killed Cindy was so you'd keep me around as your friend. I'd be the best friend of the most popular guy in school."

"You gotta burn off a little of that alcohol, Doc," Jimmy said. "Come on. Let's clear the cash out of the Swamis."

"I'm not coming."

"Yes, you are," Jimmy said. He grabbed Doc's arm, pulled him down the midway. With Slatz leading the way, they made stops at outdoor cafes, ramshackle bars, tattoo parlors, and novelty shops. They unlocked and dumped out change from the bellies of Swamis every place they went, filled the canvas bags Max had given Slatz before they'd left the Palomino.

Loaded down with quarters and dimes, they stepped into the alley behind the Majestic Theatre, found the entrance that led to the apartments upstairs, walked in.

Overhead pipes dripped brown water, paint peeled from the walls. Scratch marks left by some frantic, bloodied hand trailed down the back of the door. The carpeted stairs smelled like wet dog and vomit.

"Hey, wha'da ya think?" Slatz said, grabbing the stair rail. "Pretty cool high rise. Lot better than it looks from outside."

"I'm staying here," Doc said.

Jimmy grabbed his arm again.

Three floors up, they wandered the hallway, reading the numbers on the doors.

"Three Twenty-Two," Jimmy said, coming to a stop.

Slatz knocked.

The door opened slowly. Just a crack.

The smallest part of a sugar-cookie face peeked out at them. At waist level, between the top and bottom of a skimpy two-piece bathing suit, a bare belly button contemplated Doc like a mystic third eye.

The girl he'd first known as the nun, Sister Theresa, then later learned was likely the fabled Homecoming Queen who'd perished years ago in Carbon Canyon, opened the door as Teri, the professional dancer.

"Come on in," she said. "May's in the bedroom fluffing her eiderdown. She'll be out in a minute."

Doc hiccupped.

Slatz gulped.

Jimmy took a step forward but Teri blocked his way.

"You wouldn't have a bottle or two in one of these canvas bags, would you? Something spirited to drink? Champagne maybe?"

"Just money," Jimmy said.

Teri glanced from Jimmy to Slatz. "May will want something to drink. She's a thirsty girl."

The boys looked at each other.

"Right," Slatz said. "What's a party without a little social lubrication? How 'bout this? Doc, you stay here and keep the money warm. Jimmy and I will score some bubbly back at the Palomino."

Teri agreed.

Slatz and Jimmy took off for the stairwell.

Doc carried the bags inside, glad to get a few moments alone with Teri, Theresa, Pinkie, whoever she was.

There was a sofa covered in turquoise-tinted Naugahyde and two overstuffed chairs in the small living room. French doors led to a balcony. The back wall of the matchbox kitchen was draped in cargo netting adorned with starfish. A Felix the Cat clock hung over a turntable just outside the bedroom door.

Doc sat on the sofa, rested his elbow on a pillow embroidered with the words, "Love those coconuts." He guessed the pillow belonged to May.

Teri slipped on a white robe, sat sideways, feet up, at the far end of the sofa, facing him.

Doc looked at her pink toes, saw his reflection paint itself on the pupils of her eyes. "I don't know what to call you," he said.

"Teri's fine."

"I liked you better as Sister Theresa. Loved the riddles you dealt me, especially the one that led me to the news clippings about Pinkie the ghost girl of Carbon Canyon. That's you too, right?

"She was the first me, as far as I know."

"So now you're what? A prostitute?"

Teri shrugged her shoulders, sighed. "It's a Mary Magdalene phase. That's my best guess. I don't control who I am or where I go, Doc. The spirit just moves me. Literally moves me from one place to another. Honestly, I don't recall meeting May before today."

"So what are you doing here?"

'I think I'm trying to meet Jimmy. I have this feeling I need him to do something for me."

"If it's the pink high heels, the ones you lost in Carbon Canyon, I can bring those to you."

She wiggled her pink toes, caught him looking at them. "Well aren't you a naughty boy? Hoping to cash in on the legend? Get a little slice of heaven?"

"Blame it on the social lubrication."

She wrapped the robe around herself. "Ever thought you're like every other boy? Ever thought the problem might be you? The you that never listens?"

"Well, I'm listening now."

"You should have been listening then."

"Then?" He threw up his arms. "Which 'then?' What 'then' are you talking about?"

"A minute ago you asked me, what am I doing here?"

"And you told me you were trying to meet Jimmy."

"That was the small answer to the big question, wouldn't you say?"

Doc, exhausted, his brain numbed by the alcohol, had no idea what she was talking about.

She stood, opened the French doors, looked out over the balcony. "They'll be back any minute. I hope you'll do your best to keep our little secret, give me time with Jimmy. Pretty please," she said, "just act normal."

"Normal? A ghost is telling me to act normal. Nothing about you," he looked around the room, "or this, or my life, is normal. No, I take that back. What's normal is Jimmy gets the girl. Jimmy gets the gold mine and I get the shaft."

She turned around, let the robe drop. "How 'bout this for your shaft? You wanna be a bonafide detective? Contemplate this mystery. Tell me how I look."

She was wearing a bikini.

Doc stared at the floor. "Why don't you ask Jimmy?"

"I'm asking you."

"You look like Sister Theresa with hardly any clothes on. It's unnerving, disquieting." He brought his eyes up to meet hers. "What do you want me to say? You look normal? Divine? Out of this world?"

May came out of the bedroom. Her leopard skin bathing suit said, "And God created woman," just not in words. It answered the question, how do you put three pounds of melons into two one-pound bags?

"Styling by Frederick's of Hollywood," May said, her too-white teeth proportioned to match the rest of her. "Think your friends will like it?"

"Did it come with the meat of the animal it was made from?" Doc asked.

May burst out laughing. "This kid's funny."

Doc shot a glance at Teri. "Think I'll wait on the balcony."

Teri followed him out, stood at the wrought iron railing next to him.

"I know you don't like this place," she said, "but I can't help being here or behaving badly. It's nothing I control. I float in and out of this world, Doc. Most of the time my mind's all clouds and stardust, like a leaf in the wind. I see myself talking to you from a million miles away and it's not me speaking. All I know is there's a reason I chose you that day at the church and there's purpose in the heart of the One that wants me to help Jimmy. But you're the only one that can know who I am. Can you keep that secret?"

"It's too late. I've already told Jimmy about you."

"He can believe in you without believing in me."

"Double talk. You think that makes me feel better?"

"Just don't be upset if I seduce him."

"Upset? I'm not upset. I'm just the guy who runs around trying to help a friend solve his sister's murder. I grab up all the pieces, nearly get myself killed doing it. For that I get nothing and you give Jimmy, you—You are Pinkie, right?"

She nodded.

"No offense, but ghost sex with you would be like the Holy Grail of nooky. Sorry about my bad behavior. The sex talk. It's probably the alcohol."

"I won't hold it against you. I mean, what you're saying."

Doc stared out at the fog-shrouded horizon.

"Is it true that if I fulfilled the prophecy, ya know, brought you the shoes, and then we 'did it,' no girl could ever resist me?"

"Probably. Unless that girl was a legend in her own right."

"Is it true that 'doing it' with you doesn't count as earth sex, that, technically, the guy would still be a virgin?"

"I think that's how the legend works."

"So the guy would have 'the skills' and still be able to say he'd saved himself just for her?"

She nodded. "The best of both worlds."

"Have your cake and eat it, too."

"You *are* a naughty boy."

They both smiled in the way two people do when they reach the end of a scene in a theatrical production where both actors realize they've been poorly cast.

Below the railing, Doc could see Jimmy and Slatz in the alley. Jimmy howled in coyote talk.

"So now what?" Doc asked. "I get lost?"

"When they get up here, have a few drinks with us, then tell the guys they can catch up with you later at the arcade."

Doc heard the front door open, corks pop, glasses clinked.

May giggled.

Doc heard Slatz ask May, "Can you actually swim in that thing?"

COWGIRL AND
RENEGADE REDSKIN

Within moments, the party was in full swing. Doc did as Teri asked. Begrudgingly, he played the role of butler, third wheel, stooge. He pouted, poured champagne, watched with the other guys as Teri and May twirled across the hardwood floor, modeling their bathing suits to the window-rattling beat of the Champs' "Tequila."

"Don't you just love the lyrics?" May squealed, her face suddenly an inch from Doc's, her empty glass nudging his shoulder, begging for a refill.

He poured May a splash. "The song only has one word."

May grabbed Doc with her man-eater gaze. "I like the way you get right to the point. Really like that in a man." She hip-bumped him, winked, wiggled off backward and rejoined Teri in the center of the "dance floor."

Doc took a drink straight from the bottle. His brain sloshed as he tilted his head back. His mind went on a mean streak. He didn't like feeling invisible again.

He bobbed his head enthusiastically, toe-tapped, rolled his shoulders, thrusted his pelvis in counterpoint to the lurid rhythms of May's gyrating body. Teri would notice. She'd see him transformed into pure, eroticized male energy, see him emboldened by the superficial, meaningless, skin-deep charms of another woman. This display of shallowness, he hoped, would leave Pinkie with the same bitter taste he was left with when she'd rejected him for Jimmy. "Doesn't go down easy, does it, ghost girl?" he muttered. "All the pride you can swallow? All the crow you can eat?"

He looked at her, stopped dancing. He was wasting his time.

Teri was still dancing, but she had those stuffed animal eyes again. She'd missed out on his how-do-you-like-the-way-it-feels rejection of her. She was off somewhere a million miles away, her mind all clouds and stardust, the way it had been when she was dancing in the cemetery. He just couldn't win.

Hard as he tried, it was impossible to stay mad at her. After all, she was dead. Drop-dead-gorgeous dead.

Jimmy and Slatz were looking at Teri too. They sat at opposite ends of the couch: Jimmy relaxed and leaning back, Slatz sweating profusely, gnawing the edges of the "Love Those Coconuts" pillow.

"Tequila" ended. May went to the turntable, bent at the waist, shuffled through a stack of forty-fives. "Who likes the Coasters?"

"Who doesn't?" Slatz asked. Standing, taking a step toward May, he veered in Doc's direction. Under his breath, he whispered to Doc, "I think my mom might be worried about me, about us. I mean, ya know, us. We're lugging around a lot of loot. These girls could be dangerous. What do we *really* know about them?" He laughed nervously, turned to May. "Can Doc and I use your bathroom?"

May wiggled, spun in a circle, then pointed to the bedroom door. "Through there."

Slatz took Doc's elbow, said a little too loudly, "Need to splash a little water on this kid's face. The rookie needs a little sobering up."

Doc took one more slug of champagne, set the bottle down. "Gone chicken on us, Slatz? That's what you want to tell me?"

FORGOTTEN LORE

The next thing Doc remembered he was face up on May's bed watching his reflection spin in the fun house mirror attached to the ceiling. In the distance, he could hear "Earth Angel" on the record player. He'd lost track of time, but doubted that time had been wasted by Jimmy; he'd likely made his move. In his mind, Doc could see Jimmy slow dancing with Teri, pacing his coyote breathing to match the rise and fall of her chest, positioning himself close enough to her to feel the contour of her bare belly button against his shirt. He was soaking up Pinkie's pulse, the heat that could only emanate from the fleshy center of that little cosmic cyclone.

Jealousy and alcohol had made him pitiful, but he didn't care. He was tired of being treated like a novelty act by the girls he'd tried to help. Scarlett, Bonnie, Margaret Ann: each of them toyed with him, probably laughed at him behind his back. All he wanted them to know was that he saw the deep down part of them that was lovable, that if they played it straight with him he could be a hero in their lives. All he wanted them to say to him was, "You're a really nice guy."

What a joke, what a stupid dream. Nice guys don't win.

He stood. His mind resolved, his legs not so steady. He knew now was the moment to go back to the living room. Now was the moment to cut in on the action. He'd finish the slow dance with Teri. All he needed was props, regalia, something symbolic that would make Teri believe he had nerve, that if he wanted her, she was his…The idea was if she was a dead girl, he'd come at her larger than life.

He looked around. There were conga drums in the corner of the room, sock puppets on the bed. A raincoat made of transparent plastic hung from a coat rack. Fur-trimmed handcuffs lay on the nightstand. All these things had possibilities, he thought, but none was perfect.

Hanging on one of the bedposts was a cowgirl hat, a toy gun and holster. On the other hung an Indian chief's war bonnet.

Doc tore off his shirt, grabbed the war bonnet, put it on his head, threw back the door that lead to the living room, slurred out, "I'm on the war path for your love."

May smiled back at him. She was alone on the couch, one long leg crossed over the other. She dangled a spiked high heel shoe from the tip of a toe. "You *are* a savage, aren't you?" she said.

Doc's buzz faded. Every drop of alcohol in his bloodstream evaporated.

"Where are Jimmy and Teri?"

"They went down to the Palomino for more champagne. Your friend Slatz took off for higher ground. Sit down," she said.

Doc sat.

May took his hand. "Your friend was scared. Scared from the beginning. But not you, I could tell." She paused. "I've got a pith helmet and a whip in my closet. Grab a kitchen chair." She stroked her leopard-print bathing suit. "We could play jungle cat and great white hunter."

Doc looked around at the empty room. "Would that make Teri sorry she picked Jimmy over me?"

"If you mean jealous, the answer's maybe." She looked at his headdress, nodded. "I think we should go with your idea: cowgirl and renegade redskin. Now that'll get her where it hurts."

She pushed Doc toward the bedroom, followed him.

"I'm very reliable," Doc said, the words like oatmeal in his mouth. "And I've been told I have an excellent imagination."

May gave him one last shove. "You won't need it."

Kicking the bedroom door closed behind them, May grabbed Doc's belt loops and slung him, headdress and all, onto the bed. A sea breeze swirled in through an open window, whipped through her hair, rattled the dozens of photographs hung on the walls. She licked her lips.

"Off with the moccasins, Tonto. I see any funny moves out of you, one solitary smoke signal and it's the Happy Hunting Grounds. Got it?"

Doc slid back until his shoulders banged the headboard. He couldn't tell if he was sober or drunk, excited or scared.

May put on her cowgirl hat, tugged the brim, strapped the gun belt around her waist, climbed on the bed, stood above him legs apart, twirling the six shooter. "Your first time?"

"First time? No. When it comes to playing make believe, you're looking at the champ. I've done it all in my imagination, just never with a real girl."

"Honest and to the point," she said. "I like your style…Wanna kiss me? Want me to rub something?"

Doc thought a moment. There was one private personal place on his body he could sacrifice. He spoke the words hesitantly. "My leg's kinda sore."

May climbed on the bed, rolled up Doc's pant legs. "You want me to start with the skinnier one?"

Doc nodded, said, "Teri won't like you doing this, will she?"

May studied him. "She'll be livid." Smiling, she dropped to her knees, leaned her weight across his body, reached out, tugged open the top drawer of the nightstand next to the bed and pulled out a small leather-bound book and a bottle of almond oil. "Pretty please read to me," she said, "while I massage your leg."

Doc looked at the cover: *The Collected Poems of Edgar Allan Poe.* "Have a favorite?" he said.

"You could start with 'The Raven.'"

"Excellent choice," Doc said, flipping through the pages.

May poured a puddle of oil into the palm of her hand, smoothed it over Doc's leg. "Did you know the French symbolists, Mallarme, Boudelaire, Rimbaud, learned to speak English just so they could read Poe in the original? They thought he was…mellifluous, magnifique."

She worked magic on the muscles in his calf. Spoke of the mythic power of his Achilles tendon as she aligned its fibers. Slipping off his socks, she rubbed his toes. Never was a little piggy so glad to go to market, never had a piggy liked roast beef so much.

He read the opening stanza of "The Raven." She recited the second stanza from memory. The words of the third stanza, opening with "And the silken, sad, uncertain," they spoke together, the rise and fall of their voices, one male, one female, blended together into a sound delicious as dark honey. They alternated reading, the dual recitation lasting until the last "nevermore."

The experience was more than just pleasurable.

"You're wonderful company, May," Doc said.

She lifted a curl of blond hair that had fallen over her eyes. "I find that's what most men really want."

For some odd reason what she said made him think of the conversations and arguments he'd had with Margaret Ann over the years. He recalled the sense of—was it pleasure he experienced from their verbal scraps, how much he enjoyed the tug of war they played with words and ideas, the way her freckled nose wrinkled when they battled to a draw?

He shook the thought away. "Did you know 'The Raven' was inspired by a crow? His great, great, great grandson told me the whole story, told me Poe refused to write 'quoth the crow' because…"

May looked deep into Doc's eyes. "Because it wasn't sonorous enough?"

"Exactly," Doc said. "So you believe me?"

"Indians like you have animal spirit guides. Even a 'white eyes' knows that."

"And my leg feels fantastic," Doc said. "I don't remember anyone ever touching me that way before. Never really thought anyone would want to."

"It's part of you, Doc. Part of your forgotten lore. 'A quaint and curious and *very relevant* volume of forgotten lore.'"

"Huh?"

"Polio, right? You beat polio. That takes moxie."

"Me? Moxie? Never thought of it that way, but…someone else, a friend of mine named Patton, told me to remember that line about 'forgotten lore.' Mentioned I might hear it again someday. Didn't seem important at the time."

"Doc, I don't know who Teri is to you, but I get the feeling you're both on the run. Am I right?"

"I'm chasing down a murderer. She holds the secret."

May shifted position, sat astride him, drilled down his shoulders with the palms of her hands. "You'll need courage to catch this killer, whoever he is," she said, peering into his soul. "I know your type. You don't believe you're brave enough. Why would you? All you know about courage comes from fairy tales and novels. You think you've read them all, exhausted every source, but you haven't. You need to read the *one* book you've passed over: *your* forgotten lore, the first chapter of your own biography. Read it," she smoldered, the rhythm of her rump rocking the bed frame. "Read it and you'll learn about the boy who conquered an illness that vanquished thousands of others his same age. The strength that boy drew on wasn't inspired by great literature. No," she said, the bed springs squeaking. "No," she sighed, her eyes rolling back, her long lashes fluttering. "From the beginning that strength resided in the heart he was born with. That boy, Doc, is you."

"Me?"

She pressed the whole weight of her body down on him again, threw her head back. "Yes. Yes."

Her last words set fire to all the oxygen in the room. Doc could barely breathe. His heart pounded. The Earth tilted on its axis. The bed they lay on became a magic carpet, an island of eiderdown in a universe of falling stars.

He looked up at May. "Is this what great sex feels like?"

A horn echoed in the alley below them. Car doors slammed.

May's eyes flicked to the open window. "Great sex? Almost. It isn't really great sex till things turn dangerous."

"You mean when Teri comes back and catches us?"

She climbed off him. "What I mean is, there's a guy downstairs. He'll be coming through the door in about five minutes." She slipped on a red silk robe embroidered with tiny elephants, knotted the sash, wiggled out of the leopard-print bathing suit. "He's not the type that knocks or likes the idea of coming in second place."

"I'll leave right now," he said.

"Too late for that. His bodyguards will already be in the hall and the stairwell. They sweep the place before he comes upstairs."

Doc stood. "What do I do, May?"

"I'd take off the war bonnet, put your shirt on."

Doc tossed the headdress, grabbed his shirt, paced in circles, fumbled to close the only button that was still attached. With practiced hands, May tended to their "love nest." She shook out the eiderdown, fluffed pillows, returned the book and almond oil to the drawer, hung the cowgirl hat on the bedpost, sprayed the air with something Doc hoped was called eau de nothing-happened-here.

Facing him, she removed the holstered toy six-shooter from beneath her robe, spun the cylinder and handed him the gun.

"You're kidding," he said.

"Too soon to know."

She motioned him to join her at the window, squeezed his hand as he looked down into the alley.

A glob of something wet and slippery flip-flopped in Doc's stomach. His legs Gumbied, his mouth became the Sahara.

Through the rusted grates of the fire escape, he could see two black limousines parked in the alley below.

Doc gulped. "Who *is* this guy?"

She pointed to the wall above her bed. "Him."

Three framed photographs hung in a row above the headboard of her bed.

Doc stepped closer, studied each man's portrait: the dead sexologist Alfred Kinsey, the rebel leader Castro, the current Democratic candidate for President. "It's one of these guys?"

She nodded. "Exciting, isn't it? A man like him might do anything to snuff out a potential scandal."

"Snuff out?"

Doc could see the headline in tomorrow's *Los Angeles Times*: "Crippled Boy Washes Ashore at Pike. Dancer Vanishes." He looked at the first two photographs again. He doubted either the late Dr. Kinsey's wandering spirit or Fidel Castro's communist regime feared lurid publicity. But John F. Kennedy, a devout Catholic, a married man, wouldn't let loose lips sink *his* ship of state. Not now. Not when he was about to become leader of the free world.

Doc pointed to the candidate. "It's him, isn't it? This is one of the stops on his whistle-stop tour?"

"I met Jack earlier this summer at the Coliseum. I was a titular delegate to the Democratic Convention."

"Of course you were."

"Be brave, Doc. Pry the rest of the truth out of me. Shake me till I confess the whole tawdry thing, till I show you the Polaroids."

"You have photographs?"

"Don't make me tell you his speech writer, Ted Sorensen, wrote *Profiles in Courage*."

"Kennedy accepted the Pulitzer prize for a book he didn't write?"

"Save your leopard-pantied cowgirl, Doc."

Doc scrambled to the window. Two men in dark suits had gotten out of the limos. They stood, hands clasped behind their backs. So much for climbing out, trying to shinny down to the alley. The only way out was the front door, and by now Kennedy and the rest of his government goons were probably less than a minute from May's front door.

Doc slumped, whispered, "To save you, May, I'd have to leave here without being seen. The only way to do that is to never have been here in the first place."

"Or be the Invisible Man."

Doc thought a moment. The Invisible Man. Why not? He'd been invisible most of his life. It was a crazy long-shot good idea.

"Quick, May. Get me nail polish. Red. Black if you have it. And a tropical shirt."

"Calypso?"

"I'm going Calypso."

He hoisted one of the conga drums by its strap. "Meet me in the living room."

Next to the refrigerator, beneath the Felix the Cat clock, Doc found a mop. He sawed off its ropey mane with a butcher's knife he'd yanked from a cluttered kitchen drawer.

May joined him with bottles of polish and a shirt as bright as a bowl of fruit.

He handed her the newly fashioned "cane." "Paint the tip red."

"I see where you're going, Doc: the blind, crippled Caribbean conga player…If you can't see him, you can't identify his face. It's like you were never here." She leveled her eyes at him. "The idea doesn't have a chance in hell."

"I've been to hell," Doc said, "and gotten out."

He took off his glasses, lacquered the lenses with black nail polish. "When he comes through the door, tell him I coach tap-dance. A blind kid could do that, right?" He put on the calypso shirt, tied the shirttails just above his belly button and slung the strap of the conga drum over one shoulder.

May blew on the lacquered glasses, placed them on his face, handed him the cane. "One last touch." She scrambled back to the bedroom, returned in a heartbeat with a tin of caramel-toned theatrical makeup. "Used this in a show called *Brown Sugar*." Moments later, Doc looked "native."

Flamboyantly invisible, ready to meet the candidate, Doc tapped his way across the room. "How do I look?"

Before she could answer, the door in front of him, the door to Three Twenty-Two burst open with a bang, not a whimper.

Three shadowy figures squared off against Doc in the doorway.

The man in the middle smiled. His teeth were as big as May's. Big Bad Wolf big. It was Kennedy.

"Who's the bongo boy, May?" he said.

"A friend, Jack. A crippled friend. A ravaged young man with a humble soul. We met at an Easter Seals benefit. A production of Othello. And though he's sightless, he has a keen ear. He choreographed the tap-dance scene in the third act."

"I, sir," Doc said, "am Day-O, May's calypso accompanist. May I touch thy cheek, mon, that I might know thee should we meet again?"

Doc extended his arms, his fingers fumbled in space.

Kennedy stepped back.

His bodyguards came forward in a blur of blue serge and pinstripes. A top-to-bottom frisking ensued.

Rising to his feet, one of the agents said, "No weapons, sir. Just a withered leg. The kid probably had polio."

Kennedy nodded.

Doc bowed. "And now I take my leave, noble lady, unless your guests would like to hear a chorus or two of 'Babalu'?"

JUMBO

Doc left the conga drum at the top of the stairwell, then, scratching portholes through the black nail polish that covered his lenses, he descended to the alleyway exit of the Majestic Theatre.

No one was following him. Good, he thought, and upon reflection, decided it was better than good. It was sweet. May was right. The element of danger had definitely added excitement to the finale of their afternoon rendezvous. In fact, Kennedy showing up was the cherry on top. He took a breath, tossed away the cane. "Dan-ja," he said softly, speaking the word Massachusetts-style, the word like poetry on his lips. "Dan-ja." He could live his life falling in love with danger.

Doc threw back his shoulders, strode past the idling limousines, the wooden secret service agents in their chalk-striped suits, proud not because he had any illusion his escape had been eloquently crafted, but because his getaway had been a calamitous hodgepodge fashioned of found objects and a desperation fueled by his own imagination.

The whole thing had been ridiculously fun, and for the first time, he realized his imagination wasn't just something he could use to build fictional worlds or escape this one. Maybe this was what May was referring to when she asked him to read the first chapter of his own biography. Maybe using the imagination was a form of bravery, an exercise that strengthened the will. Maybe the imagination was an aspect of innocence, one that refused to be extinguished by logic, disease, or circumstance. "Stone walls do not a prison make, nor iron bars a cage." He'd read those words somewhere, and now wondered if, years ago, as he'd lain in the iron lung, his heart had known that truth even then.

Rounding the corner that led to the midway, Doc took one last parting glance up at May's window, envisioned the portrait photographs hung above her bed, the faces of the three men fate had recently stirred into his life, men who sought to have their names define an era. He thought of Castro, muttered the word "Reds" and laughed, then slammed smack into Slatz.

"So where's the money?"

Doc climbed to his feet. "Left the bags upstairs. Sorry," he said.

"You're gonna go back and get them, right?"

Doc took off his glasses, picked at the polish on his lenses. "Not a good idea."

"Not a good idea? Tell that to my ol' man. I come back without the money, Big Lou will have my hide."

"The place is crawling with Feds, Slatz."

"They got no jurisdiction. That money's clean."

"It's got nothing to do with your stupid payola scheme. It's more like a state secret, a secret if *they* know *you* know what it is, and *they* think you'll blab about it, they deep six your sorry ass."

Slatz tilted his head, squinted one eye, and studied Doc. "Okay," he said. "Now I get it. You chickened out. I gave you a shot at May and the best you can do is come up with some lame, chicken-ass excuse."

Doc put on his blackened glasses. "First, you were the one who chickened out. Second," he pointed to his knotted calypso shirt, "do I look a chicken's ass?"

"You look like a runaway from voodoo summer camp. Pitiful. Just plain pitiful." He pulled a comb from his back pocket, styled his Brylcreemed hair. "Well if you don't have the nerve to get the wild thing on with May, I do. I'm going back up to Apartment Three Twenty-Two. Don't bother knockin', we won't be unlockin'."

"Don't be an idiot. John F. Kennedy's up there. The guys with him have guns."

"Right." Slatz snorted. He left Doc, turned the corner of the building, and walked toward the back entrance of the Majestic. Doc heard him yell out, "May! Baby doll! Pop a cork! Your loverboy is back!"

A sickening silence stilled the air.

The sound of Slatz's footsteps stopped, then slowly, hesitantly began again. In reverse.

Pale, wide-eyed, Slatz came back around the corner at breakneck speed. "The guys in the suits. Exactly who are they?"

"Feds."

From the alley came the slap of gummed-soled shoes, the leathery squeak of shoulder holsters, the squawk of two-way radios.

"I think we should get out of here. Like now," Slatz said, tugging at Doc.

Deep voices yelled, "Stop! Stop or we'll shoot!"

They ran.

"Head for the arcade," Slatz huffed out between breaths, "Jimmy said he'd meet us there."

Dodging and weaving, Doc and Slatz scrambled down the midway. They bumped past sailors on shore leave, outflanked barkers and shills, bisected Siamese twins laden with cotton candy, knocked over an organ grinder with a monkey on his shoulder. Bobbing and weaving, sawdust flying, they hurtled the gate surrounding the carousel, dodged the moving platform of the tilt-a-whirl, crawled beneath a tethered elephant and lay on their stomachs gasping for breath.

From between the elephant's legs, Doc could see Kennedy's goons. There were four of them now, equidistantly spaced coming forward through the fractured crowd. Whispering into their wristwatches, they pushed aside small children and the infirmed.

"It's a dragnet. We're screwed," Slatz said.

"Jimmy's at the arcade, right? Where's the arcade?"

"I thought you knew."

A small man made of bones wrapped in wrinkled brown flesh leaned down and looked at them. In an East Indian accent, he said, "The arcade is closed."

"It doesn't matter," Doc said.

"You are correct, boy. There is no matter. There is only energy. But I suspect that is a subject for a different time. May I help you?"

"We're on the lam," Slatz said.

"You may be on the lamb, but you are under an elephant."

"What my friend means," Doc said, "is there are bad men after us."

"Then let Jumbo help. Slide back toward her tail and she will sit on you. Beneath an elephant's ass, all men are invisible."

Doc and Slatz looked at each other.

"Not to worry," the Indian said, smiling. "In the circus, sitting on the girl who rides him is a crowd pleaser. The animal, who tramples the jungle and tears trees out by their roots, shows his sensitivity to those with gentle souls. Let us hope he senses something of that in each of you."

A HAZE OF ECTOPLASM

Twenty minutes later, back in the Cadillac with Bunny at the wheel, Doc listened as Slatz, sitting in the front passenger seat, talked a mile a minute.

"Jimmy, you tell her," Slatz said. "Tell my mom what Doc did with the money."

"Doc gave the Swami money to a prostitute."

"Hear that, Mom? He gave all Dad's cash to a prostitute."

"He's only human," she said.

"Two hundred dollars. I bet there was two hundred dollars in those bags."

"You've got to understand, darling," Bunny said, languidly applying lipstick as she drove, "a gal can't be expected to work for nothing." She smooshed her lips together, capped the Revlon. "So how was it, Doc?"

"Great. Just great. I guess you could call it a true revelation."

"So the lady swung it a full three-sixty. Nice touch. We call that 'round the world.'"

"Mom! He said *revelation*, not revolution."

"Actually, Mrs. LaDesma, some things did come full circle. I learned a lot about myself."

"On my dime," Slatz snorted. "And what did I get? Elephant ass. A face full of elephant ass."

"Jumbo saw something beautiful in us, Mrs. LaDesma."

"You're sick," Slatz said.

"Sick, but curiously satisfied."

Bunny, nodding, said, "Darling, you could learn a lot from Doc's positive attitude." She turned down the radio, glanced in the rearview mirror. "Ready to case out that salvage yard, boys?"

Slatz turned to face Doc and Jimmy. "You prostitute-loving back-stabbers go to the salvage yard...Mom, drop me off at Fullerton Music. Think I'll spend a little time with Scarlett." He sighed. "I feel like composing something for her. With friends like you, who needs enemies?"

There was irony there, Doc thought. A title for the song Slatz might write for her.

As they drove, Jimmy finished the story he'd begun telling as the three of them had walked from the arcade up the hill to Bunny's car.

"You knew who she was all the time, didn't you, Doc?" Jimmy said, pausing midsentence.

"Before today, I'd only known her as Sister Theresa. I had no idea she'd show up at the Pike."

"But by the time she and I left the apartment, you knew she was Pinkie."

"I knew by then," Doc said.

"Why didn't you say something?"

"She asked me not to tell you who she was. Said there was something only you could do for her...So what was it?"

"All I know is she wants us to meet her tonight in the chapel at Saint Anthony's. Guess it's some Catholic church in Anaheim. There's a Chi-Rho youth dance, a big one. We're to go there, blend in. She'll find us."

"Nothing about the Studebaker? Nothing about your sister? Did you tell her we were going to Mentz's garage?"

"Doc, most of the time I thought she was a prostitute. Found out otherwise when she dragged me onto the roller coaster, the big one, the Jack Rabbit Racer. Said, 'Call me Sister Theresa,' just as the guy locked down the safety bar."

"That's when you knew?"

"The name clicked about the time we reached the top of the chute. We started down. Her eyes got that dead spooky look…like something socketed into the skull of a stuffed animal. That's when I knew. After that it was all Jack Rabbit Racer. We just flew…we just flew." He shook his head. "When the ride stopped, all there was next to me was a haze of ectoplasm."

DOLLARS TO DONUTS

Slatz got out of the car at Fullerton Music. Bunny drove south, picked up the freeway to Santa Ana. Ten minutes later she pointed out the ominous sign just beyond the First Street exit: Mentz's Tow and Salvage.

Doc crossed his fingers.

Jimmy curled his right hand into a fist.

Bunny made lefts and rights through a seedy industrial area, turned down a rutted asphalt road, slowed as she approached the entrance to Mentz's wrecking yard.

Doc closed his eyes, repeated his two new mantras: "That which I am seeking is seeking me," and "I've fallen in love with danger." When he opened his eyes, he was staring at an eight-foot-tall chain-link fence capped with cyclone swirls of razor wire.

A sign on the open gate read KEEP OUT.

Bunny didn't.

She rolled straight ahead, wound through a maze of rusted junkers with bullet-ridden windshields and stopped fifty feet short of a gray metal building the size of a small airplane hangar. She parked the Cadillac between a two-ton flatbed and a mountain of road-worn tires that smelled as though they'd recently been set on fire.

"I've got an idea," Bunny said. She stopped and buzzed up the windows to blunt the whack, bang, buzz of chainsaws, rivet guns, and sledgehammers.

Turning to face them, she said, "Why don't I go into the office, maybe just bring Jimmy with me? I do all the talking, see? The counter guy. I know the type. He'll have a pawnbroker's eye. He'll spot a con, a sob story, or a half-ass lie before either of you get two words out. He'll tell you to scram before he breaks your legs. But he won't want me to leave. He'll want me to be happy because the bozo believes someday maybe I'll make him happy. He'll talk to me. We want him to talk, right?"

They nodded. She understood the situation. She knew why they were there. Bunny had been listening.

Opening the door, she said, "Doc, it's not that I don't want you coming along. It's just that the calypso shirt and the exposed belly button might be a little distracting. Think you can occupy yourself for a while?"

"If you have some paper I could write. I've got this novel I'm working on. It's a mystery I'm going to sell to a magazine, maybe *True Detective*."

"Maybe it'll turn into a Broadway play." She reached over the front seat and jiggled his glasses. "Something Arthur Miller might write. Maybe Marilyn Monroe could make a cameo appearance?"

"I'd love to write something Marilyn would find worthy enough to appear in," Doc replied, blushing.

"Make sure it's a page turner," she said, reaching under the seat and retrieving a large ledger. "I keep a separate set of books for Big Lou. You'll find plenty of blank pages near the back."

Messing her hair to give it that I-just-got-out-of-bed look, Bunny got out of the car. Jimmy followed.

Doc, the ledger in his lap, started writing.

Using two gum erasers, a cat whisker, and a copper penny, Cinch wasted no time disarming the electric fence that surrounded the salvage yard.

"But the concertina wire, Cinch. It's impossible to get over the top of it. You'll be cut to ribbons."

Midnight could not disguise the twinkle in Cinch's eye, the glint of his pearl-white teeth as he held back a chuckle. His sidekick, the not-as-good-looking-as-he-was Jimmy, was always nervous.

"Not to worry, my compadre," Cinch said.

Slipping on kangaroo skin gloves that matched his custom kangaroo boots, Cinch grabbed two fistfuls of chain-link fencing, pulled back until the tortured wire screamed with metal fatigue, then slingshot, shooted, slungshot, whatever'd himself skyward. A twisting somersault appointed his primo landing on the other side of the fence.

"Wow," Jimmy said, bewildered.

"Just an old trick I learned from the Santinis that glorious summer I spent traveling with the Ringling Brothers."

"Wow."

Picking the gate's lock with a second cat's whisker, Cinch let Jimmy in.

"It should be easy from here, right?" Jimmy said.

That's when they heard the dogs growl.

As he waited in the car, Doc outlined the rest of the scene. The dogs would be rabid, slobbering Dobermans, at least six of them. Cinch and Jimmy would be pursued not only by the dogs but by ghostly figures captaining the gears of iron-clad monster machines, futuristic battlefield vehicles with rotating blades, cranes that swung spike-studded wrecking balls. For a moment he recalled the photo of Castro above

May's bed, and it occurred to him he might include, as villains in the scene, the Cubans who'd tried to run him down with their van, the ones who'd robbed La Paloma. But putting them in might distract from the story, slow the momentum of the narrative. He needed to keep his novel a page-turner, a tale in which, to save his best friend, the hero would suffer heroically.

Doc made a note to avoid presenting the Jimmy character as overly sympathetic. Perhaps, he thought, one of the dogs would turn out to be nice, become Jimmy's canine friend. He wasn't sure.

Catching sight of Jimmy and Bunny coming out of the office, Doc set down his pen. He tore out the pages he'd written, folded them, shoved them into his pocket.

The two of them climbed into the car. A flick of the ignition and a moment later they were on their way.

The salvage yard faded in the rearview mirror.

Pen poised again above a fresh sheet of paper, Doc waited to hear what had happened, but the pair, all chummy now, seemed, for the moment, to have formed a mutual admiration society.

"Well?" Doc said.

Jimmy turned in his seat. "You shoulda seen Bunny work the old buzzard behind the desk, Doc. She was all honey and long eyelashes. Smooth as silk."

Bunny leaned over and kissed Jimmy's cheek.

Doc exhaled slowly, tapped his pen to the page. "So what happened?"

"Here's the deal," Jimmy said. "The Studebaker *was* here. The guy we talked to was one of the mechanics that restored the Starliner Coupe after the crash in Carbon Canyon. The Studee sat on blocks for years before they found her a custom Bearcat motor that fit the engine well. Now check this out. It was stolen Christmas Eve three years ago."

"Then it *was* the car we saw that night. Wow." Doc leaned against the seat. "Wow."

Jimmy grinned. "Wanna throw in a golly gee whiz?"

Doc could feel his face redden. "What I meant was…cool, extremely cool."

"Sure." Jimmy cleared his throat. "Whoever took that car had the keys to the gate, the garage, and the Studebaker's ignition. The old man said he'd bet dollars to donuts the owner's grandson swiped the car, said it had to be the punk everyone calls Junior."

BELAFONTE'S ORPHAN SON

As Bunny drove back to Fullerton Music, Doc and Jimmy sat in silence. Though the day had brought several minor triumphs, the sad fact was no hard evidence connected Junior to the death of Jimmy's sister. And there were other questions left unanswered. There was still no way to explain the priest's silence, the reason he would collude with Junior, if or how Bonnie was involved.

"Even if we find the Studebaker," Doc said, "what good would it do? We put a car and a ghost on the witness stand? We'd get laughed out of court."

Jimmy stared out the passenger window. "If I believed in God, I'd say, 'Heaven help us.'"

"That's why we've got to meet Sister Theresa tonight at Saint Anthony's. She's the closest thing to heaven we can get our hands on. She wants us there for a reason."

Bunny stopped in front of the music store.

"Do me a favor," she said. "Keep an eye on Slatz."

They nodded.

Bunny turned to Doc. "Want me to drive you home? You can't go to the dance looking like Belafonte's orphan son."

Doc shook his head. "Can't risk it. Someone might see me."

"Got an idea," Bunny said. She pressed the release button for the trunk. "There's a suitcase in the back, check the hidden compartment below the spare tire. Big Lou asked me to make what's in there disappear, but I haven't gotten around to it. We'll pull in the alley. I think, among other things, there's clothes that just might fit you."

"I doubt it. Big Lou's…big."

"They're not Big Lou's. They belonged to a natty little weasel from East Jersey known as Eddie Two Nickels."

"Funny name."

"Not so funny when you understand 'two nickels' is what he didn't have to rub together when some business associates of Lou's asked him to pay the 'vig' on a debt he owed."

CRASH

Doc, looking slightly like Baby Face Nelson in what were probably a dead man's clothes, walked back to the music store. He'd thanked Bunny while they were in the alley. Thanked her twice, in fact. It was the second time this week she'd provided him with something to wear.

He found Jimmy in one of the rehearsal rooms practicing guitar. Word was, he said, for the past hour no one had seen Slatz. According to a fifth grade clarinet student, Slatz had gone upstairs looking for Scarlett, taking with him only an accordion and hastily written notes for an original gypsy rhapsody he'd composed. He hadn't returned.

"But he does know where we're going tonight, right?" Doc said.

"We talked about Saint Anthony's when we were in the car."

"Shall we hoof it or hitchhike?"

Jimmy held out his thumb.

Moments later, they stood in front of Fullerton Music, the sky above rouged pink like a powder puff, the streetlights on as evening approached.

Three rides took them into Anaheim. The first driver to stop was a mustached man in a European sports car. He told them they both appeared to be quite muscular, offered to take pictures of them.

The second driver was a middle-aged woman. She gave Jimmy a pocket Bible, inscribed a dedication to him, asked if he knew the Lord. Leaning across the front seat as they climbed out of the car, she said, "You're the All-Star pitcher from the Pony League Championship, right?" She smiled, her eyes eerily distant, black as coal. "You know what they say about pitchers…If they don't watch out, they'll throw their lives away."

Last to pick them up was a toothless man with a shock of white hair. He drove a battered truck, warned of the perils of scurvy. At the end of the ride, he handed Doc an orange, pointed to an illuminated bell tower beyond a cluster of abandoned industrial buildings, then gummed, "Saint Anthony's would be down that-a-way. Just follow the barranca." He rattled out a little prospector's chuckle. "This time of year that riverbed's dry as dust, and silent as an open grave."

They climbed out of the truck, stood next to each other beneath the last street lamp between them and the church.

Overhead, thunder rolled.

"Well," Doc said, jamming the orange into his pocket, "You ready to officially meet 'The Girl in the Pink Formal'?"

Jimmy nodded, squeezed the Bible he still held in his hand. They took a collective breath and started toward the church.

Paralleled by the riverbed, flanked by gray metal buildings, the asphalt alley loomed in Doc's eyes as a sinister study in collapsing perspective, a world where no matter how fast you walk, your destination keeps falling farther away. The place gave him the creeps, added to the vague sense of apprehension he'd felt in the presence of the three people who'd picked them up along the way.

"Hear that?" Jimmy asked, stopping suddenly.

Doc heard music funnel toward them.

"Probably coming from the church," he said.

"No. Not that." Jimmy looked around. "Listen."

A second sound separated itself from the darkness: the slap of shoes on asphalt. Someone running. Fast. Scared.

A shadowy figure sped past them. The runner's skinny backside, his long "Bojangles" legs, his pink and black striped shirt, his Brylcreemed ducktail gained illumination as the headlights of an oncoming car bore down on him.

"Slatz?" Jimmy called. "That you?"

The roar of the car drowned out his words.

The runner didn't look back. Gaining speed, out of earshot, he disappeared between two buildings.

The car kept coming. He and Jimmy were right in its path.

Panicked, Doc ran to the edge of the barranca, pressed his back against the cyclone fencing, expected to see Jimmy beside him.

But Jimmy wasn't there.

Instead Jimmy stood in the middle of the alley, motionless, defiant, staring straight into the headlights of the all-too-familiar beast: Junior's chop-top Mercury.

Doc tried to speak, yell out to Jimmy, "Move!" Nothing came out. His mind, like the needle of a stylus trapped in the groove of a broken record, stuttered, faltered.

Doc reached into his pocket, grasped the orange, recalled the smile on the face of the woman who'd said, "Pitchers throw their lives away."

He heard the wind whisper Jimmy's sister's name just as the Mercury drew parallel to him, sixty feet six inches away. Doc reached deep, drew back his arm, plugged in his best answer to what he guessed was a problem in trigonometry, then hurled the orange.

It traveled at biblical velocity, howled the air, its puckered skin smoothed to horsehide. Unbelievably, it headed to the point in time and space where Doc had aimed it.

The world became a slow-motion movie, spooled forward one frame at a time. He saw Fang in the driver's seat. He was laughing. A lit cigarette glowed between the fingers of the hand that held the wheel. With his other hand he poured M&Ms into his mouth, then tossed the bag aside, and lifted a half-full bottle of Bacardi to his lips.

A jet stream of orange shot through the open window of the Mercury.

The neck of the bottle exploded on impact.

Splinters of glass sprayed in all directions.

A sickening scream contorted Fang's features as his hands clawed at his face.

The last thing Doc saw before the world returned to full speed again was Fang's cigarette tumbling in the air like a fire-eater's baton toward the stack of wooden crates that filled the backseat of the Mercury.

Careening, the chop-top swerved, missed Jimmy, veered right, left, tore through the fence, exploding tumbleweeds, propelling them skyward as if some hand had prematurely lifted the lid off a giant popcorn maker.

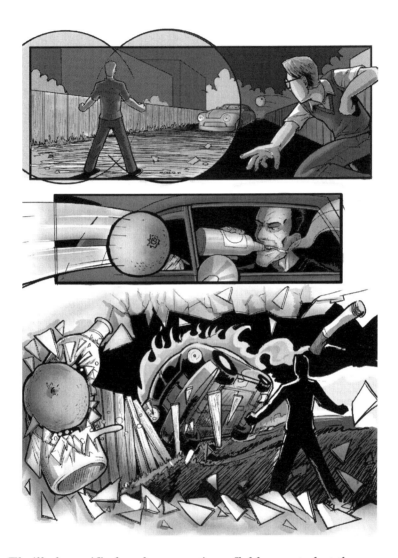

Thrilled, terrified at the same time, flabbergasted at the accuracy of his throw, Doc watched the Mercury shoot up and over the embankment, hover in space for one incredible, jaw-dropping moment, then plunge to the floor of the barranca.

The crash was brutal, cacophonous, loud as an elephant falling through a dozen skylights to the floor of a cymbal factory.

Running, meeting up with Jimmy along the way, Doc made it to the edge of the riverbed and looked over.

"Nice throw," Jimmy said. "Too bad it wasn't Junior behind the wheel."

"Don't know how I did it. Usually I can't hit the broad side of a barn."

Below them the Mercury lay flattened, squished. Its remains looked like a stomped-on scarab beetle. Its wheels, splayed out, were still spinning. A pink glow tinged with licks of flame spread across the backseat. The windshield had popped out. Fang lay sprawled across the hood, one outstretched hand clutching the car's antenna.

"He looks okay," Jimmy said. "I say we get out of here."

"We can't just leave him."

"Why not? The guy tried to bury you alive. He tried to run me down."

"He needs help, Jimmy. Take a look. The car's on fire." Doc blinked once, twice. "And I think I see someone in the passenger seat."

They scrambled over the tangled fencing, slid down the embankment on the seats of their pants and ran to the wreckage.

Doc stared into the car's interior.

"It's Scarlett," he said. "She's covered in blood."

They wrenched open the passenger door, pulled her out. Doc carried her fireman-style to the opposite embankment, set her down, kneeled over her. Limp, eyes closed, Scarlett was breathing raggedly. With one hand, he squeezed her arms, legs, ribcage. She didn't flinch. In fact she smiled, opened her eyes.

"I'll be fine, Doc," she said into his ear.

"You're bleeding."

"It's Hawaiian Punch. I stole a bottle of syrup from the church. Don't believe me, you can lick it."

"No thanks," he said.

"He won't let go of the antenna," Jimmy yelled out, motioning to Doc to help him pull Fang off the hood of the car.

Seeing a villain hurt was one thing. Letting him die was another. Doc got to his feet and ran toward the Mercury.

Flames engulfed the backseat of the Mercury and Doc, closer now, could smell gasoline. The boxes scattered through the car's interior, stenciled with "Hechos en Mexico," hissed and smoldered.

"Fireworks," Jimmy shouted. "Another thirty seconds the whole thing blows."

Together, they pulled Fang's legs. The red-hot antenna seared to Fang's hand snapped off at the hilt. They dragged him clear of the wreckage.

He fought them all the way, screaming through lips that bubbled blood. "Take your homo hands off me!"

They did. Dropped him on the pavement.

Jimmy stepped back. "Enjoy the fireworks, Fang. We're outta here."

They ran back to Scarlett, lifted her to her feet. Jimmy put his arm around her waist. Doc, standing on the opposite side, draped her arm over his shoulder. Supporting her, they headed for the top of the barranca.

Sirens wailed. Flashing lights drew near the crash site. Saint Anthony's bell clanged. Someone must have seen or heard what had happened. Help was on the way. Big trouble, too. The cops would want explanations. They'd look for someone to blame. They'd look for evidence.

Boom...boom, boom, boom.

Then again, maybe there wouldn't be any.

Roman candles shot through the broken windows of the Mercury, streaked through the sky. Strings of firecrackers machine-gunned the car's cabin, bottle rockets disintegrated the Mercury's interior. Pinwheels skittered, whirled wildly. A roar of M-80s blasted the car to smithereens. The sky became a snow globe of sparkling lights, the finale of the 1812 Overture, showtime on the Fourth of July.

Reaching the top of the barranca, Doc glanced at Scarlett. She was gazing into his eyes.

"Your secret's safe, Doc," she said. "I won't tell anyone you tried to murder us."

Doc pulled away. "I didn't try to murder anyone," he said. "Fang was gonna run Jimmy down. I had no idea you were in the car."

"She's kidding," Jimmy said. "Come on guys, there's cops everywhere. Let's get going."

Doc lagged behind them for a moment. "Kidding? This girl isn't kidding." She'd rattled him again and had loved it, had sent his mind running in circles just like she had when they were in her bedroom. He stopped. Ahead of him, Scarlett and Jimmy, dark silhouettes against a sky confettied with stars, worked their way through a section of torn-away fencing.

"Wanna tell us how you ended up in the car with Fang?" he shouted.

She turned. "What?"

"Were you the one who suggested it might be fun to chase Slatz with the car, maybe run him over?"

"I wasn't driving."

"You weren't behind the wheel, but that doesn't mean you weren't driving."

She glared at him. "What's that supposed to mean?"

"I'll tell you what it means, at least what I think it means." He climbed the slope, closed in on Scarlett. "See, I get this sneaky feeling you gave Slatz a ride to Saint Anthony's from the music store, brought him to the dance because he told you he was supposed to meet us here. Maybe before you left the store you gave Junior a call, tipped him off about where we'd be…You like to get boys in trouble, you like to see boys get hurt, don't you, Scarlett?"

Scarlett didn't budge. She blew out an oh-so exasperated breath, brushed back her hair. "You're the one in trouble, Doc," she said.

"Let's hear how I was the one who started all this. How I was the one who made you blow up Junior's car."

"Bet if we go back to the church we'll find out."

"Fine with me," she said. "It's your ass if the police stop us and force me to tell them what I know." She paused, put on her actress face. "Doc ran up to the car. He hit Fang in the face with a big sharp rock."

"It was an orange."

She took Jimmy's arm. "Come on."

A hundred yards beyond them, spotlights panned the riverbed, plumes of water arched from fire hoses, red lights pulsed through the smoke-filled air.

Scarlett clung to Jimmy, whispering to him as they walked side by side. "It was horrible," he heard her say. "I'm just glad to be alive." She wiped away alligator tears. She turned, gathered Doc in her eyes. "I don't know how I ended up in that car. I do have this hazy memory of being at the music store and Slatz asking if I'd give him a ride to Saint Anthony's. The rest is like a dream sequence from a horror movie. I have a memory of it now. It's all coming back to me: Slatz and I got to the church, we danced, but then he turned all evil on me, grabbed my arm, and dragged me to a room upstairs. He kissed me all over, talked about making organ music and I couldn't stop him." She shuddered. "It was all so confusing."

"Yeah," Doc said. "I can see how confused you are."

Glaring at Doc, Jimmy draped his jacket over Scarlett's shoulders. "First things first. We get out of here. Talk about what everybody was doing later."

Doc turned away. "Fine. Live to fight another day. I get it." He hated to admit it but Jimmy was probably right. They didn't need Scarlett talking to the police and he had to get back to Bonnie's. It was time to get Snowball home.

Clinging to shadows, ducking into doorways, the trio worked their way along the alleyway and within minutes had stirred themselves into the cluster of kids who'd forsaken the dance for the crash scene at the riverbed. Emergency vehicles were everywhere. Firemen dragged hoses. Cops shone flashlights into teenage faces, looking for telltale signs of complicity or guilt.

Out of the corner of his eye, Doc saw Detective Quinn pull up, get out of his car. Notepad in hand, he climbed through the broken fencing and began Sherlocking the crime scene.

Standing next to Doc, Scarlett made a big deal of zipping up the jacket Jimmy had given her. "Wouldn't want anyone seeing me covered in 'blood.'" She gave Doc a peck on the cheek. "See, I'm on your side."

Doc said nothing. He moved through the crowd, listened to whispers, rumors, rumors of rumors, secondhand eyewitness accounts. He overheard one girl say some chick had spiked the Hawaiian Punch, that a fight had broken out when some girl's dad busted up a mad make-out session going on upstairs.

There was endless talk of the mystery man, a dude in a pink and black striped shirt who'd been at the center of it all, a lanky kid with a lipstick-smeared face who'd come downstairs, taken on Junior Mentz and his rat-faced cousin Fang. Shaking his head, one guy added, "Couldn't throw a punch, but tell you one thing, that cat could really run."

Jimmy and Doc looked at each other, spoke the same name at the same time: "Slatz."

On the move again, they chameleoned their way through the crowd.

Near the steps that led to the chapel, there was a moment of good news. Doc heard a policeman say the kid driving the car was busted up and burnt but would probably be okay. That was followed by the statement of the parish priest. Hands clasped, he said to a reporter, "Saw the whole thing. 'Twas a bolt of lightning took the chop-top to its 'final reward.' God rest its soul."

Jimmy nudged Doc. "Let's hope that's what Quinn believes."

Ahead of them, Scarlett, who'd strayed away a few moments earlier, waited beneath a streetlight, car keys in her hand.

Jimmy went over to her, said a few words, came back.

"I told her you and I were supposed to meet someone. She's okay waiting a few minutes," he said. "I'll keep an eye on her. You take a look inside the church, Doc. See if you can find Pinkie."

Doc climbed the broad stone steps that led to the entrance of Saint Anthony's, went inside. The chapel and sanctuary were empty. Nothing there except the echo of his own footsteps. Further down a corridor, in the parish hall, silver streamers dangled lifelessly above a makeshift dance floor sticky with Hawaiian Punch. A record ticked on its last groove.

Disappointed, Doc realized he and Jimmy would go home tonight without getting what they'd come for. There would be no meeting with Pinkie, no new revelations that might unravel the mystery surrounding Cindy's death. He turned to leave but stopped, suddenly aware of the toad-like man in a dark suit standing at the far end of the dance floor: Scarlett's father, Dr. Brisco. He lifted the needle from the record, hooded the turntable with a plastic cover, clicked off the overhead light.

For a moment Doc stood in the darkness, didn't move. Neither did the shadowy form of the psychologist. Doc took a step forward. "Excuse me sir, I was looking for someone: a young nun. Maybe you've seen her?"

No words came back. Only the flick of a lighter. Doc watched the flame gather in the spectral depths of the man's coke-bottle lenses, heard the asthmatic inhalation that brought a glow to the tip of the cigarette.

"Okay," Doc said. "Guess I'll be going."

A SMALL BLACK BOOK

Doc met Jimmy and Scarlett near the streetlight, shook his head. "She wasn't there, but *your dad was there*, Scarlett. How does that make any sense?"

Her eyes filled with tears. "He helps provide spiritual counseling. He volunteers. He was downstairs. Thank God he heard me screaming. He caught Slatz trying to feel me up. I think it was my dad. I'm not sure. I must have fainted."

"Yeah," Doc said. "You 'fainted.' Just like you did when I was in your bedroom. Funny how your dad always gets there just in time to save you. Or is it that he just likes to watch what's going on?"

A horn honked. A car rolled past them. Doc looked over, recognized the battered pickup with the faded paint. It was the last car to stop for them up on their way to Saint Anthony's. This time the old man had a passenger. Next to him was the lady with the faded sugar-cookie cheeks who'd given Jimmy the Bible. She offered them a know-it-all grin, shrugged her shoulders, made the sign of the cross. The fingernails of the hand she used were *painted pink*.

They looked at each other.

Steam rose inside Doc, whistled the tea kettle of his brain. "Where's the Bible, Jimmy? The one that lady gave you?"

Jimmy patted his pants, shrugged, glanced in the direction of the wreck. Together, they watched Quinn hesitate, stoop to pick up what looked like a small black book.

BAKING SODA AND
DRY MUSTARD

Scarlett drove them north in the direction of Bonnie's house. Doc, riding in the backseat, looking out the window, watched the moon sail across a sea of clouds etched silver at the edges. The radio was up loud, the song, Conway Twitty's "It's Only Make Believe."

"So you think it was Pinkie ridin' in that pickup?" Jimmy whispered to Doc over the front seat.

"It was her all right," Doc said. "The old geezer driving was probably God. What a pair."

"Thought God was supposed to make the crooked ways straight, not put a Bible with my name in it in the hands of the police."

Doc wanted to say something like "He works in mysterious ways," but he wasn't in the mood.

Scarlett stopped the car in front of Bonnie's. She looked at the house, shook her head. "What a dump. What sort of loser leaves his little sister here?"

Doc got out of the car, slammed the door. He'd barely made it to the porch when the front door opened.

A chubby Mexican lady, the same lady Doc had first seen cooking tortillas at La Paloma, blocked the entrance. She put big hands on big hips.

"So you leave Bonnie with a sick niña," she said. "You do this to be with your freckle-faced girlfriend?"

Doc wasn't in the mood to be scolded. "Two things," he said. "What are you talking about? And how is it any of your business?"

"I'm the next door neighbor. And you're in trouble."

Doc pushed past her big hips into the living room. The television was on. No Bonnie. No Snowball.

"Hello?"

"Shhh!"

Bonnie was standing just inside the hallway. She motioned him to follow her.

The passage smelled of mustard, clove, and eucalyptus. A red glow flickered from the open door ahead of them. Doc, the condemned man, let Bonnie lead him into the small bedroom.

His stomach sank. Snowball lay sprawled on a simple twin bed, her face illuminated by six votive candles arranged above her head in the shape of a cross. She had slices of what looked like potatoes on her forehead and was...swaddled in something?

Bonnie touched Snowball's cheek. "She's asleep. The fever's finally broken."

"What's she wrapped in?"

"Cornhusks soaked in baking soda and dry mustard. Mrs. Martinez's idea. Guess it draws out the fever." She looked at him, disappointment written all over her face. "I called the music store. You said you'd be there practicing. Apparently, that was a lie." She snuggled the cornhusks around Snowball's body. "So you were out with some girl?"

"No. It wasn't like that at all."

There was a knock at the open bedroom door.

Bonnie looked up. Reluctantly Doc turned around. He had a bad feeling.

Scarlett, no longer wearing Jimmy's jacket, dressed only in a bra and skirt, leaned against the doorway. She held her punch-soaked blouse in her hand. "Mind if I toss this in your washer?"

A BALANCING ACT

Back home, Doc placed Snowball in the canopied "big girl" bed she'd been promoted to. He checked her pajamas for potato slices, bits of cornhusk. They'd be hard to explain.

Closing the door, he walked through the living room, switched on a table lamp, turned the TV on. The theme to *Perry Mason* was playing in the background when he picked up the phone and dialed Bonnie's number.

"Don't hang up," he said when she answered. "I'm coming over tomorrow. We'll babysit together. I'll cook and clean. I'll fix your vacuum. I didn't do anything wrong."

He could hear her breathing. She took short, exasperated breaths. She was still mad. "See you tomorrow," she said flatly.

"You won't be sorry."

A soft click. A dial tone. No words of goodbye.

In the kitchen, he set the stage for his parents' return. He dirtied a few plates with some concoction smothered in white gravy he found in a covered casserole dish, spooned some of the same stuff into a pan and scorched it on the stove. Filling the sink with sudsy water, he looked out through the daffodil curtains.

Gliding above Scarlett's house, a cloud like a pale gloved hand covered the mouth of the Man in the Moon. He thought about his encounter with Scarlett's father at Saint Anthony's, the image of Slatz running down the alleyway in the wake of something that had occurred upstairs in the church. There was a game going on between father and daughter, a game that produced some sick thrill for those at the center of it. The only word to describe it was "unspeakable."

Shutting off the water, he wandered back to Snowball's bedroom, smoothed her dandelion hair, lay down next to the little saboteur who tonight had been both his cohort and collaborator. She opened her eyes, blinked, spoke the word, "Dumbo," then drifted off.

Lying on his back next to her, Doc smiled, realizing for once she hadn't been referring to him. Above his head, dangling from the canopy, was a mobile. Set in motion by a breeze that came from the open window, the figures played off the tension of each other. They Caldered, floated, danced in lazy circles. A balancing act of sorts. There was of course an elephant, along with a cavalcade of other characters: a coyote, a man in the moon, a squawking crow, a sugar plum fairy pretty as a princess, a wise man, an angel, a fool. Doc wondered if, months ago, Pinkie in the guise of a shop girl had sold the mobile to his parents, offered it up to Doc now as the last punch line of the day. He closed his eyes. Dozed. Awoke and slept again.

At some point during the night, the bedroom door creaked. A crease of light fell across his face.

"Isn't that sweet?" he heard his mother say.

A deeper voice said, "Sweet? My guess is with everyone gone the boy was afraid to sleep alone. Could at least have had the good sense to turn off the TV."

MYTHOLOGY

The news was out, ears were buzzing. From the minute Doc walked on campus, talk of "the crash" was wagging the tongues of everyone from janitors to class presidents. Theories, rumors, speculations abounded. They eddied the hallways, whirlpooled through classrooms, cascaded from the principal's office all the way down to the 4H farm at the bottom of the hill. He'd gotten to class late. Took his seat and listened.

"They say he claims he's got posttraumatic amnesia, Miss Mooseman, maybe even brain damage. The whole thing sounds fishy to me and I'm not the only one." Luanne Lauderbeck, earnest-faced, stood next to her desk in the third row. He didn't know how long she'd been talking. It seemed she wasn't about to stop. "Did I mention one of the nurses told my mother who told me, in strictest confidence, some of the doctors at Saint Jude think the whole amnesia thing's asinine. Now that makes sense 'cause sure Fang's head's all banged up and blistered, but it was his *butt*, not his brain that got blasted in the explosion. Twice the normal size and brighter than a baboon's ass, that's what the nurse said it looked like."

Miss Mooseman wobbled a moment, stabilized her beret with the palms of her delicate hands. "Thank you for that contribution, Luanne. You may sit down now. I'm sure we all appreciate your...

282

enthusiasm." Miss Mooseman gave Doc one of her Jane Austin smiles. "Again, I think what we're looking for here, class, would be expressions of concern, something from the heart that might help us make sense of the senseless tragedy that has befallen a fellow Lancer."

Hands went up.

Mildred Mooseman gathered a breath, pointed. "Yes, Russell, go ahead. Your thoughts."

"Coach Ugler says the Japs are to blame 'cause they invented fireworks."

She chewed her cheek, smoothed her Indian-print skirt, forced a smile. "The coach has a novel idea there. One of many off-topic theories I've heard him express over the years. In this case he might have been referring to the Chinese. Most historians believe Marco Polo introduced fireworks to the western world on his return from China."

"Marco Polo," Russell said. "Same guy who invented the swimming pool, right?"

Doc put his head on the desk. He'd been in first period History with Russell Schliker, Luanne, Slatz too, and what Russell had reported to Miss Mooseman was true. Ugler had spent the entire hour talking about the crash, had drawn it up on the blackboard using *x*'s and *o*'s to show how the "Nips" had infiltrated the explosives trade, had used Mexican priests hopped up on fluoridated water to "mule" the stuff across the border. Pointing his coach's whistle at them, he'd said, "It's the old end around game, kids, and all the blood money goes straight to Kennedy's war chest. Before ya know it, we'll all be eating fish on Fridays."

Any other day, Slatz would have looked over at Doc and rolled his eyes at "Big Bob" Ugler's jackass comments. But not this morning. Slatz had spent nearly all of first period staring trancelike into the blank blackboard. He'd been pensive as Rodin's statue. Silent as the sphinx. He'd left class before the bell rang. Just disappeared. Doc's long-legged friend had definitely been shaken up last night, no doubt about that. But it wasn't just that he'd had to outrace a car that was trying to mow him down. Something else had sent him running down that alley and Doc was sure most of it had to do with being caught upstairs in the church with Scarlett, caught by a "concerned" father who "just happened" to be there.

A feeling of unease crawled through Doc's brain, wormed through his gray matter, the infiltration unearthing within his mind something akin to a memory: the night he'd been in Scarlett's bedroom, he recalled having the vague sense Dr. Brisco had been standing in the doorway all along, a belief the frog-eyed man hadn't "conveniently" arrived at the worst possible moment. And there was another thing that troubled Doc: the man's demeanor had been just plain creepy, and the questions he'd asked had been so weird, and yet, in a way, he seemed...satisfied.

The bell rang.

Miss Mooseman dismissed the class, reminded them to read the next chapter of *The Mill on the Floss*. "Pay attention to the author's choice of imagery: blood and water as it relates to the theme of incest."

The last word Miss Mooseman spoke separated itself from every particle of speech that came before it, wrote itself again in capital letters: INCEST. In his mind, the word became something seen from the window of a train traveling through the night. A train that carries you as the only passenger. The word lights up in the distance, illuminates the night like advertising written on a billboard. The word appears, then disappears. Doc knew nothing about this word beyond its dictionary definition. He understood the meaning, but only in the way you understand an abstract symbol, a concept or a theme. It was a word that lived in ancient mythologies, in Greek tragedies. But stories like Oedipus weren't real. Incest wasn't real, was it? He found himself staring into the blackboard in the same way Slatz had.

"Doc," Miss Mooseman said, "shouldn't you be getting to your next class?"

"Can I ask you a question? It's about a friend of mine."

"Is this friend you, Doc?"

"No. She's a girl."

"Okay. Go on."

"Let's say this girl's a character in a story I'm writing. She's not the protagonist. She was just added as a minor character, like the Cubans, but I can't get her out of the story. The whole thing takes place in a fictional world, of course. Probably a long time ago. Not around here."

"A classical tale, set in ancient times? A historical romance?"

"Sort of. There are sex things in the story but that's all right, isn't it? 'Cause it was a long time ago when sex wasn't so much a physical act but a metaphor for power or symbolic of an ultimate betrayal? It's not like something that happens in the backseat of a car. Normally I wouldn't bring up something like this with a teacher."

"We can talk about sex in the context of literature."

He took a breath. "In several scenes, this girl falls asleep or faints or something when her father gets close to her. When there's sex going on in the general vicinity of her body."

"She's having sex with her father?"

Doc couldn't bring himself to speak. For days now, he'd tried to push away the words Scarlett had whispered to him in her bedroom: "Cut me free. Let me fly." Her words painted pictures he didn't want to see.

Miss Mooseman cleared her throat. "Let me ask, why does this story take place so far in the past? Is it because you're trying to push it out of your mind?"

"I don't think things like that happen now. It's just stuff like you put in a story to dramatize a theme, right?"

Miss Mooseman took a long, deep, penetrating look at him.

"I'm going to respond in two ways," she said. "First, I'm going to comment on the scene you described. The reference to 'fainting' interests me. It reminds me of something not from the ancient past but rather from recent history...During World War II, not all Jewish women were sent to gas chambers. Some were imprisoned, forced to have sex with Nazi officers. I know a woman who survived this personal hell. She told me when the Germans would come into her room she'd close her eyes and go far away. It was her way of not being there while she was being raped."

"But what if…in the story, the girl doesn't seem afraid of the man. She acts like they're, I don't know, like they're partners."

"The answer to that is probably very complex." She put her hand on Doc's shoulder. "I need you to be honest with me. Do you fantasize that you're a girl?"

"What…? No."

"Are you confused?"

"I'm a little confused right now."

"Hmm." She took a step back. "Has Fang's accident, the injury to his buttocks, made you more acutely aware of your confusion?"

"I think we're headed in the wrong direction here," Doc said.

Miss. Mooseman stared into the distance.

"Twice in my career, troubled boys have passed through my classroom. There have been more occasions than that of course, but these two boys in particular haunt me. One involved a young man who committed suicide three years ago on Christmas Eve. The other tragically involves the boy who's in the hospital now. I tried to get them help. I don't know if either followed my recommendation. But I'm going to give you the advice I gave them: I want you to see Dr. Brisco. He's our school psychologist. He's well-respected. He's modern, post-Kinsean. I think you might warm up to him. He's frequently able to touch young men and women with identity issues."

"Dr. Brisco?"

"Get help now, Doc. Let's take you out of the classroom for the rest of the day." She went to her desk. "I'm writing out a hall pass. Tell the aid in the nurse's office I'm referring you for psychological help."

GOT A LETTER TO MAIL

Referral slip in hand, Doc took the long way around the school to the administration building. Outside, in the fresh air, this route took him past the gym, the shop building and the music department. He needed a few extra minutes to sort things out. He needed a breath of tranquility.

No such luck.

As he came around the side of the music building, he heard noises: scraping, banging sounds, an anguished cry.

He stopped, peered through the small rectangular window in the door of the first room. What he saw startled him. The blackboard had been savaged by the hand of a musical maniac. Though what was written on it looked like music, no respect had been given to staying inside ledger lines. Time signatures, the conventions of composition had been totally disregarded.

If this frenetic composition was meant for the piano, it would need to be played with fists, not fingers.

Through the haze of chalk dust, he saw Slatz in the back of the room standing over the teacher's desk. He was attacking the typewriter keys in the same way he'd apparently gone after the blackboard. He had something to say and someone he had a message for.

Doc tried the knob.

Locked.

He pounded the door. "Slatz!"

He felt a tap on his shoulder. Before he could turn, the back of his legs exploded in pain. He dropped to the asphalt, writhed, twisted, shielded his head with one arm, pulled himself with the other, slid till he managed to prop his shoulders against the music room door. The lower half of his body felt as though he'd been electrocuted. It hurt to breathe.

He looked up.

Junior stood over him. A baseball bat dangled from one hand.

"Stopped by the hospital today, four-eyes. Talked to Fang." He swung the bat again. The meat end of the barrel slammed against the door a few inches above Doc's head. "Seems you were a busy boy last night."

Doc curled into a ball, covered his head with his hands. The music room door pushed open behind him. Slatz, startled at first, stared down at him, then at Junior. The torment Slatz had expressed on the walls of the music room had apparently not quite exhausted itself. It overflowed, bubbled into rage.

In a lightning-quick move, Slatz stepped over Doc, swung a fist at Junior, missed, then stomped the heel of his skunk oxford down on the top of one of Junior's black boots.

The boot didn't move.

The bat did. Junior raised it above his head.

A coach's whistle blew. The bat froze in space.

Ugler's meaty hand was wrapped around its barrel.

He squinted down at Doc, poked a finger into the chests of Slatz and Mentz. "What are you Jackwads up to?" He grabbed the bat from Mentz. "It's not baseball season. Get off this campus. You're trespassing."

From his rabbit hole view, Doc watched Junior back away, keep going.

Ugler turned his attention to Slatz. "What's your story, pansy ass?"

Slatz dug in his pocket, held out a sealed envelope. "Got a letter to mail, Coach. It's…it's important. It's a secret…uh, uh…a surprise." He smiled. "Made a deal with a record company to record your theme: the Lancer fight song. If it goes platinum, you'll be famous."

Ugler's eyes glazed over, then brightened. "Nice thinkin', good work. Now get out of here."

Slatz ran. Ugler zeroed in on Doc.

Still on the ground, Doc held up a slip of paper. "Hall pass. I'm supposed to go to the nurse's office. I'm kinda paralyzed."

PLAUSIBLE DENIAL

Margaret Ann yanked Doc's arm, pulled him into the nurse's office. "What are you doing here?"

His answer came out as a raw yip of pain. He balanced on legs stiff as celery stalks, gathered a breath, staggered forward. "I was sent here," he said, flopping face down on the examination table.

She closed the door, slid the curtain across the window that looked out on the interior hallway, whispered, "Did you know the cops are here? I heard them say they were going to yank you and Jimmy out of class, interrogate you two separately."

Doc tried to pull himself up. His hamstrings spasmed. Wincing, he rolled onto his back. "I have no idea what you're talking about."

"The police, Doc. They've already brought Jimmy in. He's in a room down the hall. Something about an 'attempted murder' last night. What in God's name have you done?" She looked at him. "The crash at Saint Anthony's?"

"It was an accident."

"Great," she said. "So it wasn't attempted murder, it was just attempted manslaughter."

Doc struggled to his feet. From the waist down, he felt wooden, like a man on stilts. "Last night, Fang tried to run down Jimmy. I hit him with an orange."

"I assume 'him' means Fang, though you wouldn't know it from the two sloppy sentences you just strung together. If you want to be a writer, take command of your pronouns." She put on her cat glasses, buttoned the starched lab jacket. "Go on."

"After I hit him, Fang, the car went out of control. Flew over the embankment into the barranca. Fang and the car."

"So you're saying it was self defense? You were trying to save Jimmy? You hit Fang on *purpose* but the accident was…an accident? You tell that to the police, it'll sound like mumbo jumbo. When it comes to boys your age, the police don't believe in accidents."

"So I'll tell them it was something else. How 'bout this: The whole thing was directed by the hand of fate, was part of God's plan to make the crooked places straight? Or was caused by a convergence of the unseen forces from the spirit world? The more I think about it, the more I believe that's what the truth is."

She groaned. "That's going to be your defense? Listen up, pal, the courtroom isn't a theology symposium. The district attorney's not gonna put up with you babbling about God and destiny. He's gonna wanna send your sorry ass up the river. You've already got a juvenile file. They've got the word of a priest who says you're a pervert. They may know about you desecrating graves at the cemetery."

"I wasn't desecrating a grave. I was buried alive. It wasn't very deep, but there was plenty of dirt on me."

She snorted. "A technicality. The fact is you've been erratic, out of control. You're practically a menace to society. Look at the situation you've put your friend in." She stared over the top of her glasses, looked at his legs, eyed his posture. "Are you trying to conceal an erection?"

"I'm standing this way because ten minutes ago Junior bashed my legs with a baseball bat. I was sent to the office because Miss Mooseman thinks I'm having an identity crisis."

"You were sent to the nurse's office because a faculty member thinks you're mentally ill? Why doesn't that surprise me?"

"I'm supposed to get a referral to Dr. Brisco. How do you like that for irony?"

"There's no first aid for irony, but I am ethically obligated to see if I can unspaz your legs. I want you face down. Loosen your belt. Get back on the table. We need to attack those hamstrings."

Doc climbed on the table, sighed. "I think Dr. Brisco is doing things to his daughter."

She handed him a tongue depressor. "Why do you insist on making things bigger than they really are?" she said, sliding down his pants. "Now bite down."

Doc bit down.

Lotioning up her hands, she dug in.

Through gritted teeth, Doc said, "My gut tells me Brisco's somehow in the middle of all this; if not in the center of the middle, he's somewhere just off to the side. Know what I'm gonna do? I'm gonna sit down across from this so-called psychologist. I'm gonna shrink the shrink. What I uncover will blow the roof off this town."

"*You're* gonna shrink the shrink? Meanwhile Jimmy rots in jail for a crime you committed."

Doc's body sagged, everything but his rigid legs. "Okay. Fine. I'll turn myself in. Head down the hall and tell the police everything. I'm the one they want. I'll confess. But I am gonna tell them about Brisco."

"Confess and you're an idiot." She ran hot water in the sink, scrubbed her hands. "Stand up. Pull up your pants."

"So now saving my friend makes me an idiot?"

"Tell me this," she said. "What do they have on Jimmy? Witnesses? Evidence?"

"Maybe a Bible with his name in it." He buckled his belt.

She paced, Perry Masoned back and forth, tapped her chin with her right index finger. "This Bible has his signature? An inscription in his handwriting?"

"No."

"A Bible found at the scene of a crime is circumstantial at best. Your friend Jimmy's gonna walk. They can't touch him. Look, Doc, you came to the nurse's office because you were at the brink of insanity, right? At the time you were sent here, you had no idea my father wanted to interrogate you. Answer the question directly. Prior to coming here, did you know the police wanted to talk to you?"

"No, I did not."

She nodded. "The way I look at it, since Detective Quinn chooses to exclude his *own* daughter in his investigations, and considering the fact that she, namely I, therefore, have no knowledge of what he's doing here, it would seem plausible, out of compassion, that I, a qualified student nurse, would give you a ride home on my way to my next assignment. As editor of the school newspaper, *The Accolade*, I've been granted permission to leave campus. I'm going to the hospital to cover the story of our fallen classmate, Frankie 'Fang' Faletti. Your home is on the way. I'm perfectly justified in taking you there. In this scenario I have plausible denial and a perfect alibi."

"But I don't want to go home."

"I'm not taking you home, you idiot. We're going somewhere where no one will find us and I'm going to help you figure out what you think you know. I don't care if I have to squeeze your brain like a sponge. If there's a truth out there that's going to blow the roof off this town, I want the byline and the headline."

CONSECRATED GROUND

They went out the back door, Doc head down, walking better, a hospital blanket draped over his shoulders, Margaret Ann "comforting" him, supporting his stiff-legged gait all the way to her car. They climbed into her Chevy, the one painted the color of indigestion.

Pistons clattering, Margaret Ann took the back way, drove the graveled road that ran behind the 4H farm, then fishtailed onto the highway that led over the hill and out of town.

"You need more rpm. You're in the wrong gear," Doc said. "Drop it into second." The engine pinged in support of his suggestion.

Margaret Ann paid no attention to either comment.

She turned toward him, took her eyes off the road for a dangerously long time. "You understand you and I together represent a very ephemeral, event-specific destiny. There is no destiny here in any greater sense of the word."

"Fine with me." Doc looked around. "Exactly where are we going?"

"Think we'll picnic at Ascension Park. Two reasons: One, I'm still convinced there's more we need to learn about the dead. Two, I'm hungry." She made a hand signal out the window though there were no other cars in sight and looked down at the floorboard as if checking to see if something was stuck to one of her shoes. The Chevy drifted across the centerline. "Catch me up on things," she said. "I find my thought process becomes extremely acute when I'm driving."

"That's because…" He stopped himself. "Okay. I'll tell you everything that happened yesterday. Just don't get mad, promise? And please keep your eyes on the road."

Doc talked. Told her about the accident, about Scarlett, about Scarlett's dad being at the church. The series of revelations he'd had in Miss Mooseman's class.

She kept her eyes on the road, practically riveted. She gripped the steering wheel with an intensity that blanched her knuckles. He could hear her teeth grinding. "Oh really," she said. "Tell me more."

Doc did. He told her about the Pike, the fortune straight from the Swami's mouth, about Pinkie the prostitute, and his encounter with May. "With May it was a real breakthrough," Doc said. "It was like she was a genius. I left there feeling so…competent."

Steam seemed to rise from Margaret Ann's head, her curls humidified, her freckles pulsed.

"Women like that are paid to make you feel…competent. Let me guess: You gave her money."

Fifteen minutes later, her jaw still clenched, Margaret Ann drove between the giant wrought iron gates that marked the entrance to Ascension Park. Climbing the hill to the visitor's center, she rolled to a stop a dozen yards from a hearse.

She turned to him, her eyes rimmed in red. Her nose made a little sniffy sound. "I think that Swami's fortune was meant for you and me, for our partnership in solving crimes…not you and that leopard-pantied cowgirl prostitute."

He'd told her too much, had used too many adjectives in his storytelling. He felt bad. "This is really about your dad, isn't it?" he said. "You think he doesn't notice you but I'm sure he does. He knows you're smart, pretty. Wait'll we crack the one case he's never solved. It's gonna happen. It's happening right now." He took her hand. "Remember how you saw the sign in the background of the photograph in the newspaper: Mentz's Tow and Salvage? That sign *wanted* you to see it. It was seeking you…The first day, when I came to the library, you sewed my pants. I told you what I saw from the roof of the church."

She sniffed again, managed a smile. "I hated you seeing Scarlett naked."

"But don't you remember? You said, 'Blame the girl.' Turns out you were right. I had it backward. I was seeking the truth and you…threw it in my face. And now we're here." Doc looked out the car window. "Holy Christ." He yanked Margaret Ann toward him, pulled her down on the front seat, threw himself on top of her.

"Get off me, you sex maniac."

"Shhh." He put his hand over her mouth. "Father Stephen. He's out there by the hearse."

She spoke through his fingers. "What's he doing?"

"I don't know. I think he's just standing there."

"What do we do?" she whispered.

"Guess we just lie here. I could try sliding up or down."

"Don't you dare. You keep your face right where I can see it."

Outside they heard labored steps, a door swing open, the weight of something heavy fall then glide across a metal surface.

Her exhalations fogged up his glasses. He could really, really feel her breath rise and fall against his chest.

"What are you doing?" she asked suspiciously.

"Nothing…just listening."

She squinted. "What else did you do yesterday?"

The "what else" was what he didn't want to tell her. But he did.

"Bunny LaDesma, Slatz's mom, took us to the salvage yard. Sorry."

"You said *we* were going to go. Apparently that which you were seeking wasn't me when it came to the salvage yard."

"I'm really sorry, it just worked out that way. But you were right. The Studebaker was stolen from there Christmas Eve three years ago. The same night Cindy was killed. The same night Buddy committed suicide. The old guy who works the counter said Junior *had* to be the one who stole the car. I think he and Buddy were driving around together. No way to know who was driving when the car crashed into Cindy."

Two more doors slammed.

The hearse's engine rumbled. Gravel crunched beneath its tires as it rolled away.

They sat up, peered out like prairie dogs.

Ricky the giant, rake in hand, was staring at them from just outside the back door of the visitor's center.

Doc rolled down the passenger window. They both forced smiles, managed tentative waves.

Ricky walked over to the Chevy. "Good to see 'initiation' boy again. I see you pass test. Have gorgeous sorority chickie now."

Doc and Margaret Ann climbed out.

Margaret Ann pressed the pleats of her skirt, straightened her cat glasses. "I'm not some chickie, I'm the editorial director of the—"

Doc put up a hand. "Ricky, do you know why Father Stephen was here?"

"It great day. They move priest brother's body to consecrated ground. Archbishop make pronouncement, give special dispensation for suicide. The Correge of Cardinals say crazy people not know killing themselves mortal sin. Priest waiting long time to hear this news."

"Interesting," Margaret Ann said. "Think I'll get my purse and the blanket. Is there somewhere we can picnic? Perhaps a spot equidistant between the location of Buddy's grave, the grave where Pinkie's boyfriend is buried, and the place Doc's 'fraternity brothers' tried to bury him alive. I believe there might be a vortex of energy there. Vibrations."

"Vibrations? Sure. I show you."

Shaking his head, Doc followed Margaret Ann and Ricky through the maze of headstones, the sea of white crosses to the hillside above the rose garden, to the place he'd seen Pinkie dancing.

They laid out the blanket. Margaret Ann set her purse down. It tilted. A baseball rolled from its cavernous interior onto the grass. "What's this?" Doc asked, picking up the ball. He turned it in his hand. Jimmy's flamboyant signature was scrawled across the horsehide.

"It's a homerun ball. A souvenir. Might be valuable someday."

Doc chewed the inside of his cheek, put the ball back in her purse.

Margaret Ann grabbed the purse, took out a few chicken drumsticks, and unwrapped sandwiches with the crusts trimmed. She spread out the puzzle pieces. Closing her eyes, she Ouijaed the tips of her fingers over the cogs and wheels she'd cut from paper. Selected one at random.

Doc knelt on the blanket opposite her, exasperation rising in his blood like a column of mercury in a hothouse thermometer. Silently he counted to ten, asked, "What, pray tell, are you doing?"

"Detecting. Entering the field of universal thought through the portal of feminine intuition. Is Ricky gone? I don't want to begin till we're alone."

Doc glanced over his shoulder, picked up a chicken drumstick from the plate she'd prepared. Bit off a piece. Chewed. "No one here except you, me, and the dead."

Margaret Ann squinted at the puzzle piece she held in hand. "Perfect." She showed Doc the name written on it: Buddy.

"So we're ready to get started?"

"Not just yet," she said. "I need you to close your eyes. I've prepared a meditation for you. One that will hopefully bring you closer to androgyny, lower your testosterone."

"I'm not closing my eyes and I'm not lowering anything."

She sighed. "You've got to understand, a boy's mind is like a dog off a leash. Left unchecked, it runs in circles, barking and yapping, doing that disgusting sniffing thing." She patted his knee. "And we both know what that's all about. Anyway, I need you thinking clearly. I need you to work with me."

He gnawed off a piece of chicken, swallowed without "Fletcherizing."

Margaret Ann looked off into the distance. "We will be using Occam's razor if you have no objections."

He had no idea what she was talking about, but whatever it was made him smile. She never gave up. And there was that annoying look in her eyes, that persistent, irresistible, conniving innocence that made him believe when she asked him for something, the request came with an unspoken "pretty please" on top. He acquiesced. "What's Occam's razor? Better not be something in your purse."

She sparkled. "No, silly. It's a detective's tool." She steepled her fingers, leaned in conspiratorially. "Sherlock Holmes used it all the time to solve mysteries. Occam's razor is the principle that says the simplest explanations are usually the correct ones. It says stay away from complex assumptions, motives that only make sense in the rarest circumstances. Let's try it." She held up the puzzle piece with Buddy's name on it. "He committed suicide. Why?"

Doc used the "razor." "Do we know it was suicide? How do we know Buddy wasn't murdered?"

"The police said it was suicide."

Doc shrugged. "The police said Cindy's death was an accident. When I first talked to your dad I told him I wanted to help find the person who *murdered* Cindy. He didn't correct me."

"I'm sure he meant—"

Doc stopped her. "Why would you assume your dad meant something else? If he had, he would have corrected me." He grabbed the puzzle piece from her, rifled through the others till he found Junior's card, held them both up. "I think these two guys were in the car together. Everything points to the fact Junior stole the Studebaker. He had keys to the gate, knew where the keys to the car were. His grandfather never reported the car stolen. He's not the type to let someone else be the guy behind the wheel. How 'bout that for Occam's razor?"

"So if we assume Junior ran down Cindy, how does that begin to explain why Buddy would kill himself? If that, in fact, is what he did."

"I don't know. But I think Father Stephen does. And I think Scarlett does too. I think Buddy was Dr. Brisco's patient. Miss Mooseman practically told me that, and I think—"

Margaret Ann put a hand over Doc's mouth. She took the puzzle pieces from his hand, tossed them back into the pile. "When you say, 'I don't know,' you're supposed to stop. It's not your turn anymore. That's how Occam's razor works."

Pinpricks of heat rifled Doc's scalp. "What are we doing here? Playing 'Red Light, Green Light'?"

"I don't make up the rules."

"Of course you make up the rules."

She selected another puzzle piece, held it like a card in a poker hand. "I think we should talk about 'the girl.'"

"Sorry, I thought I was already talking about Scarlett when you stopped me. I was about to offer up a theory."

"What you have is likely a hypothesis. I doubt it meets the criteria of a theory." She glanced at the paper circle she held in her hand, smirked. "Go ahead."

"I think even before the accident Buddy was upset, in some sort of trouble. Someone like Miss Mooseman notices he's gone mental, he's ready to crack. He ends up seeing Dr. Brisco, spills his guts to the 'good doctor.' Scarlett gets wind of the deep dark secret. I don't know how. She eavesdrops, reads Buddy's file. Something like that. Whatever it is she knows, I'm betting Father Stephen knows she knows it. The priest is scared, afraid of her. That's why he didn't say anything about what happened at the church."

Margaret Ann pushed her tongue into her cheek. "He's afraid of a naked girl? Maybe she has a reason to believe he likes naked girls. What is he, maybe twenty-five, twenty-six years old? Maybe she was offering an invitation or a dare."

"Doesn't jive. I believe, deep down, she wanted the priest to help her. I think all the sex stuff she does is a cry for help. I've read about girls like Scarlett in *True Detective* and *Real Crime*. Learned a lot more from Miss Mooseman, too. They're victims of circumstance."

She slapped his face. "You love that tramp, don't you!" Margaret Ann exhaled, shook her head. "What girl do you know that isn't worth fighting for? I can't figure out if you're fickle, naïve, or just immature. You're a mess!"

"She's *not* a tramp. She's a girl in trouble. I'll admit she's dangerous, maybe even evil. But it's not all her fault." Doc leveled his glasses, moved his jaw around, looked straight into her eyes. "I'm *the bonafide* detective, and here's what I know: Three—"

"'Boner-fide' would be more like it."

Doc paused, kept the expression on his face resolutely, indelibly, unalterably serious. "Three days ago, I followed a kite. I was looking for a girl who would lead me to a killer, and it lead me to Pinkie, a lost soul trapped between Heaven and Earth. Then I saw Scarlett from the roof of Saint Mary's. Every girl I meet along this journey is like a tumbler in a lock. They're part of the unraveling of this mystery. That's what I'm focused on." Doc looked at the puzzle piece in Margaret Ann's hand. "You can toss that back. I'm finished talking about Scarlett. We're done talking about 'the girl.'"

Margaret Ann turned the piece around. Bonnie's name was on it. "What about this little tumbler? Your babysitter. The girl the priest keeps his eye on. The girl Junior 'kidnapped.' I've done some snooping on my own. All 'hush, hush.' There's a rumor out there, you know. She was gone for a year, went to 'school' at Saint Anne's in Los Angeles. That's where unwed mothers go to have their babies. Maybe that's what was upsetting Buddy: he'd gotten his girlfriend, Bonnie, pregnant. With that on his mind, maybe it was hard to keep his eyes on the road."

Doc's heart curled into a stone fist.

"You're wrong," he said. "You don't know what you're talking about."

But she did.

He could see it in her eyes.

IMPRISONED YEARS AGO BY ORTHODONTURE

Margaret Ann shut the driver's side door to the Chevy with a polite, soft click. She didn't fuss with mirrors, didn't grind the starter. When she drove over the speed bump just beyond the open cemetery gates, the *clunk-clunk* of the car's frame barely rattled his teeth.

"Sorry," she said.

"Didn't feel a thing."

"That's not exactly accurate. You apparently felt something. You practically screamed at me." She took a breath. "I only mentioned the rumor because I considered it pertinent. I wasn't trying to be mean."

"Didn't say you were."

Margaret Ann looked at him sheepishly. "Bet you're thinking what I'm thinking. We made a lot of progress today. I'm pretty excited. I think we're closing in on the truth."

"There is no truth, Margaret Ann. There's just reality."

They drove in silence to the hospital, stopped in the wide semicircular driveway near the front of the entrance.

Margaret Ann got out, pinned a press pass to her sweater. "There'll likely be a police presence in the burn ward. They do that in cases of attempted murder."

"It wasn't attempted murder. It was an accident."

"Sorry. Anyway, this won't take long. Just need to interview a few nurses, see if I can get a comment or two from Fang. When I get back, we'll go to Dr. Brisco's office. See if there's anything that proves Buddy was his patient."

"Fine with me."

She leaned into the Chevy. "Look, Doc. I'm sorry I slapped you. It was for your own good. You're so gullible. It's infuriating. When are you going to learn not every girl's some 'Poor Pitiful Pearl.'"

"Just for you, Margaret Ann, I'll toughen up. Touch my skin." He held out an arm. "See, thick as an elephant's."

She opened the door, slid back into the car. "Hey, I've got an idea. Why don't you head into Emergency? Sign in. Say you're there to see a psychiatrist. It'll give you an alibi for leaving school. Take my purse. Swish when you walk, hum a Broadway tune. Cry. Say you're in crisis. Wait ten minutes, then head back to the car."

"I'll think about it."

"Just trying to help." She got out of the car, waved goodbye.

He watched her walk away, socks sagging, skinny legs and all. He was mad at the world, confused and upset by what she'd told him about Bonnie, but for some reason, it was hard to stay mad at Margaret Ann.

He waited a few minutes. Two cop cars rolled by. A third parked behind Margaret Ann's Chevy. His pulse rose. Margaret Ann's suggestion began to sound pretty good. He got out of the car, grabbed her purse, and followed the arrowed walkway around the corner of the building to Emergency. She was right. It might not hurt to have an alibi.

Five ambulances, their lights still flashing, clustered near the entrance. Doc stood next to one of the ambulance drivers outside the double-wide electric doors and watched as attendants wheeled in stretchers. The victims lay beneath blankets. They writhed, stared wide-eyed into space from behind skin smeared with blood-red goo. It was like a horror movie, an Italian horror movie; the air smelled like vinegar and tomato sauce.

"What's happened?"

"Accident at Hunt's Foods." the driver said. "A real mess. Ramp gave way. Ten males, one female ended up in a cooling vat of ketchup. Could have been worse. Could have been chunky marinara. That stuff will take you down."

Doc nodded. "Chunky marinara, huh? Well, let me tell you, friend, if that's the stuff that takes you down, plenty of it's out there in the world waiting for you. I took a big gulp today. Found out my girlfriend's got a baby by another guy. It's just not fair." Doc sighed, walked into the emergency room, signed his name at the desk, and took a seat.

He'd barely taken a breath when Grill sat down next to him.

"What's up, Doc?"

Doc looked around, confused. "What are you doing here?"

"Preoperative physical."

"You're having surgery?"

"Yep. Dad says I need my jaw broken. There's been a problem in the final phase. Something doesn't quite line up. Looks like I'll be in braces another two years."

Doc fumed. "You can't do two more years, Grill. It's ridiculous. Your dad's running some sort of con job. Let me look at your teeth."

Grill grinned.

"Your teeth look fine," Doc said. "Straight as an arrow."

"Yeah but…"

"But nothing. You need to rise up against authority. People lie, Grill. They come into the emergency room covered in blood, but it isn't blood, it's ketchup. Girls have babies they don't tell you about. Presidential candidates accept Pulitzers for books they didn't write. Psychology, politics, girlfriends, dentistry: They're all frauds."

Doc reached into Margaret Ann's purse, dug around, pulled out pliers. "I'm cutting those braces off you."

Grill put up his hands. "Wait just a second, cool down. What are we really talking about here?"

Doc squeezed the pliers. "Bonnie…her little brother's not her little brother. The kid's her baby. The first girl I've ever loved and she's not—"

"Intact?"

"I was going to say, not who I thought she was."

Grill shook his head. "Seems the Gigolos have fallen on hard times; I'm getting ready to go under the knife. I hear Jimmy's looking at a stretch in the crowbar hotel. You've been duped. And then there's—" Grill took a letter from his pocket, started to hand it to Doc, stopped. "I ran into Slatz today at school. He told me what happened to him last night at Saint Anthony's. Said Scarlett lured him upstairs, seduced him, then humiliated him. Fell asleep on him. There he was with his pants half down when her father walked in. But her dad didn't just walk in. Slatz is pretty sure he watched them for a while, peeked at them through a keyhole in the door."

Doc stopped him. "Slatz told you Scarlett fell asleep?"

"Yeah. She just conked out. Went limp as a dish rag." Grill handed Doc the letter. "It's a carbon copy. Slatz gave it to me because for a time the three of us were involved in a love triangle. He thought it might interest my biographers. He wants the letter to get Scarlett in trouble, embarrass her. Give her a taste of her own medicine."

Doc took the letter and read.

Dear Playboy,

My name is Scarlett. My father thinks I look beautiful when I'm naked. Oh, I mean nude. He says when you're nude, it's art.

He takes lots of pictures of me. When he does, I wear extra red lipstick and flutter my peek-a-boo eyelashes.

My Dad loves everybody, but especially me.

When boy scouts have no dad, he takes them on camping trips and teaches them to kiss. He lets them practice on him. It's okay because he's a psychologist. Sometimes he watches them kiss pictures of the pretty girls in your magazines. You can kiss magazine girls anywhere you want.

I want to be in your magazine so the boys can learn on me. Do you have to be out of high school? Write and tell me.

Love,
Scarlett

Doc set the letter down. His heart ached for Scarlett, for Slatz too. "Where's the original?" he asked.

Grill shrugged. "In the mail?"

"It's an upside-down world, Grill. You know that, don't you? The ones who are hurting just keep getting hurt. I should have talked to Slatz. I should have stopped him."

"So the letter wasn't such a great idea?"

Doc wasn't listening. He had his eyes on the crowd. Amid the swirl of nurses and doctors, the clattering carts, the restless, waiting ill, Doc caught a glimpse of a girl for whom neither rain, nor sleet, nor gloom of night could keep from her appointed rounds. She carried a mailbag draped over one shoulder, wore a gray shirt, shapely knee-high socks, and comely orthopedic walking shoes.

Doc pointed. "You've got to talk to her, you've got to get Slatz's letter back," Doc said.

Grill glanced at the girl then lowered his head. "Forget it. I don't stand a chance. Just look at her. She's pretty. Smart too, I bet. Probably nailed the civil service exam. She'll never track down that letter for me. Even if she has the letter with her, she'd never let me near her pouch."

Doc pressed his palm against Grill's forehead, pinned the back of his friend's head against the plastic seat. "We'll see about that." He raised the needle-nose pliers, took aim at Grill's mouth. "It's time you become the gigolo of gigolos. It's high time a girl says 'yes' to you. Open wide…"

Doc commenced war on metal. He excavated. Broke the chains that bind men's souls. Sparks flew, rubber bands twanged in all directions. The mail girl, as if drawn forward by the force of a magnetic field, came and stood next to them, dabbed perspiration from Doc's forehead. He nodded thanks, probed the gummy maw one last time and stood back.

A crowd had gathered: Attendants, interns, candy stripers, several men smeared in ketchup looked on as the transformation began.

Her pouch swaying as she looking into Grill's eyes, she asked, "What's going on?"

"My friend's true face was imprisoned years ago by the orthodonture his father wired into his mouth. He's free now."

She knelt in front of Grill. As though mesmerized, she stared at the young man seated before her. She whispered the words, "It's like watching a frog turn into a prince. It's practically mythic."

Even Doc was amazed. What the mail girl said was true. Letting the pliers fall, Doc watched Grill's neck and shoulders thicken. His jaw squared. His nose exquisitely aquilined. In profile, he looked like a teenage Paul Newman, a young emperor memorialized on a Roman coin. When Grill finally spoke, he directed his words to the mail girl. He said, "May I introduce myself?"

He didn't lisp.

She leaned in, held Grill's face. Exchanging whispers, the couple rose and walked off together.

The liberation of Grill had been like a dream sequence, something you'd read in a fairy tale. At the same time, what he'd done with the pliers had required no imagining. He'd simply seen a wrong and righted it. No more messing around. From now on, he'd do the right thing without hesitating. He'd act and move on.

It was time to find Margaret Ann. He was ready to step out of the marinara. He was ready to face Bonnie knowing the truth. Love, if it was love, always finds a way.

Invigorated, undaunted, Doc pushed through the double doors at the far end of the waiting room. He'd look for the stairs, the elevator, a way up to the burn unit. If there were police waiting for him there, so be it.

He found himself in a long, winding corridor, the porcelain-tiled walls bathed in an eerie, blue fluorescent light, the air cold and foggy as a meat locker.

A figure appeared out of the mist, an old woman in a tattered translucent bathrobe, her body a tangle of dry sticks.

"I know you," Doc said. "You're Jimmy's grandmother."

She held a framed photograph in her hand. It was the one taken on her honeymoon, the one he'd seen at Jimmy's house.

Circling, she showed him the portrait, then said, "The lady in this picture? She used to be my best friend. But when I ask about her, no one seems to know where she's gone."

He could taste her breath. It was acrid and sulphurous.

Doc stepped away from her, turned to go back the way he came. His knees slammed into a shrouded gurney. The wheels rattled as it rolled a few feet. Twisting, he slammed into another gurney. A hand shot out from beneath the bloody blanket draped over it, grabbed his wrist. The fingernails, long and splintered, were painted pink.

Doc froze.

Pinkie sat up, her crimsoned torso stiff as a bedspring, her eyes milky obsidian, lifeless as a stuffed animal's.

"It's all right, Doc," she said, wiping her hand across her chest. "It's only ketchup."

"You scared me...I mean, startled me for a second." Doc looked around. "What is this place, Pinkie? Where am I?"

"Limbo, Doc. I've brought you here to visit me. Just want you to know I think it was nice what you did for Grill. It's nice what you're *going* to do for Bonnie tonight. Remember the promise you made to her on the phone: make dinner, fix the vacuum. It's important you fix the vacuum. I mean that. We've got to get the cheerios off the floor. Promise me you'll fix the vacuum."

"I'm going to fix everything."

"Look at me, Doc. I'm fading away. We're running out of time, you and me. Take the noble path. Fix the vacuum."

Doc stepped backward. A mist surrounded him. He heard the *ding* of the elevator. Doors slid open behind him. He stepped in, pushed the button that said Exit.

LIMBO

Back in the car, playing it cool, Doc said for probably the third time, "I'm telling you, Margaret Ann, I'm just going over to Bonnie's to find out what she knows. Work my way into her confidence. Sleuth around. Maybe tonight I'll tell her I know about the baby. She might break down, tell me who the father is. If it's Buddy, that would explain why he might have been out drinking the night Cindy was killed."

Margaret Ann wheeled the Chevy onto Doc's street. She stopped just beyond the corner, eyed him suspiciously, peered into his soul as though her cat glasses gave him x-ray vision. "Ever since we left the hospital you've been acting weird, fidgety. There's something you're holding back."

"I told you I ran into Pinkie. It was a little unsettling."

"No. It's more than that. You have a crush on Bonnie and it just kills you that she's not some delicate wildflower you've stumbled upon in the wilderness, that she's probably been banged more often than an outhouse door."

Doc breathed in slowly through his nose, chewed the inside of his chewed-up cheek. "How wrong you are, my dear," he said, climbing out of the car. He shut the door carefully, leaned in through the open passenger window. "I don't love her. She's just the babysitter. Someone

I took advantage of so I could play in the band." He turned away. "I'll walk from here. Pick me up at three o'clock. If we're partners, you'll drive me to Bonnie's. In the meantime, see if you can get into Dr. Brisco's office and find out if he has a file on Buddy."

HE SET THE KEYS FLYING

Coming through the front door, Doc saw his father sitting at the kitchen table, sipping coffee, smoking a cigarette.

Dad looked at his watch. "You're home early."

"Teacher's meeting," Doc said, heading straight for his room.

He could hear the kitchen chair slide back. The last thing Doc wanted was to have his father follow him.

"I've got reading to do," Doc yelled out. "Big test tomorrow." He shut the door to his bedroom, sat down at his desk, picked up *The Mill on the Floss* and opened to a random page. He didn't see the author's words. Instead he saw a future with Bonnie. He couldn't get her out of his mind. He pictured their future beginning in a snowy field, beneath which lay a parchment landscape. Letters from the alphabet ran into the distance, formed sentences that became the rails of a train track. He saw Bonnie, himself, her small child. The three of them, hobos on the run. In his heart, there suddenly arose a blossoming dream of freedom. Draped over his shoulder, he had a nearly completed manuscript tucked into a tattered canvas bag.

When all this was over, when Junior was locked behind bars, he'd ask Bonnie if she'd like to run away with him. He'd tell her he knew about the baby. That it was all okay, that he would take care of them.

She didn't need to worry. He'd written a book, a real moneymaker. Just a hundred pages more and he'd be done.

The bedroom door opened. His father walked in holding Snowball in his arms.

Doc closed the book. "Where's Mom?" he asked.

"They offered her an early shift. She'll be back in a while. Thought we'd give you the night off. Why not? Turns out you've been a pretty good sport. A real team player."

A pang of guilt twisted Doc's stomach. He breathed through it. "You still going in to work?"

Dad bounced Snowball in his arms. "You're not trying to get rid of me, are you?"

Doc looked down at the book.

His father walked over, put his hand on Doc's shoulder. "Yeah, I gotta work. Leaving in just a bit. So, what you got there?"

Doc was tempted to tell him the truth, that *The Floss* was a tale of incest that ends with a brother and sister drowning in each other's arms. Instead he said, "Sophomore year we read books with water metaphors: *The Mill on the Floss, Huckleberry Finn,* and *The Old Man and the Sea.*

"*The Old Man and the Sea,*" his father repeated, slowly stretching out the syllables, gazing up, drawing into his lungs what Doc guessed was a breath of salty sea air. "Now there was a good yarn."

"Well, the 'yarn' I'm reading now's a little different, Dad. It's about a girl who covers up a murder so she can keep her baby. But actually the story's about the guy who wants to save her. He's just a kid, but his plan is to expose the killer then run away with the girl before the police can charge her with 'conspiracy after the fact.' They go someplace where no one will find them, maybe India. Someplace where they'll be understood."

"They can't be understood? What's the problem? They don't speak English?"

Doc took a breath. Nerve endings in his brain burned. "They speak English, Dad."

"But apparently they don't speak reality, do they? You see, son, that's what's wrong with novels. They don't solve for *x* like men of science do." He set Snowball on Doc's desk, lit a cigarette, puffed. "All well and good, if you like that sort of drivel."

"It's not drivel. It's life viewed through the writer's artistic vision."

"And in this vision the characters don't need a roof over their heads or food to eat? They live on love?"

Doc bristled, composed himself. "No, they don't just live on love. See, the boy in the story has a secret talent, a gift he was born with. When the chips are down and the cupboard is bare, the young hero turns that talent into money."

"So what's his talent? Crime?"

"I don't know. I'm only on chapter three. I've only been back in school for a month. But I imagine it's like if you and Mom couldn't work and our family needed money. I'd start writing stories and novels like great-granddad. The public would gobble them up. I'd sell a million copies. The idea's not so farfetched. I've got writing in my blood."

"You've lost me, kid. Your great-grandfather was a citrus rancher. Far as I know, the only thing that old goat ever wrote was a bill of sale."

"No, Dad, your *real* grandfather…Rudyard Kipling. I know about the piano. I know all about their secret marriage. Grandma Nana told me the whole story. I remember her showing me the wedding photograph of her and Kipling."

Snowball began to giggle.

The floor beneath Doc trembled. A sickening sensation climbed his legs, dragged his heart into his stomach.

"Dad, I know Kipling ran off with some other woman after the wedding."

"Yeah, his wife. It's called a honeymoon." His father started laughing. "Nana was never Kipling's girlfriend, let alone his bride. It's true she was at his wedding. Know how she got that photograph? The old bat slipped the photographer a few bucks. Nana grabbed Kipling at the reception and kissed him. The photograph was a practical *joke*, not a family secret. And you fell for it hook, line and sinker…That's priceless. You're such a bozo."

"Bozo," Snowball squeaked.

Heat rose in Doc's face, a fever raged through his body. His vision warped.

His dad fell back against the bedroom wall, laughing uproariously. "Secret talent, secret talent." Tears spilled down his father's cheeks, and Doc could smell the ammonia scent of freshly dampened diapers. He couldn't believe they'd topped off their humiliation of him by throwing in the water metaphor. But they had.

His father wiped his face with his sleeve, dried his glasses on his tie. "Don't be so thin-skinned, son. Roll with the punches a little."

Doc swiveled in his chair. "Is that what you do, Dad? Roll with the punches?"

His father lifted Snowball from the desk, hoisted her onto his hip. "You have something you want to say?"

"How is it you order me to give up my life, become some girlie family babysitter, force Mom to take some crap-ass job, and that makes *you* the one who rolls with the punches?"

"You watch your language, young man."

Doc stood, pushed his chair back, stared up at his father. "What's wrong, Dad? The words lack precision? Did I leave the *x* out?"

His father offered up a smile, an expression that struck Doc as both wry and mischievous. His features hardened. "You're such an ingrate."

"Glad I'm great at something."

His father laid Snowball on the bed, studied Doc, nodded knowingly. "Be right back."

He left the room, left Doc wondering.

The bedroom window was open. For a moment Doc entertained the idea of running. He looked over at Snowball. She was lying on her back counting her toes. "Crap-ass, crap-ass."

Doc looked at her, said, "Well he shouldn't have sold the piano."

His father marched into the room, a typewriter cradled in his arms. He dropped the Remington on Doc's desk, rolled in two sheets of clean white paper with a carbon in between. "I've got to go to work," he said. "You're going to spend your 'night off' right here. Write me a story. Show me the pen's mightier than the mouth. I'll read whatever you've written when I get home. If that's okay with you."

"I guess that would be okay."

"If it's a love story, here's a little tip: True love doesn't start off all hot and heavy. It doesn't happen in an instant. It grows over time. Something else: When I was a boy, Nana told me my dad was sired by Buffalo Bill. I thought I was destined to join the rodeo. Become a bronc buster."

"She made a bozo out of you, too?"

"Every chance she got. Put five husbands in the grave. One last thing. When I was at Stanford, Aldous Huxley came to speak. Know who he is?"

"*Brave New World?*"

His dad nodded. "The guy came out on stage, asked the audience who wanted to be a writer. I think every hand went up, including mine. He said, 'Then what are you *doing here?* Go *write!*' That's what he yelled at us. That was it. That was his speech."

"So?"

"So I went back to engineering. Math. Science. I didn't have the nerve to believe in my imagination. I thought Huxley would disclose some great secret, something better than 'just go do the work.' But in the end he was right. I did the work. Found out I loved science and engineering. I have a talent for it, maybe not a great talent, but I do my best. And what comes of it is…what it is." He paused and Doc could see himself gathered up in his father's eyes. "I'm sorry I sold the piano," he said. "I didn't know how much it meant to you. Anyway, I think your mother's home. I'll take the baby. You write. If you have a 'secret' talent, don't keep it a secret."

Alone in his room, Doc sat down at the typewriter ready to write the prologue to his *A Murder in Sunny Hills* novel. Pausing, his fingers floating above the keys, a thought crossed his mind. Maybe a dad's job wasn't just to teach his son how to roll with the punches. Maybe a dad's job wasn't done until he turned his son into someone who would punch back, win or lose. He took a breath, punched the keys, typed "Christmas Eve 1957," swung the carriage back.

"Shall we press ahead?"

It was Kipling's voice. Doc turned in his chair. The novelist wore a white linen suit, sported a bowtie adorned with tiny imperial elephants.

"Think I'll do this on my own."

Kipling rolled his sleeves, raised a finger to the sky. "I keep six honest serving-men (they taught me all I knew); their names are What and Where and When And How and Why and Who."

"I'll keep that in mind," Doc said.

"This is our big chance. It's time we take on a little thorn and bush, lad. Go to the banks of the great gray-green, greasy Limpopo River, sit beneath the fever-tree and write this story."

"Think I'll just stay here."

Kipling polished his glasses. "You're sending me away?"

"Don't get me wrong. I love your books and poetry. You've been an inspiration."

"Sorry about the bloodline," Kipling said. "But you know things like that don't really matter."

"Guess I'll find out."

"I'm always available for a pithy adjective, a brocade metaphor, an editorial tweak."

"I know," Doc said, turning back to the typewriter. He decided to tell the story in the spirit of the truth, allow himself some dramatic license. "Here it goes," he said softly to himself, then set the keys flying.

Junior took the corner fast, bat out of hell fast. But that was the point, wasn't it? Half the fun? The other half was watching the blood drain from the face of the guy sitting shotgun. It had been a bad news night for Buddy and, if Junior had any say in it, the night was going to get worse.

"Gotta slow down, Junior. You're going to get us killed."

Buddy's voice came out pale, panicky, barely audible over "Jingle Bell Rock," the song blaring on KFWB. He fell silent, lifted the half empty fifth of Bacardi to his lips, took a pull, then stared at his reflection in the window.

Junior took his foot off the accelerator. "See Buddy, I'm slowing down, anything for you. It's cool."

The Studebaker snaked through the neighborhoods, prowled through the light rain that had begun to fall. Every house they passed was resplendent, decorated to the hilt. Strands of Christmas lights, rows of colored lights, white and red, raced along the rain gutters, swirled up columns, twined the trunks of trees. There were Santas on roofs, reindeer on lawns. "O Holy Night" played on the radio.

"Want me to change the station, Buddy? Don't know about you, but man, this music's puttin' me to sleep." Junior closed his eyes, conjured a demonic grin, then pounded his foot down on the accelerator. The Studebaker blew through the intersection.

"Stop it. I mean it. Stop playing games."

"Can't hear you, Buddy," Junior said, his voice a sarcastic singsong. He lifted his hands from the wheel, thrust his arms toward the rain-splattered windshield, let his wrists go limp. "Look at me, I'm the ghost of Christmas past."

319

Buddy grabbed for the wheel. Junior's eyes opened, his pupils swirling black water. He slapped Buddy's hand away, glared at him. "Don't do that, Buddy. Don't ever do that." Junior reached out, grabbed the bottle from Buddy.

"I'm so screwed," Buddy said, sinking back into his seat.

Junior took a swig, threw back his head, and gargled, "Poor me, I'm drowning in sin. I knocked up my girlfriend. Save me, Lord."

"Shut up."

"Shut up?" Junior punched the accelerator, swerved to the opposite lane, clipped a mailbox ribboned in scarlet, tore into the Styrofoam postman Santa that stood beside it. A second later, he was back on the road, laughing.

A hundred yards past the house, Junior stopped the car in the middle of the street. Dangling the empty bottle in one hand, he climbed out, staggered in front of the car, displayed himself triumphantly in the headlights, then threw the bottle at the Studebaker's windshield. It bounced off the roof, shattered on the pavement. He came around to the passenger door and jerked it open. A porch light turned on. Up the street a car approached.

He pushed Buddy over to the driver's seat, got in. "Drive," he said.

Buddy, behind the wheel now, looked around, saw the porch light and oncoming car. He threw the car into gear.

"Gotta get to my brother's," he said. "Gotta tell him about Bonnie. He'll know what to do."

"Take the shortcut, the back way around the stables."

Passing the last house on Valencia Mesa, Buddy sped down the hill. The paved road turned to gravel, then to dirt. Buddy wheeled left, took the fork, the rutted bridle path that wound down to Basque Avenue. No cops would come this way.

Ahead was a redwood barn. At the peak of the roof, beneath a weather vane, a tungsten light burned blue, illuminated a corral, a hitching post, a galvanized water trough and a sign that read "Shorty's Stables."

The Studebaker clattered over the cattle guard, bounced through the open gate. A form, running across the path, appeared in front of them, its yellow eyes burned in the beam of headlights. The bumper struck its hindquarters. The animal spun, its body twisted into brush. Buddy kept driving, his eyes drawn to the barn, to the lights that shown down on the celebration. Along the east side of the structure, a spotlight played on bales of hay that formed a backdrop to a nativity scene. Jesus, Mary, Joseph, the wise men, each figure life-size, all humbly made, gathered there together in the falling rain.

Junior said, "Looks like a party. How 'bout we crash it? Do it now, Buddy!"

"No."

Junior lunged, grabbed the steering wheel, twisted it to the right. He pressed his left foot down on Buddy's right. The car veered, smashed into the figures, plowed through the bales of hay.

Buddy struggled against Junior's grip, tried to pull the car back onto the bridle path.

Straight ahead a girl was leading a horse out of the barn. She had blond hair, the horse had a blaze on its forehead. The horse reared in the headlights, its body filled the left side of the windshield. The girl remained frozen, motionless, her mouth open, the reins stripped from her hand as the horse jerked its head.

A thud hammered the grill of the Studebaker. The girl disappeared beneath the driver's side amid a series of sickening, thunk thunks *and other sounds like flesh being chewed by the blades of a lawnmower.*

Twenty feet past the nativity scene, Buddy skidded the Studebaker to a stop. He got out, ran back to the girl. Junior slid into the driver's seat. The horse was trying to stand. It twisted and fell on its side. Now the girl was standing, her chest and hair drenched in blood, her arm dangled forward, dropped, ripped away at the shoulder. She dropped to her knees, fell on her face.

Buddy tried to pull her up. Couldn't. He turned her over and dragged her onto the grass. He ran back through the rain and leaned into the open window of the Studebaker.

"She's still alive; we've got to get help." He climbed into the car.

Junior threw the Studebaker into reverse and backed over the girl as she lay in the muddy grass. He pulled forward and looked at Buddy. "She's dead. You killed her, Buddy. And now we're going to drive to your brother's and you'll tell him how it was an accident. How both Bonnie and this girl were accidents. You'll tell him, Buddy, and he'll forgive you: he's got the power. And he'll never say a word about this to anyone, he can't, so help him God."

FRUIT OF THE POISONED TREE

A few minutes before three, Doc folded the carbon copy of *A Murder in Sunny Hills* along with "the originals" of everything he'd written. He took the two bundles and shoved them into his back pocket and left his bedroom. It was time to meet up with Margaret Ann. He shouted, "Class project. Be at the library. Back around ten. Bye, Mom."

His mother was standing by the table in the dining room, sorting laundry fresh from the dryer. "You say something?"

He passed by her, beat it out the front door before she could turn around.

From the top of the driveway, he spotted Margaret Ann's car parked halfway down the block in the shade of a pepper tree.

He closed the distance, popped open the passenger door, slid in, then swallowed hard.

Quinn was behind the wheel.

Frankie Lane sang "Cool Water" on the radio.

The detective turned the volume down. "Lock the door," he said. "We need to talk."

Doc smacked the knob down with the flat of his palm and sat back. "It's not Margaret Ann's fault," he said. "I conned her."

"I doubt that. She couldn't take the smirk off her face when she told me what you and she'd been up to. Can't fault the detective work. Explains why Father Stephen wouldn't want you snooping around."

"Pretty wild stuff, huh?" Doc said, breathing a little easier.

Quinn frowned. "And dangerous."

"Not really."

"Tell that to Fang."

Doc tried to look mystified. Puzzled. Wide-eyed. "Heard he was in some sort of freak accident. Guess how it happened is a mystery."

"You're a bad liar, Doc. Your friend, Jimmy, even with his hand on a Bible with his name written in it, is still a lot better at it than you are. That's why I let him go." Quinn started the car, put it in gear. "I'm taking you to Bonnie's house. Gonna let you run your game of cat and mouse a little longer. But you have to let me know if you get in over your head. And whatever you do from this point forward, you'll do it without my daughter's help. Understand? You're going to stay away from Margaret Ann till this is over."

"It's probably over now," Doc said. "We haven't found the Studebaker, haven't come up with a shred of hard evidence. If Bonnie's hiding the truth, she's not going to say anything now. She wouldn't risk going to jail. She'd lose her baby. If Junior was behind the wheel, there's no way to prove it."

"So what's your plan?"

Doc shrugged. "Don't have a plan. I'm just making dinner tonight for Bonnie, helping her with some chores. It's not like I'm gonna help a girl who probably hasn't done anything wrong flee prosecution."

Quinn lit a cigarette, gave Doc a mind-reader's stare, then drove in silence all the way to Locust Street. He stopped four houses down from Bonnie's front door. "One last thing," he said. "Margaret Ann wanted you to know she went by the 'doctor's' office. Said to tell you there was no file on Buddy, but she did come across an empty file with Fang's name on it."

"You think..."

"I don't think anything, Doc. I can't. You understand, don't you? Any evidence obtained as a result of someone's daughter breaking and entering would be thrown out of court. It's called fruit of the poisoned tree. But you might ask Bonnie why Fang—if it's true he was upset about Buddy's death—would go to Dr. Brisco instead of seeking help from Father Stephen. I'll be back to pick you up around seven."

THE SMILE OF AN ASSASSIN

With the carbon copy of what he'd written this afternoon curled in his hand, Doc climbed the steps to Bonnie's door. She was still mad at him, he was sure of that.

But he had a case for being angry, too. From the beginning, she'd led him to believe she had a little brother, as much as sworn nothing close to anything romantic had gone on between her and Buddy.

He took one more breath before knocking, felt a thorn rake the walls of his heart, had to remind himself again that nothing in the past mattered. He was here to have her read what he'd written. She'd, of course, compliment him on his compelling prose, admit to him that the story he'd written about the accident was probably true. He would ache with her as she choked back tears, console her as she fell silent with resignation. Holding her, he'd look into her eyes and tell her everything would be okay.

Before he could knock, Bonnie opened the door.

She looked, not really at him, but instead gazed out at the shabby lawn, the rusted cars parked along the street as though the view from her porch held more significance in her life than he did.

"Where's Snowball?" she asked.

"I have the night off."

"No 'band practice'?"

He shook his head. "I have something I want to read to you. I want to talk."

"About what?"

His vocal chords knotted.

"About what?" she repeated, glaring at him.

"About…dinner. And the vacuum. I'm here to make you dinner and fix the vacuum. Later I thought I'd read you a story I've written." He stepped past her, walked into the living room. The carpet crunched beneath his feet.

She eyed him cautiously. "There's a couple of cans of SpaghettiOs in the cupboard. If you're serious about fixing the vacuum, there's a screwdriver on the toolbench in the garage."

"Just point the way."

"Are you all right?"

"I'm fine."

She closed the front door and followed him.

"That's your story there?"

Doc looked down at the sheets of paper as though the hand that held them belonged to a stranger.

"Sort of."

She snatched them from him, her icy expression replaced with a coy smile. "You've written something just for me. What is it? The next chapter of our steamy Nazi adventure? Something sweet and wonderful?"

He stepped forward, reached out his hand.

"I need to explain."

She wagged a finger, danced away from him. "No explanations. I want to be surprised. You go play with the vacuum. It's in the kitchen. I'll check on my little brother. Hopefully, he's napping."

She disappeared down the hallway.

Doc stood in the empty room, stared into the paint-by-numbers portrait of the Pope. The crooked places weren't getting any straighter. He'd had it all worked out and now nothing was happening the way he'd imagined. She wasn't supposed to improvise, run offstage with what he'd written. Now all he could do was pray and wait and fix the vacuum, hope she'd come back before reading what he'd written.

Numb, he walked into the kitchen. The vacuum, dumb as a stone, leaned against the refrigerator just beyond the door that led into the garage.

"Get the tools."

It was Pinkie's voice talking to him. Another woman inside his head, running the show, telling him what to do.

"Okay," he said.

He flipped the latch, opened the door that led into the garage.

In the half-light, he saw a car covered by a dusty moss-green tarp, a slumbering beast in hibernation.

He went to the tool bench, pushed aside a flashlight and pawed through a box of wrenches and hammers looking for a screwdriver.

Behind him, he sensed something stirring, felt the rise and fall of an oily breath on the back of his neck. He grabbed the flashlight, held it like a weapon and spun around.

From beneath the tarp came the faint *tick, tick, tick* of a cooling exhaust. In the next moment, the shadowy form beneath the tarp seemed to heave, give rise in Doc's mind to a memory, a reminiscence from a recurrent dream, a dream that despite all efforts, had, in the past, always seemed to fade upon wakening.

Positioning himself in front of the car, he switched the flashlight on, threw back the tarp. What he saw dropped him to his knees.

Inches from his face, the Studebaker's grill greeted him with the smile of an assassin. A flash flood of images swept through Doc's brain. He saw the fiery crash in Carbon Canyon that had claimed Pinkie's life, the burning nativity scene at Shorty's Stables, the glowing eyes of the coyote, the ceaseless sorrow in Jimmy's eyes.

He kicked the cold, indifferent metal and stepped back. "So we finally meet," he said, then walked around the car like a prison guard, shining the flashlight's beam into the Studebaker's interior.

Though his hand held steady, his mind reeled with the sinking realization Bonnie's involvement in the cover-up reached far deeper than he'd ever imagined. His trusting side struggled against primal instincts. Rage gathered in his gut like a lynch mob even as his heart rose to plead her case. His gullible side stammered excuses, explanations, shouted out what he wanted to hear: She was backed into a corner. Facing the loss of her baby, she'd been left with no choice but stay silent, let the killer hide the car in her garage.

The beam of light froze.

The incurable romantic stepped aside as Doc's eyes focused.

Centered in the circle of light illuminating the backseat was a scattering of green M&Ms and, on the floorboard, the ragged brown packets that had once contained them.

His brain sopped up the image like a long-hungry sponge.

Fang: the little weasel had been there that night. He'd been in the car, knew who was driving. With a certain vindictive pleasure, Doc imagined Junior's cousin in the dark days and weeks following the accident, pictured him squirming in his bed, sweating out nights plagued by guilt and nightmarish dreams. Scared and confused, Doc guessed Fang had acted oddly at school. Miss Mooseman had noticed. She'd talked to him, encouraged him to see Dr. Brisco.

Unwittingly, Fang had ended up seeking consolation from the Devil himself, from a man who would use the knowledge of Buddy's involvement in Cindy's death to blackmail Father Stephen, jeopardize any hopes the priest might have of receiving a dispensation that would allow him to move Buddy's body to consecrated ground. Scarlett probably knew Fang's secret, too, and Doc wondered if, as she was taking off her clothes in front of the priest, she was saying, "Tell anyone about this, tell anyone what you think my father might be doing to me, and I'll destroy any chance your brother might have of making it into Heaven."

Even in the dim light, everything became clear. What Doc had seen from the roof of Saint Mary's was a mortal man put between a rock and a hard place. A man forced to make a choice between the welfare of a living girl and the ultimate fate of his only brother.

There was nothing Doc could do about that situation now.

He needed to get back in the house.

Reaching out to replace the tarp, the flashlight fumbled from his hand.

It rolled beneath the Studebaker.

Doc dropped onto his stomach, crawled beneath the shadowy belly of the car, and grasped for the rolling cylinder. The flashlight spiraled off his fingertips, rocked back and forth. The beam, like a searchlight, illuminated a strip of chrome riveted to the inside margin of the wheel well.

Wedged beneath the metal were bits of saddle blanket and blood-clotted strands of blond hair.

As vile, as sickening as the sight was, his heart couldn't help but swell with a sense of triumph. He'd found the Studebaker. He had a reason to believe Fang was a witness. He had irrefutable physical evidence linking Junior to Cindy's death.

"Thank you, Pinkie."

As his whispered words faded, he heard voices arguing. One of them glacial, familiar, pitiless as a nail gun.

Junior was in the house.

He heard Bonnie shout back, "I told you, no one's here."

Quickly switching off the flashlight, Doc climbed onto the tool bench, pulled himself into the rafters, chimpanzeed his way to a span of plywood that supported an array of battered cardboard boxes. He burrowed out a hiding place, slowed his breathing.

The rafters, still vibrating from the weight of his body, creaked, and above his head, two boxes teetered on a pallet. One was labeled "The Harvard Classics," the other held holiday decorations. Strands of Christmas lights spooled from the torn sides like snakes from a Swami's basket. A ceramic icicle slid over the edge, fell. Doc snatched it from the air, breathed a sigh of relief.

"Nice catch."

Doc looked over his shoulder. Silhouetted just outside a small ventilation window, a black bird postured like a little general. He beaked aside the screen and stepped in.

"Patton? Is that you?"

Patton brought a wing tip to his beak. "Shhh!"

The inside door to the garage burst open.

Junior pushed Bonnie into the garage, looked around.

"Satisfied?" she said. "He's not here. It's like I told you. I just baby-sit for him. I don't know him. He doesn't know me. He doesn't know anything about me."

Junior pressed his thumb against Bonnie's windpipe. "He knows you go to the cemetery. He's been shadowing Buddy's brother...the 'good' Father. His friend Jimmy was at the salvage yard."

"If my mother catches you here she'll—"

"Your mother's a whore and a lush."

"My mother's in the bedroom and she'll hear you."

"Really? Is she flat on her back or on her face? Guess if she's entertaining company, it doesn't really make any difference."

"You're such a bastard."

"Is that what you call your precious baby before you tuck him in?"

Bonnie struggled against his weight, tried to get away.

He threw her onto the hood of the Studebaker, stepped back, came forward again, stopped just below Doc, and fingered a wrinkle in the canvas shroud that covered the car. "Someone's been messing with the tarp. If that four-eyed freak knows something, I'll beat your face in."

From his knees, Doc calculated. Without hesitation, he took aim. He hurled the ceramic icicle like a javelin, kicked at the boxes. The missile found home, its tip splintering between Junior's shoulder blades. Doc kicked at the boxes again. This time the force pushed the containers past tipping point. Cardboard gave way. Ceramic wise men, shepherds, a miniature manger, and ornaments of every description rained down within a cyclone of tangled garland. The books avalanched, too. All hardback editions. The power of great literature pummeled Junior, raked away a section of the tarp that covered the Studebaker.

Flailing, shielding his eyes, Junior looked up just as the metal stand that had likely held last year's Christmas tree cracked him on the head.

He screamed, howled like a wounded animal, pawed at the bits of glass embedded in his face...looked up. "There's someone in the rafters."

In the midst of the sound and fury, Bonnie scrambled off the hood of the Studebaker, her momentum carrying her into—Doc had to look twice, blink his eyes and look again—Margaret Ann? Margaret Ann in a pink prom dress was standing just inside the kitchen doorway that led into the garage. Had she somehow, someway, for some reason he couldn't fathom, followed Junior to Bonnie's? He prayed she'd run, get the holy heck out of there. Instead, hands on hips, she shook her head dismissively.

"No one's falling for your stupid 'look up' trick, Junior. I see the Studebaker."

Bonnie looked from Junior to Margaret Ann, "Who are you?"

"I'm Junior's kidnap victim. He grabbed me from the changing room in Thelma Ray's dress shop. I was trying on gowns for Homecoming. Now I'm what you'd call 'leverage.'"

Junior wasn't listening to them. Squinting upward, he grabbed for the ladder that leaned against the tool bench. "Whoever's up there's a dead man."

There was nothing Doc could do. He looked around for something, anything that might give him an advantage. The only thing in sight was Patton. Perched on a beam above Doc's shoulder, the bird was grooming his feathers, off in some world of his own. Doc shot a desperate look that said, "How 'bout some help here?"

Patton looked back. His beady eyes declared, "No problem." He narrowed his palate, squawked out *caw, caw*. Gathering up a glass dove that teetered on a crossbeam, he rose in the air and dive-bombed Junior. He circled, released the dove; it dropped, detonated on the concrete. Patton swooped, sortied, flew in crazy circles around the inside of the garage.

"See," Margaret Ann said, "See what all your yelling and pushing gets you? There's no one in the rafters. All you've done is scare some bird half out of his wits. Now don't you feel foolish?" She took a deep breath. "This is the last time I'm going to ask. Where's Doc? What have you done with him?"

Junior whirled, glared at her. "Don't you ever shut up?"

Patton buzzed between them one last time, scattering their words as he flew by, his fluttering finale ended with a soft landing on Doc's left shoulder.

Margaret Ann's eyes had followed Patton's flight. "I'm not answering your questions. I want answers."

Junior snapped open the switchblade he called *Persuasion*, grabbed Margaret Ann by the neck.

Bonnie stepped between them. "Leave her alone."

Junior slapped Bonnie with the back of his hand. "Get back inside now or someday you might come home to find your precious baby drowned in the bathtub."

Bonnie cowered, stepped back. Stumbling, she ran back into the house.

Junior turned to Margaret Ann. "Where were we?" He rubbed his head. He looked a little unsteady on his feet.

"I imagine we're at the part where you threaten to kill me. But you won't do that. Not now. You're too smart for that."

Her eyes flicked up to Doc for just an instant. Her look said, "This guy's no match for me. I'm going to play him like a banjo. Just you watch."

Doc didn't want to watch. He wanted to act. But with a knife so near her throat, watch was all he could do.

She took his hand from her neck. "You need to listen to me," she said. Her posture became a mirror of Junior's. Her voice became the whisper of a coconspirator. "Now's not the time to hurt anyone, is it? You've got a plan and it's all coming together perfectly. You can hardly believe your luck."

Junior rubbed the lump on his head, again. "Yeah. Yeah," he said. "My plan."

In a soft, hypnotic voice, she said to Junior, "Yes, the plan. The plan came to you when you cornered me in the dressing room at Thelma Ray's."

"Yeah. Thelma Ray's."

"You saw me wearing the pink formal. I could see you thinking."

"You got that right." He tilted his head, studied the blade in his hand. "So what was I thinking? *I* know what it was I was thinking, but I dare you to tell me."

"Your idea was very clever, practically genius. You were thinking, here's this girl wearing a pink formal…I do feel compelled to pause a moment and interject *I'm supposed to have an invitation to Homecoming,* but I guess that's a matter for another time…anyway, you put two and two together.

"Huh?"

"Two and two, Junior. You put it together. You knew I'd already figured out the Studebaker you stole from the salvage yard Christmas Eve three years ago was the car Pinkie died in. You knew I'd figured out you were behind the wheel the night the Studebaker plowed into the Nativity scene." She took a breath. "Then, remember, in the dressing room you went through my purse, the purse that is now *in my car* with my *extra* set of car keys still in it. You found my case notes. You figured your psychologist friend Dr. Brisco could use those notes to prove I was obsessed with the legend of 'The Girl in the Pink Formal.' A disturbed girl like me might just commit suicide tonight. It's the perfect night, the eve of anniversary of Pinkie's death. So you thought—and this is where it gets really brilliant—'Why not kill two birds with one stone?' You take me and the Studebaker out to Carbon Canyon, mile marker forty-three. Just a few hundred yards from the *abandoned limestone quarry.* You send the car over the edge. So long physical evidence. You rig it so it looks like I committed suicide somewhere else. Remember, somewhere else, definitely not in the car. Maybe you make it look like I let myself be ravaged, dismembered, eaten by wolves. That's how a crazy, love-sick girl would do herself in. It would be deliciously ghastly and totally consistent with the psychiatric profile Dr. Brisco would lay out for the police."

Junior nodded. "Make it look like suicide. Just like I did with Buddy."

Margaret Ann swallowed hard. "Buddy?" She gathered herself. "But this time, you'll be nowhere near the scene of the crime. You'll have an ironclad alibi. You'll be back in town beating up some poor schmuck in some random parking lot. Something like that. You'll figure it out later. Just like you'll figure out a way to snuff out Doc."

"Yeah. Two and two and the bird with the stone thing…but how do I get back to town?"

"You'll get the Blutos to grab my car. They'll meet you out in the canyon."

"I like my plan." He put away *Persuasion,* grabbed a roll of duct tape from the tool bench, slapped a strip across Margaret Ann's mouth. Using the rest of the tape, he twisted her like a top, mummied her arms and legs together, and tossed her in the backseat of the Studebaker. "Be right back."

He slammed the car door closed, headed inside.

The coast clear, Doc climbed down, opened the door to the Studebaker, reached into the backseat and ripped the tape off of Margaret Ann's mouth.

"What are you doing?" she whispered.

"Helping."

"Helping us get killed. Right now Junior's operating on about three cylinders. I think that clonk on the head gave him a concussion. Trust me. We've got a better chance if you wait till he takes me to the Canyon. Now get out of here. Hide. Get back in the rafters."

"How do you keep your cool? You were amazing. You were beautiful," he said. "You didn't even flinch when Junior admitted he'd killed Buddy."

"It wasn't easy."

He turned to leave and she called, "Doc."

For a second, he thought she wanted him to lean back into the Studebaker and kiss her. A kiss goodbye in case they both died.

"Put the tape back on my mouth," she said.

SOMETHING YOU
SHOULD KNOW

Seconds after Doc reached safety, Junior was back. He held a grocery bag that clattered when he tossed it on the front seat.

Glancing up at the rafters one last time, tossing aside the tarp, he lifted the garage door, slid in on the driver's side, and started the engine. The Studebaker roared to life. Junior dropped the transmission into reverse, backed out the driveway, and sped away.

In that moment, Doc felt as though his heart had been torn in half. An emptiness he had never known overwhelmed him, an anger he had never known raged. He scrambled down from the rafters, burst through the door into the kitchen.

Red-eyed, Bonnie sat at the kitchen table, holding her baby, Doc's pages in front of her.

He picked the pages up, shoved them in his back pocket. His voice cracked. "Junior took Margaret Ann. Tell me everything he did inside the house before he left," he said.

She sniffed. "He grabbed six cans of SpaghettiOs. Called the Blutos. Told them he was ditching the Studebaker in Carbon Canyon. They're coming over here to get Margaret Ann's car."

Doc grabbed the phone, dialed the Fullerton Police Department. The dispatcher answered. Collecting himself, Doc said, "Detective Quinn's daughter's been kidnapped." A tinny voice asked his name. "You're speaking to Dewey 'Doc' Ruggles, and I'm dead serious." He listened a moment, set the phone in its cradle, picked it up again and dialed Grill.

The phone rang once, twice, kept ringing.

"That girl looked really pretty in her dress," Bonnie said. "And she was so brave."

"She's not afraid of anything."

Grill answered on the sixth ring. Doc said, "Tell Jimmy and Slatz to stand out by their mailboxes. You, too. I'm on my way. I'll explain later."

He hung up the phone.

Bonnie looked up at him. "What did the police say?"

"They said, if you know what's good for you, you'll let the girl go free, turn yourself in. Guess I wasn't clear. They thought I was saying I was the kidnapper."

"Maybe when you said 'dead serious' it came off wrong."

"Adults just hear what they want to hear. Anyway, I'm not waiting around to explain myself again."

Tears rolled down Bonnie's cheeks. "I'm sorry, Doc. Sorry for so many things."

Doc stroked the little boy's head. "I'm sorry, too."

For a moment their eyes met, and in that moment Doc turned the last page of the last fairytale he would ever need to read. "I think you're a really nice person," he said.

"You too, Doc." She took a breath and changed the subject. "I read the pages you gave me. I'm not sure about everything, but I think you got it mostly right about the crash, what happened that night. There's something else," she said. "Something you should know. Buddy wasn't the one who got me pregnant."

CARBON CANYON

In the rearview mirror, Doc could see Grill in the backseat, the strap to his Polaroid around his neck.

Sitting shotgun, Jimmy asked, "What's the plan?"

Doc wheeled Margaret Ann's car onto Brea Boulevard, leveled his glasses. "Get to Carbon Canyon before it's too late"—he looked around—"Hope I'm going the right way."

Pushing Grill aside, Slatz leaned forward and pointed over Doc's shoulder. "Past the Union Oilfield, turn at the water tower."

Doc nodded, stomped on the accelerator. "Here's the deal, guys. Junior's got a twenty minute head start, Margaret Ann bound and gagged in the backseat, six cans of SpaghettiOs and *Persuasion* in his pocket...and the Blutos are probably right behind us." He glanced around at his three friends.

Minutes earlier, he'd told them what had happened in the garage: What he'd seen, what he'd heard, the way Margaret Ann had held her ground, how she'd bought time by playing to the ego of a concussed psychopath, gotten him to confess he'd killed Buddy to keep him from talking about the accident. He told them about the priest, a real shocker. Buddy's brother, Father Stephen, was the father of Bonnie's baby. Looking at each of them, Doc said, "Junior plans to tie up every loose end. He'll kill anyone who tries to stop him."

Grill's new handsome face, though pale, was etched with resolve. Slatz softly hummed something with a martial air. Jimmy's eyes steeled with visions of retribution.

No one asked to get out of the car. No one said they should go back or call the police for help.

Doc turned at the water tower. The highway narrowed to a ribbon of asphalt. The sky turned to indigo. A full moon rose above the hills and howled white light.

Through the windshield, Doc watched the world play games with gravity, the road dip and dive, the valley carve itself into a gorge. The landscape turned primeval. Nature left the color wheel behind.

"Into the Valley of Death..." Doc said.

Someone spoke the Lord's Prayer.

They were descending into Carbon Canyon.

Doc took a breath, thought of Margaret Ann, recalled what his father had said about true love. He steadied the wheel as though it were the rudder of a storm-tossed ship. Gusts of wind tilted trees inward over the road: black leaves tumbled down from dark branches. Tiger-striped shadows raced across the hood of the car.

He turned the headlights on.

White wooden stakes, like posts of a picket fence, strobed past: mile marker thirty-eight, mile marker thirty-nine.

"Mile marker forty-three's where Pinkie died," Doc said. "The quarry's just beyond it. Get ready, guys."

"And do what?" Grill asked.

"I don't know. Go through Margaret Ann's purse. For all I know, she's got an arsenal in there."

Slatz grabbed her bag and rummaged. "Here's a flashlight and—whoa."

"What?" Jimmy turned. "Gimme those," he said, grabbing the high-heels by their straps. He dangled the pink stilettos in front of Doc's eyes. "We might just run into Pinkie. Couldn't hurt to bring these with us."

"This isn't about 'The Legend' anymore, Jimmy. It's not about you giving Pinkie the shoes and her giving you total sexual knowledge. Besides, these shoes belong to Margaret Ann. She must have been trying them on at Thelma Ray's when Junior kidnapped her. Put them down. Tonight's about your sister and Margaret Ann."

"I don't care about the legend, Doc. I know tonight's about the girls we care about, and justice. We're gonna save Margaret Ann, and I'm gonna bring these shoes to Pinkie 'cause she wants me to."

Doc twisted in his seat. "She told you that?"

"At the Pike. On the roller coaster." He spread the collar of his shirt. A small cross hung from a fine gold chain fastened around his neck. "She gave me this," he said. "She's more than a ghost. What I know now is she's the guardian angel you found for me, an angel who knows my sister's in Heaven. Don't you see how it all ties together? Don't you see what this has been about all along? Pinkie wants to go to Heaven, too. She wants to be where Cindy is."

"That's right," Doc said. "She wants to be in Heaven but she can't get there because she hasn't been baptized. It said so in the newspaper. I can't believe I missed that clue."

"You missed that clue," Slatz said, "because nobody believes that superstitious bunk anymore. And I'll tell you one more thing—"

"Stop." Grill pointed out the windshield.

Doc hit the brakes.

The coyote stood motionless in the middle of the road, his yellow eyes illuminated by the headlights. Off to his left, a white post read mile marker forty-three.

"We're here," Jimmy said, getting out of the car, the straps to the high heels gripped in one hand.

The coyote turned in a circle, ran into the woods.

"Gotta follow him," Jimmy said.

Doc nodded. "I'll hide the car. Slatz, Grill, you guys go with Jimmy."

Switching off the headlights, Doc pulled to the shoulder, edged down an embankment until the wheels found the graveled surface of an ancient riverbed lined with scrub oak and pepper trees. He guided the car beneath a canopy of branches, switched off the engine, grabbed Margaret Ann's purse, emptied his pockets of everything he'd written, stuffed the pages in her purse. If he died tonight, his partially finished novel would give his father something to remember him by. He snapped the purse closed, got out, and worked his way back to the highway. When he saw oncoming headlights scorch the tree-lined road with light, he pressed himself against a rock outcropping.

The truck slowed. Voices yelled out, "Junior, hey, Junior!"

The Blutos had arrived.

From his hiding place, he could see the idling red pickup. Giant heads leaned out each window. "Check the quarry?" they said over one another, then sped off.

From across the road, a flashlight's beam winked Morse code.

Doc crossed the highway. "Grill?"

Grill, out of breath, said, "We think we see her...This way." Following Grill, Doc climbed over boulders, roots as thick as anacondas, trees flattened by lightning.

A second canyon, deep as the interior of a cinder cone, lay below them. It was windswept, inexplicably barren, hostile as the dark side of the moon. A solitary oak, the only living thing in sight, stood equidistant from each canyon wall, its giant branches chalked with moonlight. It was all he could see until he noticed the wriggling figure tied to its trunk.

"Margaret Ann!"

Grill grabbed Doc's forearm. "Wait for Jimmy and Slatz to get back. This whole thing might be a trap."

"I don't care." He broke free and ran toward her.

Nature fought him all the way. Rocks banged his shins, shale slid beneath his feet, brambles lashed out, joined with the forces of darkness to spin a web around his legs. His feet tangled. He tripped and fell a thousand times before he made it to the bottom of the canyon. He sprinted the last fifty yards, then stopped.

In the moonlight he could see her face, her mouth taped closed, her pupils fixed and dilated. She was either really angry or dead. Her pink formal was covered in red sauce and meatballs. "Bait" cans, now empty of SpaghettiOs, lay scattered around her. Pinned to her chest, a suicide note of sorts read, EAT ME.

He knelt in front of her, tore the tape from her mouth.

Jimmy, Slatz, and Grill, catching up with him, gathered around to help Doc free the ropes that held Margaret Ann to the tree.

"You're alive," Doc said.

"Maybe not for long," she said, her freckles suddenly fading.

Doc turned around.

Out in the darkness, there was movement.

Eight pairs of malevolent red eyes stared at them, a palpable hunger, a blood thirst pulsed from their animal skulls. Muzzles bristled, retracted, bared sharp teeth. The better-to-eat-you-with kind.

"Dogs? Just lost dogs, right?" Grill said. "Maybe they're friendly. Maybe they're more afraid of us than we are of them."

"Raise your shoulders, stand tall," Slatz said. "They'll think we're bigger than they are."

Doc stepped in front of Margaret Ann, turned, and looked at the beasts. "Nothing's bigger than they are, except my desire to save this girl."

The guys groaned.

"Take a picture, Grill," Jimmy said sliding in next to Doc. "Maybe the flash will scare them."

Fingers fumbled. The bulb popped.

Eight low growls slowly joined in a chorus.

A second sound, almost imperceptible, caught Doc's attention. It came from behind him. The *zip-zip* of a zipper.

He could feel the heat of Margaret Ann's body, smell the scent of her skin.

Stepping forward, wearing only a slip and bra, she threw her pink formal at the dogs.

They went crazy, pounced on the sauce-marinated dress, tore at the meatballed fabric.

"Get in the tree," Doc said. "Climb!"

THE ROMEO IN HIS BONES

Panic. Desperation. Wide-eyed, adrenaline-injected looks at one another. Somehow, without a word between the Gigolos, a plan took form.

Scrambling onto Jimmy's shoulders, clawing, climbing, clutching bark and the stumps of broken branches, Slatz and Grill orangutaned their way up the moonlit oak.

Jimmy took a running leap and grasped a curving, outstretched limb, eight, maybe ten feet above the ground. Swinging his legs over the branch, he hung upside down like a trapeze artist awaiting the arrival of a second aerialist.

Doc glanced over his shoulder. Three of the dogs were closing in, heads low, snarling, teeth smeared with spaghetti sauce.

He knelt before Margaret Ann. For a split second, he wondered if the last thing he'd see in this life was her underwear. He grabbed a breath, laced his fingers together, and quickly made a cradle with his hands.

She placed one bare foot into his open palms.

He vaulted her skyward. Her stomach, the valley of her belly button brushed his lips, his nose. Her last words, "Don't forget my purse."

Jimmy's grip was sure. He lifted her into the tree, then hung upside down again, waved his arms.

Doc jumped. His outstretched arms fell short of the target.

Margaret Ann screamed down at him. "My purse."

"You want your purse?" he said.

"No...*use* my purse."

"Oh...yeah." Doc picked up the handbag. On tiptoes, he lifted it high above his head.

Jimmy grabbed one strap. The purse tilted. Doc curled his fist around the other strap.

Jimmy hoisted.

Sockets stretched. Biceps burned. Doc drew his knees to his chest. He rose, kept rising. Pinking shears, nail files, cuticle clippers, straight pins, a dozen deadly instruments designed to enhance feminine beauty rained down on the dogs as they tore at his pant legs and shoes.

Doc kicked, kicked again. Suddenly, like music to his ears, he heard the sound of sharp teeth snapping at thin air.

He wrestled his way over Jimmy's body and onto the limb.

The three of them climbed, didn't stop till they'd joined Grill and Slatz among the leaves, thirty feet above the valley floor.

They were safe. At least safe for now. One thing was sure, they wouldn't be going home soon.

Below them the dogs swirled around the base of the oak: a procession of malevolent forces, a river of black molasses reminiscent of the swirling tigers who turned themselves into syrup in the *Little Black Sambo* story. But tonight was no fairy tale.

Doc looked at Margaret Ann. She was shivering.

"You can have my shirt," he said. "If you're cold."

She reached out. "Hand me my purse…and stop looking at me."

"I'm looking at you with genuine concern. I'm not looking at you literally." He handed her the purse. It was light as a feather.

She reached into the bag, undid a few snaps, and removed a small plastic packet no bigger than a deck of playing cards. Unfolding the contents, she produced what looked like a raincoat or a windbreaker. She shook it out, slipped it on. "It's made in Japan," she said. "It's thermal."

Above them, perched side by side on a branch, their jaws still dropped like drawbridges, Grill and Slatz stared down at the dogs. Below Doc, Jimmy, resting on an outstretched branch, serene as a saucer of warm milk, leaned against the trunk of the tree, his eyes scanning the starry sky.

Nodding in Jimmy's direction, Margaret Ann whispered to Doc, "Jimmy doesn't even look nervous or scared."

"He never looks nervous or scared, but something's happened to him, he's changed. Told me he believes in God, says Pinkie's an angel and that if angels exist there must be a home in Heaven for his sister."

The branch Jimmy balanced on creaked. He looked over at them. "She needs to be baptized. She believes you can't get into Heaven unless you've been baptized. It was never about the pink shoes. The shoes were just a legend."

Doc sighed. "Gotta admit it was a pretty good legend."

Margaret Ann frowned. "Just when I start to think you're nice, you give me every reason in the world to hate you again."

"You love to hate me and I hate the fact that—"

"Keep it down, Doc," Jimmy said. "Junior's gonna be back any minute to make sure your girlfriend here's dead."

"You hate the fact that what?" she whispered.

"That I probably care about you more than you can ever know—"

"You love me? How did that happen?"

"Over time. It's like looking through binoculars. You keep turning the knob and then suddenly things come into focus."

"Oh," she said, then glared at him. "It's taken you seven years to focus your binoculars?"

Suddenly a bolt of lightning sawed the night sky. Thunder, in a voice as serious as an admonition from God himself, rolled across the landscape like a freight train.

The largest of the beasts stopped in his tracks and stared up defiantly at the heavens. Like an incarnation of the Devil, he was ready to take on the Author of Creation. Furious, he contorted his body, snapped at the others, then viciously attacked the tree. He slashed at the bark with teeth as sharp as razor blades. Rising on their hind legs, two of the dogs leapt forward and pushed at the oak's trunk with paws as big as catcher's mitts. The other five tore at the root system.

The oak swayed.

Deep within its core, Doc heard wood splinter.

"My whole life's flushing before my eyes," Slatz wailed. "Right down the toilet."

Tilting next to him, holding onto a branch, Grill shouted. "At least you had a life. I turn handsome for one day, now I'm gonna die and I don't even have a picture of myself."

Lightning exploded the ground around the tree. The brilliance left Doc momentarily blind.

He rubbed his eyes, tried to focus. All he could see was prismed light spreading out across a world, shredded pieces of Margaret Ann's dress scattering in the wind.

Above his head the stars blinked back to life. The moon rose and raced along the horizon. Silhouetted on the rim of a distant hill, three figures paused, then disappeared down the opposite side of the ridge.

"Junior and the Blutos," Jimmy said. "They're leaving. They think they've won."

"They're wrong about that," Slatz said. "They might leave but they won't get far. We cut the brake line on the Blutos' pickup. They won't get back to town before dawn."

"We still got a problem, guys." Doc said, looking down.

Globs of blackness again, the dogs sat silent, motionless around the base of the tree.

"Junior's gonna go after Fang when he gets back," Jimmy said. "You know that, don't you, Doc?"

"Yeah. Fang's a loose end. Guess I'm a loose end, too."

Doc's eyes met Margaret Ann's. "You've got to get to the hospital and save Fang. You've got to tell your dad the whole story—"

Margaret Ann put a finger to his lips. "Tell me again," she said.

"The whole story?"

"No. I want to hear you say it again. What you said just before the lightning struck."

"That I love you?"

"Yes. Wanna know something...? I actually like you, too."

She wrapped her arms around him, pulled him close, lightly kissed, in perfect order, the pulse in his throat, the corners of his mouth. She brought her lips to his. The kiss she gave him was deep, warm, and absolutely delicious. It whispered to his heart something beyond the reach of language, strummed his insides with music only angels could hear. It heated the Romeo in his bones, caressed his soul, distilled all eternity into one breathless moment. It was really good.

A twig snapped. Doc looked up, saw the guys grinning down at him. He pulled away from Margaret Ann. "As wonderful as this is, my darling, I must, as the poet says, leave thee. I must not...tarry."

Margaret Ann, her lips still lingering in a pucker, opened her eyes. "What?"

"I'm climbing down. I'm gonna distract the dogs so you guys can get away. It's your only chance. The next time they come at us, they won't stop till they take the tree down."

Her mouth hung open.

A cool rain fell from a cloudless sky.

"No," he said. "Don't speak. Just know I'll take this memory, this little bit of heaven with me if I die." He kissed the back of her hand and descended the tree.

SONGS OF NIGHTINGALES

Rain ticked the leaves, slicked the bark and branches. The world around Doc collapsed, narrowed to a funnel of blackness.

Over the rush of wind, he could hear the others yelling down at him, "Stop! Don't do it! You've lost your mind!" He could hear Margaret Ann, too. She was crying. Her tears spilled down on him, splashing his cheeks and shoulders, the singular sensation of each tear warmer than the falling raindrops.

Numb, without a plan or stars to guide him, Doc, undaunted, laddered down the tree.

Ten feet closer to his inevitable death, he paused, yelled, "Jimmy, if—"

His foot slid, slipped. As if a rug had been pulled from under him, he fell. Frantic, his arms swiped at empty space. A branch slugged his ribcage, another lashed at his face. Fistfuls of twigs disintegrated in his hands. Somehow a flailing elbow hooked a mossy limb. Dangling, he held on, his heart hammering in his aching chest. He drew in a slow, deep, painful breath, said again, "Jimmy, promise me if something happens to me you'll look out for Margaret Ann."

Silence.

The oak creaked. Heat lightning flashed, faded.

"If?"

Doc glared up. "I heard that, Slatz. Thanks for the vote of confidence."

Jimmy quickly answered back, "Don't listen to him, Doc. You're doing great. Nothing to worry about. Remember, when you hit bottom, get as far away from the tree as you can. Run like there's no tomorrow. At the last second, take cover, climb another tree. We'll get help. We'll come back for you."

"Got it," Doc shouted. He worked his way down a few more perilous feet.

There was just one problem with Jimmy's idea. Below him there was no cover. There were no other trees.

As strategy abandoned him, as hope faded, he found himself savoring the memory of Margaret Ann's kiss. Other memories, too, flooded his mind: the last conversation with his father, moments of music shared with the Gigolos. He smiled knowing he would miss forever the jabs, the sarcasm, the slapstick camaraderie of the ragtag friends who tonight dropped everything and without asking a single question had set off with him to save the girl he loved.

He had never been so sad, so scared, so grateful for every day God had given him. He didn't know whom others thanked. Maybe they thanked randomness or the guy who came up with existentialism. Maybe they believed the earth was this insignificant little blue ball flying though space. Maybe it was, but funny how it turned out so many wonderful things happen here.

Hanging from the lowest branch, he could see the canyon's floor. The moonlit dogs sat just beyond the faint shadow of the tree.

He dropped the last eight feet, landed hard, but didn't stumble. He roared at them, bared his teeth, Elvised his hips, stutter-stepped.

The dogs didn't move.

Doc picked up a rock. Threw it at them.

Still the dogs didn't move.

Slowly, drawn in by an inexplicable curiosity, Doc walked toward one of the creatures.

It didn't growl. No animal stench emanated from its body.

Backlit by the blue-black night, the animal appeared curiously abstract, its contours smooth, almost sculptural. The closer he got the more it seemed fur, blood, and sinew took on the rarified form of polished obsidian.

Tentatively he extended his fingers. His hand touched cold stone.

It was a trap.

He spun around, prepared to see the dogs charging at him, ready to gobble him up.

Nothing.

Nothing but sagebrush and desolate wasteland as far as his eyes could see.

Moving around the tree, Doc touched each stark, monolithic form one at a time: Boulders. Each dog had been transformed into a solitary boulder.

He yelled up, "Get down here. You guys aren't going to believe this."

From high in the tree he heard Grill whisper, "That's not Doc's voice."

"Of course it's my voice, Grill."

"Prove it. Tell me something only you and I know."

"You've got to be kidding."

Silence.

"I cut off your braces at the hospital. I know you were the first male candy striper at Saint Jude's."

A conference of whispers ensued.

Slowly everyone, Jimmy carrying the pink stilettos, Margaret Ann clutching her purse, Slatz, then Grill, the Polaroid dangling from the strap around his neck, made their way to the valley's floor.

Margaret Ann rushed toward him, flew into his arms, and smothered him with kisses. "You were so brave. So stupid. I just love you." She slapped his face. "Don't you ever do anything like that again!"

Looking around, Jimmy said, "I think pure evil took one last shot at us, created a legion of demons to scare us to death. I think Doc's courage broke the spell. You were like Daniel in the lion's den."

"That's quite a compliment, Spartacus."

Grill walked over and kicked one of the boulders.

"Mass hysteria," he said. "We got suckered into some sorta mass hysteria."

The others eyed him warily.

"It happens," Grill said. "You can ask my mom."

Margaret Ann paced in circles. "No. There's got to be a better explanation. Someone needs to make sense of this. Maybe the dogs just ran off."

"I never took my eyes off them," Doc said.

Slatz stepped forward. His collar, the sleeves of his shirt looked singed, scorched black, burnt at the edges. His pompadour sparked intermittently, frizzed out as though it had Einsteined. One eye looked slightly crossed.

Doc looked at him. "You all right?"

Grill said, "I think the grease in his hair caught a stray nip of lightning."

In a voice that sounded almost professorial, Slatz, one index elevated, began. "I think Jimmy's postulate, namely that the dogs were a manifestation of pure evil is, in part, correct. I might point out, however, that Jimmy failed to identify the central irony, that being Junior's witnessing of the dogs savaging Margaret Ann's dress contributed to saving us. Junior erroneously assumed Margaret Ann had been consumed. Destiny, or so he thought, deemed he would 'be' and she, and we by extension, were 'not to be.' Doc's actions, and the keyword here is action, trumped all that...Did I work in a little Shakespeare? I believe I did."

"Wow," Grill said. "That was erudite. Way to go!"

"Somehow," Slatz said, "I even know what 'erudite' means."

As they stood there talking, wondering, proposing explanations, Doc noticed pink lightning splinter the eastern horizon, the sky overhead glow the color of cotton candy. Sensing a new wave of change was about to crest, he turned to Slatz and Grill. "How 'bout you two guys bring the car up to the road. We'll catch up with you in a few minutes."

"Sure," Grill said. "We're on a roll, right? Time to get to the hospital before Junior can shut Fang up for good."

Doc watched as the two of them headed for the western slope, heard Slatz say, "You look quite dashing, Grill."

"Yeah," Grill answered back. "Doc cut my braces off. It was my 'to be or not to be' moment."

The two figures continued climbing the rocky hillside, their silhouettes slowly absorbed by the blackening bubble gum sky. A lone coyote howled.

Margaret Ann tugged at Doc's sleeve. "Why did you send them away?"

"I think Pinkie's about to make her appearance." He took Margaret Ann's waist and turned her till they both faced east. Jimmy joined them.

Cascading moonlight silvered the hillside. Slowly, the smell of dead earth and rotting wood was supplanted by the perfumed fragrance of night-blooming jasmine and bougainvillea. A breeze carried the songs of nightingales.

Around the base of the ancient oak, water bubbled up. Crystal clear, it spilled outward, pooled and deepened, its surface frosted by the reflection of a million stars. On the opposite side of the pond, Pinkie appeared. Dressed for Homecoming, she was barefoot, vaporous, beautiful.

"I want to baptize her," Jimmy said. "It's time she had a real homecoming. But I'm scared, Doc. I'm not sure I'm, ya know, qualified to do it. I'm not a priest or anything."

"There *is* a way," Doc said. "It's called baptism by desire. You speak your mind with a pure heart and it'll work out fine."

Jimmy gave Doc a hug. Then, stilettos in hand, he walked the outer perimeter of the pool.

Doc and Margaret Ann looked on as Jimmy took the hand of "The Girl in the Pink Formal" and guided her along a path ribboned in wildflowers.

"Baptism by desire?" Margaret Ann whispered. "I'm not even going to ask how you know that."

"It's true, my darling. Be still. Let's listen."

Dropping the shoes, Jimmy lifted Pinkie, carried her into waist-deep water. He cradled her head, lowered her body. The tips of her hair spiraled outward in swirling eddies, forming a crown of star-splashed light.

Looking heavenward, Jimmy said, "Here's the situation, God. As you know, Pinkie's got no earthly voice. She can't ask you to receive her into your heart, so I'm speaking for her. Doc says I can, says it's legit. She's your child, God, and she wants to come home to you. It's only right." Dipping his hand, Jimmy poured a palmful of water over Pinkie's forehead. "I wash away all her sins; the holy spirit dwells within her. I baptize this girl in the name of the Father, Son, and Holy Ghost. Surely goodness and mercy shall follow us all the days of our lives, and we shall dwell in the house of the Lord forever."

Margaret Ann snuggled up next to Doc. They watched as the two emerged.

Standing at the water's edge, Jimmy picked up the stilettos, handed them to Pinkie. Joyful, radiant, she whispered something to him. He nodded, then walked back toward them.

Doc shook his head. "Got to hand it to him, Margaret Ann," he said. "The guy gives Pinkie salvation and cashes in on the legend at the same time."

"What do you mean?" Margaret Ann asked.

"The prophecy, the shoes, the legend. I wanted all that so I could understand you, romance you when the time is right." He lowered his head. "Never mind."

Jimmy came to a stop in front of Margaret Ann. "Pinkie has something she wants to give you."

"Me?"

"Yes, Margaret Ann, you."

Margaret Ann smoothed her raincoat, straightened her cat glasses. "Okay," she said. "Here I go."

Barefoot, she walked forward, awkwardly navigated the outer rim of the pond. Beneath the full moon two girls came together. Pinkie cupped Margaret Ann's ear, said something. They both giggled. Then Pinkie knelt, slipped the pink stilettos onto Margaret Ann's feet. Margaret Ann clicked the heels together and both girls giggled again.

"What's going on?" Doc asked.

"I didn't *give* Pinkie the shoes. She took them from me. I didn't fulfill the legend, Doc. Didn't want to."

"It doesn't really matter, right? The legend's not real. It's just...a legend...Tell me it's just a legend."

"The legend's real, Doc."

"You're telling me Pinkie's just given *Margaret Ann* total sexual knowledge? That's not right. That stuff is for guys to know."

"It's a changing world, Doc," Jimmy said. "It's a changing world."

DRIVE

Outside the car, next to the signpost that read mile marker forty-three, there was a discussion of sorts. Not about the disappearing dogs, not about the pink shoes, the baptism, or Jimmy leaving the others to spend time hugging and petting a coyote who'd appeared at the side of the road, but about who would drive.

Margaret Ann prevailed. After all, it was her car. She was the only one who had a license. But, in "fairness," she did let it come down to a vote, a show of hands.

Jimmy, not interested in worldly matters, abstained.

Slatz and Grill, apparently unable to recover from the way Margaret Ann had said, "Pretty please with sugar on top," seemingly "transfixed" by the way her words had come out velvety as the darkness that swirled around her translucent raincoat, raised their arms like prisoners surrendering to a higher power.

Doc knew what was happening. She was using her newly found "talent" and he didn't like it one bit. He jerked the purse from her hand, fumbled through the contents until he found her keys. "Here," he said, handing them to her. "Have it your way."

"She's not getting her way," Grill said, pulling his beret from his back pocket and putting it on. "We voted. It was fair and square."

Doc yanked open the passenger door, tilted the seat forward. "Yeah. Right."

The guys piled into the back. Doc slid in opposite Margaret Ann. "Go," he said.

Margaret Ann turned the key; the ignition fired. She put the car into gear, pressed a pink heel to the accelerator, and fishtailed onto the highway. The speedometer climbed to seventy miles per hour.

They were on their way back to Sunny Hills.

"So we head to Saint Jude's?" Grill said. "Stop Junior before he puts a pillow over Fang's face?"

Doc turned to Margaret Ann. "Time to catch you up on a few things you missed out on, unless, along with everything else, you're now clairvoyant."

She downshifted as they approached a hairpin turn. "Fang was in the backseat the night Cindy was killed."

"Rrright." Doc ran his tongue across his front teeth. "I guess your gift of 'total knowledge' reaches beyond the realm of the sexual to include what? Omniscience?"

"I was tied up face down in the backseat of the Studebaker," she said. "I saw the M&M wrappers on the floorboard."

Slatz leaned forward. "Tell her about the baby, Doc. It's a jaw-dropper."

"Turns out," Doc said, "Father Stephen is the one who got Bonnie pregnant. Buddy found that out just hours before Junior stole the Studebaker the night of the crash...Pretty good bit of sleuthing, huh?"

Margaret Ann nodded. "Buddy's girlfriend and his brother, a priest, made a baby together? Didn't see that coming. That must have torn Buddy up. No wonder Father Stephen didn't question his brother's motivation for suicide. When exactly did you 'sleuth' that out?"

"Bonnie told Doc everything this afternoon," Grill said. "She laid out the whole sordid tale while Junior was hauling you out to the canyon."

Margaret Ann pulled to the side of the road and stared out through the windshield. "Let me get this straight," she said. "While I was tied up, on my way to certain death, you and your *ex*-girlfriend chatted. Did you listen to records? Did you make out?"

Doc threw up his hands. "She was never my girlfriend."

"Just your kissing partner?"

"I, uh, uh...I need to clarify something. It's kinda funny if you think about it. Ya see, in a way, Bonnie was a girl I made up. A product of fantasy. A projection of my imagination. I wasn't actually kissing her, I was kissing the idea of her."

"So you admit you kissed her."

"Mostly she kissed me."

Jimmy put one hand on each of their shoulders. "Drive, Margaret Ann. I'll explain."

Angry, glaring at each of them, she drove.

Jimmy picked up where Doc had left off. "It happened like this, Margaret Ann: Bonnie followed Doc out to the street. He was on a dead run to save you. I'm sure of that. She blurted out, probably a million-words-a-minute, everything that had happened between her and the priest. The conversation lasted only as long as it took Doc to dig the car keys out of your purse."

"Yeah," Grill said. "The sex was a one-time thing."

Margaret Ann bristled. "What?"

Doc shot back, "He means between the priest and Bonnie. Technically it was statutory rape, but of the consensual type."

Slatz interjected, his voice still sonorous. "I think a bit of perspective, some distancing might be needed here. I picture Stephen in Seminary, a young man facing a crisis of faith. At the same time Bonnie, a lost soul, is living in a fatherless home with an alcoholic mother. Their vulnerabilities brought them together. How can we call what happened between them a crime?"

"They were left with nowhere to turn," Jimmy said. "All they could do was to try to make things right. After Buddy died, Father Stephen returned to Seminary. Took his vows, resolved to make amends, find a way to get Buddy's remains to consecrated ground. And the baby? The baby gave Bonnie a reason to live, to hope somehow God's mercy would lead her to a brighter future. The price they paid was keeping what happened a secret."

Margaret Ann looked into the rearview mirror, studied the three guys in the backseat. "Did you rehearse this whole thing?"

"No," Slatz said. A few sparks sizzled his pompadour. "Absolutely not."

She stared at Doc. "So how long did this 'conversation' with Bonnie last?"

"Maybe a minute," Doc said. "The longest minute of my life because all I wanted was to get to you. You've got to believe me."

She gazed down at the shoes Pinkie had placed on her feet, closed her eyes. "I *do* believe you," she breathed. "With these shoes on I can actually, just barely, but actually understand what it must be like to be a confused, horny, bonafide brainless teenage boy. We can talk later, but now it's time to focus. Where do you think Junior's headed? What do you think he plans to do?"

"Hard to know for sure," Doc said. "We've got a few problems: The Blutos probably told him your car wasn't at Bonnie's house. That Bonnie didn't stop me from taking it. That puts her in danger. He's probably looking for me, too…but my best guess is he'll head to the hospital. We need to get a confession out of Fang before Junior gets to him. It's not gonna be easy."

"I know how we get into Saint Jude's," Grill said. "We do it under the radar—something Junior and the Blutos will have a hard time doing in the dead of night. Margaret Ann, head for the corner of Harbor and Las Palmas."

"But drive slowly. Keep an eye out," Doc said. "Remember, you're a kidnap victim. Once we're near town, there'll be police on the lookout for your car."

POKE AND PLUNGE

Ten minutes later, Margaret Ann, switching off the headlights, pulled in behind a brick and glass building. Lettered in gold, the sign read, "Sunny Hills Smile Center."

"Your dad's office?" Jimmy asked.

Grill nodded. "Let me out. Gimme a few minutes." He grabbed the flashlight and headed for the door.

Lightning flashed overhead. Thunder rolled.

Rain thumped the roof of the car, splashed the windows.

Margaret Ann turned on the windshield wipers, clicked on the radio.

As the Everly Brothers softly sang "Let It Be Me," Doc watched Grill tilt a potted bird of paradise, reach under it, and retrieve what he guessed were keys. Seconds later, Grill was through the back door into his dad's office.

Taking Doc's hand, Margaret Ann said, "After I drop you guys off at the hospital, I'm going home. My dad must be worried sick. I won't tell him about Fang or what you plan to do, but I'm going to tell him everything else." She smiled. "Except the supernatural parts. He'll send deputies to the quarry to look for the Studebaker. He'll want to go after Junior."

362

"With your dad," Doc said, "it'll be personal. I should have asked for his help days ago."

"He would have come at Junior hard, Doc." Margaret Ann said, "But you're the one who's meant to take down Junior."

Doc pushed her words aside. "You'll make sure your dad tells the deputies there's evidence in the car? If they look they'll find bits of saddle blanket, horsehair, and blood under the wheel well on the driver's side. I know that for sure…One more thing—and I hate to ask this of you—but could you, maybe, get your dad to help Bonnie, see if he could think of some way to keep her safe from Junior, find a loophole that would let her keep her baby. You do believe she deserves a second chance, don't you? Maybe a fresh start?"

Margaret Ann nodded. "It's nice of you to want to help her…as a friend."

The back door to the Smile Center opened.

Grill stepped out. He wore a trench coat, carried a rectangular metal case. His beret had been replaced by a small white triangular cap.

In the rain-scattered glow of the security light, Grill's features appeared altered. It was more than the absence of braces, it was the whimsical fullness of his lips, the lilting arch of his eyebrows, the blush that set off his cheekbones…the bangs. In an odd way, he looked disturbingly beautiful.

Margaret Ann flipped on the headlights.

Grill fanned open the raincoat.

"What's he supposed to be?" Slatz asked. "A French maid?"

"No," Doc said. "I think he's wearing a nurse's uniform."

Grill slid into the backseat next to Jimmy. "This outfit will get us into the hospital. What I have with me will seal the deal." He pulled a handful of syringes from the pocket of the coat. "Sodium Pentathol," he said. "My dad uses this stuff to induce twilight sleep. We double, maybe triple the dose, we're talking truth serum." He patted the metal case. "Got a tape recorder. Battery operated. Put them together, we've got a recorded confession admissible in court."

"You ever inject anybody, Grill?" Jimmy asked.

"Poke and plunge," he said. "Think that's all there is to it."

CALL ME NORMA JEAN

Hoping the darkness would wrap a cloak around them, praying the wind-swept rain would blur the car into anonymity for just a little while longer, Doc sat next to Margaret Ann as she put the car in gear and pulled out onto Harbor Boulevard.

She drove like a model citizen, didn't change lanes or flash her high beams. No one spoke. The only sound Doc could hear was the rattling of syringes in Grill's pocket and the vibration of the car's frame as they traveled the winding road. It was a crazy plan. They had less than a mile to go. They were almost there.

The signal turned red at Hospital Road. Margaret Ann slowed, stopped, clicked on the turn signal.

Tick, tick. Tick, tick.

Doc turned, looked out the back window. No red truck following them. No cop cars, no flashing lights, though he knew Quinn had likely thrown a dragnet over the town. In his mind he heard an overlay of gravelly voices on two-way radios: "Be on the lookout for..."

Green light.

Margaret Ann turned left, followed the circular drive up the hill, then drove past the main entrance to Saint Jude's.

Ahead of them, beneath the shock of light that illuminated the entrance to Emergency, Doc saw two men in suits: big, square built, steely eyed. Local cops? No, but he had a feeling in his gut he'd seen these guys before.

Slatz leaned forward. "Doc, aren't those the goons from the Pike, the guys who chased us?"

Doc nodded slowly, imperceptibly. Slatz was right. They *were* Kennedy's guard dogs. "Wonder what they're doing here?"

"The whistle-stop tour. The campaign," Margaret Ann said. "Remember? I told you I read about it in the newspaper. Wha'da ya bet Kennedy's gonna make an appearance at the hospital? Get himself photographed with some sick kids."

Doc glanced up at the rearview mirror. Slatz and Jimmy had slid low in the backseat, but Grill, lipsticked, preoccupied, Margaret Ann's purse on his lap, sat upright applying mascara. Behind him, through the back window, Doc watched the men turn, their eyes fix on Margaret Ann's car.

Grill smushed his lips together, made a smacking sound, said, "Drop me off here. I'll go in through Emergency, slip down to the lower level parking area. Let you guys in through the loading dock."

"No," Doc said. "We stay together. Go, Margaret Ann."

She wound the car around the perimeter of the hospital, descended to the outside lot on the lower level.

There were only a dozen or so parked cars. The scattering of light poles, like too few candles on a black birthday cake, did little to illuminate them.

The rain stopped. Moonlight glistened the asphalt.

Maybe a hundred yards away a few trucks, quiet, unoccupied, abandoned for now, slumbered in the neon thrum of the loading dock.

Here, Doc thought, they still had the cover of night. If they hurried, they should be able to make it onto the loading dock and into the hospital without being seen.

Margaret Ann let the car coast, then stopped between two cars: a white Cadillac and a Ford station wagon.

Doc opened the passenger door, accidentally banging against the side panel of the Cadillac. Jimmy and Slatz climbed out. Grill followed, steel case in hand, syringes chattering like wind chimes in the pockets of his dress.

Doc, one foot out the door, reached back, took Margaret Ann's hand and looked into her eyes.

She pulled him close, kissed him lightly on both cheeks. "I never wanted to need anyone, but I need you. You're the opposite of everything I ever thought I wanted...Now go."

"Find your dad," he said. "Tell him I'm sorry for getting you into this mess."

He watched as she drove away. When he glanced around, his friends were crouched low between the two cars.

He dropped down beside them. "What?"

"The Feds," Jimmy said. "They're coming this way."

Doc rose, peered through the back windows of the station wagon. Jimmy was right. One of the men was already descending the loading dock. The other, pointing in their direction, marched down the hill toward them.

An electric window hummed. A latch popped. A woman's voice behind them said, "Get in."

Doc looked in through the open window of the Cadillac and watched as a woman leaned, ever so languorously, across the front seat. She opened the passenger door. The cabin light switched on. In its radiance, beneath the scarf that covered her head, he saw the signature platinum blond hair; the face like a poem perfectly punctuated by an exquisite beauty mark; and, blossoming lower down, straining the buttons of what looked like a safari shirt, the legendary cleavage.

"Miss...Monroe?"

"Call me Norma Jean." She opened the car door a little wider. "You're all very welcome to get in."

Slack-jawed, stumbling like blind men awed and mystified by the sudden gift of sight, the boys climbed into the backseat of her Cadillac. Doc slid in next to the most famous woman in the world and introduced himself.

"Are you boys in trouble?" she said, the words Marilyning in her mouth.

"Uhhh...no," Jimmy answered. "We're here to surprise this kid in the burn unit. Do a sort of...skit for him. Cheer him up."

"Oh. So you're actors." She turned and looked at each of them. "I'm impressed."

Grill, beautiful in his nurse's uniform, leaned forward. "As you might suspect, some of us are more accomplished at the craft than others, less reluctant to take on complex roles...I'm actually a male actor."

Slatz snorted. "You, an actor? Let me tell you something, Miss Monroe. The last time this guy was on stage, he played an undescended testicle."

"It was symbolic," Grill barked back. "*Waiting for Gonad* was a tragic parody. At the most primal of levels, my character was forced to endure an existential crisis."

Doc interjected, "To Grill's credit, there *were* several critics who felt he stole the show. In the last act, just as the final curtain dropped, so did his voice."

She giggled. "You boys are very funny...Make a girl laugh, you can just about make her do anything."

The boys in the backseat fell silent.

Outside the window, two men in lockstep, their shoulder holsters bulging beneath their jackets, were closing in on the car.

"We *could* do with a little help," Doc said. "We've got to get into the hospital."

"I'm here to surprise someone, too. Why don't you join me? You could be part of the surprise. I'm very sure Jack would like that."

Doc couldn't get over the way she shaped each word, the way she formed each of the syllables as though she were making them up in her mouth for the first time, as though, to her, the taste of each vowel and consonant was unexpected. "That would be great. Thank you," he said. "I really mean that."

A heavy hand pounded the driver's side window. "Okay, you inside, let's roll it down. Secret Service."

Doc whipped off his glasses.

Marilyn, looking at him, said, "Anyone asks, I'm your Aunt Norma Jean." She buzzed down the window. Removed the scarf. Shook out her hair.

"Oh!" the man said, stepping back. "It's you. I mean, I'm sorry, Miss Monroe. My apologies."

"May I help you, Officer?" she asked.

"My partner saw a car drive down here. It's late. Seemed a little suspicious."

"The press," she said. "Reporters are always looking for a story. They sometimes follow my car...I think you frightened them off."

"Glad to be of help. Anything else we can do for you, ma'am?"

Jimmy said, "You can have your partner bring us some sandwiches. Maybe a few Cokes."

Doc groaned.

"Could you do us that little favor?" Marilyn cooed.

The man nodded. "Roger that, ma'am."

"If possible," she said, "we'd like to rest awhile. We're very sleepy. I'm meeting Jack this morning. Would you come back at six and wake us up?"

The man glanced down at the illuminated dial on his wrist.

"Two hours, fifteen minutes from now? That would put you at the rendezvous point on time?"

She giggled, the sound delicious, playful. "I've been on a calendar, officer, but I've never been on time."

The other agent came around to the window, swept a flashlight across the faces in the backseat.

"What we got here?"

"My nephews...and niece," Norma Jean said.

He looked at her, paled, clicked the light off. Jaw rigid, he studied Doc and Slatz one last time. "Not a make," he said, shaking his head at the other officer. "The kid we chased at the Pike was a gimp, wore glasses. The string bean with him had a greasy pompadour. Punk looked a little like that one in the backseat, except this kid here looks like some squirrelly version of Einstein."

"A gimp? A string bean? A squirrel?" Marilyn said. "These were children you were chasing? Dangerous criminals?"

"Just a description, ma'am," he said.

"A description where you make fun of people? I stutter. Did you know that? In the eighth grade, I was elected secretary of the English Club. I would stand up and say, 'The mm...mmminutes for the last mm...mm...meeting.' How would you describe me? What would you reduce me to? Big breasts and a stutter?"

They walked away quickly, heads down. Ten minutes later they were back...with food, drinks.

Everyone ate except Norma Jean. While the others shoved in sandwiches, Doc told Marilyn what had brought them to the hospital, what they planned to do. He told her about Junior's brutality, his determination to get away with murder. "It'll be tough to go toe-to-toe with him," he said.

She blinked eyelashes as long as curb feelers, studied him. "The boy who wishes to be the mere equal of his enemies lacks ambition, Doc," she said. "You'll need to do more than match good against evil. You'll need another arrow in your quiver."

"What arrow? Junior's bigger, meaner, scarier than all of us combined."

"But you can be crazier than he is, right?" She drew in a breath, smoldered a little. "I grew up in tough neighborhoods, foster care.

There were lots of mean people, dangerous people. But there was usually one guy in every town even the baddest of bad guys couldn't intimidate. This guy was hardly ever big or strong. But he was crazy. Looney-bin crazy. Didn't understand intimidation, didn't understand he was supposed to be afraid. That made him unpredictable, and no one, not even a guy like Junior, wants any part of that."

"So we'll need to be unpredictable, crazy, if we want to beat Junior?"

"Like a fox," she said, then smiled. "I do it all the time. Reporters ask me, 'Do you walk around the house with nothing on?' I get little lewd questions like that. I say, 'No, I have the radio on.' And they're the ones who laugh nervously and walk away a little less sure of themselves."

"So we should double down. Take it over the top. Act as though we don't understand we're supposed to feel intimidated?"

"Why not?" she said. "It's always been the right answer for me."

Doc ate his sandwich and thought about what she'd said. The rain stopped again. Clouds, like runaway boxcars, raced across the night. His eyelids felt heavy. The car grew quiet. Through the windshield he thought he saw the Dog Star chase Pegasus across the sky, the image of night drawing closer, staring in at Norma Jean, its black breath condensing on the glass. In her reflection there was a look of longing as though, between the pools of light and shadow outside the car, she hoped to find the answer to some question. Dreamily, she said, "I think every star, every girl, deserves a chance to twinkle, don't you? No matter what they've done, what they've suffered?"

Doc nodded. "I feel that way, too." He looked over his shoulder, made sure the other guys were asleep, then added, "You know when I really fall for a girl, Miss Monroe? And in some ways I think it's the same sorta thing you're talking about. It's not when I see her in her perfection, it's when, for the first time, I see a certain sadness in her eyes, it's when this I'm-too-good-for-you, know-it-all-girl raises her hand in class and I see the tear in her sweater she wears more often than she wants people to know. It's when I notice the ear that sticks out a little too much, and then, all offended and angry, she starts chewing me out for staring at her, and there I am again; I can't take my eyes off the crooked tooth she's always trying to hide. It's the imperfections, the sadness that tells me things have happened along the way that make this girl feel not so good about herself…the broken places. I see those broken places and fall in love."

"You have a good heart, Doc, but some people might say that's a crazy reason to fall in love," Marilyn said.

"But that's what you said I needed to be, right? A little crazy? Maybe I've got a lot of crazy in me."

"Well, I'd say you've got a good start."

Doc closed his eyes. A parade of memories, visions of all the twinkling girls he'd come to know: Bonnie, Scarlett, Pinkie, May, Norma Jean, Margaret Ann, the moments spent with each of them collapsing one into another in his mind, folding up like the cylinders of a seafarer's telescope…then disappearing into the soft, warm fabric of a dreamless sleep.

A tap on the window.

Daylight.

Norma Jean sat up.

Outside the car the two Feds balanced hot chocolate, sweet rolls in their hands.

Doc reached over the seat, shook the other guys. "It's time we have a little talk with Fang," he said. "I say we go."

"What about you, Marilyn?" Jimmy asked.

"Me?" she said. "I've just become part of the plot. I'm coming with you."

They all climbed out of the Cadillac, Doc first, tilting the seat forward, holding it there as Slatz's long legs stepped into the morning sunlight. Yawning, stretching, he pulled a comb from his back pocket and ran it through his hair. With one stroke his whole look changed. The Brylcreme-saturated teeth seemed to slick away the electricity, short-circuit the Einstein effect. His pompadour, licking up the lanolin residue in the comb's teeth, rose to new heights.

This is not good, Doc thought. He glanced over at the agent. The man's pupils dilated as though he'd suddenly found himself in the presence of a distasteful memory, a memory that Doc feared might include carousels and an elephant swaying to the music of a calliope. The man's molars locked at an offset angle. The corners of his mouth twitched, twitched again as Jimmy, shouldering out behind Slatz, took a cup of hot chocolate from his hand.

Jimmy swigged it, smacked his lips, and handed it back.

The agent threw the cup on the ground.

"We should go now," Doc said, shooting a look at Grill.

The "nurse" wasn't listening. He was standing on the other side of the car absorbed in conversation with Marilyn. She whispered something in his ear. He blushed, adjusted the mounds of tissue paper he'd shoved down the top of the white uniform. Turning to Doc, he falsettoed, "Marilyn thinks my lipstick's a little overdone." He pooched his mouth. "What do you think?"

"I think it's time to go."

BANG!

The sound like a gunshot.

Blackbirds chattered from the eucalyptus that swept the hillside above the parking lot.

Marilyn's eyebrows arched; her lipsticked mouth formed a perfect, bright red O.

Doc whipped around.

BANG!

A bus, black smoke belching from its exhaust pipe, Servite Catholic High School stenciled on its yellow side panel, pulled up to the loading dock.

Leaning out its open windows, Doc saw a gush of pimply faces, a blur of boys' hands waving miniature American flags.

BANG!

Hoots and hollers erupted from the bus.

Its frame rocked.

Red, white, and blue balloons bubbled out the windows, a dozen or more effervesced skyward as the double-wide doors in the back of the bus were flung open.

The G-men had seen and heard enough. A commotion that mimicked the sounds of gunshots was a breakdown in security. Protocols needed to be enforced. The suspicious Fed, the one who'd shined the flashlight into Marilyn's car, scowled, jabbed an I'll-be-back-for-you finger in Doc's direction, then took off after the second agent who was already marking double-time in the direction of the school bus.

Now was the moment, Doc thought. They could ditch the Secret Service, sneak into the hospital, get to Fang without being followed.

He motioned to the others. "Move."

Marilyn, Doc, and the rest of the Gigolos slipped into the wake of the agents.

Grill, in his tight skirt, taking three steps to Slatz's one, pointed up at the hospital. "Fang's on the third floor," he said. "I called the nurse's station from my dad's office." He grabbed a breath. "Room Three Twenty-Three."

Marilyn wiggled her way up to Jimmy. "Tell me again, how did the poor boy get burned?"

"Doc blew him up. Saved my life. Took out Junior's chop-top Mercury with an orange."

Marilyn paused, breathed out mostly vowels, "An orange what?"

"Just the citrus," Jimmy said.

Ahead of them, the agents yelled, "Out of the vehicle. Everyone, out of the bus, now." Corralling the boys from Servite, the agents began sitting them down on the asphalt below the driver's side window. The Gigolos and Marilyn peeled right, dodged behind the bus. Through its open back doors, amid the balloons, Doc saw a clothing rack filled with maroon blazers, a stack of straw bowlers banded in patriotic colors.

"These guys must be Servite's chorus," Grill said. "The 'Altar Boys.' I recognize the jackets."

Jimmy climbed into the back of the bus. Pulled a blazer from a hanger. Tried it on. "Wha'da ya think?"

Looking up at him, Marilyn squealed. "Incognito. Jimmy, you're very smart. Go into the hospital as part of the entertainment? I love that idea. It's crazy." She winked at Doc, took a breath, then descended into "character." Her posture changed. Her voice liquefied, every cell in her body began to smolder. "I think I'll go up front and introduce myself to the boys from Servite. Give them a show. You hold onto my broken places, Doc. I'll catch up to you and your friends later."

Joining Jimmy, Doc and Slatz scrambled into the bus, frantically tore through the racks till both found a coat that fit.

Grill crouched, not so ladylike, behind the rear wheel of the bus, stood guard.

Buttoning the borrowed coat, leaning out the back of the bus, Doc asked, "How's Marilyn doing?"

Grill peeked around the corner. "We'll know any second." He counted down, "Three, two, one. Curtain going up."

There were audible gasps in the distance. Frenzied howls and wolf whistles. Vocal chords squeaking, dropping two octaves, then resonating at frequencies unavailable before puberty: the blond bombshell had detonated at ground zero.

Coats buttoned, hats in place, Doc and the gang jumped from the back of the bus then climbed onto the loading dock. Grill, metal case in hand, hustled up behind them.

At the edge of his vision, near the opposite end of the platform, Doc saw a van pull up: Red's Sanitary Supply. Four burly men climbed out. They were dressed like either ice cream men or orderlies.

"What are they doing here?"

"Who?" Jimmy asked.

"The Cubans! The Communists!"

A second later, sliding in behind the van, a red truck skid to a stop. Two giant faces leaned out the windows and grinned at them.

"It's the Blutos!" Jimmy said. "No Junior. Must have let him off at the entrance."

Doc took one last look at the Cubans and Blutos, then ran.

They all ran. At break-neck speed, they serpentined between crates, leapt over stacks of boxes. One by one they disappeared into the bowels of the hospital's basement.

EVERYONE HIT THE FLOOR

Low-lit corridors.

Green walls.

A maze.

Lead changes, like a horserace. Slatz in front, then Doc, then Jimmy…then Grill?

They pinballed off gurneys, IV stands, monitors on rolling carts.

A blind turn.

A dead end.

In front of them, a freight elevator. A staircase.

Doc stopped, pushed the button. An eternity of silence, then the drone of cables.

Ding.

The elevator doors opened.

Doc leaned in, hit the button for the third floor, shoved Slatz and Grill forward.

"You guys get to Fang," he said. "Do what you can. Keep an eye out for Junior."

The doors faltered, jerked, closed.

Booming down the corridor, vibrating the walls were sounds of bulls in china shops.

Jimmy and Doc, their backs to the staircase, stood their ground.

Twin shadows that, even disembodied, possessed the power to tear them apart climbed the green walls. A reek of animal odor overpowered the smell of ammonia and disinfectant. The floor shook.

The Blutos turned the corner, stopped, stared at them with slitted simian eyes, eyes that had missed the invention of the wheel, the discovery of flint for making fire.

"Wha'da ya say, guys?" Jimmy said. "In the mood for a little fe-fi-fo…fun?" He flashed his Davy Crockett smile.

The Blutos lunged.

Doc and Jimmy scrambled up the basement stairs, made a hard right at the first landing. Climbed. Another right, then right again, each flight more dizzying and disorienting than the one below it, the whole thing like a trip through an Escher drawing.

Out of breath, they reached the ground floor of the hospital.

Two giant stainless steel laundry carts heaped with dirty linens rested against the wall. A short hallway ahead of them led to three doors.

Jimmy wrestled the carts into position at the top of the stairs.

Doc ran to the door that read Exit. Tested the handle. Locked.

They looked at each other, then studied the signs above the other doors: Crisis Psychiatric, Active TB Ward."

Jimmy shoved the carts. The wheels clattered, frenzied like cymbals in the furry fists of a mechanical monkey, *bang, bang, banged* down the tile steps. Metal screamed as the cart careened off the walls. Impact. Profane echoes. Angry expletives…It was a nice try, but the sound of heavy footsteps persisted. The Blutos were still coming.

"Which way, Doc?"

Doc recalled Marilyn's advice: "Do something crazy." That's what she'd said. He glanced at the doors. "We stay. I'll take it from here."

"That's crazy, Doc."

"I hope so."

Aping up the last step, the Blutos, bruised and brooding, one of them tearing away a sheet that twisted around his head, the other sniffing a soiled towel, stopped at the top of the landing. They hulked forward, stopped. Their meaty foreheads wrinkled. The towel and sheet dropped to the floor.

"Why aren't you running?" they said in unison.

"We give up," Doc said. "You guys caught us fair and square. You win. Junior's gonna be proud of you."

The bones of their skulls shifted, their scalps stretched. Something intracranial writhed for room to process what, to them, must have seemed an abstract idea. They winced, looked migrainous. "We win?"

"Good," Doc said. "We've reached a meeting of the minds." He pointed to the door that led to the TB unit. "I think through there's the best way to take us out of here."

They frowned. "Why not take the stairs?"

Jimmy shook his head. "The door over there's locked. Can't go upstairs, can't go back down either. You morons aren't the only ones chasing us. Check out these maroon blazers. They're stolen. They're disguises. The Feds are after us."

The Blutos sniffed the air, cocked their heads. Listened. "The Feds is cops?"

Doc nodded. Then, to his surprise, he thought he heard distant words mumbled in Spanish, the faint squish of gum-soled, agrarian shoes creeping up the lower staircase. "Hear that?" he said. "I'm telling you there are guys with guns who want us more than you do." Again, Doc pointed to the door. "Let's go this way."

"You think we doesn't read. That sign says Active TB Ward. That stuff makes you sick."

"Think about it," Doc said. "It says *active* TB ward. They're *active*. How sick can they be?"

The sound of climbing footsteps grew louder.

Pointing to the door to "Crisis Psychiatric," Jimmy said, "On the other hand, we could go the 'mental health' way. It's not like anyone's ever tried to have you both declared insane...or have they?"

One Bluto looked sheepish, the other swallowed hard.

"Okay," they said simultaneously. "Start walking. No funny stuff."

Manhandling them, the Blutos twisted Doc and Jimmy's arms behind their backs and marched them forward.

There was a small chicken-wired window cut into the door of the TB unit. Through it, Doc could see maybe twenty men, most of them gaunt, unshaven, clad in dreary bathrobes and rubber slippers. Some wandered the room like derelicts; others shot pool or sat at tables playing cards and checkers.

"Wha'da ya see?" Jimmy said under his breath.

"So far nothing that looks like help."

A Bluto shoved Doc flat against the door, his cheek pancaked against the glass. He reached down and turned the knob. The door opened. Doc and Jimmy, followed by the Blutos, stepped into the unit. The door behind them clicked closed, *whooshed* as it hermetically sealed. An alarm rang.

Every head turned. Unblinking, medicinally modified bloodshot eyes stared at them.

A hand holding a checker stopped in midmove.

A poker chip on its way to the pot froze in its flight path.

"Hi, everyone," Doc said. "Just passing through."

"STOP WHERE YOU ARE!" The voice boomed down from loudspeakers. It crackled with feedback as its magnitude scratched holes in the sound barrier.

"YOU HAVE ENTERED AN AREA OF ACTIVE INFECTION. YOU WILL BE ADVISED AS TO THE PROCEDURE FOR COMPLETE, FULL BODY DECONTAMINATION. YOU WILL BE EXPOSED AND HOSED. REMOVE YOUR CLOTHING."

Panicking, grabbing Doc and Jimmy by their collars, the Blutos reversed gears and bolted for the door that led back to the hallway.

Skidding on his heels, Doc spotted the source of the voice. Within a glass-enclosed nurse's station, manning the helm of the TB unit, was a massive wimpled nun in a white "Army of God" nurse's uniform. She had a forehead like the Blutos. She scowled, squinted. Her bulldog face pruned into the microphone, "Howard? Clarence? Is that you?"

Dragging along beside Doc, Jimmy said, "Who the heck are Howard and Clarence?"

"Us," the Blutos huffed. "That's our aunt."

Doc heard a *whoosh*.

The entrance door to the unit burst open. Orderlies rushed in from the exterior hallway.

Auntie Bluto screamed, "CHLOROFORM THEM!"

The brothers Bluto braked, picked up Jimmy and Doc, threw them over their shoulders, reversed gears, and ran deeper into the unit.

The speakers rang out, "IF YOU KNOW WHAT'S GOOD FOR YOU, YOU'LL FOLLOW THE RED LINE ON THE FLOOR. YOU HEARD ME. FOLLOW THE ARROWS."

Doc twisted, tried to break free.

Jimmy mounted the Bluto beneath him. Threw his legs over a Bluto's—was it Clarence's—shoulders? He rose erect and rode the Bluto like a Brahma Bull down the red tile pathway.

Tables toppled, decks of cards played fifty-two pick up, tubercular bones snapped as the infirmed were trampled, checkers scattered like buckshot. Reaching up, Jimmy grabbed a pool cue as it javelined through the air.

Ahead of them, with no way around it, was the decontamination unit. It looked like a glass boxcar derailed on the outskirts of hell, an airless enamel prison cell with doors reminiscent of a meat locker. White steam pumped into the chamber through pipes, fogged its interior. Vents added to the chemical concoction a haze of pinkish gas.

The Blutos stopped at the meat-locker doors, turned, and faced the patients and hospital staff.

Waving straightjackets, brandishing chloroform-soaked towels, the orderlies cautiously inched toward them.

Doc glanced over at Jimmy.

Jimmy was staring upward intently eyeing what Doc guessed was the master valve, a red wheel, its fittings clamped around the massive pipe that led into the decontamination unit. His fingers coiled around the thick end of the cue.

"Do it," Doc said. "Batter up."

Jimmy swung for the fences.

Whack.

He swung again.

Whack! Whack!

The wheel bent, dislocated.

Rivets pinged, gaskets blew, enamel tiles disintegrated into white confetti, steam erupted, hurricaned, Nagasakied into an apocalyptic avalanche of chemically infused fog.

Everyone hit the floor.

Choking sounds. Visibility zero. Aftermath.

Pawing through the pinkish, pea soup haze, Doc and Jimmy Brailled their way back through the unit, crawled out the front door and back into the hall...

"Buenos dias, chico."

Doc looked up at the sound of the man's voice.

Leaning against the opposite wall were the Cubans.

The leader, the one with the gold tooth and the milky eye, the one who'd held a gun to Doc's head in La Paloma, came forward. He jerked Doc to his feet, stuck a finger in Doc's chest. "Why you keep following us, chico?"

Jimmy jumped up, slapped the man's hand away. "'Chico's' not following you anywhere. We've never seen you before."

The leader's five o'clock shadow darkened; his good eye marbled from Jimmy to Doc. "Tell your friend the truth."

"I've run into these guys before," Doc said. "They're communists. Reds."

"Please," the Cuban interrupted. "We prefer the term 'freedom fighters.'"

Doc scoffed. "They were looking at maps in the library, Jimmy. Circling stuff in the newspaper. They held me hostage in a Mexican restaurant a couple of days ago. My guess is they have beef with Kennedy." He turned back to the Cuban. "That's why you're here, right?"

"The light bulb it go off in your head, si? Muy bueno." He lit a cigar. Puffed dismissively. "You read too much *Time* magazine, amigo. We are simply freedom fighters here to exercise our freedom of expression as guaranteed by your Constitution."

"Yeah? Well," Jimmy said, "we're freedom fighters, too. Our battle's upstairs. We plan to nail the guy who murdered my sister. We're one confession away from getting that done and we're running out of time. So step aside...amigo."

The Cuban came closer. "Let me understand this. You are here on a matter of family honor? Like ours, yours is a noble cause?" He glanced over at the TB unit, sniffed the noxious fumes that snaked from beneath the door. "And you will apparently stop at nothing to complete your mission?"

"I have a holy fire burning inside me. My best friend here, Doc, he's the one who struck the match. We're on a mission from God."

The Cubans leaning against the wall crossed themselves.

The leader nodded, then as if holding a red cape, made the sweeping gesture of a toreador. "Then go. The door that leads upstairs has been 'unlocked.' You are free to go."

Jimmy took in a slow, deep breath, spread his arms wide and embraced the Cuban. "Familia," he said. "It is everything, yes?"

Looking over Jimmy's shoulder, the leader grinned at Doc, winked. It was a taunt. Definitely a taunt.

Doc challenged him, stood tall on two strong legs. "So why are you all dressed as orderlies? Where's that gun you had at La Paloma?"

Jimmy stepped back from the Cuban. "It's okay, Doc. Relax. We have an understanding here. The generalissimo believes us, we believe him."

Doc pointed at each of the Cubans. "I want you guys to swear you're just here to protest something. Nobody gets hurt, right?"

The leader relit his cigar, puffed out a quick succession of ever-widening smoke rings. The circles formed a bull's-eye.

Jimmy fanned the smoke away. "Come on, Doc," Jimmy said. "Let's go."

KENNEDY

They climbed the stairs, their shoes slapping the concrete steps.

Doc said, "You believe him? You don't think they're gonna make trouble?"

"If they do, they'll have a hard time making a getaway." He reached into his pants, pulled out a set of keys.

"You picked his pocket?"

"Viva la Revolucion, Doc."

"I don't know," Doc said, pushing open the door to the third floor. "I still think we should blow the whistle on them."

"We'll tell someone about them on the way to Fang's room. It should be down the hall to the left."

But exiting the stairwell, Doc realized they couldn't turn left. The corridor in front of them was jam-packed, busy and bustling with nuns coming toward them. Every Catholic in town it seemed, wanted to see Kennedy. Italian nuns with vacant faces swayed their arms in the air. Girls just off the boat from Ireland pushed kids in wheelchairs. Older Spanish nuns held newborn babies in their arms. Polish nuns herded cripples on crutches. An unending international procession of nuns and more nuns blocked their way to Fang's room.

Doc pulled Jimmy by the arm. Together, the two of them muscled their way into the fray. "We've got to get Fang's confession before

Junior gets to him. Let's just beat our way there. How tough can a bunch of penguins be?"

A tidal wave, a trample of black and white, engulfed Doc and Jimmy and buffeted them backward, spun them, pushed them toward the distant double doors and a sign that read Dayroom.

Doc took one last shot at getting the attention of the crowd. He shouted out, "Cuban assassins! Make way, everyone. Kennedy's in danger!"

He might as well have been speaking to the children of Hamlin. No one was listening. He felt like he was in a movie where what was supposed to happen next wasn't happening next. They had to get to Fang and time was running out.

He looked around for someone who'd take the threat to Kennedy's life seriously. Someone whose face wasn't illuminated by a rapturous glow, anyone who wasn't transfixed by the anticipation of impending epiphany.

Bobbing in a flashflood of religious ecstasy, Doc spotted two maroon jackets. He grabbed Jimmy's arm. "Over there," he said. "I think I see Slatz and Grill."

Flailing, sinking, and surfacing, the other two Gigolos dog-paddled their way through what, to Doc, seemed the entire convent scene from *The Sound of Music*, then finally arrived at Doc's and Jimmy's sides just as they reached the double doors that led into the Dayroom.

Grill, his forehead bleeding, came up for air. "Geez, you'd think Kennedy's the Second Coming."

A nun pointed at Grill's bloody face. Wide-eyed, sobbing, she screamed, "Stigmata. A crown of thorns. It's all true." She swooned, collapsed to the floor.

"All this for Kennedy?" Doc said. "What's the big deal? The guy's a plagiarist. He fools around on his wife. He's gonna break Marilyn's heart."

"It's a Catholic hospital," Slatz said, elbowing back a priest. "Wha'dya expect?"

A chant rose from the clergy. Rosary beads rattled out rhythms like a thousand maracas.

Jimmy gripped Grill's lapels. "Did you get to Fang?"

"No chance," Grill yelled. "He has this Nazi nurse. Really brutal. She's only letting adults in. Something about Fang being a victim of a violent crime. Said she already tossed his cousin out."

"So Junior *is* here?" Doc said. "Either of you see him or Marilyn?"

They shook their heads.

The double doors opened, opened wider.

The procession pushed forward. Ahead of them a podium, a microphone, a grand piano, an arcing array of flags in flagstands.

The Dayroom began to fill.

Now flanking the Gigolos, there were reporters, camera crews, puffed-pigeon dignitaries, blue-haired matrons, and aides to the candidate. Security was everywhere.

Even worse, Doc realized he and his friends were inadvertently leading the way. They were at the front of the pack.

Kennedy's entourage burst through the double-wide doors at the opposite end of the room.

Impending convergence. Believers now stood in the presence of the one they believed in.

As though it were a reflex, the Gigolos straightened their jackets, buttoned buttons. Grill adjusted the slip underneath his nurse's uniform.

An ethereal voice announced, "The Democratic candidate for President of the United States, John Fitzgerald Kennedy."

Like the skin of a banana, the entourage peeled away. Kennedy, big-toothed, tanned, a sculpted stack of politically perfect hair, admittedly handsome, took the microphone in hand, claimed his place at the podium. He looked through Doc, past him, smiled confidently at the adoring crowd and said, "In Americah, no stah shines brightah than the smile of a healthy child. The Democratic Pahty has always and will always fight for our children."

Wild applause.

Kennedy beamed, then slowly his features iced over as his eyes met Doc's.

Though Doc wasn't where he wanted to be, where he needed to be, he was where he was: face to face again with the man he'd met upstairs above the Majestic Theatre. He could feel his blood boiling.

"Greetings from May and Marilyn," Doc said softly. "So, Jack, gonna tell Jackie about your day at the Pike?" He mouthed the words in a way that made his meaning perfectly clear.

Kennedy lowered the microphone to his side. "So it's ah bongo boy, Day-o...I see your sight has been restored. Too bad you keep sticking your sniffer in the wrong place. You're a clear and present danja to the campaign, young man. We'll need to have a long talk with you."

Kennedy nodded, the gesture a coded order to his security staff.

Two Feds put their hands on Doc.

Jimmy stepped forward, took the microphone from Kennedy's hand. Full-throated, in perfect pitch, he sang out "God Bless Amer-i-ca."

Everyone who could stand, stood. The Feds let go of Doc, put their hands over their hearts.

Jimmy handed the microphone to Doc, and Doc tentatively sang, "America?"

Jimmy leaned in and tenored, "Land that I love."

Making it a four-part harmony, Slatz and Grill joined in: "Stand beside her...ba ba ba boom...and guide her...ba ba ba boom...Through the night with a light from above."

The Gigolos marched in place. "From the mountains," then over to a grand piano, "to the prairies."

Every eye was on them now. Every hand clapped in rhythm. Every voice raised in song.

When they got to "foam," Doc spotted Marilyn in the crowd, Margaret Ann standing next to her.

The gold-toothed Cuban was right behind them, pistola raised. Both girls, arms linked, swayed back and forth in front of the gun barrel pointed directly at Kennedy.

HIS HANDS DECIDE
THEY'RE BULLETPROOF

Suddenly, Doc is present in a world where everything is immediate, real in a way he has never experienced before. He hears the crowd singing, "My home…sweet…home."

He hears a *click* as the hammer is thumbed back. The weapon, cocked, magnified, is all he can see.

Doc has a memory of hearing himself yell, "Gun! Take cover! Run!" but the words are in a place somewhere behind him.

There's a stinging sensation as his knees bang wheelchairs. He's in the crowd. Airborne. Flying over the audience.

Marilyn and Margaret Ann look up at him curiously, mouths wide open as he vaults over them. Traveling through space, his hands decide they're bulletproof. They reach out.

The Cuban becomes a giant, rising Cheshire cat. He's taking aim. His gold tooth glints as he shouts slow-motion words that stretch out in Spanish, "Muerte a los tiranos!"

Time jerks, freezes, then starts again. A dream-like vision sweeps into Doc's periphery. He sees a piano bench propelled by long legs. It reminds him of a hermit crab carrying its shell, a life form frantically running for its life. It blasts past him.

It's clear the bench is a battering ram, an irresistible force held aloft by hands that know the instrument: Slatz's hands. Blind, Slatz is unaware he is charging into the line of fire.

Bang! Bang!

Ceiling tiles explode in a sizzle of white dust. Chunks of splintered wood fly in all directions.

Doc is on the floor. He has a vague recollection of colliding with Slatz when the two of them barreled into the Cuban.

Men in suits climb over him. He hears struggling, the ratcheting of handcuffs. Rights are read.

His head rests on something soft. In his ear there's a heartbeat.

"Doc? You okay?"

The voice is Margaret Ann's.

He opens his eyes. Opposite him on the floor a few feet away, he sees Marilyn. Slatz is cradled in her arms. Smoke wisps up from a hole in his maroon jacket. There's blood dripping down Slatz's arm.

"I got shot," Slatz says. "Just the shoulder. Still, pretty cool, huh?"

"Doc?"

Margaret Ann's voice again.

He looks up. "It's wonderful being close to you."

"You're lying on my chest," she says.

"Can I stay awhile?"

"What about Fang?" she says.

He exhales, grabs a fresh breath, stands, remembers he's on a mission.

INDIANA

With time back in one piece again, Doc took Margaret Ann's hand and pulled her up. Together, they navigated through the crush of stunned onlookers, pushed past nuns making the sign of the cross, Feds shoving reporters back, doctors kneeling over the apoplectic.

Clear of the crowd, Doc righted an overturned chair, stood on it, looked over the room. Kennedy was gone, had been whisked away. No sign of Jimmy or Grill, though he did catch a final glimpse of Slatz. Assisted by Marilyn, Bobby "Slatz" LaDesma agonized to his feet, winced theatrically, waved off the army of photographers.

Shutters flurried in rapid fire in Slatz's direction. Flashbulbs *pop-popped*. The press shouted out, "Young man, what made you do it? How did you find the courage?"

Looking on, Doc smiled, shook his head, hopped down from the chair. Landed hard. Odd, he thought, his gimp leg didn't hurt. It hadn't hurt for days. He led Margaret Ann through the double doors into the corridor.

"The police recovered the Studebaker," she said as they moved quickly down the hallway. "My dad picked up Bonnie and the baby, took them over to our house. She and I talked for a long time."

"Is she okay?" Doc asked.

"Safe for now. My dad's gonna get them out of town, put her and the baby on a train."

Doc stopped. "A train? A train to where?"

"Indiana. Bloomington. Near the college I'm going to. My aunt and uncle's place."

"I guess that's good," he said. "She wanted to go to India. Indiana? Guess that's close enough."

"Doc, my dad hasn't told anyone what he's doing. No one will know where she is. As far as the world will know, she's disappeared. She'll never go to jail. She won't lose her baby."

"Why is he helping her?"

"I asked him to. Had to. You can't fix everything."

"What about Father Stephen? He knows. With everything coming down on him, he might talk."

"Father Stephen's gone," she said.

"Gone? Like dead?"

"No. Like gone to Rome. My dad went by the church. Father Stephen was 'called' to the Vatican. He left last night. My guess is he knew it was only a matter of time before the truth came out."

"Yeah," he said. "You're probably right." He took a breath, pictured the puzzle pieces he and Margaret Ann had laid out on the blanket in the cemetery only a few days ago. Now he sorted through them again in his mind. "Junior's got no one left to lie for him," he said, "no one left he can threaten."

"Except Fang."

Doc nodded, stared down the hallway ahead of him. "You coming with me?"

SOLVING FOR X

They found Room Three Twenty-Three around the next corner, walked in. Margaret Ann stayed by the door. There were voices from behind a green curtain: Jimmy and Grill arguing, Jimmy saying, "Geez, Grill, this is ridiculous."

"There are critical variables at play here. As a nurse I have a professional obligation to—"

"You're not a nurse, Grill."

Doc pushed through a flap in the curtain.

Jimmy and Grill stood bedside. The tape recorder, its reels slowly turning, sat on a tray table. Fang lay face down on a motorized bed, his blistered buttocks elevated, teepeed in the middle. Tubes wormed in and out of his veins. His left arm, encased in plaster of Paris from wrist to shoulder, was suspended in midair by a system of pulleys.

Jimmy grabbed the syringe from Grill. "I say we juice him up again. See what happens."

"How's it going?" Doc asked.

Jimmy shook his head at Doc, glared at Grill.

Grill shrugged. "I made a little mistake. When I started the tape recorder, I swore Fang in. Told him he had to tell the truth, the whole truth, and nothing but the truth. I wanted the confession to be legit."

"So?"

"I think he's into this regression thing, Doc. Apparently, his whole truth begins at conception; must have been pretty traumatic."

Jimmy ground his teeth. He tore away the tubes and cables, flipped Fang on his back and jabbed the needle into Fang's right arm. Pushing down on the plunger, he growled, "The only truth I want to know is what happened Christmas Eve. Remember Christmas Eve three years ago, Fang? We know you were there. You were in the backseat of the Studebaker. We found the empty packs of M&Ms. Your prints are all over them. You're gonna tell me who killed my sister."

Margaret Ann pulled back the curtain, joined them. "Did any of you notice there's no flowers in this room, no get well cards. I think we're Fang's first visitors. It's sorta sad."

Grill nodded. "You should see his cast, Margaret Ann. Only one signature. He signed it to himself."

Margaret Ann walked closer to the bed. "Maybe we should…"

Fang began to twitch. His eyes bugged out, crossed. His cheeks ballooned in scarlets and purples.

Doc tensed. "I think he's choking."

"No," Grill said, calmly. "He's reliving his embryonic journey: intimations of sperm penetrating egg, the beginning moments of consciousness. In his case, his journey into the world was a dark and dirty process."

Jimmy retracted the empty plunger, pushed it down again. "Process this, Fang."

Like someone strapped into a jet car speeding across the Bonneville Salt Flats, Fang's lips began to jiggle, his skin stretched flat against the bones of his skull. His bloodshot eyes seemed to stare into an abyss haunted by demons hungry to devour his soul. In a tiny, helium voice, he screamed out, "I've defied the laws of nature. All that matters is I'm here. It doesn't matter how I got here. I have life."

"What's he talking about? Doc asked.

"The truth behind the circumstances of his birth. He's approaching catharsis," Grill said solemnly.

The metal bed rattled. IV lines snapped. Fang's eyes settled back into their sockets. His crazed look seemed to melt away. He sat up, smiled, burst out laughing. "I'm not telling you guys nothing. You're suckers, idiots. Junior Mentz rules." He sneered, glared at Jimmy. "Maybe I watched your sister die, maybe I heard her bones snap, maybe I saw her crawl in the mud, crying 'boo-hoo, help me.' If I did I'll never tell you." Chuckling, he leered at all of them. "Sodium Pentothal. What a joke. I could eat that stuff for lunch. So now you know. So what if I was conceived rectally? My dad swears that's the only way he ever did it to my mom and I'm proud of it, so the joke's on you." He closed his eyes.

Doc looked around at the others in the room. "What?"

Margaret Ann said, "I didn't know you could get pregnant that way."

Grill shook his head. "I doubt he was conceived that way. His mom must have had a fistula, a rip between the two walls. But I see in his declaration the seeds of irony: Because Fang believed he was conceived *in* an asshole, he became one. There's one more thing. We have, in the makings, the possibility of a literary connection. A homage of sorts. If it turns out his confession puts an end to Junior, it'll be like the prophesy in Shakespeare's *Macbeth*, the second prophesy the witches made: 'None of woman born shall harm Macbeth.' Fang will become a Macduff of the modern era. 'Twas he who killed Macbeth. Neither he nor Macduff was born the regular way."

Doc rolled his eyes. "That's the stupidest thing I've ever heard."

"Yes," Grill said. "You're right. 'Stupid' is the operative word, though, perhaps a bit too strong. See, it may turn out that Mentz's fatal flaw was he didn't stay in school, never took literature or learning seriously. Rather than read, rather than battle a book or a play from cover to cover, he decided to torment the weak. Fang was probably one of his first victims. My guess is Junior, knowing the circumstances of Fang's birth, threatened to tell every girl in school that his cousin was born, and would forever be, a piece of crap. Fang couldn't let that happen, so he did what he was told to do."

396

"That's just so sad."

It was Marilyn's voice.

Doc looked over his shoulder.

Standing just inside the doorway were nuns, priests, the police... and Marilyn.

She stepped forward, glanced at the chart chained to the foot of Fang's bed. "It's all so horrible. I wish I could help."

Doc had an idea. He took Marilyn's hand. "Don't open your eyes, Fang. Just listen."

"Sure," he said. "I'd love a bedtime story."

Doc steadied himself. "Here's the rest of the whole truth, Fang. That last injection Jimmy gave you? It was a syringe filled with air. You've got air bubbles working their way to your brain."

Fang's face paled. He squinted up at Doc. "I don't like bubbles."

"Too bad. You're probably gonna die, though I can't say I know that for sure. Maybe you'll just end up a vegetable. But I can tell you this: If you don't tell Jimmy what happened to his sister we're gonna leave you here. Let Junior kill you. And he will kill you. Bonnie's gone. So is Father Stephen. That's the God-honest truth. You're the only one left who knows what happened Christmas Eve. You have a choice. Confess and you're redeemed. Stay silent and you go to hell."

"Junior's my cousin. He's my friend. We keep each other's secrets."

"Buddy was Junior's friend too," Doc said. "Junior killed him."

Fang was silent. He squirmed in the bed. "I'll take my chances. Besides, there's no Heaven up in the sky. No Heaven on Earth either."

"Feel the bubbles in your brain?"

Fang's face greened a little. "I feel sick, really sick." He burped, burped again, blanched. "Stop them! Stop the bubbles!"

Doc nodded at Marilyn. "An angel's about to appear in front of you, Fang. She wants you to know Heaven is real. Tell her the truth and she'll give you a peek at what lies beyond the Pearly Gates."

Leaning close to Marilyn, Doc whispered, "I need a fantasy for a sex-starved teenage boy. I'm sorry I have to ask."

Reluctantly, she knelt beside the bed, gathered Fang in her eyes.

Fang blinked. His pupils dilated.

"You'll need a sponge bath," she said, "before you go to Heaven. Let's both of us get comfortable." She undid the top button of her blouse, breathed in; the inhalation released another button.

Fang's eyes opened wider.

"Confess," she whispered. "And I'll open my heart for you to see."

Fang's swollen jaw hung open.

She came closer, took a breath. Another button popped. "Whoops. Only three more to go," she said.

The tape recorder whirred.

Fang moaned, "Glory Be to God."

She started to undo another button, stopped, perked an ear. "I'm so very sorry. I hear the angels calling. It's time for me to go."

"No, no," he screamed. "Stay. I'll talk."

They all froze in their tracks. Silence teetered at a tipping point, reached out, gripped the room by the throat.

Marilyn glanced back at Doc, mouthed, "I can't do this," then gazed at Fang. There were tears in her eyes.

"Frankie?" she said. "That's your name, right?"

Fang nodded.

"Your Christian name?"

"Actually, it's Francis."

"Well first of all, Francis, I need you to know I'm no angel. And I can't tell you for sure that there aren't air bubbles going to your brain. I will tell you this, and it's straight from the heart: I'm not here to get you to tell the truth if it means making a fool of you, and I don't think Doc would want that either. People have made a fool out of me, used me. It's not very kind. Like you, the circumstances surrounding my birth weren't so wholesome. I've lived life as an orphan. It hurts. People have hurt you, too. I see the broken places." She took a breath.

"I'm like this friend of mine. All my love just pours into the broken places." She took Fang's hand, Doc's too. "We're all orphans of the storm, outcasts till someone tells us it's time to come home."

Fang began to cry. "I tried to be a regular guy, tried really hard when I was a kid. I wasn't very good at it. I was always so scared they'd find out about me. If they did, Junior said my nickname would probably end up being something like Fudge, not Fang. I'd end up with a stink on me that wouldn't wash off. I didn't have friends who could show me what you have to do to make people like you. I just couldn't figure it out on my own. A guy like me hasn't got a chance when everyone around is already the star of the show. It's easy for everybody else to be the best person in the room when all you're up against is me... when you compare yourself to me."

"You can be the best person right now, Francis," Marilyn said. "You can do what no one else in this room can. You can take away Jimmy's pain. Tell him what happened to his sister."

Doc held his breath. Every molecule of air in the room stood still.

Fang reached up. Slowly, fingers fumbling, he refastened her buttons. Looking at Jimmy, he said, "Junior just...Junior said he wanted to crash the birthday party."

Doc, pointing to the buttons on his own shirt, gave a thumbs-up to Margaret Ann. Smiled.

Margaret Ann didn't smile back. She looked from Marilyn to Doc, folded her arms across her chest, rolled her eyes, and walked out of the room.

Fang kept talking: "Jesus's party," he said. "The Nativity scene? It's a birthday party, right? It was all supposed to be a joke. The girl on the horse, she came out of nowhere. Junior steered the car right into them. She was hurt bad, but she wasn't dead. Buddy got out of the car to help her. Buddy and I said we should take her to the hospital, get someone to help the horse. We begged Junior...He threw the car in reverse and ran over her again. Said if we told anyone he'd kill us." Fang sobbed.

One of the cops stepped forward, said, "What you did with Marilyn's buttons…that was pretty dignified, kid. Still, I gotta do this." He handcuffed Fang's broken arm to the metal bed.

"It's done," Doc said, turning to Jimmy. "Now we track down Junior."

A nun approached them, Margaret Ann's purse in her hand. "Junior? Your friend, Junior?" she said. "He wanted me to tell you that he and your little girlfriend were leaving…the pouty girl with the freckles." She handed Doc the purse. "She'll probably be lost without it."

"Where did they go? Which way?" Doc asked, panic rising in his voice.

The nun smiled. "Junior said to tell you they were going to church. Saint Mary's."

Doc lunged forward, fingers ready to throttle the nun, every cell of his body desperate to choke more information out of her.

Jimmy held him back. "Thanks for letting us know, Sister."

Through gritted teeth Doc whispered. "We need to tell the police. Quinn needs to know his daughter's been kidnapped."

"No, Doc. Cops show up at the church, Junior's gonna hurt Margaret Ann. Don't you get it? He wants us to come alone…he wants me." Jimmy pulled the stolen keys from his pocket.

Doc stared down at the purse he held in his other hand. His shoulders sank. "Kidnapped again. Twice in twenty-four hours. That never happens to anybody. It's my fault. I *never* should have given her the thumbs-up when Marilyn started popping her buttons. She completely misunderstood me. I was excited about Fang's confession, impressed with what he did to preserve Marilyn's modesty. I didn't mean I liked Marilyn's breasts."

"You wanna apologize? Deliver the message in person. Come on. Let's go."

They took off along the corridor; scrambled down the three flights of stairs; pushed through the broken door at the bottom of the stairwell; passed by the TB unit, where Doc, at the last moment, caught a glimpse of the Blutos' slackened, sedated faces peering through the chicken-wired window of Crisis Psychiatric.

Together, Doc and Jimmy rushed through the double doors, through the warehouse, and outside to the loading dock.

The Blutos' red truck was gone. No doubt Junior was behind the wheel now, Margaret Ann his prisoner.

The Cuban's unoccupied van was still parked at the bottom of the ramp. Jimmy got in through the unlocked door, jammed the key into the ignition.

The van's engine faltered, then roared to life.

Hopping in, Doc climbed over the passenger seat. "I'll look around back here. See if they left any weapons."

"Check Margaret Ann's purse."

"Good idea," Doc said, bracing himself, stumbling, standing as the van wound up the hill. Jimmy's last hard left onto Harbor Boulevard tilted the van on two wheels, knocked Doc to the floor. The purse went flying.

Scrambling to his feet, Doc grabbed the purse, a few items from the floor of the van, and climbed into the passenger seat. The speedometer climbed from fifty to sixty. The oil pressure held stout and steady. Out the window, an armada of clouds the color of burnished pewter chopped through the leaden sky. Doc could feel the power of destiny gather near them. He remembered what May had said to him about the "forgotten lore" of his own life, the first chapter of his own biography. The strength he'd drawn on to defeat polio hadn't been inspired by fairy tales or great literature, it resided in the heart he was born with. He could feel that heart beating now.

"What ya got, Doc?"

"Courage."

"No. What did you find? In the back? In the purse?"

Doc looked at the things he'd gathered in his lap. "I've got a length of braided rope, a red enamel lighter commemorating the

Rose Parade, a baseball signed by you, an eyebrow pencil and three Tootsie Rolls."

The van's engine coughed. A sound like an iron horseshoe clattered in the engine. The gas gauge pointed to empty. It started to rain.

The van ran out of gas at the corner of Wilshire and Harbor Boulevard, less than a mile from the church. They coasted into a loading zone in front of Fullerton Music.

Through the store's plate glass window, Doc could see the owner, Mr. Lunde. He was helping a customer. Doc stepped out of the van, waved frantically, motioned for the man to come out.

The owner frowned.

Jimmy got out. "What are you waiting for? Let's go."

Doc handed the baseball to Jimmy. "Hold on a minute," he said, cramming the three Tootsie Rolls into his mouth. Nodding, he chewed vigorously. With the eyebrow pencil he scrawled on the backside of the candy wrapper: Police. Call Detective Quinn. Margaret Ann kidnapped. Go to Saint Mary's. He gummed the message to the inside of the windshield with a globby wad of caramelized chocolate, licked his sticky teeth. "Throw the baseball, Jimmy!"

"Where?"

Doc pointed to the music store. "Through the picture window."

Jimmy wound up, delivered the pitch.

They ran in the direction of the church, glass crashing behind them, the wind a flat hand against their backs, thunder rumbling overhead like cannons booming. In the distance, a rainbow arched over the church.

Pointing, Doc said, "It's a sign. We're gonna make it in time."

Three blocks, two blocks, one block to go.

They pounded up the rain-slicked steps of the church, the great wooden doors moaning as they pulled them open.

With the coil of rope fashioned into a lariat looped over his shoulder, Jimmy led the way up the center aisle. Stopping, he yelled out,

"Junior," his breath exploding from his lungs. "Junior," he yelled again, the words bladed with anger.

No answer came back.

The sanctuary was empty, silent. Light spidered down through stained glass windows. Dark shadows skittered across the floor. The air was a stench of dying roses, dead earth, things less than holy.

Doc recognized the smell, remembered the moment he'd breathed in this odor before. He knew Jimmy would remember the odor too. The sanctuary smelled exactly as it had the day of his sister's funeral. The day services were held for Cindy.

Doc's skin crawled. He sensed something: His gut told him the church had been abandoned. With no priest watching over it, with Father Stephen gone, the place felt spoiled, leached of all goodness, corrupted by the Devil.

All around him, beneath the golden altar, within the naves, tiers of votive candles bloomed in a hellish raspberry light, glowed like jars of radioactive jam.

Saints pictured in scenes painted on the walls glanced down at them, then looked away as though he and Jimmy were invisible. Smug, prideful, the saints seemed to withdraw into egos enchanted with their own righteousness. Even Christ in the glory of his crucifixion looked scared for what awaited them.

"Let's look around outside," Doc said. "I don't like this place."

"No," Jimmy said. "Junior's here. I can feel him."

"Let's check somewhere else. The prelate's office. Maybe there's a priest around."

A corridor behind the confessional led to the office. The door was half open. They walked in, looked around. The desk was scattered with the manuscripts. Pages had been torn out.

Standing over the desk, Jimmy fingered a letter opener with a pontifical seal on its hilt. "Junior's been here too."

Shadows crossed over them.

Doc looked up. Above him were the stained glass skylights he'd looked down through less than a week ago. Each panel now seemed like a prediction, each parable whispered a story that now seemed ultimately personal, a Biblical message meant just for him: the Prodigal Son, Jesus with Mary Magdalene, Lazarus rising from the dead. Their themes were not unlike the elements of the mysteries, the dilemmas he'd dealt with since the day he'd chased the kite.

The glass panels shivered.

"Up there," Doc said. "Junior, Margaret Ann, they're on the roof."

"There's a ladder above the choir loft, a hatch that opens to the roof. We can go up that way."

Doc looked at the skylights. "I'm going to climb up from outside. Wait here a few minutes." He pulled out the Rose Parade lighter, the flares. "I'll come up behind the cross. I'll hide behind the bell housing. You keep Junior busy. Act crazy. Use the lariat. Make him ask himself why you're not acting like you know he's King of the Mountain. He'll lose sight of Margaret Ann. He'll lose sight of everything but himself: that's when we'll strike."

Doc hurried out the side door and into the alley. Just beyond the metal trash cans, tilted up against the outside of the church, was the ladder Pinkie, the nun, had conjured up the day the kite had gotten tangled on the cross. Somehow, even before he'd left Jimmy's side, Doc knew the ladder would be there waiting for him.

He ticked up the rungs lickety-split, hooked his fingers into the rain gutter that ran beneath the second floor balcony, wrenched himself up and tightroped his way along the railing to the drain pipe that ran up the side of the steeple. He didn't look down, didn't look back. He cleared his mind, brought his focus to a pinpoint, but nothing was there. His mind was blank. He had no idea what he was supposed to do. He had no plan to take down Junior. What had he told Jimmy? He couldn't remember.

A scream ripped the air.

Doc looked up.

Margaret Ann's upper body tipped over the edge of the roof. Outstretched hands gripped elbows, rag-dolled her back and forth over the void. One leg lost its footing, a red shoe toppled through space. He could see up her skirt. Her skinny legs, double-jointed at the knees, trembled like pipe cleaners.

He heard Junior laugh.

Doc's blood ran cold. Anger raced through his body like an epidemic. He monkey-fisted the drainpipe, dug in his heels and shinned, shinned, shinnied upward to the bell tower below the cross. He braked at the last moment when he heard Junior yell out, "For the last time, bitch, I'm telling you to sit down and shut up. It won't be long before the fun begins."

The words told him that for now, Margaret Ann was safe.

He lowered himself out of sight, straightened his glasses, hugged the wall. Took a peek.

Margaret Ann, cat glasses crooked on her face, sat on an air conditioning unit facing him. Junior, his back to Doc, paced in front of her.

The wind picked up, howled.

The bell thrummed a sound as ancient as a Gregorian chant.

The shadow of the cross swept across the roof of the church.

A popping sound, a *whoosh* of paper wings.

He looked up. His jaw dropped.

Lancelot, the kite, bigger now than he'd remembered, more menacing, its serpent's tail still lashed to the cross, spiraled above him in a widening gyre.

He looked across the roof, watched as Jimmy, coiled rope in hand, lifted the hatch, pushed back the lid, and rose to his feet.

Junior, all big boots and black leather jacket, snapped open *Persuasion*, squared off against his friend, Gunfight-at-the-O.K.-Corral style.

Doc's eyes flicked to Margaret Ann.

She hadn't moved, hadn't turned to look at Jimmy. Staring straight at him, she mouthed, "Do something."

Doc shook his head. Pulling himself up to the roof, he mouthed back, "Not yet."

He watched as Jimmy, cool as a cucumber, sly as a fox, leisurely twirled the noose at the end of the rope, its diameter doubling, tripling as he spun it. Hopping into the center of the loop, Jimmy flicked his wrist upward. The noose, a blur of white, climbed his body, cycloned above his head.

"Well yippy-ki-yo," Junior said. "What now, little cowboy? Gonna lasso me? Gonna hang yourself?"

Jimmy smiled, "I'm here to send you to hell, Junior."

"I go there occasionally," he said. "I just don't stay." Slicing the air with his knife, Junior savaged to the left. Jimmy danced right.

Margaret Ann screamed. It was an earsplitting do-something-now-Doc scream.

Junior tromped over to Margaret Ann and grabbed her by the hair. "She just never shuts up, does she?" He muzzled her mouth against his leather jacket, dragged her over the tiles. *Persuasion* pressed to the back of her neck, he turned to Jimmy. "Where were we? Ah, yes. Now I remember...I like the idea of you using that rope to hang yourself. I can hear my friend Dr. Brisco saying, 'It's a shame. The little man couldn't live without his big sister. Tragic. But things like that happen. Nothing we can do about it but pray for his soul.'"

Grinning, Jimmy leisurely twirled the rope above his head, then asked, "You and Dr. Brisco are friends?"

"We both have our secrets, just not from each other. He works things from the inside. People talk, do what he tells them to do when he gets them on his couch. Outside, I let *Persuasion* do the talking. We'll just leave it at that."

Dark clouds marched in and suffocated the sky.

Lightning cracked.

Jimmy eyed Junior's knife. "I understand Buddy needed a little *Persuasion*, too."

Junior scoffed. "Buddy was weak."

"Cowards always pick on the weak."

"What did you call me?"

"Bye, bye, Junior." Jimmy slung the noose. It flew. A rush of wind sent it spiraling off course, the force of the gust jerked the rope from Jimmy's hand. The lariat, twisting upward, sailed over Junior's head, disappeared into the darkening sky.

Junior burst out laughing.

Doc wasn't laughing, but he *was* smiling. The lariat wasn't gone. He'd watched it drop down from the sky and loop over the top of the cross twenty feet above his head. The free end, trailed down the side of the bell tower. It dangled in front of him. His mind flashed to movie images. He could see himself grabbing the end of the rope, slinging himself through space, the burning flare held high overhead, his knees flexed to his chest ready to kick. Plunging down in a high heroic arc, he'd blindside Junior, sweep the lovely princess, Margaret Ann, into his arms. He would be Zorro, Tarzan, Captain Blood, every hero who'd ever come to the rescue by rope or vine.

Doc grabbed the bottom of the rope, jerked down. The noose tightened around the cross. He pulled out one of the flares, the Rose Parade lighter. Estimated the angle of attack.

From across the roof Jimmy nodded. He brandished the letter opener, pointed his weapon of last resort at Junior.

Junior howled with laughter. "A letter opener?"

"Thought you might need it when you got the message, Junior. It's a message I'm sending air mail."

Air mail, that was the signal. Doc lit the flare, tightened his grip on the rope. Below him, the shadow of the cross made an X on the roof. It passed over Jimmy, stopped when Junior was in its crosshairs. The equation was perfect. "Time to solve for x," Doc whispered. He leapt into space. Centrifugal forces accelerated him in a wide arc. Doc, the predator falcon, descended on his prey. He was right on target. Five, four, three seconds from impact.

Then everything changed.

Margaret Ann broke free from Junior's grip. She grabbed the letter opener from Jimmy, charged at Junior.

Junior swatted the letter opener from her hand, then…bent to pick it up.

Doc, helpless, riding the backbone of momentum, sailed over Junior's head and kept going. One hundred and eighty degrees, back to the bell tower, back to the base of the cross. The wind died. The kite above him fluttered, drifted down. The flare he held above his head sent Lancelot up in flames. He watched it float away like some Nordic funeral pyre. He did his best to maintain the posture of a hero. He shoved the flare forward. It fizzled out.

"It's still three against one," he said.

Malevolence saturated Junior's pupils. The earth and sky seemed to shift. A crosswind billowed Junior's jacket away from his body. Black leather became black wings. He pointed the blade at Margaret Ann. It doubled in length. Junior smiled at Doc. "Seems *Persuasion*'s got a hard-on for your girlfriend. Maybe I'll just…"

The flaming kite hit Junior like a freight train, like the axe blade of Dante's pendulum. It erased him midsentence from the place he was standing. Its fiery tail wrapped around him like a boa constrictor. The kite's paper skin suctioned itself to his face, sizzled something Biblical, something in Latin. Junior's hair caught on fire. He flailed, whirled, ran at Jimmy.

Jimmy drove his fist into Junior's face, the impact sending Junior spinning across the roof. His head clonked into the church bell. He staggered, wandered cross-eyed in a circle, stopped in front of Doc, slurred, "You're the gimp who had polio, right?"

"That's right," Doc said.

"Doesn't your leg hurt?"

"Sometimes it hurts. I just decided not to limp anymore." Doc took *Persuasion* from Junior's hand, wound up, and delivered a haymaker of his own.

Junior Mentz wobbled, his eyes rolled up in his head, a front tooth tinked onto the tiles. He drifted back, back, back and fell. His scream faded as his body disappeared down the shaft of the bell tower.

Doc, Margaret Ann, and Jimmy looked at each other.

There were sirens in the distance.

"Think I killed him?" Doc said.

Margaret Ann looked around, then at Doc. "Where's that flare?"

"It's burnt out."

"We'll see about that."

Doc and Jimmy walked over to the bell tower, peered down into the cavernous darkness. Margaret Ann joined them. She lit the flare, dropped it down the hole.

One second. Two seconds.

Yelps. Curses. Threats. Sobbing.

Jimmy tucked the letter opener in his pocket. "My guess is he's stuck about halfway down."

They turned at the sound of footsteps approaching.

Detective Quinn, standing by the open hatch, was waving cops and firemen onto the roof.

THE SWEETEST PART
OF FOREVER

Doc and Jimmy were led down to the sanctuary and questioned by the chief of police, a big-bellied man named Holbrook. Stopping them every minute or two, he licked the tip of a pencil, stubby as his thick fingers, and wrote down what they said.

Two men in black suits stood behind the chief. Arms folded, they leaned against a pew, saying nothing at all.

Jimmy kept the story simple: Margaret Ann had been kidnapped by Junior. He'd taken her to the church. That's what a nun had told them at the hospital, Jimmy explained. "With everyone busy dealing with the attempt on Kennedy's life, there was no one to chase after Junior. No one would listen to us," he said. "We should have tried harder to find an adult to help us. We know that now. We're sorry."

His back to the altar, Doc, responding with "yes, sir" and "no, sir," watched as police brought Junior Mentz down through the hatch above the choir loft. He was strapped to a stretcher, looked pretty bad. His hair was fried wire, his face a busted tomato, his leather jacket a scorched carcass shoveled up after a prairie fire. When the pace of questions slowed, Doc asked, "Is Margaret Ann okay?"

"Her father's taken her to the station. Poor little thing, imagine she's quite shaken up." Holbrook flipped a page in his notepad, licked the pencil. "When we're done here," he said, "I'm gonna need you boys to head over there, too. We'll get this report typed up. You'll put your John Hancocks on it, make it official."

A half hour later, another twenty questions, and they were done. At least for now. Apparently the chief didn't know the whole story. Later, when he found out about Jimmy's sister, the Studebaker, the priest, Buddy's murder, he'd sit them down again. It would probably be in a windowless room with bright lights shining in their faces. But for now, he and Jimmy were free to go as long as they promised to walk straight to the police station.

They went out the side door into the alley beside the church. The ladder was gone. The storm had passed. A fleet of small silver clouds, sleek as flying saucers, scooted beneath the sun. Taking a moment, Doc imagined these futuristic images of the modern age escorting Pinkie to Heaven. She'd like that, he thought. She'd like going home in style.

They turned, walked east on Commonwealth.

Jimmy threw his arm over Doc's shoulder. "It's been quite a day. Pretty good. Loved you coming out of the clouds like a secret weapon."

"I liked your Wild West show with the lariat."

"We make a good team, don't we?" Jimmy said.

"Yeah. Wish we could spend the rest of the day hanging out together, but I gotta get home. Gotta babysit."

Jimmy stopped. "Don't know about that. We might be at the station awhile."

Doc stopped, too. The police station was at the end of the block. The place was chaos. "Something must have happened," Doc said. They walked a little faster, then ran.

Outside the station there were cars parked everywhere, skewed at crazy angles, wheels over the curb. There were cop cars from other cities, ambulances, fire trucks, a van with a press pass in the window.

Double-parked in a red zone in front of the entrance was a black limousine from the Kennedy campaign, Bunny LaDesma's Cadillac, and Grill's mom's Lincoln. Crossing the parking lot, deputies with white gloves and whistles swirled around them directing traffic. A herd of citizenry swarmed the station like ants at a picnic.

On their way to the entrance, a fireman tipped his cap to Doc, a police attack dog wagged his tail, a square-faced sergeant with salt-and-pepper hair gave Doc a knowing nod, the old crow from the library gave him a kiss on the cheek then shouted out, "I gave this boy his first library card."

Doc wondered what this show of respect was all about. "Think what's going on here has anything to do with us?"

Jimmy pulled open the door to the squad room. "Guess we'll find out."

Inside, the place was a madhouse. Twenty cops sat at twenty desks interviewing people of every description: nuns, other police, politicians, choir boys from Servite, a man who looked like Francis Scott Key, even the Blutos' aunt. In one corner of the room, Slatz and his dad were yacking it up with a guy who looked like Hugh Hefner. Slatz was wearing a China-red smoking jacket with black satin lapels. Big Lou was beaming.

Center stage, Grill, shouting, "Yes, you may quote me," stood on a desk surrounded by photographers, his mother's ermine coat draped, impresario style, over his shoulders. The mail girl from the hospital was taking pictures of him. When Grill spotted his fellow Gigolos, he hopped down, pushed through the crowd, wriggled in between Doc and Jimmy, raised his arms, snapped his fingers. The press corps hopped to it, gathered around.

"Everyone, check it out. Headline," he shouted. "Kennedy Crooners Crack Cuban Caper, Assassination Attempt Foiled."

There was furious applause, frantic note-taking by reporters.

"I don't get it," Doc said.

Like a ventriloquist, Grill slid the words out of the side of his mouth. "Publicity for the band. They've got pictures of us singing to Kennedy. We're famous."

From the press pool, a woman reporter asked, "Grill, is it true you spent the night with Marilyn Monroe?"

Grill smiled a Paul Newman smile. "Let's just say there's talk of a three-picture deal."

Slatz walked up, pressed down his lapels, joined them.

Another round of applause.

A shotgun blast of questions from reporters.

Microphones were jammed in their faces.

Wanting no part of this craziness, Doc ducked under a TV camera, slipped into the crowd, then turned back to watch and listen. There were only two Gigolos left "on stage." Jimmy had gone somewhere too. Doc looked around but didn't see him. Didn't see Margaret Ann either.

Around him, voices shouted over each other:

"Slatz, Grill, is it true your mothers will be posing for *Playboy*?"

"Can you confirm the Castro connection?"

"Vatican involvement. A missing priest. Your comment?"

"The letter to *Playboy*, Slatz? A conspiracy of silence? Charges of molestation? Is it true? Speak to us, please."

Slatz stepped onto a chair, rose to his full height.

Grill, ringmaster, standing next to him, raised both arms. "Ladies and gentlemen of the press. Headline: Pianist Pens Plan, Pervert Pinched."

Slatz cleared his throat. The reporters' pencils poised, waited. He began with a brief treatise on shifting mores in a post-Kinsean American. The audience, enraptured, listened, wrote down every word as though each sentence he spoke carried the force of a mystic haiku, as though every quip he uttered was saturated with subtleties, laden with layers salient with meaning. He explained the procession of complex clues, including the recovery of his own underwear from

Dr. Brisco's mailbox, that had led him to believe the respected psychologist was deeply involved in deviant behavior. "These factors," he said, "resulted in the letter I wrote to *Playboy*, a letter that led to the issuing of a search warrant and today's arrest."

"Is it true that along with nude photographs of Boy Scouts and girls from the 4H Club there were several revealing photographs of Grill's mother?"

Grill spoke up. "We like to refer to those photographs as French postcards."

Doc felt a tug at his sleeve.

Bunny was standing next to him, all smiles. She whispered, "Thank you so much for helping Slatz become a genius. Big Lou's so proud."

"He was struck by lightning, Mrs. LaDesma. It was an accident."

"His father and I don't care how you did it."

"I'm not sure the genius part is permanent."

She put a hand over Doc's mouth. "My son's granted the press one more question." She stood on tiptoes, looked over the crowd.

"Slatz," a reporter said, "I'm sure every American appreciates and respects the courage you showed today in saving Mr. Kennedy, but I'd like to get back to the letter and the response by the legal staff at *Playboy*. Might one say you used double reverse psychology to expose an expert in that very subject?"

Slatz thought a moment. "Yes," he said. "One might."

"One might?" Doc shook his head. When he turned, he saw Jimmy with his mother. She was crying. He was crying too. Each was in the other's arms for the first time in many years. For a moment, he thought about Scarlett, wondered if he'd ever see her again. He said a little prayer for God to heal her broken places, that time would be her friend.

Doc glanced at Slatz and Grill. They were soaking up the spotlight.

Despite the silly vanities, despite the fact that the press had so many things all wrong, there was a certain poignancy to it all. In almost every way, his friends had found themselves arriving at a heroic ending. This was as clear to Doc as a color illustration in a storybook, as illuminating as the last page of a cherished fairy tale. In less than a week, Grill had gone from ugly duckling to Swan Prince. Slatz, like Dorothy's straw-headed scarecrow, had discovered he had a brain. And Jimmy, shedding his armour at battle's end, had allowed himself to feel the exquisite sadness that comes from great loss and the expansion of the heart that derives from the resurrection of faith.

Doc took off his glasses and wiped his eyes.

"So what's your story?"

He put on his glasses, blinked the world into focus. Margaret Ann was standing in front of him. She handed him a handkerchief. There were fiery streaks of red in her auburn hair, lustrous highlights he had never seen before. The dusting of freckles across her perfect nose reminded him of the Milky Way. And that scrubbed fresh little Irish face—he could never grow tired of looking at it. She wore a pink cardigan sweater with pearl buttons and a fluted navy skirt with tiny Swiss dots. And nylons. And the pink shoes. My God, she was something to look at.

"Are you gonna keep staring at me all day or you gonna answer my question?"

"What question?" Doc asked

"So what's *your* story?" She had a pen in one hand, a notepad in the other. "I'm a reporter. Remember?"

"The story's up there on stage."

She poked his chest. "No. You're the story, you're the hero." She brought her lips close to his. "You're my hero, that's for sure."

Coming out of nowhere, glaring at Doc, Quinn pried them apart. "Young lady, you're coming with me. Doc, your father's here. He's got your little sister with him, the sister you're supposed to be *babysitting.*" Quinn pointed over the crowd. "The back door's over there. Get going. They're waiting for you in the garden by the jail." He put a firm hand

416

on Doc's shoulder, handed him a small Bible. "Found this at the crime scene. Turned out it's worthless as evidence. Take it. You might need it."

Doc took the Bible, then looked up at Quinn. "Want to thank you for what you did for Bonnie."

"Don't mention it." He stared at Doc. "I mean that literally."

Doc nodded. "Just one more thing. I can't help thinking about Scarlett."

"Once the detective work is done, once the truth is known, there are limits to what we can do. At this point, Doc, she needs a savior. You're just a hero." He took a breath. "Maybe she'll be helped by therapy. Maybe it'll just take time. A detective's gotta realize cracking a case doesn't put the world back together. That's why people pray. My guess is, even atheists sometimes pray for girls who've gone through what Scarlett has." Quinn looked at the exit that led to the garden. "Better get going, Doc. Your dad's waiting."

Doc's weak leg jellied. A steel band tightened around his ribcage. He was out of gas. He could see the lies he'd told his parents waiting for him at the far end of the road.

Margaret Ann looked at him. "Are you in trouble?"

Doc didn't answer. Against the grain, his body numb, he slowly pushed through the crowd. The world narrowed. His eyes became a hand-held camera in a foreign film, a black-and-white movie. Cinema Verite. Everything zooming in and out. Distorted. Fellinied. Too close, too real.

Coach Ugler's face lunged in front of him. "Hand-eye coordination. That throw you made with the orange? Got me to thank for that, don't you? Just remember: Life's like football, or is it baseball?"

Rusty Richards threw an elbow, knocked Ugler to the side, cleared the way. "Life's not like anything else," he said. "Put that in your playbook, Coach."

Doc moved forward. A girl kissed his cheek. It was Raylene, the girl Jimmy had talked to at the Teen Center, the one who'd said she was

Junior's girlfriend. "I'm free," she said. "Free to be with the boy I really love: Fang. I'm going to stand by him through thick and thin. He's not really that bad, you know."

Miss Mooseman, magnified, loomed toward him, arms outspread, Bake-o-Lite bangles chattering. "*The Mill on the Floss.* You see its relevance in our lives? Tell them to keep it in the curriculum. Be a voice against censorship."

Doc stumbled, banged against a chair. Grill's mom looked up at him, grabbed his wrist. She was sitting at a desk with a detective. Photographs were spread out between them. "We're picking out the best ones. Care for a peek?"

Doc staggered out the back door and into the garden.

His father stood in the shade of a solitary pine at the edge of a grotto, the borders of the flagstone pathway leading into it plush with Saint Augustine grass, limestone hydrangeas, and roses the color of paprika. Snowball on her hands and knees splashed water in the small pool beneath Bernini's statue: The Ecstasy of Saint Theresa.

Margaret Ann, panting, out of breath, clutching her purse, came up behind Doc, took his hand and squeezed it.

Beside him in his darkest moment, they walked forward.

A gust shuddered the branches of the pine and needles rained down on their shoulders. The shadow of a crow crossed their path.

Doc spoke into the wind. "I wasn't in school today, Dad. I guess you know that."

His father sat down on a wooden bench and motioned for Doc to join him. His tie, loose at the collar, his butch cut still at attention, he had that meet-your-maker look in his eyes. "Would you ask your little friend to play with…Snowball? I'd like to speak with you."

Margaret Ann let go of Doc's hand, pulled a rubber ball from her purse, and tossed it in the direction of the pool.

Snowball ran after it, shouting, "We play chicken."

Doc watched the long legs and the little legs chase each other in circles: a last fond memory.

He sat on the bench, stared straight ahead, swallowed, waited.

Never looking at him, Doc's father took the Bible. "When I was your age, I earned the rank of Eagle Scout."

"I know, Dad. You did everything the right way."

"Not exactly. A month later, I was caught shoplifting. Bet you didn't know that. A few months after that, I went on an overnight camping trip. Told my parents I was going with a scout named Bill. Actually her name was Jill."

"Jill was a girl?"

"Don't tell your mom...I *did* volunteer for World War II. I was one of the last, not one of the first. I was busted back to private three times. Told myself private was the only rank you could hold without compromise. Don't know if that's true. My grades were good; I was near the top of my class. But I always had the feeling a friend of my dad's pulled strings to get me into Stanford. I've really only been scared twice that I can think of. The first time was when you had polio. The second was when you didn't come home last night. Don't know why but being scared makes me mad. When I'm afraid for you, I get mad at you. Understand? You mean the world to me." He looked up into the pine tree. "I was going to get my haircut today. But then I decided if it turned out you were safe, I might just let it grow out."

"I think it might look good that way, Dad."

His father ran his fingers through his hair. "It's not a big thing, of course, but I wanted to get your advice on that." He slapped his hand on his knee, stood. "Now you go play with that girl over there, play as long as you want to, and I'll take Snowball back home...One more thing. Quinn told me what you've been up to. What you did. Pretty cool." He walked over, nodded at Margaret Ann, picked up Snowball, slung her onto his hip, and walked off across the grass.

"I love you, Dad," Doc said in his deepest voice.

His father nodded but didn't look back.

Margaret Ann sat down next to him.

"I thought what your father said was sweet, even if it was a little flat."

"Took a lot for him to say what he did."

"So where do we go from here?" She smiled, flicked her eyebrows, Groucho style. "I like what your father said: 'Son, you go play with that girl as long as you want.'"

"Guess we could go to the library."

"We *could* go pick out my corsage and your boutonniere. You owe me a night on the town. A romantic evening. Dinner? Dancing."

"Thought your dad was mad at me."

"He is. Never wants me to see you again…I'll sneak out. Even let you drive."

"We'll ask him. He says yes, you'll drive. I'm done with trouble."

Margaret Ann walked over to the flagstone pathway and picked a rose. Walking back, she tossed it into his lap.

"I need to ask you a question. Give me an honest answer, okay?"

He turned the rose in his hand, didn't look up. "Okay."

"Are you in love with Bonnie?"

"No."

"Were you ever in love with her?"

"I don't know. No. It wasn't like that, not in the way I think you mean. I felt bad for her. I wanted to help her. I liked it when she kissed me. But I don't think I ever kissed her. Honestly, I don't ever think I did. I should have said goodbye to her. Would have said something if I'd known I was probably never going to see her again."

"How 'bout this?" Margaret Ann said. "I'll be her. Right now. Right here. Look at my feet. I've got Pinkie's shoes on. The prophecy guarantees me total knowledge of the male mind. I'm the essence, the embodiment of understanding. I'm like sunlight. Turn over the dark rock. Let me shine down on you."

"I don't know," Doc said.

"Look into my eyes. You know you need to say something to Bonnie. Hopefully it's going to be goodbye, but whatever it is should be the truth. I'm Bonnie. Talk to me."

"Okay, I'll try." He took a breath. "I think, in a way, Bonnie was my first love. But for me, maybe for lots of guys, the first girl you love is really just a girl you make up. You get a crush on a girl you've never spoken to, you don't know a thing about her. You give her qualities, make her a mystery. She's unattainable. Then she startles you one day. Gives you attention. A kiss from her and you're flying high. She's your first love. But it's not true love."

"I'm not here to be someone in an audience. I'm not a generality. I'm Bonnie," Margaret Ann said. "Talk to *me*."

Doc tried again. "Bonnie, I wish you all the best. Hope you and your baby build a new life in Indiana."

Margaret Ann sat next to Doc, took his hand. "Wish you were going with me, wish we were bound for India, not Indiana. We could dance beneath the Punjabi moon, listen to tigers in the night. Hunt for rubies."

Doc looked at Margaret Ann. "What are you doing?"

"Bonnie told me about the Galaxy Glider, about you playing make believe with her. Come on," she said. "Stay in character."

"Okay," Doc said, "here it goes. Bonnie, you *don't* wish I was coming with you. I'm *not* the guy for you. You never thought I was even for a second. You let me be in love with the idea of you. And it was sweet, and fun, and it took both of us away from our troubles."

"Kiss me," Margaret Ann said.

"I don't want to kiss Bonnie, I want to kiss *you*. I love *you*, Margaret Ann. Even though you annoy me and boss me around, I think you're the most wonderful girl in the world. I'm crazy about you. You'll probably ruin my life, but I don't care."

"Ruin your life? Boss you around?" She picked up her purse, walked a few steps, then lay on the lush green grass. "I dare you to kiss me now."

"Think I'm afraid?"

"I know you're afraid."

He lay down next to her, pulled her close, and kissed her. Eyes closed, he made the kiss last the sweetest part of forever, anchored in his memory each sensation: the fragrance of her skin and breath, the jazz dance her tongue did in his mouth, the salty taste of tears that made him feel she was already missing him before he was even gone. In his mind, Doc wandered upon a treasure chest. In it he placed the moon and stars and all the memories he hoped they would share together.

They kissed until each heart surrendered to the other, until each took on the other's heartbeat.

They lay on their backs. Doc shifted, then shifted again. Something was poking him. He moved, got up. He was lying on her purse. Scattered around him were pages from the book he'd been writing. There were doodles, drawings scribbled all over them. "What's this?" he asked.

"Sketches. You're a good storyteller. Sometimes you're a little hard to follow, but all in all, you're not too bad. However, you're clearly missing one thing."

"And that would be?"

"Me. I thought maybe I'd illustrate your novel. It'll make your story complete."

"You want to turn my novel into a comic book?"

She stared up at the sky. "That cloud over there looks just like a hippopotamus." She pulled him down on top of her. "Don't you just love that word?"

The End

Made in the USA
San Bernardino, CA
22 December 2018